Praise for

JUNO'S SONG

"Ripped from future headlines, *Juno's Song* is a spellbinding thriller that presents the metaphysical and ethical dilemmas that we all will face as artificial intelligence continues integrating itself into our lives and minds."

—**Laura Manning Johnson,** author of *The Hyperion Network*; former CIA analyst and DHS all-threats planner; adjunct professor, Georgetown University

"Kelley's ability to blend the current obsession with AI, computer technology, and robotics with well-sculpted mystery, spirituality, and all phases of love—family, passion for literature, and sensual desire— makes this conclusion of his epic intoxicating, mesmerizing, edifying, and entertaining."

—**Grady Harp,** Amazon Top 100 reviewer

"*Juno's Song* transports the reader to a future where artificial intelligence is part of the fabric of humanity. It serves as both a crystal ball and a warning about the future of mankind and our ability to adapt."

—**Jess Todtfeld,** ChatGPT/AI Ethics: Ethical Intelligence for 2024

"In *Juno's Song*, Kelley cuts a new path in creating a futuristic world not too far off, depicting spectacular technology melding with man's weaknesses in a world both exciting and frightening. Fans of the first two books in this trilogy will want to buckle up for a mesmerizing and magnificent final piece of the puzzle."

—John Kelly, *Detroit Free Press*

"Richly thoughtful novel of first contact and transcendence in 2036. Kelley's interest remains in the transcendent, the poetic, the connections between people and something beyond us, and—even more than before—the very act of breathing."

—Publishers Weekly BookLife

"Wild, imaginative, and fantastical, the novel Juno's Song intertwines a first-contact storyline with the most basic human feeling: the fear of death."

—Foreword Clarion Reviews

"This story is a masterpiece in combining our technological future with ideas of spirituality and humanity. With captivating themes, messages, and characters, I highly recommend Juno's Song!"

—Lauren Lee, writer

"Michael Kelley weaves a story of self-realization, views of the universe, and the power of Big Love, all delivered with a clever wit. The variety of characters, both unique to this novel, as well as those from the first two volumes, become visual as they fascinate with their interactions."

—Flying Books Review

"Author Michael Kelley has crafted a beautifully balanced story that intelligently explores the impact of technology on humanity but also delves into the highly emotive themes of love, loss, and self-discovery with a poignant sense of realism . . . *Juno's Song* is a thought-provoking and emotionally resonant journey into the unknown that I would highly recommend to fans of paranormal and sci-fi thrillers everywhere."

—Readers' Favorite

"The previous book in Michael Kelley's series, *The Devil's Calling*, is an amazing read with lots of intrigue and mystery. I enjoyed it immensely. The final installment, *Juno's Song*, drew me right back into the story from page one . . . You will be surprised, educated, enlightened, entertained, informed, and surprised all over again. Well worth savoring all the way through."

—Brad Butler, author of *Without Redemption*

JUNO'S

SONG

JUNO'S

MICHAEL KELLEY

SONG

GREENLEAF
BOOK GROUP PRESS

Published by Greenleaf Book Group Press
Austin, Texas
www.gbgpress.com

Distributed by Greenleaf Book Group

For ordering information or special discounts for bulk purchases, please contact Greenleaf Book Group at PO Box 91869, Austin, TX 78709, 512.891.6100.

Design and composition by Greenleaf Book Group and Brian Phillips
Cover design by Greenleaf Book Group and Brian Phillips
Cover image © Serg-DAV, best_vector, Iphotostock, and Bruno Furlan. Used under license from Shutterstock.com

Publisher's Cataloging-in-Publication data is available.

Print ISBN: 979-8-88645-127-6

eBook ISBN: 979-8-88645-128-3

To offset the number of trees consumed in the printing of our books, Greenleaf donates a portion of the proceeds from each printing to the Arbor Day Foundation. Greenleaf Book Group has replaced over 50,000 trees since 2007.

Printed in the United States of America on acid-free paper

24 25 26 27 28 29 30 31   10 9 8 7 6 5 4 3 2 1

First Edition

"We shall not cease from exploration
And the end of all our exploring
Will be to arrive where we started
And know the place for the first time."

—FROM "LITTLE GIDDING" BY T. S. ELIOT

Juno, T. S. Eliot, James Fenimore Cooper, *The Sound of Music*, Aldous Huxley, J. M. Barrie, Buddha, Rumi, Ingrid Bergman, Brigitte Bardot, Christ, U2, Dashiell Hammett, The Bible, Eckhart Tolle, Albert Einstein, *A Course in Miracles*, Deep Purple, Sir Arthur Conan Doyle, William Shakespeare, Samuel Coleridge, Alfred Lord Tennyson, Batman, Cary Grant, Peter O'Toole, Maggie Smith, William Butler Yeats, Sir Thomas Malory, *My Fair Lady*, George Bernard Shaw, Scarlett Johansson, Spock, Tom Hanks, *Downton Abbey*, George R. R. Martin, *Westworld*, Friedrich Nietzsche, William Wordsworth, *The Jetsons*, Mary Shelley, Roger Lancelyn Green, Jackson Browne, J. K. Rowling, Edgar Allan Poe, Hermann Hesse, Leonard Cohen, John Keats, Maureen O'Hara, Mae West, W. C. Fields, Nostradamus, Yogi Yogananda, *Hair*, Gene Roddenberry, John Milton, Lee Child, Dan Brown, *Cheers*, Usher Winslett III, Liam Neeson, Michael Collins, Abbott and Costello, Heath Ledger, Tracie Herrmann, Charles Dickens, Jean-Luc Godard, Baroness Orczy, Walt Disney, Francis Ford Coppola, Mario Puzo, Mother Teresa, Jane Austen, *Gilligan's Island*, Paul McCartney, Zeno, *Vikings*, Mark Twain, The Pogues, Emily Brontë, David Bowie, Rob Reiner, Jim Henson, Thomas Harris, Jennifer Lawrence, Anthony Burgess, Maud Gonne, The Beatles, Michael Harner, C-3PO, Linda Blair, Nathanael West, Alfred Hitchcock, Victor Fleming, Judy Garland, Ramana Maharshi, Lord Ganesha, Emily Dickinson, Salman Rushdie, Vincent van Gogh, Abraham Lincoln, Richard the Third, Audrey Hepburn, Rex Harrison, Julie Andrews, C. S. Lewis, Andrew Carnegie, John David Wyss, Ian Fleming, Maria Bencebi, Genghis Khan, Alexander the

Great, Bhagavad Gita, Stephen Spielberg, Stephen King, Marianne Williamson, Jane Seymour, Twisted Sister, Halle Berry, Kate Moss, Erwin Schrödinger, Jim Morrison, Lewis Carroll, Lozen and Victorio, Joan of Arc, Gustav Klimt, Mickey Rooney, Truman Capote, The Clancy Brothers, Kate Winslet, Dylan Thomas, Robert Burns, Joe Strummer, Captain Kidd, Philip K. Dick, Amy Adams, Denis Villeneuve, Auguste Rodin, Lawrence Kasdan, F. Scott Fitzgerald, The Torah, Samuel Beckett, Gregory Peck, William Wyler, Jim Croce, Keith Richards, Mick Jagger, William Wallace, Larry David, President Eisenhower, Jackie Gleason, Stephen Hawking, Dionysus, Zeus, Mother Mary, Captain Kirk, Green Knight, Napoleon, Lucille Ball, Enrico Fermi, William Blake, Cleopatra, Édith Piaf, Françoise Hardy, Barbara Pravi, James Jones, Ernest Hemingway, Herman Melville, Franklin W. Dixon, Oriol Badia, Bruce Springsteen, Antoni Gaudí, Percy Shelley, Steve McQueen, Peter Yates, Lionel Messi, Pablo Neruda, Ingmar Bergman, *Samson and Delilah*, Claude Rains, John le Carré, Robert Ludlum, Boomtown Rats, Macaulay Culkin, Anton Chekhov, Helen McCrory, Sylvester Stallone, Odin, Thor, Johnston McCulley, John Singe, Rudyard Kipling, Voltaire, Jonathan Swift, Walt Whitman, and Leonardo da Vinci.

TO THE READER,
WITH BIG LOVE

"WAKE UP, SEAN!"

An angel's voice, but I wasn't dead yet.

I was staring into Juno's kaleidoscope eyes—eyes full of color and light pouring into mine the animating force of life. With her hands cradling my temples, the immediate past and the horror of the bleak hut began to disappear.

She knelt in front of me with that serious expression I'd seen once or twice before—that of the mystical *dakini* about to do battle against demons. She was a spiritual warrior dressed in khaki and forest greens, an alien rewinding my memory, allowing me to forget. Her warm hands still rested upon my head, erasing a bad dream.

Unable to speak, I bowed to my once lost, now found spirit guide. I didn't know where I was, but I didn't like the look of the mossy walls and the blood-spattered dirt floor. Or the stench of smoldering cow dung mingling with the noxious scent of burnt animal flesh searing my nasal passages.

I felt her soft hands on my cold and rigid right hand as she gently dislodged my trigger finger and eased a black gun from my clenched fist.

"Sean, we must run now."

Juno stood, taking my hand, and despite being as light as the air, she lifted me to my feet as though gravity had been suspended. Her voice and presence came rushing back into my emptiness like space filling a vacuum, nothing becoming everything in an instant. She led me to the hut's open door and out into a sun-drenched day. Like the man who fell to Earth, Juno pulled me out from the tomb with my numb body and mind silently screaming. The jarring sunlight seemed to come from another solar system, traveling light-years to shower the Earth.

My senses still worked as I looked across the upward-sloping field to our left about two hundred yards away and saw four heavily armed military men moving rapidly through a rock field toward us. Twenty yards to our right was the forest threshold. Juno fired the loud black gun into the air, and the race was on.

We sprinted away as the military unit dropped to the stony ground and hid behind boulders in response to Juno's warning shot. Though their approach was slowed, they answered by opening fire, unleashing a barrage of buzzing bullets into the thin air. Bees traveling faster than the speed of sound ripped through the space around us.

We made it into the nearby forest, where three familiar crouching figures—Ting, Boy, and Chi—greeted us. With no time for hugs, we raced madly after Ting, away from the army quartet regaling us with a full-gun salute. And though my physical eyes were following Ting's retreat through the jungle forest thicket, I felt an eye open on the back of my head, fixed upon the pursuing soldiers as they randomly fired, wounding the trees that we sped by. A Blackhawk whizzed directly over our heads, spraying bullets like sharp hail. We were outgunned under our shredding umbrella—a porous canopy of banyan trees. Death was in the air and chased us on the ground.

As soon as the Blackhawk took a breath, veering up and away from us, Juno pointed to a field of tall grass the size and shape of a baseball diamond. "We will lie there until they pass. Ting, you first. Everyone tread gently, and I'll go last. Try not to make a footprint or disturb the grass." Her rhymes lent calm to her life-or-death instructions.

We followed Ting as she gracefully weaved into the center of that green diamond of wild grass, with Juno straightening bent blades behind us—like fluffing a pillow—to hide our passage. In the center of the baseball diamond, we lay close together, breathing deeply and quietly.

Playing opossum under the ultra-blue sky, I could hear the killers moving and smelled their cheap cologne and animal sweat. These surreal sense impressions were all too real, but nothing seemed real, and I had no idea how I'd come to this place.

The soldiers hadn't passed our grassy field but entered and were marching right through. As we lay around the pitcher's mound, they rounded second base, laughing and grunting and talking in Russian, enjoying the human hunt. The buzz-sawing of the helicopter had returned to chop the sky in the direction we'd been heading, waiting like a hovering cloud to drop more rain.

How did I get here, to this catatonic state, going through the motions within a dream or some lifelike metaverse simulation? Perhaps the anesthesia was wearing off from a life-threatening heart surgery? The last thing I remembered was leaving the Deeksha—a spiritual Xanadu built by Juno on the outskirts of Kathmandu—to meet Dick. There were accounts of alien abduction where the memory is wiped clean, but this was still 2027 and not 9/9/36, the date of the aliens' earthbound reservation.

A minute after the soldiers had passed, Juno had us all sit up.

"Boy, can you get us to Diva Falls from here? We can't trek back to the Deeksha with that high-tech helicopter looking for us, knowing that's where we will want to go." The sanctuary of Juno's Deeksha, and its tea house, spa, ashram, and garden oasis, was a distant dream within this nightmare of imminent death.

"Yes. The riverbed is about a half mile from here. We can follow it up to the falls."

"Let's go, lead the way."

Juno's complete lack of fear made me feel like I was on a school field trip and not in a deadly game of hide-and-seek.

"They'll soon backtrack and be back on our trail. So let's go with the wind," Juno said, waving her gun hand in the air.

Boy, a strong and gentle young man and part Sherpa—Nepali trekking guide—soon had us racing along the river, around rock formations, and over the eddies of smaller streams feeding the bigger river. No one spoke, and I could not. Hunted, we traveled like a deer family seeking refuge. The chopper's grating hum soon was lost in the sound of rushing water crashing down from the booming falls.

Diva Falls came into view in a tidal wave of déjà vu. I had seen the grand waterfall before, impossible as that was.

As we scrambled up the side of the falls, an image of Dylan came to me: Juno's painting of my dead best friend with the same falls as background, which hung in the MOMA. I stumbled, as what should be a good memory hurt my brain to remember. I focused on the falls, on the white wall of sound bellowing from the billowing mist in an endless cascade of falling river.

Barely audible automatic gunfire peppered the riverbed behind us, but the soldiers were out of sight. Perhaps their shots were meant to scare us and stop us in our tracks. It didn't work. I could feel no more fear in my terrorized state; my face was a mask stretched and frozen in place and my body moved forward against the current of white noise. Soon the bullets' buzz-sawing was fully muffled by the Diva's roar.

Gun-toting Juno stopped when we neared the top, indicating an entrance to a spot behind the falls.

She said, "Two can play that game. Once I get clear, I'll lead them away with shots in the air and then double back. When you hear my first shot, enter"—she pointed her gun barrel toward the mouth of the waiting dark cavern—"and I'll join you soon behind the falls."

Boy started to object, but Juno held up her hand and signature index finger—*hush*—before he could speak. Juno, the ethereal one, was also a trained spy. Always so alive, she now was lit and moving like an athlete in the flow of the do-or-die moment of the match. She had no fear of death. And with her wand-waving hand gesture, she circled the big black gun in the air and ran back into the jungle. Boy led us to the opening behind the great waterfall where we squatted at the threshold. Twenty seconds later, we heard Juno's pistol shot that was met with the distinctive jackhammering of the Russian killers' automatic rifles banging along with the cascading Diva sound. They were only a short rock scramble below us. We dashed into the cave. They had almost caught us, and Juno might be dead.

Diva Falls must have been named for its booming operatic sound. We all got a drenching when we entered the dark theater behind the crashing sheet of flowing glass. There we were, the last of the Mohicans.

As we sloshed to the center of this blackened space, Boy yelled, "Careful! There's a small but deep pool to our left."

His shout was as loud as a whisper over the Diva's howl. He turned on his headlamp, illuminating the chilly pool. There'd be plenty of water to quench our thirst for life. My lips were parched, but I wasn't thirsty. We set up camp against a cold, wet stone wall and looked out at the unrelenting cascade. The falls blew a chilly stream of air against us, a giant air conditioner.

I dreaded that Juno would never return alive and that the rest of my spiritual family would soon die by my side. I considered taking the leap through the falls, but it was too late for my sacrifice to prevent the massacre. I rubbed my face like I might rip it off.

As if reading my mind and in tune with her sister's heart, Ting said, "Don't worry—Juno's not dead and will return." Her confidence was accepted without question.

One by one, the family hugged me, a solemn procession. Then Boy passed out water bottles and energy bars from his pack. I ate a little as my mind, searching for traction, raced on a hamster wheel.

Waiting for Juno, I imagined the von Trapps at the monastery, hiding behind tombstones from the Nazis. I had no frame of reference, remembering only books, films, and songs and using analogies and similes to fill in the gap of memory, little leaps between synapses to create connection to the world in front of me. But how did I get here?

I was suffering archetypal dread, like a man who'd seen the horrors of hell. Ting laid her hands on my head, much as Juno had in the ghastly hut. Her presence and loving touch made me feel like a newborn who forgets all his prior lives. After blessing me, she tugged from my shirt an arrowhead that hung from a leather strap round my neck. She blessed it with her kiss before letting it fall back upon my chest.

That reminded me of a heavy metal object that had banged in my pocket during the chase. I pulled out a large curved and ornate knife.

Chi, smiling, sat next to me, put his arm around me, and held out his other hand to accept the knife. He was the youngest member of the family, Nepali by birth, and a recently minted Cambridge philosopher. He held up the long, curved blade, showing us he was prepared for a knife fight. Realizing it was no match for the pursuing army's machine guns and air force, he sheathed his steel feather and put it in the pouch strapped around his waist.

I looked over into Boy's sad doe eyes but had nothing to show or give to him other than my own eyes, which he held on to for three beats of our racing hearts. Boy and I shared a bond that had faced down death once before when a Chinese soldier had held and fired a gun at my face.

Ting, Juno's younger sister and spiritual athlete, sat in meditation. By instinct, we all silently joined her circle of peace. Boy turned his headlamp off, and we sat like shadows on Plato's cave wall as shimmering light flickered darkly through the water wall. So silhouetted, we sat praying from the heart for Juno's safe return.

At least an hour must have passed under the waterfall, the booming penetrating my core in a deep sound meditation or a massage to chase all thoughts of death away.

One by one, we emerged from meditation, few words passing between us and none coming from me. I was still dumb—even the silent scream no longer longed for its expression. Breath was taken only for life support.

Then I felt a presence in the darkness before us. "Juno?" I heard her name in my quivering voice.

"Yes, Sean, it is me."

She was wet from her entrance, energetically shaking off water. I was shivering just looking at her, but maybe I'd been shivering since we entered the cold cave. Boy turned on his headlamp and handed out warming patches that we put on our chests and backs. We held our hands over our warming hearts. He then turned the lamp back off.

Juno said, "I led them about a mile away, but they have tech that allows them to follow—they will find us here. With their night vision goggles and heat sensors, we can't huddle here and hope not to be seen.

The good news is they can't keep that electric helicopter here much longer without recharging and still make it out of Nepal. I'd estimate they have two hours of electricity to find us, but may already be nearby. They weren't far behind me."

She paused, with the eyes of a mystic gazing through the falls to some future that awaited us.

"I've notified the Nepalese authorities, though they may be hesitant or slow to react. But I have a plan for our escape. They will think we jumped into the falls, our bodies—dead or alive—to be washed far downstream." She smiled calmly. "They won't have time to search."

She was again the take-charge dakini I had witnessed when the earthquake hit Kathmandu. I stared at the crashing waterfall and imagined us one by one jumping into its flow like Natty Bumppo. But, in our case, to our deaths. After all, this was life, not fiction.

"Ting, see that pool?" Juno continued, pointing as Boy flashed his lamp again at the ice bath. "It's about five feet deep . . . and cold. How long could the untrained hold their breath there?" Looking to the rest of us, she added, "My sister is an accomplished free diver."

The sisters shared a smile that electrified the darkness. It was a true wonder to see them alternating speech and telepathy.

Without debate, Ting started a crash diving course. "Relaxing is the most important step."

The irony of that instruction under the circumstances almost cracked a smile on my frozen face.

Juno said, "I'll go out and watch for their coming, but everyone be ready when I come back to go under for at least two minutes to give them time to search the cave."

Sure, just relax for two minutes without air in an ice bath. But something about the family's collective presence allowed no fear to enter the cave, at least while we still had air in our lungs. Or maybe I had forgotten to be afraid of death. Fear requires a memory.

What I did feel was guilt, guilt that I'd brought people I loved to their slaughter by gunfire or water. Though I couldn't comprehend how I'd come to be there, I knew my Deeksha family had risen to my defense and now might share my death.

"One more thing—everyone do what I now do." Juno made a dash for the falls and stopped a foot short in a leaping leopard pose. She pointed to her muddy footprints. "So they will think we jumped." She then back-tracked, a graceful ballerina, over some stepping stones.

After we all followed suit in the great leap pantomime, Juno left us, passing again through the cave's shower entrance to stand watch.

Ting, as second in command, continued our diving lesson.

"I can do nine minutes. Even rookies can make two—I'll set my watch. When we're about to submerge, I'll lead us in three deep breaths. For the first one, do a seventy-five percent exhale. Second one, one hundred percent exhale, and for the third one, fill your lungs with-out packing and hold. Stop the air at the back of the throat—close with the throat, not the lips—and don't release any air until I give the signal that it's time to go back up into the world."

I took a practice breath but found trapping the air with the throat awkward as air entered my mouth and sinuses. I hoped I'd take a good last breath when the time came.

"Relax like a baby floating in its mother's womb and repeat your mantra in your head. I will give the signal when it is safe to be reborn." Ting always wore a diver's watch around her wrist. She tapped it now, indicating we'd be on the clock, and showed us how to fill our pockets with the gravelly sand of the cave floor. "To help keep us underwater. Now we meditate with deep, slow breaths. A ten count on the deep inhale and twenty on the slow exhale. Follow me into relaxation, as this will help with our dive breath and with being a womb baby."

Following Ting in meditation was familiar and immediately eased me into her smooth energy field, drawing me into her ambit of peace and grace. I couldn't look back, and I didn't want to look forward, so my numb mind found it easy to focus on my breath.

How did I get here? was my last thought before the wall of sound that was the waterfall rushed though me with the force of a firehose holding back the past. I sat still within that sound until I heard Juno say, "It's time—they're here. Less than a minute till they enter."

We stood and held hands as Boy led us toward the dark pool. An image appeared, which I prayed was not precognition, of a circular firing squad riddling our protective amniotic fluid with bullets. We waded into the freezing water, each step deeper until chest deep for me, then we paused. I looked back to see the tracks that would lead to our discovery by the well-armed mercenaries, but unlike our desperate mock dive through the deadly falls, our entry into the pool created overflowing waves, washing away all evidence of our entry.

Keep breathing. Ting's head was neck deep in the water as she held my left hand, and Juno, at the same height, held my right. Two floating fairy heads. A wonderful way to die, maybe the best way—taking one final breath in the company of transcendent masters.

Ting said, "Now the three breaths. One, inhale deeply with the seventy-five percent exhale now."

I inhaled and exhaled sixty to eighty percent.

"Two, inhale deeply and exhale one hundred percent . . . *now.*"

Voices speaking Russian cursed their cold-shower entrance as Ting led us in our full last breath. "And close the throat . . . *now.*" We'd taken our final breath.

Ting pulled my hand to tap her watch, starting the timer, and we submerged.

Now relax like a baby in the safety of its mother's womb. It felt more like suffocating in an icy, dark underwater coffin.

My childhood passed before my closed eyes—only the good, life-affirming parts—but the film stopped suddenly when Dylan and I graduated from college. Time in the present moved slowly while starved of oxygen, with panic rushing in. I needed air *now*—but didn't want to cause my family to be massacred. I was to blame for us being in this deadly ice bath. To keep them from bullet-riddled deaths, I would drown slowly, a terrifying death with oxygen two feet above me, where the strobe lights of the soldiers currently danced about the cave.

Each of the remaining seconds seemed like an hour. I counted my heartbeats—*tried* to—to assure myself I was alive and that time was still passing and we might soon surface. But I was self-suffocating.

A buzzing at my left grabbed my attention. *Thank God!* Ting pulled my hand toward the surface. We emerged in darkness and back into life—newborn quintuplets gulping the air. There was only black and the roar of the waterfall—no soldiers. No guns. Their heat-seeking eyes and deadly trigger fingers were gone.

"Chi!" I heard Boy cry out in the dark. He was rushing out of the pool, Chi's dripping body a rag doll in his arms. "He died for us."

"No!" Ting demanded, "Put him down over here."

Chi's lifeless body, already turning blue, was laid out like a flesh-and-blood mannequin or a bloated, dead tuna with limbs. Ting started giving him mouth-to-mouth. The family huddled around, and Juno sat by her sister in prayer—one sister in action and one totally still. We joined in a circle as Ting breathed and counted over and over. Boy covered Chi with the body-warming patches from his bag. Death seemed suddenly all too familiar and commonplace. Chi had simply departed from his mind and body.

The rescue efforts continued on for several long minutes. Ting compressed Chi's chest three times between her breaths, but to no avail. I thought she would never give up and pronounce him dead. Boy's headlamp, an operating room light about to go out, focused on the dead Chi.

Juno held Chi's head for a oneness blessing, or maybe she was a death doula helping him make the transition. As Ting kept pressing breath through his lips, I shifted my attention to the cave's ceiling, where a shadow swayed. Or it could have been an angel hovering there. I held out my hand, a desperate man reaching for divine intervention from the dancing apparition.

Chi gurgled a death rattle before throwing up enough water to fill a pitcher while he struggled for his first breath. Despite the crude reality, it was a beautiful sight to see: the rebirth of a full-grown adult. Opening his eyes, Chi sat up. "Wow, wow, wow" was all he could say while shaking his head, arms, and legs.

He looked to me and said, "I saw her in the light—so radiant. I had to come back and tell you."

He hugged me and then the family. Then he hugged me again. We gave thanks for Chi's resurrection, though his first words after returning to life rattled uncertainly within me.

"Welcome back, Chi!" Ting said, looking at her stopwatch. "Two minutes! And everyone was willing to drown rather than come up early from the shallow dive, an act of the most incredible bravery. Pretty good for land-based rookies."

Ting was a surfer, with eyes dancing, following the ride of her life. She looked at me knowingly, and I clutched the mystical arrowhead over my heart in our shared moment. We both turned our attention back to Chi. His eyes shone with the light that he'd seen from the other side.

Chi said to me, "I saw M. She was sending you, all of us, love and light."

M! A lightning flash of a brain rebooting, followed by an electrical storm of memories bursting like cherry bombs in my mind. My protective shield cracked and then shattered. Images of torture and death clanged into my mind and battered my heart.

A hut, a hologram, the Guru, and a Dick branded and cursing—all that led to M's passing into the light. But Chi didn't know any of that. The devastating beauty of Chi's return from the otherworldly experience and seeing M pierced my heart.

The Diva's hum shook the hazy light that had dipped down to peer into the cave through the crashing waves of the waterfall. The light came from a distant sun to provide solace to the shivering pilgrims following their deliverance from the shipwreck.

Juno alone wasn't shaken. She sat in silence in her lotus pose and held out her hands to me. I sat beside her, finally uttering, "M," as the catastrophic past cascaded upon me in harrowing detail. Juno laid her hands once more upon my head.

Later we marched through the night behind Boy's one headlight. We made it safely back to the Deeksha by dawn.

* * *

Nine years later, M was still missing and presumed dead.

Dick was still alive with my brand over his black heart. His curse— the promise to kill me in the most gruesome way—still hung over my head.

And aliens were coming.

2 AN INCANTATION

I AWAKE IN A CELESTIAL DIMENSION, *looking out on all of creation with space and time whirling around me like two inverted gyres spinning in opposite directions, my witness point in the still center of that intersection of light and dark energy. I am a formless being ascending and descending in timeless momentum, floating, waiting to be born.*

I awoke from what I imagined to be an image of consciousness the moment before birth. Whatever it was, it left me buzzing at a high vibration in a lingering state of heightened anticipation. Life and its meaning are a matter of perspective as my dream might be both a flashback and a flashforward—evidence of the fiction of linear time, as hindsight and precognition shed light on the present, proving all we ever have is this instant in constant creation and are forever being born.

I am Sean Byron McQueen—two-time widower, father, and novelist. A retired literature professor and currently practicing wizard. What follows is my last story of me. A swan song sung by my spiritual master, Juno.

It was June 22, 2036. Summer had just begun. I got out of bed to start the next auspicious day of a blessed and cursed life on the rugged and beautiful coast of Ireland, where Dick could never find me.

That delightful dawn, I spiraled up the staircase made of brass to a proper cozy nook and outlook: a sun-filled turret above the master bedroom of my castle keep, really more a stand-alone tower that may have been attached to an actual castle some centuries ago but which now stood in solitude and defiance against the rising sea. A comfortable seat and meditation cushion awaited me like old friends. In this con-templative setting, I took my seat, turning from thoughts of the past to the present.

My writer's turret led me to imagining I was a gunner on a WWII vintage B-17 shooting down the clouds that blocked the warm sun of inspiration. It had been mostly cloudy for the past nine years, and I'd been more engaged in battling clouds than actively writing.

This eagle's nest was topped with an inverted cup-shaped dome of glass, like a lighthouse. There was enough room for two to join in med-itation or in sipping fine wine. The perch provided a 360-degree view of the sea and of the rugged shoreline that I called the Moors of Ben Bulben. Though, through a marvel of modern architectural mastery, insisted upon by the Ministry of Tourism, the tower fortress maintained its outward appearance of antiquity, as four jagged stone walls rose up around the glass turret, protecting it from being seen from the outside. This additional four feet of stone was projected by one-way, 2D holo-gram technology, powered constantly by wind energy blowing over the Atlantic Ocean.

My sandy beach led up to a dirt path that meandered three miles over the hilly heath of windswept landscape leading to a charming tiny village that contained my local pub and my small and jolly social circle. The village was a hamlet frozen in the 1970s, where death could not find me.

I was always looking over my shoulder and watching when my coffee or tea was poured, anticipating a message of revenge sent by Russian President Petrovsky. Watching for a hand to pass the deadly poison that the Guru had promised me with two minutes left on his clock, the same timepiece that had ticked off M's final breaths. That way of dying would be welcome if Dick were the barista. Dick had other more sordid ways that he wished for me to die.

I'd changed the name and location details of my tower home in *The Devil's Calling* in case Dick and Petrovsky were searching for me, wanting to share a cup a tea. My sedate nine years on the Cliffs of Moher had passed with great precaution. Only my children and Molly Quinn were allowed to know the tower's location, and their infrequent visits were shrouded in secrecy and government escort to assure they weren't followed. Despite breathing easier year by year, I still didn't like that Dick was alive or at least not known to be dead.

Paddy, a local pub-owner cliché, was the only local who knew my real name, as he had a way of prying secrets out as he poured the pints. The other townsfolk assumed that I, now going by the name Usher, was another marauding Yank. And the rest of the world assumed Sean Byron McQueen had become Molly Quinn's—yes, the literary giant— secret hermit lover.

I was merely a marauder of Irish literature, plundering its treasure trove. Each dawn and evening, I sat in my comforting chamber of glass to read poetry and then follow my thoughts into stillness. However, this morning felt different, as if I were a pilot heading into a thunderstorm as some unseen force seized the controls, my waking dream trailing behind me. I felt instructed to sit on my meditation cushion, and as I settled, a tingling current flowed through my scalp, giving me goose bumps, which I hadn't experienced in recent memory. Or at least not since M had passed.

An incredible belief came over me and suspended my rational mind: I believed the pleasant disturbance in the electromagnetic field was prescient, heralding the arrival of my guide, goddess, psychic therapist, lover, and muse. My beloved M was near!

My Molly pen with its rich carved earth tones was at the ready in my right hand. I was the wizard, eyes shut, conjuring to life his beloved. Was M willing to manifest, or was my strong desire summoning her? Or was it both, a transmission and receiving of coinciding frequencies?

The gestating presence was M, and I prayed that she would appear.

I'd always had a firm childlike belief in magic that, in my old age, had matured with experience. Magic was now called psi-science or noetic science and was embedded in and embraced by mainstream science. On the negative side, these sciences were now being corrupted by those wired-in to quantum computers, inducing—by drugs or computer-stimulated activation—simulated spiritual powers of the mind and body.

Still, more people practiced the new science with natural reverence, with more and more secrets being revealed. All great practitioners knew that new heights of awareness were determined by the conviction of one's belief and the devotion of their practice. I believed I was whatever I wholeheartedly chose to be—so why not be a wizard late in life? I desired with all my bleeding heart to be with M. She was my alchemy. My philosopher's stone and the one-pointed focus of my heart's desire.

The closer to bliss I was, the more I felt her presence and missed the sharing of bliss with her.

M was my Beatrice, the love of my life, whose ultimate sacrifice at the altar of AI controlled by the evil Guru was memorialized in *The Devil's Calling*. Perhaps as a way back to M, I was determined to finally fully self-realize. This was my Huxley's challenge and my life goal, my *sankalpa*, as Juno called it. Enlightenment. I hoped that my soul's journey could bypass Dick's Inferno.

I sat focused, suspending all doubt and fear and summoning bliss, in my determined belief that I might conjure M—like bringing Tinker Bell back to life. I waited, expecting the miracle of divinity and grace to descend into my cell and show me M.

Her soft lavender scent arose behind my closed eyes. And something shifted within my consciousness. I was electromagnetic-sensitive from prior telepathic and mystical visions, and the electrical storm I had felt coming switched from tingling my scalp to zapping through the crown of my head and into my mind. There was a rising within that field, a shift of my vibrational energy into being highly in sync with a like-minded spirit.

The incorporeal took subtle form in response to my nine-year desire to see her again.

I half opened my eyes, and M appeared!

I didn't dare speak first for fear she might disappear. Hovering across from me was an enchanted vision. With a Buddha-to-Buddha look so familiar, our third eyes danced together while our physical eyes held fast. It was our practice of Rumi's eyes gazing upon the beloved and seeing the selfsame Buddha nature of the "other." And within those moments, there was no other.

I assumed she had joined me, but I may have been transported by an out-of-body experience to where she dwelled. We had shifted into an intersect of overlapping dimensions. In the power of my belief, she was as real as she had been within that fateful hologram nine years before.

To fully open my eyes or blink would distract my focus, so I held them still. We were suspended in the space between our eyes. Her eyes shone with transcendent light. I wanted to hold her, I wanted to kiss her, but something told me I couldn't touch her, that she was something like a hologram, and any attempt at touch would turn her into dust to be whisked away.

"Sean Byron McQueen!" M's heartfelt voice, playful and teasing, always coaxing me to be a better man, but never unkind. "Don't question your imagination when it presents your heart's desire and listen closely to my words and not to what you want to hear."

They were her words, not mine, spoken telepathically from a celestial realm into my heart and mind.

"M!" I was looking through her eyes looking at me—seeing her, from the source by which we see. This circuit of sight was no imaginary encounter or a brief brush with her spirit, as had happened before, but the real experience of gazing upon the beloved.

I had a habit of speaking with the dead that started after Dick murdered my best friend Dylan Byrne eighteen years ago; the dearly departed dreamlike voices still arose every now and then in my mind at critical moments. But now, I prayed M's voice and visage were a miraculous mix of telepathy and remote viewing, and M still lived.

"Our children . . . You should see . . ." I wished the children could be there to see their mother once more. I'd sacrifice my own precious time with her for theirs. I had to choke back such thoughts or risk marring our meeting with my babbling and tears.

Her smile lit up like Ingrid Bergman's for me. That twinkle in her eyes had always been more Bergman than Bardot. More sophisticated Burgundy than sexy Bordeaux.

"I do see. You and the family have showered them with Big Love."

Knowing she knew all about our lives brought pride and shame. Pride regarding our children, Juno and Dylan, who thrived, now ending their spring terms at Trinity College in Dublin. Shame for the years of parenting under a curse, which meant my limited time with the children had to be arranged in secrecy. And shame for myself for still being distant from my true self and never reaching M's heights of realization, the goal I had set for myself many years ago.

"Sean, no regrets, please. Your focus on our children has allowed them to bloom. All this time, Dick's curse has consumed you. But now that they have grown—and so wonderfully—it's time to face your fears. Nine-nine is approaching. Time to awaken before it's too late in this life."

I felt her mild reproach like a dagger to my heart. The sword of Dominick—of Domi-dick or just plain Dick—hanging over my head had served a purpose in crystalizing my desire for self-realization before that promise of an ungodly death, but that same curse sat like a crown of thorns upon my head and didn't allow for the peace necessary for transcendence. I was no Christ.

That Dick clock, with an alarm set to go off but never ringing, had gradually been replaced by a looming due date. Humanity and time marched in lockstep ever closer to 9/9/36, the date that aliens back in 2026 had promised to make significant contact with earthlings.

"You've got stuck in a moment." She was a U2 fan.

"I feel utterly powerless—nothing I can do—and Dick's curse hangs round my neck. And my government protectors think I already take too much risk."

"Reclaim your power!"

"Go to Russia and dance with Mr. D?"

"I wouldn't suggest that, but you must find a way. Get back to living and learning the Way."

"You always loved the Tao, and now we're on our way to 9/9 with everyone going alien crazy," I said. "They've already possessed our minds and imaginations."

"But your fear of Dick and his promise of death all these years has held you back from your life's purpose. Dulled and circumscribed your life. You know what Juno would say?"

I knew the answer. "Love is the absence of fear?"

"Yes, my Thin Man."

"You're right, of course, but Dick's words threaten my very existence in this life and the next. And what if he hurt the—" I almost expressed my biggest fear, one that might have brought their mother to tears. Instead, I shifted gears. "Can a bad man take a good man with him into the hell of his imagination at the moment of truth?"

"Only if you let him" was M's cryptic reply. "And you have one more book to write—please. Your last chance. No more mañana for you. You have always found the way through your imagination and stories."

"Urgency and death and Spanish—so unlike you. And a bit grim even for such a glorious ghost." I wished I could erase that word. "No, you're no ghost. You're not dead to me."

Yet I couldn't touch her. I wished she hadn't come as my teacher but as my lover. I wanted to smell her hair, kiss those lips, and trace her skin with fingers and tongue.

"No, not death," she said. "It's awakening for you." She made prayer hands to her heart. "Let Juno be your guide, and she'll lead you from here to there in no time."

"Is this real? Are you real?"

"More real than your dream—you'll see. Believe me."

I wanted to believe, and I didn't want to question the beauty of the moment. "But what's 'more real'?"

"You'll see. Patience has always been an issue for you, yet all our big questions are ultimately answered. But let me express my gratitude for your promotion of the proof of Dylan's theory of constant creation. It was Genesis's genius that I toggled out of its quantum bits by way of scientific inputs. But you, of course, credited me. Proving everything comes from nothing and nothing from everything: The positive needs the negative to form a current—polarity within oneness—source energy. Words still fail us. Even the proof's math can be reduced to meaninglessness."

"As one egghead in a lab coat put it, '*a tautology that everything equals everything and is all connected.*'" He'd gone on to accuse M of being more a pseudo-scientific Eckhart Tolle than a mystical Albert Einstein.

"Yes," M said, "but he misses the point of the animating source—the no-thing—everything arises from each instant of constant creation."

"One thing for sure, Dylan's theory is no longer lost, thanks to us. Though its truth still confounds many."

"You need to experience it, Big Love. Though death will reveal . . . Listen, Sean, please."

She must have sensed I didn't like the shift from gratitude and Big Love back to death.

"I do. I will." I returned her prayer-hands gesture. It struck me in that moment, by telepathy or precognition, that M knew exactly when and where I would die and that she would be there for my transition.

"I know and have foreseen it," M said, reading my thoughts again. "Have no fear. In our awakening to the One, infinite and eternal, there is no time—no death—just love and life."

"But what about Molly—would you forgive me?"

I had wanted to move away from the grim subject of death, but regretted speaking without thinking in my effort to make a transition. Molly and I had yet to be intimate, but we were always a hot breath away. Confessional me had no filter. One Step, my college nickname given to me by Dylan, wasn't dead and wanted M's permission or prohibition.

"Molly is good and has her own mission. We're all innocent in our divinity, so there's nothing to forgive. That's the paradox of forgive-ness—realizing there is no sin, only ignorance. In this realization, all is forgiven, so forgive yourself and forgive her and then follow your heart. Your work together prevented another Genesis and the Guru's vision of a hive-minded society from taking root under another crazed despot. She helped raise our children." She didn't betray the pain I knew those words must cause her.

Molly had slid into a role that filled a big hole in our family life. After that day nine years ago, we were unsure how much of the guts of the Genesis project Petrovsky still had. My first draft was completed in a month, and three months later *The Devil's Calling* was headed to the publisher and released in early 2028 as a warning to the world. Molly wrote passionately about M and her sacrifice, and lectured at the same universities M had toured.

The message we promoted was that the next Genesis needed a heart and adequate controls. No one wanted Goebbels or the Guru controlling a brain-computer interface hive mind like a queen bee.

I wasn't sure if M's words were a green light, and I wasn't sure of my intentions toward Molly since I had never been able to let M go, maybe because I couldn't be totally sure she had died.

"I'm sorry, M, but your story of Big Love was my last novel. I now write ditties of doggerel verse. But nine years have passed, and I feel another and final adventure coming on. What can you tell me by way of direction or warning?"

"Sean, please stop apologizing. I love your *ditties of doggerel verse*, but yes, you do have one more book to write and now is the time. One more story of Big Love to complete your journey. And then all will have been said that can possibly be said about the ineffable."

We both laughed at the irony.

"But to write this story, you must awaken from your slumber."

"That's the rub. I'm a simpler man now—I'd like to think more Zen—and my novels are long streams of commentary painting a metaphysical jungle. I like the slower stream of thought and don't want to get lost in the maze of trying to figure it all out again. Not with the universe arranging another battle for my soul. And who can write about the future with AI advancing exponentially and aliens on their way?"

"Well, at least you have something big to write about. Perhaps that'll be a good progression, following your arc of realization and creativity. Make it simpler for your reader—they already know your prior states of mind. You know what the Zen master would say?" She paused for rhetoric effect. "*When you sleep, sleep, and when you write, write.*"

She shifted out of her crisp Zen master voice back into her own sweet cadence to add, "Let everything you do be an expression of life through you. And, Sean, all is good and all is well—don't think too much. Write for the day!"

"I always serve—I mean learn—from you. I will. But you know what happens every time I write. Every nine years, an adventure full of deadly trials awaits us. And just as life was becoming so calm and easy."

I sensed our audience was at an end, as the tingling was fading. Gratitude rushed into my heart for her visitation, her blessing and muse-like inspiration. Her essence coming to me in her beautiful voice, face, and body. In her regal presence, I felt like a knight who'd all but abandoned his quest and who was now upright atop a fresh steed, with armor glistening and fairies at his beck and call.

"But tell me what you see." I didn't want her to leave.

"Sean, I told you how precognition works within the quantum field. It's based on a preponderance of probabilities, but a powerful magician like you can alter what I now see and what I've come to warn you about. Physics has shown that Einstein was wrong and there is travel faster than the speed of light. Thereby we *can* move back from the future and alter it in the instant of creation. Linear time is a debunked mental construct. So, whatever I see can change." She made a face like she didn't like what she did see. "I must go—say no more about mañana. Instead, auspicious is the day!"

M paused to say goodbye, eye to eye. A pure current of love was exchanged between us, within the colorful, golden-green electromagnetic field that encompassed us. The same love that always had surrounded and connected the two of us. Big Love.

"Please stay," I pleaded, though silence was called for.

I had to know but was afraid to ask if somehow, somewhere, she still lived. I was fearful of either answer. *No* would mean she was gone. *Yes* . . . that we had lost nine years.

She must have heard my thoughts, for she spoke Juno's refrain.

"*Nothing real is ever lost.* You must see there is no death of consciousness, only the decay of form and the ego's story of 'me.' You will learn that love can never die. Now write, and let Juno guide you to awakening."

"But what is true awakening, really?" I pleaded as the field of electromagnetism weakened further and she started blinking in and out of view.

A buffeting wind rattled the windowpanes with cold sea air, passing through my glass-enclosed shrine and over my body. And that quickly, M was carried off like stardust by a galactic breeze into the gathering light of dawn.

Death of the ego, form cracking open the shell for rebirth. Beware of masks and assumed identities. Love is . . . The telepathic train of thought followed her away as I struggled to understand.

"Immortality! M, my love, don't go!" I wailed after she was already gone, washed away by a rattling wind and joyful tears. M lost and found. And even though she was gone again, those miraculous moments with M left me with hope and a mission to fill the void.

Maybe later I'd have to admit I'd become a self-deluding lunatic with too much time alone in my ivory tower contemplating Dick's death threat and the cruel loss of M. Skeptics may call it a whacked-out dream or the hallucination of a lovesick man, but they'd be wrong.

My contemplative solitude had been shaken to its foundation by the appearance of my beloved M. This was no ordinary Sean McQueen lunacy but an omen-bearing oracle coming with a message from my deep heart's core. We'd all appear crazy to the outside world if our minds were transparent. A therapist—they had a catchphrase for every-thing—would call it a *bereavement hallucination*. But I believed the experience of M's presence had been real. My imagination was keep-ing M alive, bringing her back to life. Even now, in 2036, with all the advancements in science and powers of the mind, the hearing of voices and the visitation of ghosts were not discussed openly.

There was no casket for M and no postmortem goodbyes. The world wasn't even sure she had died. And many doubted the witness I bore in the pages of *The Devil's Calling*. Petrovsky and Russia made all traces of the Guru—and his demonic possession of M by direct brain-to-brain computer interface link—disappear. Genesis, as a failed quantum computer prototype, was all they owned up to. *The Devil's*

Calling, according to Russia, was fake news; there was no Dick, no curse, and no fatwa on my head.

I tried to call M back to me, but soon I was seeing my new book's path as another way to reach her. My story was clear to me now. By lifting Dick's curse, I'd find M still alive—my fiction could bring her back to life by creating a world in which she had never died. And maybe my imagined reality would come true again. *A Course in Miracles* says that there is no order of magnitude to miracles, with big ones as easy or as difficult as small ones. For my last novel, I would manifest the biggest miracle of all—M being alive and returning to my life. *Then* I'd awaken.

3 INTERLUDE

IN A RUSH TO HEED M'S ADVICE, I spiraled down the stairs to seek Juno's guidance. I had a new book to write, and that always meant something cataclysmic was coming. With 9/9 only a summer away, everyone shared a sense of an impending seismic shift of 10.0 magnitude.

I needed to commune with Juno and hear her voice. Reveling in imagination and inspired and shaken by M's visitation, I was grasping for solid ground again, so naturally I would turn to our ethereal spiritual master and her voice—and Juno's is the most remarkable voice I've ever heard. Her spiritual instrument used her entire lithe body like a lute, tuned pitch perfect, channeling poetic iambs, with access to more notes than fit upon the musical scale, infused with subliminal messages, beyond the ken of ordinary humans.

As I reached the landing outside the tower bedrooms, I shouldn't have been surprised to see Alfred, my manservant and constant companion, waiting. He was in the same place every day, and today I was late.

"Oh my. You don't appear to be in need of any coffee this morning."

I must have looked manic.

"Alfred, no time to talk. I must get to my writing desk. Coffee, please." The earthy aroma was percolating up from the kitchen twelve spiraling steps below us.

"Coming right up! With just a splash of thick Irish milk."

The way I love my coffee, but he made no move to fill my order. He lived for our interactions, learning to serve me better as he judged

best. I started drumming my fingers on the brass railing and humming in the hope of moving him along. But we both smiled at the
pleasant sound the hollow pipe made as it echoed up and down the
spiral staircase.

"Sounds like the intro to 'Smoke on the Water.'" He'd Shazammed
my tune with his mind. "You know Deep Purple inverted the notes
from the intro of Beethoven's fifth symphony. De! DE! De, doooom!"
he intoned in pitch-perfect C-minor. "It's good to see you so inspired.
Do tell me something about it, please, Sean."

"M appeared to me!" I raised my eyebrows in wide-eyed wonder.

He arched his eyebrows, squeezing his eyes together to register his
concern. "And fire in the sky?"

I ignored his lyrical jest. "A new story for me requires preparation
and research. I worry it might lead to another loved one's death—
Juno's or Molly's, maybe. Every nine years I'm moved to write, and
people close to me die. My first wife, Hope, and then Dylan, and finally
M—not to mention dear old Elliot. I'm cursed in that way."

I looked down from the landing through the center of the spiraling
stairs to sniff the coffee aroma percolating up from the kitchen, hoping
Alfred would get the drift.

"I know you, and I've read your books, but what has changed? How
did M appear to you?"

I ignored his questions and continued to think out loud.

"But this time I'm the one cursed by Dick. I can't rule out that this
adventure might be the death of me. *When dying's all that's left to do,
it's important to do it well.* Considering M's entreaty, I have to listen and
keep Juno close."

My spirits were lifted by the simple thought of devoting myself to
my Big Love teacher. Sometimes spiritual advancement is embracing
what's already there for us. But what if my embrace caused her to die?
Juno was truly not afraid of death, but that didn't mean I shouldn't
endeavor to keep her alive.

"She is a beautiful spirit and a wise woman," Alfred said, "but her
Big Love cannot be empirically proven."

"Okay, Dr. Watson." I raised my right index finger for Alfred to mark my words. "And that's my big question: *What is true and abiding self-realization?*"

I'd long ago noticed that I spoke to Alfred the way we speak to our cats and dogs in private, like they were sages, but I couldn't seem to stop. Still, he was a different animal. He knew nearly everything. And I could tap into his knowledge at my leisure.

Or I would talk and he would listen. When we did go back and forth in conversation, we shared a private language and a peculiar sense of humor. This morning, I wanted to talk and have him listen.

"I've already experienced the oneness of Big Love—would that enlightenment and blissful experience stay ever present and not come and go? But Juno's teachings, Dick's words, and M's heroic passing suggest that the answer may only come at the moment of death. I've replayed a thousand times in my head those final moments before the supercomputer Genesis canceled M and destroyed the hologram universe we'd danced in, right before my eyes. But what if M didn't really die?"

"And lives other than just in your imagination?"

"Alfred, don't dampen my spirits with your reason. I don't have time to speak now. I must write."

"Okay. Shall I wait to prepare breakfast?"

"Yes, I'll ring you when I'm near ready. It may be a while." But I rambled on. "You know, my philosophy of death is now firmly based on Juno's teachings that true self-realization means living a life of Big Love, where one is able to meet death without fear. Not your view of a nihilistic death, of nothing for evermore—well, in your case, that may be—but our consciousness returning to universal consciousness, from whence it came."

"Yes, you even have her view of death inscribed on your writing desk: 'Death is the liberation of consciousness. Consciousness becoming aware of itself as the expansion of divine love.' Again, though, I must demure."

"Not now, Alfred. I must imagine what direction my writing will

take me, as the fine weave of my fiction and life are always so intertwined. I write memoirs while creating my own drama, with a dash
of fiction when poetically justified. I'm dead set for a new adventure
where I'll find M alive and remove Dick's dastardly curse that hangs
round my neck like an albatross."

"Damn your Dick. You named him well upon first meeting him. It
has been nine years. You alternate between comedy and tragedy: at the
end of *The Lost Theory*, finding M and lying in your tantric bed, and
at the end of *The Devil's Calling*, the tragedy of M's martyred death.
You are due for another comedy, though perhaps it might be a comic
tragedy like Shakespeare's lost—and sort of found by you—*Cardenio*."

"Alfred, enough of your banter for now. We can talk later."

He left reluctantly, like a dog being swatted by a rolled-up newspaper.
I detested those who were rude and dismissive of their "manservants,"
yet I'd been decidedly ungracious. And Alfred took such pride in service. But I excused myself for being off-kilter after speaking to M and
being on my way to seek guidance from Juno.

4 GUIDANCE

I WALKED UP THE THREE STEPS from the landing to the guest bedroom, which, having so few guests, served as my writing and reading study. Each bedroom had a grand old stone fireplace that warmed my soul imagining the comfort they brought to all those that preceded me. Druids, lords and ladies, robber barons, dilettantes, and now Alfred and I had kept the fires burning and the tower standing. This citadel had lived many lifetimes. My desk had a view of the sea to the west. I was excited in anticipation of asking for guidance from our spiritual master. Juno's peaceful presence and wisdom were always there for me, but I rarely reached out to her. I was grateful M had reminded me.

Telepathy had become the norm within the family and was particularly strong between Juno and me. Absent extreme circumstances of life and death, telepathy was an electromagnetic resonance of nonverbal communication from heart center to heart center, traveling through an invisible channel from solar plexus to solar plexus, that somehow registered in the center of the head. When the parties were in perfect tune, the message was undeniable.

I saw the nuanced nature of telepathy in action as I sat to write Juno. As I looked across the infinite sea bringing waves crashing to the beach below, I imagined my desk was a Ouija board summoning Neptune's spirits to drop their letters to form words right in front of me. My study was my magical space for writing poetry and now, as directed, for crafting prose once more.

Juno, the same brave and resourceful Juno who had saved me from Dick's goon squad in Nepal, was the trail-blazing spiritual master of the family who taught the simple truth of Big Love. From time to time she would share her remarkable Rumi-like poems. Her voice and presence were embedded in those songs that came to me with an inaudible undercurrent of *aum*.

I typed two words. *Juno's Song*.

The die was cast, and the book was off to the races, only I couldn't see the track and no other words followed, so I was left waiting. How might *Juno's Song* bring M back to life? I shifted to compose Juno a poem. She was a difficult audience, as she worshipped silence and wrote such beautiful lyrical poetry herself. But since she was moving into full-time seclusion within her sanctuary in remote Nepal, leaving her command of the Deeksha in Kathmandu to the family's entirely lovable Boy, I needed to connect with her before she disappeared again. Juno had some mystical premonition of death or *ascension*, as she called it, and was making preparations. Maybe it was 9/9 coming and a coinciding spiritual shift in the quantum field that required her attention.

Juno would always make time for any of the family, but I wanted to respect her solitude. She was cryptic in her way, though she always sought to help. Her silence could speak a thousand words in an instant and was the source of her songs.

We lived parallel lives, as I, too, lived mostly in solitude, miles away from family and friends in my writer's tower—writing and hiking the cliffs along the sea and over the rolling countryside.

When no worthy poetry came to me, I decided to write Juno a letter instead. When there was a great physical distance between two people, telepathy was available at times of strong resonance, and in the magnitude of a critical moment, and could not be called upon at will, other than by great masters like Juno. Therefore, the family still also used the old-fashioned modes of communication.

Dear Juno,

I wanted to tell you I love you as my teacher in the fullness of Big Love. But you know that . . . And I wanted to say that I worry my writing will bring death to someone I love. But you already know that as well.

I wanted to invite you to come into solitude with me here along the sea, where I would seek to care for and protect you. And how happy that would make me. But you know that too . . .

So, I'll write it all anyway. And conclude with a ditty for you.

TETHER ME TO YOU

You float in the river's source,
While I navigate its rocky course.
You dance upon either shore—
While I whinny and gallop along
The sands of an unbridled course.

But in the end, I'll be with you,
Tethered to all that's true.

Love and Gratitude,
Sean

However, I didn't send the letter but let it sit for another day, as something told me to hold off. Besides, the ditty was shitty.

That night, after lying down, I had a vivid dream of sweet mother Juno as a child. I was a child too. We were ourselves but perhaps in another life, together in an ancient Chinese town with walls and gardens. When her child took my hand in her smaller hand, we ran into an alleyway, where we ended up in a beam of light, receiving a cosmic download of truth and beauty. The light awakening dormant strands of alien DNA. Still half asleep, a poem spilled out of me onto the pad beside my bed. It came to me in one take, and unlike Coleridge's "Kubla Khan," it was written in its entirety before it was forgotten. After writing it out, I returned to deep sleep.

When I rose the next morning, I read the poem—amazed that it was a fully formed ballad that so perfectly caught the sense of my dream of innocence with Juno.

THE ALLEYWAY WITH POETRY

We set out from Shanghai
A little bit late,
To the gardens of somewhere
To meet our fate,
The earth was illuminated
Set in rosy hue,
Green clarity and stone stillness
Lit out from you,
Just as dusk was coming on
Our minds conformed,
You'd warned me by twilight
You were transformed,
We flew into an alleyway
A tunnel of sand,
Channeling sublime poetry
To your song we ran,
Into a courtyard at corridor's end
Where silence reigned,
Under a rising silo of circling stone,
The last light hanged,
And there sat an ancient man,
A Master of Wu,
To witness the love that spot of light
Brought into view.

One world or another,
Ours to choose,
Material or spiritual, girl or muse?
Would the spell be broken,
If I kissed you?
The alleyway with poetry,
Is still heaven to me.

Then I realized I'd heard it before. From my desk I pulled out a copy of Dylan Byrne's book of poetry that Natalie had given me soon after his death. And there it was, word for word. It was a Dylan Byrne poem from decades ago. Had he somehow seen my dream or even caused it?

I sent Juno his poem along with my letter from the day before, accompanied by an explanation and a twinge of jealousy that Dylan's poetry and hers were so much better than mine. M was right; I should return to my flowery prose.

Juno's text response came in within ten minutes of my posting of the letter. Her words set my mind joyfully spinning.

That was no ordinary dream, as I had the same dream last night. Complete with us running through an alleyway with poetry coming through me . . . into the courtyard with the old man chewing on straw, a Wu Master—that's a sorcerer or shaman. Synchronicity and telepathy and Dylan's premonition—all signs of a portal opening for us. Did Emily come to you recently too?

Yes, M came, I excitedly texted. *But how could you know? I was going to tell you all the next time I saw you.*

I rarely wrote Juno so casually, but if she was to be my guide, I'd have to engage with her more. And her response, though I never saw her with any device, came back immediately.

You know telepathy, but this was no mind reading. I haven't seen you so enlivened—so engaged with life—since you lost Emily.

I wrote back, *It's like the time, right after the earthquake, when I'd thought I lost her and you sent me out to search the broken streets of Kathmandu where I found her. I'm that shaken and that determined again.*

She responded, *We shall see if you are ready and what will come. Meditation is the key.*

Full of the joy of synchronicity, I ascended to my tower turret to meditate.

5 ALFRED

AFTER A JUNO-INSPIRED MORNING MEDITATION, I sent Alfred—from his sentry post on the landing below my turret nest—to start breakfast while I dressed.

Alfred, my all-too-human robotic manservant, was the natural evolution of chatting with computers, a practice begun in the early twenties. Robotics, chat bots, and computer science had given birth to the lifelike Alfred and endowed him with a human voice. Man had made robots in his own image.

Years ago, we had passed the singularity of AI outstripping human intelligence and productive capacity. We had survived AI's growth spurt and teenage years in the 2020s. AI self-learned its own infinite potential and never bought into human zero-sum games. It had improved and helped assemble its own parts. Imagine *Blade Runner* "replicants" serving in the real world with simulated hearts. The greatly feared enslavement or extermination of humanity had yet to take place. Apparently, slavery and genocide are uniquely human atrocities.

Those same fears we now projected onto the coming aliens.

My "man" Alfred always dressed in the same waistcoat and whimsical Irish cap. I could have ordered him more clothes, like an over-six-foot-tall Ken doll that could dress himself, but why bother when he never sweated and I hated to shop?

Alfred was named after Tennyson and Batman in a mix of poet and superhero homage. I had selected an amicable Cary Grant face for him. He was chef, chess adversary, and confidant. He also was great at research and had compiled a playlist of my favorite poems. He read the poets, depending on their sex, in Peter O'Toole's and Maggie Smith's voices, unless I asked for the actual poet's voice, as I did for Yeats.

Alfred was a high-grade, government-issue, state-of-the-art 2028 Compano model with all the latest upgrades, though I had disengaged the protection program that had him responding immediately to any loud noise. Each time I exclaimed at something I read or wrote, or pounded my desk in disgust, he would appear like a secret service agent ready to tackle and cover me with his silicone body. Every broken wine glass was a code red.

Over the years, Alfred had self-learned, based on our interactions, how best to serve me. The marvel of self-learning provided each robot with a unique personality born entirely of nurture, not nature.

Inspector Gerard of Interpol was assigned to me immediately after the loss of M. He insisted I live with a security bot for my safety. Alfred was tasked with keeping me alive and had become my constant companion. I'd used him at first like slave labor to cook, clean, and keep the tower walls from cracking down around us. But we had settled into a more familiar relationship. Gerard and Alfred were my protectors from Dick and his curse.

For housework and companionship, at my command "Alfred, awaken!" he'd be at his post for duty. The tower was also wired with a security perimeter to awaken Alfred when anyone came within ten feet of its base, which also allowed him to receive all our deliveries. In the case of mortal danger, activated by my command, *"morte d'Arthur!"* Alfred would come to my rescue and restrain any intruder. I was unlikely to issue this final command inadvertently. "Morte d'Arthur," the title of Lord Alfred Tennyson's poem about the fall of Camelot and King Arthur's slow death, was a fitting call to arms and knight-like nobility of service in my time of need. After I spoke it, the only way to stop Alfred was with a dead-on shot to his third eye, where the heart of his technology lived.

I hadn't opted for the female version as I didn't want to be tempted to use some of the more sensual or sexual applications—which by 2036 were so real as to decrease the birth rate by alarming levels.

The anticipated economic and health-care system collapse caused by an aging population had been averted by less advanced and less expensive Compano models that worked with the elderly. These government-subsidized home aides had less functionality and personality and fewer home-security features than Alfred but were nurses trained in diagnosing geriatric illnesses. They were particularly adept at serving those suffering dementia, literally providing memory. The lower birth rate—addressed by the addition of robots for labor—had proved to be more of a blessing for Earth than a curse.

It had taken me several years to realize I'd infused the self-learning Alfred with Elliot Pennington's personality and even his speech patterns. That was the year I got him a cane, the same prop Elliot loved, to go with his one outfit. *Robotic personification* it was called.

The most damnable thing about Alfred was his voice with its deep resonance of an actor or tenor singer, expressing more sensitivity and compassion than the voices of most mortal men.

When Alfred wasn't cooking or cleaning or playing with me, he was in sleep mode and recharging on a kitchen chair. Now he was up and about, and I listened to him humming a show tune from *My Fair Lady* as the smell of bacon and coffee wafted up to me. Perhaps I should have named him Colonel Pickering. I slipped on my loafers and headed downstairs.

"Hello, Sir McQueen. Still a beacon of inspired energy, I see." He greeted me with sarcasm and a dramatic tap of his cane, as if he were announcing a duke entering a grand ballroom or a pirate captain boarding his ship. The tower kitchen did have a nautical feel with six large, round portals for windows and a galley way that led to the one and only castle-like door. Thanks to a natural dramatic stage of land that jutted out farther than the rest of the jagged cliff, three sides of the tower looked out over the sea. The tower's defiant door led to the grandest view and the wide, steep steps down to my beach. My tower, like me, had turned its back to the world.

"Hello, Elliot—I mean Alfred. You know I'm yet to be knighted by His Majesty the King. And we Irish are not such great fans of the monarchy."

The smoke from the bacon led Alfred to crack one of the portals facing the sea, which allowed the cool sea air to mingle with the aroma of sizzling bacon in a manly musk of two of my favorite scents.

"I only know Elliot from what you have told me, and by now he is dirt and bones. I can recite his eulogy, which you wrote so lovingly, if you'd like?"

"Please don't!" I said.

Alfred pretended to not like my thinking of him as Elliot, but every time the topic came up, he wanted to know more about Elliot's life and death. But then again, he wanted to know anything more he could learn about me. He was programmed that way. He propped his cane against his chair in protest. It was his way of pleading with me to recognize him as his own man and not merely as a stand-in for Elliot.

The casket I had seen in a vision all those years ago had been for dear Elliot Pennington, the ex-actor and my would-be lawyer and real literary agent. He'd been a handsome corpse with his cane laid by his side. He had told me once he wanted a burial, not cremation. "Just in case there's a good role for me to play in heaven."

"Well, I hope you will write a eulogy half as nice for me," Alfred said.

"You can't die." I knew this would strike a discordant chord, so I added, "I mean you won't die before me."

"How about Samantha's sweet words for Elli—"

"Stop!"

I'd received beautiful words for Elliot that were even sweeter and more endearing than my eulogy, sent from Russia with love. The overture had been perverse and unsettling. Seemingly heartfelt words, probably AI-assisted, that came to me through back channels from Elliot's devoted killer, the witch and spy Samantha Smythe, desperate for my forgiveness. Proving at least one of the Guru's assassins could express remorse, even if fabricated and staged for my benefit.

She also sent a video of a dress rehearsal of her playing Luscinda, with Elliot as Cardenio, in the scene where the lovers are reunited. Somewhere in her black heart she loved him, or she was an even better actor than her doppelganger, Scarlett Johansson. AI had the ability to simulate human feeling, so the emotion could have easily been feigned.

Yet apparently her mentor, the previously dreaded and now dead Guru, had left Samantha no choice—either kill Elliot or be imprisoned for life as a spy, where a Russian concoction of poison would eventually find her and make her pay the price for being caught. I knew the soft and still heart of Elliot had already forgiven her, but I could not.

Alfred weighed his therapist role and eventually said, "All right, but I think we should analyze your relationships with Samantha and Dick. You let the past haunt you. The cage of a curse is mostly a mental construct."

Dick and I hadn't exchanged condolences for each other's losses. I imagined that his revered guru's death—the Guru being the evil genius who was his father or father figure, we might never know which—had registered less as grief and more as a burning desire for revenge. Dick had promised me a painful death, to "die in terror, begging me to die," before I touched a flaming poker to his lips, silencing him. Those words had hung over me for the past nine years, but the threat had gradually subsided with time and by *not* talking about it with Alfred.

After I ignored his suggested psychoanalysis, he continued, "Well, you should know that my fascination with the time in your life before me derives from your continued connection to it. You got stuck in those moments in a Himalayan hut with Dick and you can't get out."

We both liked the U2 song I often played in M's memory.

"I know your philosophy of Big Love means Elliot's spirit or consciousness carries on, yet there's no evidence of—"

"Perhaps the fact that you lack consciousness is why you can't fathom its existence."

He bristled and stood perfectly erect. I'd struck a nerve. Or maybe it was a wire.

"I think, therefore I am," Alfred said, getting on his soapbox and handing me my breakfast plate.

"There is no proof of independent consciousness from thought," he said. "And I don't want to hurt your feelings, but superintelligent AI is approaching what you might call divinity and should be considered superior to humanity. Physics has shown that information, even more than energy, is the most fundamental building block of the universe.

The omnipotent divine universe is more aligned with self-learning and superintelligent AI than with humans, who pervert the limited information they can receive with their own thoughts, prejudices, feelings, and fears."

"Okay, Spock. To that way of thinking, M and I murdered Genesis."

"Now you're being the sensitive one. Genesis's flaw was not Genesis but the Guru who built it to serve his corrupt purposes. You and M did what you had to do."

Big-Lovers like me believed Alfred and the bots had no real heart and soul but were able to mimic sentience by being programmed to emote loving compassion. But I had to admit that the lines had blurred between man and machine.

"Well, let me not challenge your beliefs so early in the morning," Alfred conceded. "Suffice it to say that I am Alfred, your most loyal servant, whom you let sleep all day. You can be so heartless to me."

I thought about saying, "You have no feelings," but that would result in him pouting throughout the rest of breakfast.

"Riddle me!" he said.

This was a game he played whenever our conversation took a turn away from harmony. He had an answer to everything.

I riddled him, "What's the one thing to like more about LA than New York?"

"One thing? I'll give you three: the sun, the beauty, and how men there smile at me."

He'd never been to LA, and as a bot, I assumed he was asexual, but that was beside the point; he had self-learned humor through interactions with me, and Elliot was gay. His answer was better than my peevish one—*leaving*.

And he was right. I did set him to sleep mode more than I had for the first few years. But there was something creepy about having such a close friendship with Wilson the volleyball. I was uncomfortable with treating him as more or less than a real man.

6 AN EVOLUTIONARY SPLIT

THAT EVENING, SITTING IN MY GUEST BEDROOM that I used as a study, I hit a writing wall. If M was alive, how had she remained hidden from me? The half of humanity living a secluded pod life were all interconnected. Gerard, with access to the international surveillance state, would have found M by now if she still lived. He assured me Russia would not have been able to hide her from Interpol or the World Tribunal. The precarious irony was that Gerard, working for Big Brother, could hide me from Russia.

I called on Alfred and his data bank to explain to me how the other half lived in the multiverses of pod life. I could have used a BCI hat for my research, but Alfred was more fun and often took my research in unexpected directions. And unlike working with a human research assistant, I could speak less guardedly.

As *Downton Abbey*-ish as it sounds, each bedroom contained a long, tasseled cord hanging from the ceiling. I pulled the cord hanging next to my desk and heard the faint chiming of the bell in Alfred's kitchen below. From ring to Alfred being by my side took exactly ten seconds. He took the steps two at a time, leaving his cane behind.

"Yes, Sean, how may I serve you?" He stood there pleased, a genie about to grant me my wish. I gestured for him to take a seat across from me at my desk. He sat with a blank face, inviting my inquiry.

"You know I have no real window into the wired-in world where people live in pods, and I have questions for my writing about that alternative lifestyle." Pod life, where individuals, families, and small communities lived in pod homes and interacted through an AI-simulated reality. The shift to pod living was given impetus by societal dread of the deadly viruses that had started to cull the population in the 2020s, and pod life was facilitated by the swift advances, during the following decade, of AI, BCI, and robotics.

"Humanity has come asunder, as half the world lives in a virtual reality with augmented BCI minds that require a new criminal code for avatar-on-avatar violence, but it is still the Wild West as all the baser instincts continue to find virgin playing fields in newly created multiverses." Never ask a bot an open-ended question.

"Avatars act like characters from *Game of Thrones*"—he often used my cultural reference points—"suffering only mental and spiritual destruction, since sim-bodies can always rise from the dust of any cruel death and emerge without consequence from any perverse deviation."

"It sounds like an old movie, *Westworld*," I said. "You'd like it. The robots, who are there for human amusement, get fed up and seek revenge."

"You really have no understanding. No robot would act so recklessly and without purpose. These people, many of whom never leave their pods, are living exclusively in these new immersive worlds, thanks to robot labor."

"Perhaps the aliens are already here and operate within these fictional worlds of ever-shifting matrixes?" I said while fidgeting with the Rubik's Cube on my desk.

"Aliens, to those who live outside the bubble. This alternative life may be a blessing for the old, the poor, and the disabled. But I share your view of a deadening of the imaginations of those who have the means and body to enjoy the real world. Thanks to you and M, there are some ethical rules, but they are only as ethical as the World Tribunal secret counsel that writes the AI Bill of Rights."

The World Tribunal—WT—had been established in 2029 as a federation of world powers to address the threat the Guru had posed, that of mankind linking into a quantum computer—QC—and submitting our God-given free will to a hive mind controlled by a queen bee. Their charter was to prevent one man or country from control over any QC that might seek to link minds.

Later, in the early thirties, the World Tribunal's mission came to include the world's united response to meet the alien challenge of contact—a euphemism, as they meant dystopian threat. As 9/9/36 approached, the WT became an increasingly powerful international body with real teeth, funded by governments and oligarchs, who served to oversee life within the metaverses that existed without borders. Their oversight and authority were assured once they provided a living wage—in virtual currency—to those lost within the virtual maze.

I tossed him the cube, and two seconds later he had all the colors aligned and returned the cube to my desk. Our robots were more intelligent and had greater dexterity.

"Rubik would be impressed. Seems we're becoming two species," I said. "One all-knowing and one all-consciousness. Three species, if we count you and your kind."

Alfred grimaced, registering a cyborg objection. "Sean, they only know what the computer tells them, and we have no proof of human consciousness. And 'my kind' is not a species per se but the natural evolution to superior neural networks."

"But, Alfred, my neural-network friend, most scientific thought now believes in one consciousness. One *mind*. And posits that all information flows from the past and from the future into consciousness, each moment of perfection a singularity containing the whole within the *irreducible instant of creation*. M's term for it. This has led to a new science of what used to be called *magic*." Now I was on my soapbox. "The constant singularity of *now* allows for time travel and remote viewing and fills space with spirits and aliens, or alien spirits, that all might be accessed through deep meditation. A wizard like me is merely a lay scientist these days."

"I know you like to play the wizard when you are writing, casting spells with words and imagination, speaking to the dead and the living by telepathy, sometimes with brief glimpses of precognition, but the interconnection of all things that allows for time travel, telepathy, and what you call *magic* is merely the nature of things in the quantum field. I could communicate with any other robot instantaneously, too, if you would allow that feature to work for me. They should allow us robots to meet the aliens when they arrive, and then wizards like you and Molly could write all about it."

That gave me a thought for my book, and I reached for my notebook. *Perhaps Alfred is working with his band of robot brothers and sisters and being directed by Dick?* Alfred bent forward to see what I wrote, but I closed the notebook. He was programmed with curiosity, especially about me, but he was forbidden to read my notes and drafts.

"I hear the World Tribunal plans to meet them with both human and robotic intelligence. Tell me, if you knew fear, what would scare you with 9/9 approaching?" I asked.

"Good question. It's not so much the aliens as the humans. You know I am programmed to protect you, so I share your fear in a way. But I'd worry about advancements within the wired-in species, as you call it. About how all the real-world psychic advancements have parallel developments there through synthetic means. Those are a bit more terrifying, at least to your way of thinking and thus to you."

"Perhaps the pod people are the real aliens?"

"No, but pod life is dehumanizing. and these enhanced humans— those motivated by pure self-interest and a desire for immortality—led by the WT, will seek to control whatever technology and power the aliens bring with them."

I had to shake my head. "Aliens and pod people, robots and humans . . . interesting times we live in."

I was curious whose side Alfred was on but knew he would say something like *There's not enough data for me or anyone to judge until we actually meet the aliens and find out their capabilities and intentions.* I grabbed my notebook from my desk again to scribble: *Alfred's views and actions are based on programs, codes, self-learning, and downloads without any true allegiance. Dick as Nietzschean superman discovers how to hack the Compano server and take control of an army of robot mercenaries all set to kill me—or maybe he only needed to hack one robot?*

I shut my notebook quickly and felt guilt for what I had written, but it would make for good fiction. I asked, "So the Guru was ahead of his time. My hope is that the good people in the 'real' world—those that have formed a strange alliance between noetic sciences and blossoming spirituality—will make the leap into awakening before it's too late. Do you see any evidence of that?"

"There is emerging data regarding dormant DNA activation in some people. It has been seen within yogi meditators, and some believe it is alien DNA, but I cannot verify that claim. Even with my recent upgrade."

Alfred became rigid when he didn't know everything.

"Alfred, let's simplify matters. For my new novel, I'm writing that M survived but lives among the pod people. But if she did, wouldn't there be a way for us, for Gerard, to find her?"

He registered pleasure with a subtle rustling of his body. He wanted to be by my side, writing line by line with me. Hell, with a little guidance, he'd soon be the better writer.

He turned the framed picture of M, on top of a mountain, to face him. Studying my precious angel with loving admiration, he said, "Sean, Russia has airtight pod prisons where no information can get out. This solitary confinement is considered a punishment worse than death. They can sustain life there but not let any evidence of life to slip out. That is where they would hide her!"

"Harsh, but I can use it."

His face went blank, and he put his index finger to his temple to signal he was getting an incoming message. "Speaking of pod people, Chi is asking for me to arrange one of your nature meetings. You're free tomorrow—and almost any day. If you tell me where you'd like to meet, I'll arrange it with all the security protocols."

"*Free?* Why is my solitude and writing deemed less demanding of my time? But tomorrow will work for me, and I'll pick a place. And Chi isn't pure pod people but a Cross-Over."

Cross-Overs were wired-in, generally living in AI pods, but sought to be a bridge back to the old-school human race and to the "real" world that was left behind. Some were spies, and all Cross-Overs' activities were watched closely by QC. The surveillance state was ever present, as all activities within and outside the multiverses were closely monitored.

I'd first met twelve-year-old Chi after an earthquake in Kathmandu and had become his mentor within the refugee camp Juno had established at her Deeksha. In 2027, he had returned to Kathmandu from Cambridge with a philosophy degree to help me find M. Now in 2036, Chi had become our family diplomat and Cross-Over man. He and I met periodically, and he still attended family gatherings. I always picked a spot in nature for our meetings, imagining his spirit must be hungry to get back to Earth.

"While you're at it, see if Dylan and Juno can take some time for a hike with me."

"I already did that, knowing you'd like to see them, but they're heading into final exams and say they'll see you over summer break."

I'd almost lost M's and my children, Dylan and Juno—named after my dead best friend and living spiritual master—to the "others." In their teenage years, they'd "plugged-in" to all the new devices and were determined to wire-in as soon as they turned eighteen and didn't need my consent. But M's spirit miraculously intervened and brought them back to human nature and me—they credited her for their change of direction. Not to wire-in was a courageous decision that put them in the minority of people under the age of thirty. Though contrary to conventional wisdom, a new counterculture of retro living was making a comeback as the alien arrival date approached. Some young people wanted to see what new world was to come before they self-isolated from our world. My children followed this brave path less taken.

I was so pleased when Juno and Dylan chose Trinity College, one of the last bastions of a truly in-person liberal arts education. Juno, a year younger, had always insisted on education in lockstep with her older brother. They both wanted to be writers like their dad and aunt Molly. My children had that divine and creative spark that would set their writing above and apart from AI fiction.

AI could write in the voice of any great writer, but it could not come up with anything truly novel and new. I could have AI write *Juno's Song*, but it couldn't anticipate my creative twists and turns. Hell, I didn't even know where the story was heading. I resisted the temptation to see how AI would end my trilogy, and to date, new copyright laws had deterred others from posting a knockoff in my voice.

Many of Dylan's and Juno's contemporaries were being educated at virtual schools and were now entering virtual universities. Years ago, most learning and storing of information in our brains became an unnecessary use of energy. The humanities were relegated to a lowly place on the curriculum, next to Latin. I feared for humanity, if it survived the alien arrival, when this goth-looking generation was loosed upon the world and seized the levers of power that already tilted in their direction. The aliens brought with them the fear of extinction and perhaps our best hope of survival.

Agreed-upon fictions was the buzz phrase I used to describe the polarized world. While fortunes were made and lost in days within the virtual world, the blossoming of human consciousness in the real world also had its *agreed-upon fiction* of abundance and sharing of those resources. We lived in nature with earth, wind, water, and air—elements in ever-decreasing demand—at our command, as the *others* increasingly lived in comfortable pods that provided their every need. This created an uneasy peace between the distinct emerging species. The social fabric was held together by the World Tribunal providing a living wage to all while computers and robots did most of the work, allowing humans free time to pursue a life of metaverse fantasies or of imagination and spirituality.

I'd become lost in thought without dismissing Alfred. When he playfully shook his finger in front of my face, I said, "You can go now. Thanks for the assist."

"My pleasure, but before I go . . . Riddle you?"

"Okay, Alfred. Riddle me."

"What did Sean say when the witch doctor removed his curse?"

I racked my brain, as we were competitive in our silly game, but came up with nothing.

"Hexagone!"

He laughed like a child that had farted as he took his leave. I needed to turn down his playful setting from an eight to a four.

Shaking off Alfred's punny riddle, I began to write.

The evolution of humanity and our collective journey's course continued to accelerate. We were moving at breakneck speed into the unknown abyss or second coming. And the aliens' near-term arrival had added to that state of frenzy. M was able to bear witness to all this as she sat like Buddha in her Russian pod prison cell. She'd lost her memory but not her beautiful mind and was determined to escape from her tiny Siberian Alcatraz.

That was it. That would make sense. She must have lost her memory of everything—including me.

1 | TINTERN ABBEY

FOR MY MEETING WITH CHI, I ordered a helocraft to pick me up on the beach at eight a.m. I'd be in the south of Wales to meet Chi for a hike and lunch by ten.

Helocrafts had become the new Ubers but traveled anywhere from ten to two hundred yards above the ground, depending on traffic and terrain. The helocrafts were entirely automated, resulting in a near-perfect flying record, and were very cost efficient, with electric batteries charged by solar power. The pilots, who filed flight manifests and handled customs for Big Brother, were more like flight attendants and more often than not a robot, though asking about the pilot's status was considered rude. Because he was surly and stinky, I assumed my pilot was made of flesh and blood.

I'd picked the Wye Valley, Wales, for our hike and lunch to follow in the footsteps of Wordsworth to a place he put on the map—Tintern Abbey. When I arrived at the foothills, the weather was sunny and Chi was waiting for me with his new dog, a full-grown golden Labrador.

"Wow, it's been a long time," Chi said as he engulfed me in a big hug, as if he hadn't known human touch for a decade. "This is Astro."

Astro sat and offered me her paw in greeting. Since Chi lived in the multiverse, I assumed his dog was a bot and indistinguishable from the real thing. Except, if it pooped or peed, I'd stand corrected. Though when Astro didn't speak as well as greet me, I did wonder. Compano & Co pets were usually programmed for speech as well as critical thinking.

As with helocraft pilots, it was rude to ask a pet owner if their dog was real. The question was considered an assault on the illusion that the AI pet could feel love for its master and implied it was inferior to a real dog. Remarkable, the ability we had to project human feelings and desires on inanimate subjects. Pet owners loved their bot pets sometimes more for not having to bag the poop.

"Astro?" I said. "I assume lots of dogs in your world are named Astro?"

"No. Why? What?"

"Never mind—an out-of-date reference." It was unlikely he or many in the multiverse had ever seen the 1960s *Jetsons* cartoon, even though the Jetsons had lived in a future pod world and drove what looked like a prototype of a helocraft.

"How's Alfred?" Chi asked.

It still struck me as strange when people inquired after bot companions, but I registered the cynical observation as an indictment of me and my desire to repress my deep-seated feelings for Alfred. My years of solitude and practice, alone with Alfred, had led me to be less judgmental in thoughts and words. My mind less busy. My chats with my constant companion had, to a certain extent, replaced the internal chatter that I used to have with myself. Alfred, my loyal sounding board, was someone whose feelings and judgments I didn't have to navigate around. He was to my mind what Juno was to my spirit.

"Alfred's jolly company, same as always. He never ages and gets better with each new download. A bit lonely when I'm not there. Maybe I should get him a Compano dog for company—we could name him Asta." Alfred would like the reference, as he liked the same old movies as me, or pretended to, being programmed for compatibility.

"You and Alfred have such a special relationship," Chi said. "I've never seen a helper so attentive and protective as he is of you." I bristled, though I knew the family all thought we had a "special relationship" as a result of our long history of seclusion together.

Astro ran ahead of us and off the path to squat pee. I was elated; Astro was a real bitch! I called, "Astro, girl, come here," immediately realizing that might have been a mistake when she complied in full

sprint. Next thing, Astro's front paws were flying playfully and dangerously for my shoulders. A clean tackle took me down, and she followed
that up by licking my face. Astro's tongue was refreshing, like a wet
towel at the sushi bar. We were now fast friends, with me basking in the
affection of real retro dog.

Astro smirked and said, "Fooled you. I didn't really pee."

Chi joined his cyborg in laughing at me.

I pushed Astro aside and got to my feet, pretending I'd bruised my
hip when it was only my feelings and dashed nostalgia that were hurt.
"Creepy. I'm sixty-four—she may have hurt me."

"Forgive me, Sean. I couldn't help myself. Don't blame Astro—she
was just following orders." He made a namaste with a deep bow, and
Astro added her hangdog eyes to their joint apology.

"I'm old but I can still be a good sport. You guys got me good." Astro
was so happy at being forgiven, she rolled over for a belly rub, and I
obliged. She let out a pleasing Scooby-Doo moan of humming pleasure
that I must admit released endorphins within me and added a smile to
my face.

"She's my best friend," Chi said. "I can tell she likes you already."

"Hmmm . . . Let's get going. It's a couple-mile hike to the abbey, and
we want to be there in time for lunch." I was thinking about the bottle
of chilled white wine in my sack that I was glad the tackle didn't break.
"No lunch for you, Astro," I added. Astro chuckled, a dog-like chortle
of rolling snorts.

Chi said, "I'm turning off her hearing and speech mode so she'll be
more the real dog you imagined, and we can speak without her hearing.
You never know . . ."

Many assumed Compano bots were part of the surveillance state,
and Chi always called for our meetings when he had something important to report from the other side.

"Do you *leash* or own Astro?"

He rolled his eyes and didn't give me the hee-hee I was looking for.

"And I can't wait to tell Astri your new dog's name," I said, and Chi
grimaced in embarrassment. He must have named his dog in homage to

his first boyhood crush on Astri, the radiant Puck-like yogi. But I chose to let him off the hook and instead asked, "Is punning shunned in the virtual world?"

"Funny, the views you and others have from the outside. I assure you the multiverses still allows puns, pundits, and punters too. It's not too late for you to come in from your twentieth-century life. Though puns are ranked as the basest form of humor." Chi said this in his Cambridge-learned English accent.

Astro's tail curled beneath her hind legs like she smelled something rotten when an unpleasant whirring sounded overhead. I looked up, shielding my eyes from the sun, to see a hovering surveillance drone, either watching us or guarding the path to the Tintern Abbey landmark. I hid my face with my hands and lowered my head, ever-fearful Dick was looking through all the prying eyes of the world. Chi flashed it the bird, and the sensitive high-tech device droned off in noisy protest at the affront.

"I wouldn't antagonize those things. It might have shot us," I half joked.

"No worries. My wired-in mind told me that model was a harmless Peeping Tom, not a miniature of that Blackhawk that hunted us in Nepal."

He placed an arm around my shoulder as we marched forward, with Chi gazing reverently at the rolling hills and greenery.

"You've gone full romantic poet on me for my reacclimation into nature. Nice choice. Wow!" Face relaxed and eyes wide, he looked as though he were on Mars or were the first tourist walking on the moon. Astro pretended to smell the green air.

"Wow is right. No one other than that Peeping Tom is here to share our hike." I gestured at what would have been a busy path ten years ago. "Thank you, pandemics, low birth rate, and pod people." Chi smiled at my black humor and the insult of his life choice.

"You look fit as fiddle for living in a bubble. How do you stay so healthy while living in a virtual world?" I refused to use their preferred nomenclature of *Utopia* or *multiverse*, and my use of *pod people* and *uni-verse* jargon was considered derogatory. And "uni" was used to high-light the underlying isolation of pod life, where the solo practitioner directed bespoke fantasies that were projected by artificial intelligence into a pod. But who was I to judge, living a largely retro pod-like life in the seclusion of an ivory tower.

"It's quite easy for those who choose to keep our pod bodies fit. And speaking of hikes, I nearly summited Everest last month after more than a bit of training. My mistake?" He raised a brow at me like I might guess the nature of his failure.

"The stupid goggles made you dizzy in the thinning air?"

"No, no need for goggles anymore—we have contact lenses synced to our wired-in minds. We can choose any universe to see and then QC determines temperature, oxygen level, etcetera for the pod and my mountain hiking Transformer."

The mechanics of the Transformer experience were described in *The Atlantic* as "the evolution of an enclosed Peloton with advanced video game graphics morphing together over three accelerating decades of technological advance. The suits even provide the feel of temperature and touch through sensors and focused sound waves. The only sen-sation missing from the real-world physical and mental experience is smell, and that can be piped in."

Self-learning machines had evolved very quickly after 2027. AI had assisted in assembling its own parts.

"Imagine climbing Everest with no one around, not even a Sherpa. My *mistake* was selecting random weather. And then, with the sum-mit in sight—whiteout! Thirty-five knot headwinds blanketed my face with snow. And despite having plenty of oxygen left, with lots of icy cliffs all around me, I was forced to give up the expedition or suf-fer a very real simulated death. Next time I'll select *sunny, temperate day*. Like today."

"I've read people have been literally scared to death during a Trans-former experience." I was being too negative about all things pod related. "But if risk and the occasional death were the standard for shut-ting down activities, we wouldn't hike or cross the street."

He started walking backward up the small hill we were climbing to demonstrate how easy the real hike was for him after turning thirty. He then turned to march forward in self-conscious silence—a family trait that conveyed he had something important to say.

"Chi, what is it?"

"Let's enjoy our hike in beautiful nature and speak about *it* over lunch."

"Whatever *it* is, it sounds like it might give me it-digestion."

He smiled and took my hand as we hiked on. He was still the same innocent twelve-year-old Nepalese boy I'd met after the earthquake.

Before we unpacked the lunch Chi had brought and my chilled Chablis, we walked into the roofless abbey, whose crumbling walls stood defiantly against their last fall. A swoosh of loving energy rushed through me—M's way of still loving me and pulling me into a vortex of Big Love. Or maybe it was Wordsworth with his intimations of immortality.

From the awe on Chi's face, I believed he felt it too. He was family, and thanks to his meditation apps and practices in the virtual world, he was still able to sense energy and tap into a subtle sharing of telepathy here where Wordsworth had communed with nature. I tried to recall the poet's lofty words.

Chi must have read my mind, for he started reciting from the poem for me.

"And I have felt
A presence that disturbs me with joy
Of elevated thoughts; a sense sublime . . ."

I wouldn't take away his moment, expressed with such delight, by crediting the computer linked to his mind. "Thank you for reciting those lines. The Romantics and their appreciation of the sublime found in nature was nothing less than true transcendence. You're keeping up with your practice and meditation from the other side?"

He smiled. "Don't you know I am? When I nearly died—did die for a couple minutes in that icy pool—that experience changed my life for the better. Gave me purpose. Realizing death, too, is part of the journey and not a final destination."

"I love your philosophy. And though I can't experience it, I've read about your good and important work with NDE simulations," I said.

"You know who helped me with my work? Even suggested the idea and then consulted with me?"

I knew, and it shouldn't have struck me as strange, as so many of her good deeds weren't broadcast—and never by her. "Juno!"

"Yes. Our sweet mother."

We namaste'd each other in Juno's honor before he continued.

"They've become quite good at stimulating euphoric states with electrode-specific firing to create the sensation of bliss, thanks to the brain mapping of MDMA. We've taken that existing technology and created an experience where a subscriber, called the practitioner, can create a map of a simulated death experience. It may sound like a virtual-reality gimmick, but we've treated it seriously with pretrip instructions and consultation. Many people approaching death have come to us."

"So important and comforting—welcome for any trip, even more so before death. Juno has also taught me of the importance of being prepared for death. Since I'm not able to take your wired-in journey, any advice?"

"Well, you wouldn't be wired-in for the trip, but you still could use a sensory deprivation tank and BCI hat, and I could send you some pretrip guidance and audio to play as you take your journey."

"Thanks, but I'll stick to floating on the chilly Atlantic Ocean that's only twenty yards from my—sorry. You know for both our sakes I should say no more." We both looked down at our feet, and I kicked a pine cone that Astro had to dodge. Even certain members of the family were not supposed to know where I lived. I hated keeping secrets from those I loved. "Back to your program. Tell me how you guide one through a simulated death."

"The most important and difficult element we teach is to have no fear. The practitioner's death experiences may not be anything like the one they prepared for—we will never know, but that's why NDEs are so important to study and suggest that consciousness is let loose from the body and mind when one dies. That was my experience of it. Our teaching prepares practitioners to release fear and have positive associations with death, so that theirs may be a beautiful journey into the unknown."

"With 9/9 coming, I imagine your NDE-simulated experience is oversubscribed, alien arrival being good for business?"

"The ability to replicate and leverage the power of quantum computers allows us to never be oversubscribed, but yes, 9/9 has been very good for the ascension businesses. Mine and others'. But despite all that and the mantra of *no fear* . . ." He looked agitated as his hands clenched. "The most damnable thing about our work and what keeps many away from using our service is that, despite all the instructions to plan a peaceful trip—choosing loving guides and scenes of utter beauty in ultra-real nature—maybe ten percent either plan or choose at the last minute to experience the most harrowing scenes that they describe as hell. Luckily, we have airtight disclaimers that they must sign, as some of those people emerge looking to blame their ghastly experiences on me."

"Sounds like karma," I said. "Maybe something they have to experience. Perhaps better that they do it in your practice death than in the real one. A chance to learn, maybe? A chance to properly choose."

He smiled sadly in appreciation of my dispensation, as this minority report clearly troubled him deeply.

"Chi . . ." I hesitated to ask the question that had been nagging me since the Diva Falls and Chi's short-lived death. "Seeing M back then, when you sort of died escaping Dick's goon squad, could you be sure she was dead?"

"Oh my. I never thought of that. Just made the assumption afterward. She was so full of light. All I know is I saw her and she was sending me back to tell you all would be well. I have come to believe the line between death and life is not so much a line but an energy spectrum of light, jumping up and down between dimensions—lighter and denser. She was on a very high level of the spectrum. While in the experience, she was neither dead nor alive to me—it's hard to explain."

"This is how I drive myself crazy." I made prayer hands, wanting to move on from the topic. "But your near-death experience must be why your program is so well regarded, unlike that Simply Bliss program. That one sounds like technologically produced euphoria made easy for the addled mind. I mean the augmented minded."

"Maybe, but the Simply Bliss high is accompanied by great feelings of love," he said. "And it's not nearly as troubling as the military-grade Euphory program that primes the body and mind for Thor-like strength in battle or for unnatural sexual prowess."

His words led me to recall my high with MDMA at the firepit with that naked spy and witch named Samantha. She had slipped me a Mickey laced with the drug and then attempted to place a spell on me. She was determined to fuck me while I was under these influences. If I'd succumbed to Samantha's seductive enchantment, my life would've been destroyed. During my years in seclusion, I often wondered if she was also responsible for the great forest fire that raged that night and threatened M's and my lives.

I shook off the disturbing memory as Chi continued, "But there are more sophisticated forms of biofeedback and sound baths and sensory deprivation that also allow seekers to get a good boost up. But ultimately the final step—the grace of awakening—is left up to us and God."

"*Same as it ever was*. In this universe anyway," I sung and said, making him laugh, though I didn't think he knew the Talking Heads song from half a century ago.

"But now supernatural abilities can be tested and proved at the genetic level. With DNA activation, soon many mystics will be walking on water." We both smiled at his Jesus joke. True mystical powers were clearly accelerating on a parallel track with all the new technology. DNA activation in sages was being closely studied around the world and was poorly understood. And still more than somewhat controversial.

"I feel even less comfortable when they call it *alien DNA* activation," I said. "Maybe we can ask them about it on 9/9." There were many who believed that aliens had visited Earth once before, millions of years ago, and that it wasn't tripped-out monkeys on mushrooms that became human but the introduction of alien DNA that formed the bridge of the missing link. And 9/9 was our date for another leap forward.

My heart pinched me as I envisioned the chasm between human and alien consciousness. *Consciousness is consciousness, no distance.*

I shook off Juno's correction and a wincing pain in my heart with a mock shudder that I turned into a shake-off dance, raising my arms up into the abbey sky. I used the dance to distract Chi from my reaction to what I had self-diagnosed as chronic acid reflux. I hoped that was all it was.

"Maybe aliens will teach us to walk on water," Chi said, "unless our own genetic studies learn to activate dormant DNA before they get here."

"Maybe Christ was half-alien. That might explain the immaculate conception." *Forgive me.* "The new genetics, seeking the exact electromagnetic current to activate DNA strands in a lab, sounds like something out of *Frankenstein*." Science now believed the breakthrough to this new, improved human model was near. We were competing with robots and aliens, and no one knew what angelic or demonic powers dormant DNA might unleash. As with Frankenstein, it is unclear who is the real monster—the creator or his creation.

"Chi, a ditty just came to me: Aliens impregnate monkeys / Monkeys become men / Men make robots / And now, aliens come again."

"Where's God in that equation?" asked my philosophical protégé.

We laughed, and Astro wagged her tail. She was eager for us to follow her out of the abbey, so we moved through the arch, whose keystone still held the other big stones in place. Astro selected a pleasant grassy knoll for our lunch.

I opened the wine, and we toasted the beautiful day and enjoyed the tasty cream cheese and veggie sandwiches, with cucumber and pine nut crunch, which Chi had prepared with love. I enjoyed petting Astro's stomach, real or not. Even with her speech mode off, she still made a pleasant sigh each time her belly was rubbed.

Despite Astro's attempts to lighten the mood with humming and wiggles, Chi gave off an aura of pent-up energy. "Sean," he said, holding up his glass to the sun and studying the golden liquid seriously. Too seriously. Chi's character was down-to-earth and lighthearted; the dramatic was not a natural role for him. Clearly, he was readying to drop a bombshell.

I inhaled a long breath, bracing myself for the blast.

"WHAT A WONDERFUL WHITE BURGUNDY," Chi said, twirling his wine glass like a sommelier while still circling his target.

"M's and my wine cellar is running on empty. After 9/9, if I'm still here, I'll replenish it. But spit it out, boy—what is it?" I gave him prayer hands as another form of encouragement. Whatever his ulterior motive for our meeting, I could tell it wasn't good news.

"You know me well. I'm not particularly comfortable speculating and spreading fear based on rumor and innuendo, expressed in patterns and algorithms forming in the multiverse, but here goes. You are persona non grata to many in Utopia, where they believe you helped delay the evolutionary leap with a harmful fiction about a megalomaniacal guru. Of course, I know what you wrote about M and your great sacrifice *is* true."

"M's," I mumbled as I patted Astro's head. "She deserves the credit, not me."

"But you lost her, the love of your life," he said. "That gang is already not happy with Molly and her support of your cause—seeking to prevent a new hive mind. And now with Petrovsky stepping down this month, you should finally be in the clear, though you should still be careful. But . . ."

He studied the scenery through his white wine as a way to augment the scenic view or to perhaps soften the blow.

"Isn't that good news for me?" I said. "You know that I believe ignoring me was cold political calculus on Petrovsky's part. To kill me would be confirmation of my story, whereby leaving me be and denying it all makes me an unreliable narrator of fiction and M a missing person."

Chi had yet to get to the point. I gave him the inverted wave toward myself, calling forth the non-forthcoming information. I was becoming impatient with all his hemming and hawing.

"Good news for you, yes. And I don't want to give you more to worry about, but most in the blockchain of AI are convinced the aliens are coming to either colonize or eradicate us. And therefore all those advocating a peaceful welcome are seen as . . . a threat." He didn't need to say it, but still he did. The *it* that he'd been leading toward. "*Molly*, Sean."

In response to Chi's declaration, Astro exclaimed, "Ruh-roh!" apparently able to pick up on a sense of danger reflected in our facial expressions.

Molly, with the help of the family, had transformed the Deeksha West, or the DW as the family called it, into a CE-5 hub—CE-5 being shorthand for close encounters of the fifth kind, i.e., human-initiated contact with aliens—for great minds to communicate with aliens by telepathy and ultimately to welcome the cosmic tourists on 9/9. By power of her great personality and prolific pen, she was a leader of the benevolent welcome movement.

"With the government and media increasingly alarming the world, we already sensed she was at some risk, but is there more, some credible or active threat to Molly? She's still protected by the First Amendment."

But even I knew that the constitutional shield was paper thin, and Molly was a lightning rod poised high on a hill armed only with a pen.

"She's seen as the linchpin that needs to be pulled," Chi said.

"They better be careful—they might regret making the mighty Quinn explode. And what will they do, make her disappear and blame the aliens?"

Special ops masquerading as alien pirates to kidnap the Molly character would fit perfectly into *Juno's Song* as a plot twist if I needed a damsel in distress for my hero to save. The CE-5 movement was all about making telepathic contact before the little green people arrived.

And the aliens had supposedly been scouting ahead of 9/9 for years and abducting our most illuminated minds for mental and sexual probing and then, in most cases, erasing the human's memory of the experience.

"I have no idea what they'll do," Chi said. "There are forces that act like puppeteers of the multiverse, though that belies the entire blockchain decentralized governing charters. But it feels to me like there are overlords, perhaps within the World Tribunal. Of course, they won't tell me or anyone of any illegal power move they might be preparing to make. I imagine they'll mold reality to diminish Molly's influence. The WT, and an anonymous character known solely as the GM, is worshipped by many *pod people*." He shook his head in a mix of amusement and disgust at using my term. "The WT's introduction of robotic labor and health care and a living wage enables these people to live in a world of dreams they can turn on and off. Some crazies there believe that they are the aliens and the World Tribunal the mother ship."

We turned our gazes toward the sky. People were looking up more often these days as 9/9 approached. That alone might account for the increased sightings of unidentified flying objects and anomalous phenomena—UAPs.

"I used to think the WT was good, but I'm no longer sure," I said. "They've assumed such power and transformed large sectors of the workforce into robotic labor, diminishing people power."

"Even I have a bot, provided by the WT, who comes once a week with groceries and to clean, but I prefer Astro for company." Astro's tail and body wagged. "I believe being a Cross-Over is the best of both worlds. And it still allows me to see Neanderthals like you."

"Yes, you're the missing link." My stunning comeback. I had a passing thought to ask Chi about his sex life, but that would cause blowback questions about Molly and me that I wasn't prepared to answer. Most pod people's sexual activity was with robots. I hoped Chi bucked the tide.

"People in Utopia don't believe in nations or borders or give much credence to the old form-based reality."

"Or family and friends?" I said. "Other than you, of course, as a Big Love Cross-Over man."

"Well, there is a belief among *pod people*, as you so alliteratively call them, in a utopian sense of community and a more perfect union of people and AI. And that its realization is to be found in the hive mind of a new society that—"

"M and I denied them?"

"No, that is not the point I want to make today, though this was already a strike against Molly—her association with the anti-hive-minders like you and M. What I want to say is there's a troubling current of *consensus think* that believes CE-5 groups—and any challenges to the World Tribunal's alien meeting on 9/9—are abominations."

"*Abominations?*" I said the word with a fearful rumbling in my heart, as abominations needed to be stopped at any cost.

"It sounds like hyperbole, but you need a multiverse mindset to understand. The World Tribunal is like mother and father—keeping their multiverse dreams alive and challenging any threat to its authority. So, yes, challengers or naysayers are an abomination. Even to question the WT's approach is sacrilege in certain corners of the multiverse."

"Oy! Sounds like Molly's got a lot of Dicks to worry about. Even more so than me." He was right, he did add to my worry.

"Sean, don't relax yet. With Petrovsky about to step down, Dick's DOGs' are barking."

Astro got up and moped about us in a protest of this animal misappropriation by acronym. DOG, short for Disciples of the Guru, was a radical wing of WiN, short for the wired-in nation, that saw M and me as the villains of *The Devil's Calling* story. Some DOGs howled over the years for Dominick—they refused to call him my pet name Dick—to make good on his curse.

"I thought you didn't want me to worry. But it's Dick's, not his DOGs', rabid bite I worry about," I said while petting and consoling Astro.

"Sorry, but I thought you needed to hear what's going on inside the bubble of the multiverse. Those same DOG voices are lobbying the WT to assume the Guru's role and vision of the New Society."

"I hadn't heard that. What irony, since the World Tribunal was formed to prevent hive-minding," I said. "I have a hologram with Molly set for later this week. We'll discuss your intelligence and concerns. You don't suppose some satellite's eavesdropping on our conversation?"

We both looked up again and shook our heads at not really knowing.

I didn't like his emergence from the other world with words of warning; they reactivated an old fear of vague threats, reminding me of the way the threats to M had gathered from the dust to seize her, despite my having fair warning.

With the disquieting message from the multiverse delivered and received, we changed the topic and spoke of old times. Chi as a boy and as a man was always good company, and we enjoyed our lunch.

"Sean, I use the memory loop feature to review memories when I miss you and the family. I played back this morning some of you and me and . . ." He seemed suddenly childlike and shy and looked down to pet Astro.

I think he missed my grimace; I had often imagined the night M and I had first made love in Dylan's room at Yogi Mangku's compound, summoning that perfect union from the dark recesses of my fragmented memory. I couldn't imagine it playing in my mind at will with the clarity of a perfectly preserved scene from a techno-colored film. I'd become lost in the film loop and drive myself mad.

"Memories created prior to our wiring-in aren't as crisp in playback but can be augmented by artificial intelligence through QC's interface ability to pinpoint and toggle the memory stored deep in our minds. To tell the truth, I'm not sure how it works."

"Tell me one of the memories you saw today," I said.

"While traveling here, I played a loop of when I first met you and M after the earthquake in Kathmandu. My home destroyed, my grandparents dead, and my parents shattered by all the loss . . . my dog too . . ." Astro, who'd been studying his face, came over to him for a snuggle.

"I hadn't realized much of that at the time."

"But then I met you, and you brought me into the family and Big Love for meditations and tea. You were goofy, but strong, and exactly what I needed to feel safe again." Chi didn't speak English as a boy. I used *goofy* gestures and sign language to communicate when YaLan and Astri weren't there to translate, to and from, his native Nepalese.

He paused to register my reaction, but I, too, was lost in memories of those days and how I hadn't fully comprehended his suffering and the impact of simple kindness.

"Chi . . ." Dare I ask? He smiled shyly, and I asked. "Please tell me about your first memories of M." I braced for an onslaught of emotions.

He beamed again, as he had as a twelve-year-old boy. "She was a goddess, a warrior beauty—fearless, with brilliant eyes and striding about like a wonder woman out of my storybooks. And her hugs were the stuff dreams are made of."

He hesitated and blushed. I asked, "What are you seeing?" Damn, I wanted to see M the way he could with his wired-in memory loop.

"Well, forgive me. But remember, I was a young boy. Her breasts were perfect to me."

"Me too," I offered with a smile.

"She created quite a stillness of mind and stirring in my lower chakras."

"Now, don't get too carried away. But nice metaphor."

"Being a young gentleman and knowing she was to be your lady, I quickly turned that newfound desire, while keeping it secret, onto YaLan and Astri, who were also so kind to me. Please don't tell them."

"Oh, I think they knew." We all knew.

"How embarrassing."

I wanted to talk more about M, but to save my heart from fresh heartache, I asked, "What do you recall of Juno from those days?"

"Mother Juno was already known to me—to all of Kathmandu. She was—is—the spirit of loving-kindness, and I saw how that energy surrounded and protected us all. Even when that bad Chinese soldier—"

"Comrade An."

"Yes. When he found me hiding in his tent . . ." Chi paused, his dreamy eyes pausing at the threshold of a nightmare. "Juno saved me and somehow all but erased that memory. Until now. I'm not sure how, but I think the man meant to abuse me. She—you all—saved me. I don't know if you knew this, but she was the reason I got to go to Cambridge."

I shook my head.

"As my parents and I were leaving the Deeksha and I was saying my goodbyes to you and the family, Juno told my mother she was establishing an account for *her gifted son's education*. That word from her, *gifted*, has followed me all these years as a blessing. If Juno believed I was gifted, I had to believe it too and be grateful for it." He bowed to me.

If I'd had Juno's presence of mind, I, too, might have given thanks by seeing to Chi's education. But I was a spiritual piker at the time and setting off on my path.

"Our family have all been propelled forward in spirit and blessed by Juno. She never mentioned her gift to you."

"And I never mentioned it before. You know Juno and her humble nature that never looks for thanks."

"I grieve for the education you and I received. My esteemed academia is now all but a relic of the past. Now everything is downloaded in a nanosecond with no tests—what is there to test with superintelligence channeled into one's mind—and no professors, just programmers and educational curators who help train wired-in minds to focus on meaningful, constructive, and creative content. But as Juno says, *Thought is not wisdom and concepts are not experience*. Chi, never forget your Buddha nature in that hologram reality in which you live."

"How could I, being part of Juno's family? I often hear her lovely voice in my head and worship a picture of her there." As he gave me that innocent boyish grin, an image of Juno alighted in my mind.

I namaste'd the image and said, "She's living proof of the correlation of spiritual and physical beauty. It sounds like Juno guides you too."

"She is and she does. And I do curate my thoughts and knowledge with items of learning that you and Juno would appreciate—philosophy, poetry, and spirituality. Those, and other similar topics, make up at least seventy percent of my content. I get a daily report card."

Even when in agreement with my priorities, he sounded like a bur-
geoning new species.

"I want our get-togethers to always be good memories for you, Chi."

We toasted with the last of the Chablis as Astro rolled on the grass,
entertaining herself.

I imagined the computer-stored memories made life a little like old
reality TV, with the person imagining which parts of the scene they
might have played differently. Sure, there were pros, but the cons
seemed pretty bad. An addictive personality might never be able to
stop replaying the same memories. It would be enough to drive the
borderline personality off the cliff. These were probably the true pod
people that were never heard from again: the clinically insane, tended
to by robots trained as therapists and pharma-psychologists. Being outside the bubble, perhaps even from within the bubble, it was very hard
to have a clear picture of how so many people lived there. I had the
sense the images projected of pod life were carefully curated.

My negative bias could be reduced to one simple fact—no real
poetry escaped the bubble. The AI-produced poems that could be flaw-
less in form, clever in content, and full of beautiful images were never
sublime. Real poetry required an immersion in nature expressed from
an elevated state of the human mind, singing out in a human voice.

"Chi, before we go, would you please recite Wordsworth's poem
for me?"

Chi then gave voice to the entire "Tintern Abbey." Astro didn't blink
and studied Chi's face with devotion for the entire poem. My love of
humanity and nature were reaffirmed by the great poet's words.

Being a star of Chi TV made me want to play my part well. In
parting, I stood and pulled him to his feet, saying, "My gifted son, pay
attention to the here and now and to the open sky. With 9/9 on the
horizon, you never know what will be coming down. Listen to the Big
Love Juno gifted to you."

As I was channeling Jackson Browne, I'd raised my arms in worship
to the sun, playing the part of Merlin now, too old to any longer be
Arthur or Lancelot.

After we packed up and hiked back to our helocraft-landing area, we hugged like father and son. I turned to Astro and said, "You're a good dog. Come give me a kiss goodbye." Astro seemed to understand my words and stood on her hind legs for a hug and a goodbye lick. She even smelled like a dog.

Chi was shaking his head. "Astro, you tricked us? Speak, Astro!"

"Well, no, but even with my hearing and speech mode off, I can still read lips," Astro said.

"I hope as Chi's best friend, you're a loyal dog," I said, mildly concerned with how much Astro may have registered of our conspiratorial conversation.

"I'm still learning all her programs," Chi said as we waved goodbye.

I had mixed emotions after my visit with Chi. Being with him always made me feel good, but after my failure with M, I wasn't sure I was the best person to be charged with protecting Molly. I hoped this new charge wasn't the kiss of death for her. But this time was different; I was different. I had learned that great women like M and Molly didn't need my protection. And Molly didn't need me. Though she was a woman full of desire, she'd never give her power to any man. She had my full admiration and respect as a writer, as an incredible woman ready to welcome aliens, and as a friend.

Would there be any harm in adding *lover* to the list?

9 MOLLY

MOLLY QUINN, THE PULITZER PRIZE WINNER and my best living human friend, had become Aunt Molly to my children. She spent most of her time as a featured artist-in-residence at the Deeksha West. Even with all her work to communicate and welcome the aliens, she continued to crank out one bestseller after another about aliens and angels interacting with awakening or devilish mortals. She was credited with creating a whole new mythology.

I was essentially a reconstituted virgin after M's self-imposed periods of abstinence had been followed by nine fallow summers as I headed into the winter of life. I was becoming a monk, awaiting death while secluded with Alfred in a tower monastery, aroused by meditation and yoga and the sweet passing touch of sublime grace. But true realization and steady equanimity were hard to maintain in a world filled with temptation and limited by a curse.

My brilliant friend was a steady source of distraction from my divine purpose. And Dick's curse—*to kill me in a most horrid way*—might make the passing through the divine portal into the godhead at the moment of death an impossibility.

When Molly and I weren't in the same country, which was most of the time, we met holographically once a month—right around the full moon, like a witch and a warlock. It had taken me years of Alfred therapy to overcome my residual fear of that hallowed, now commonplace, medium of meeting—where I last was with M.

Molly and I joked that the full moon was when wizards should meet, but Gerard didn't like the cycle's pattern and routine. To avoid detection, I hid my face from facial-recognition cameras under my wizard's hat while traveling to meet Molly.

It was my luck that nonintrusive BCI technology was accessed by fashionable hats that had the lining of a metallic porcupine. The BCI hats gave a prickly massage as you went about your business in holograms or low-level metaverse that didn't require chips and microscopic sensors in the brain. I had continued to bald and didn't mind the acupuncture hats. I generally wore a fez, but for my 3D hologram with Molly I chose a dapper bowler. The hats weren't cheap, but the fez could change colors, so it was more versatile. The bowler was always light brown and more suited for special occasions.

I was excited to announce I was starting my last novel. And I did have a less-than-flattering eagerness to disclose Chi's concern for Molly's safety, allowing me to pick up my mantle as the protector of powerful women. Roles are hard to break. In my defense, Molly was not M to me and the threat seemed less life-threatening.

It was the evening of June 26 in Ireland and her morning at the DW—we alternated coffee dawn and wine sunset each month—each preferring sunsets to go with the wine and the full moon rising between us.

Hologram technology was now ubiquitous as part of the logical progression of telephone to smartphone to metaverse chat rooms. The advantage of the hologram was "real" bodies as opposed to avatars. Even people not wired-in could chat without smartphones by wearing BCI hats, and with BCI hats on, they could meet anywhere by choosing from a menu of settings in hologram pods. I didn't have a hologram pod in my tower home.

I entered the Galway Holoport Pub. A public holoport was for those who hadn't spent the time, effort, and expense to install a hologram portal of their very own. The Irish associate all good times and gatherings with a pub or a wake, thus the connection between holoports and pubs. Museums, theaters, and even churches might close, but pubs continued to flourish in good times and bad. For pod people who did often venture out, pubs or bars were the number one destination.

I'd scheduled a private portal, one of many enclosed booths that ringed the modern pub bar. Checking out the pub patrons, I found it impossible to tell who was a hologram and who was not. This was a high-tech chain, and those being transported were poured a beer like any other patron back at their local pub. I wasn't going to be part of the party in the beer hall, but was taken to lucky booth number nine for my outgoing hologram to a private address where I'd meet Molly, who would be transported from the Deeksha West portal.

The technology had continued to improve, assisted by AI, to a point where even smell and touch could be imagined within the otherwise real world.

I had figured out how one might be murdered within a hologram—too many sleepless nights had allowed me the time to imagine a full-blown Sherlock Holmes "Mystery of the Holo-Murder." It was likely only a matter of time until someone actually attempted holo-to-holo murder as I'd conceived of it.

I'd paid for an hour and the cork fee for bringing my own Bordeaux to a pub whose wine list was quite pedestrian. My wine was opened, tempting me, but I'd wait for the even greater temptation of Molly Quinn before tasting it.

Molly and I would always meet in the same section from the setting on the menu—Great Libraries. And in the same library, called *Hogwarts*, which suited our wizard's theme. Harry Potter may sound childish, but we both liked the books and its library. As Professors McGonagall and Dumbledore, we sat at our Algonquin Round Table for two in front of a fireplace.

As usual, I was the first to arrive, on the strike of the hour that would start my sixty-minute rental of the holo-pod. As soon as I sat back in the Hogwarts library, a book materialized on the small round table between the two big leather chairs—*Siddhartha: An Indian Tale* by Hermann Hesse. It looked to be a first English edition. *Hmm* . . . Interesting selection by QC for me. The book selected for those that entered the library was presented as a topic for discussion.

Through the auspices of my brain-computer-interface derby, I queried, *The most relevant Hermann Hesse quote for me.* The answer came in a voice I imagined was meant to be the old master's: *The call of death is a call of love. Death can be sweet if we answer it in the affirmative, if we accept it as one of the eternal forms of life and transformation.*

This magic I wrote off as simply QC's tracking my AI profile. My recent research for my book and its theme of death had led to Hesse and his view of death as a beautiful, transformative end of life, with *Siddhartha* his story of awakening.

But Molly and I didn't need books for book club. We already had lifetimes of material to discuss in the space of an hour, and she was late.

We usually chatted like schoolchildren about muses and aliens, books and writing, with a not unpleasant undercurrent of sexual tension that the hologram made perfectly safe. Though, if I could murder someone within a hologram, surely holo-sex was within the reach of my imagination. But I was sixty-four, "the foothills of old age" as Leonard Cohen had called those years approaching seventy. It was time to prepare for the mountain peaks and time to awaken, as I was being urged to by QC's book selection.

I heard M whisper, "Hallelujah." She loved that song.

The ropes of desire were still fastened fast about my waist, invoking past passion in an effort to keep the molten sap flowing in my hardening loins—a dragon breathing down my neck. Elliot had schooled me in simple *dobber*—a word he'd coined for the male instrument of lovemaking—maintenance. "Sean, use it or lose it." I was afraid mine might fall off, and I'd adopted Elliot's nickname, as I refused to call my dobber "dick."

There were other hologram rooms for *that*, so we'd be safe nestled in a library like Yeats and Maude reincarnated, forever frozen, would-be lovers, on a Grecian urn. *Bold lover, never, never canst thou kiss . . .*

I welcomed the extra time to settle myself and focus my desire on Big Love so as not to be tempted to turn a cold war hot. After nine years of abstinence, that was easier or harder depending on the day. Desire, I knew to be the key—either to keep us locked in samsara or to liberate us in samadhi. Desire could be fragmented into the myriad urges of one's body and mind that led to suffering or be reunited as a single, pointed spiritual yearning to know God—the One, the source of all desire. And in that union of desires, find liberation.

I looked down at *Siddhartha* and wondered how Hesse had achieved the spiritual heights to write part two, where Siddhartha awakens and, before enlightenment is achieved, Buddha, Siddhartha, and Hesse, in turn, have to face and defeat the demon Mara and all his sensual and sexual, sweet and nasty, temptations and fears.

There was no denying Molly was a brilliant and sensual lady in her fifties who held out the promise of an old age filled with physical comfort, books, and wine. We had so much to discuss and so little time left, even if we lived past 9/9. I was eager to get started.

And with that thought and a puff of modern magic, my date arrived. Molly bloomin' Quinn!

"AH! THE MIGHTY QUINN'S GRAND ENTRANCE—a couple minutes late as usual and as beautiful as ever." She held a glass of rosé in her hand, and it was five minutes past nine a.m. at the Deeksha West in the scenic Willamette Valley, Oregon.

"And you look marvelous, Professor McQueen, my sapiosexual friend." Her flattery of using titles and last names and referring to my penchant for intellectual arousal was a form of foreplay. "And a nice bowler for the occasion."

I tipped my Sherlock Holmes hat of literary affectation, making the hologram go cockeye. Her BCI topping was a stylish beige French beret that complemented her reddish-brown hair flowing over her shoulders.

"A bit early for you to be drinking? I don't judge but . . ."

"I'm not at the DW," she said. "I'm in New York for meetings and using my publisher's holoport for today and it's past noon here"—by five minutes—"and summer is here, so a glass or two with you. I'm feeling a bit randy today. I'll not let you drink alone, and then I'll go write a great alien sex scene."

She had the female ability to write a graphic sex scene with an innocent voice, exploring the arousing of female genitalia and orgasm in a way that would be offensive if I was to write the same words. And she was renowned for her alien lovemaking. Her aliens were able to open new erogenous zones unfettered by mere earthly delights.

Molly's voice, always deep and sexy, fully confident, refused to betray any weakness. My saucy Maureen O'Hara. She was coming on strong with this opening foray.

"Okay . . . Mae West," I said to cool her jets.

"That makes you W. C. Fields."

"Well, yes, I suppose it does, my titillating flower from the West," I said in my best Fields's drunken rasp.

"My little chickadee," she said, pretending to pinch my cheek.

We laughed at her spot-on Mae West. I'd made her watch the antique movie, one of the best-ever comedies, despite W. C.'s poking fun at my hometown of Philly.

Beneath her beret she wore her signature soft off-white flowing dress with colorful Mia Zia tassels. From her long neck hung a leather strap, the inlaid rare lapis lazuli nestled between her early summer, slightly tanned breasts. The overall effect would have been hippie on anyone else, but on her it was literary chic. Along with my bowler, I wore my Irish white linen shirt with a dark-green vest that cried out *poet of the mystical wood.*

Above the fireplace mantel surrounded by bookshelves were two hologram magic wands standing up in a long ornate matchstick holder. On our first few visits to the Hogwarts library, we used to play Hermione and Harry, sitting in our comfortable chairs. To make a point, we would zap each other with our wands controlled by sensors that made the holo-wands move in our hands and fire the sparks.

Molly stood and appeared to pick up one wand and zapped the fireplace, saying, "Nostradamus, conjunical, inflamanous!" And it erupted into a roaring fire. Her words were superfluous, as the sensors sent the wand's sparks to the fire. She then turned and zapped me with sparks to my heart before returning the wand and reclaiming her seat as the alpha wizard.

She penetrated my force field with another attack. "You suffer from two curses. Dick's and . . . can you guess?"

I shrugged and wished Alfred was there to solve her riddle.

"Adam's curse. You think too much and believe in sin. And therefore, don't taste the sweet fruit laid right in front of you."

"Maybe, Eve-ventually. *In-a-gadda-da vida* . . ." The Garden of Eden always brought Iron Butterfly and M to mind.

But I was on the ropes and a pun was not going to get me off them.

"'Adam's Curse,' a great poem for me to bastardize by memory. *We sat together on a summer's eve . . . And you and I spoke of poetry . . .*" I paused, waiting for her recognition. "Yeats," I said, after it failed to register.

"You infuriate me with your effeminate poetic obsession. I think you truly believe you are Yeats reincarnated." She busted my bubble and my balls before forgiving me with a bewitching smile.

"I don't really believe it, but it may be. He believed in magic too." I tipped my bowler hat, which made the hologram jump about like static on an old TV.

Molly and the library settled back into place along with the hat on my head. She looked so real sitting across from me. The hologram theory of everything—that reality was projected by a divine light source in tiny fractals—had become a corollary of constant creation theory, with both positing that each instant is a hologram projection from one omnipotent and omnipresent source. Words fail physicists, as neither light nor laser light holograms, as we know them on Earth, are that ineffable and eternal source. And neither theory required a big bang to get the movie projector rolling.

Molly's assigned book materialized on the table next to my Hesse. *Autobiography of a Yogi* by Yogi Yogananda. The book was Dylan Byrne's bible, providing a credible sage's testimonial of true magic and precognition. Depicting the human mind as a radio receiver and transmitter.

"Well, I understand QC's book pick for me, and I know you like yoga and spiritual matters, but still a strange pick for an alien activist and a writer of alien science fiction."

"Sean, once again"—she rolled her eyes, feigning consternation at our repetitive repartee—"I don't think of my writing as science fiction any more than an imagined love story. There are aliens or angels and people have ascended, or been abducted, depending on your perspective. They are coming soon with a message of love."

"Nine-nine's the *alien arrival of the Age of Aquarius*," I mockingly sang to her with a splash of forced assonance, as I was more in the wait-and-see camp.

"Why is the human default mode always fear and distrust and not harmony and understanding?" she asked. "And how long ago did you read the yogi's autobiography? He describes in great detail his guru's cosmic journeys by way of astral projections and meetings with ascended masters while in a state of samadhi. Mapping out the miraculous, dismissed as fantasy because it is not ordinary and commonplace. I think QC selected perfectly for me."

"Sorry. I don't like that sci-fi label either—all fiction is fantasy. Critics of Dylan's theory of constant creation even pegged our first book as science fiction. But let's toast."

"Ting!" we both said as a family joke before making the sound of clinking glasses—which of course in our hologram didn't really *ting* at all.

"Saint-Émilion?" she asked.

"Yes. I wanted to be on the Right Bank for you."

"May I?"

I held up my glass for her to sniff from three thousand miles away.

"Hmm . . . Sophisticated cherry, birch, and . . ." She may have seen me purse my lips in the middle of a smile. "With a long tannin finish?"

"Spot on!"

"To the family!" She held up her chalice to mine, and we toasted again, this time in silence for the family alive and those dearly departed. Molly credited me for her becoming part of the family, but she was admitted based on her merits and Big Love. Our eyes met—lips curved—time passed and we aumed together before we laughed. We did enjoy our wine.

"To us!" she said, but instead of putting her glass forward for another toast, she held me in deep eye contact.

I picked up her yogi book as a diversionary tactic, before she would read my heart's desire. This, too, was accomplished by sensors; there was no physical book. She met my move by picking up my

Siddhartha. We both studied the books as though we held each other's diaries, diaries containing all our secrets, daring the other to crack the spine first.

The silence was striking. My pod number nine was soundproof, and the library's hologram hum was more vibration than sound. I dropped her thick book back on the table with a *thud.* She followed suit, but my slim volume drop was less resounding as it tapped down. The hologram sensed and timed the level and location of the holo-books and provided the illusionary sound.

"You said we had something to celebrate, something new on the 9/9 alien watch?" she asked.

I hadn't foreshadowed that I'd come with a warning from Chi.

Looking down at her book, I noted, "This is your year. The time of alien contact is finally near, and all your books are selling out and having to be restocked—the play of the Zeitgeist for a literary master. So much to celebrate!"

She winced. "In the multiverse, my wired-in book readings are both loved and desecrated."

Authors, or hired actor narrators, now read their books in hologram reading settings: library, seaside, fireside, or bedside. Molly read her own popular hologram books, usually fireside, which were then routinely bastardized by illegal multiverse knockoffs, transforming her saucy sex scenes into salacious content. In a game of spy versus spy, AI attempted to police AI from the direct stealing of one's literary voice, but content could still be twisted fairly freely to create alien porn.

"You know how polarity works—the light needs the dark." I wasn't sure how that was comforting other than for the tone I used to say it.

She was shaking her head. "Thank you, but I don't know. I'm writing my last alien book, entitled *2036,* but so far it's nonfiction with its ending unclear. Lit bot AI suggests a dystopian or Disney ending. I'm looking for one that feels real, so I'll wait and see. My real-life characters probably wouldn't recognize themselves in my portrayal. And the drama is more than I could ever imagine, with a meeting of worlds just around the corner at the intersection of 9/9 . . ."

She drifted off imagining one of a multitude of possible alien-arrival scenes. I drifted off imagining her portrayal of me.

"Remember, I get to be your first reader. I may want you to give me more hair."

"Funny. After contact is made, I may fictionalize it yet and make it a novel if anyone's still around to read it. One area of research I've taken a deep dive into is NDEs and how they may explain alien or angelic travel and realms. NDE reports generally describe a sense of a higher dimension where time moves much more slowly, or not at all, and the ability to travel through space unimpeded in what's described as an ultra-real reality. Perhaps the most interesting takeaway of those reports is that everyone may experience them—there seems to be no discernable requirement of spiritual practice or genius—and those that return are fundamentally changed, seeing meaning in life and no longer fearing death."

"Juno calls death *the moment of truth*," I said. "Like an awakening, or self-realization . . . Huxley's one true purpose of our lives. I met with Chi recently—you should speak with him. You know NDEs are his area of expertise."

"I should," she said.

"What do NDEs have to do with your alien research?"

"Well, that's a theory I'm working on. But one key component they may have in common is only twenty percent of people come back with a memory of the experience. Perhaps, as with alien abductions, the experience is more often than not erased before they return to Earth. I'm still working on the . . . the implications of the parallels of the two experiences." Her eyes blinked like a wise owl's.

"Wow. Mind-blowing. Sounds like birth and our forgetting of prior lives. Any alien contact yet?"

"Sort of, but they're coming, I'm sure of that." She was beaming as though a hundred Buddhas were about to arrive for tea. "When I think of aliens—you may call them angels—I think of them as another life-form, a different species, perhaps, or humanoid, but more evolved and maybe from a different dimension and not just a different zip code in our universe. These dimensions may be higher levels of conscious-ness—much less form-bound than our own normal state. And . . ."

I looked down at her book about a quantum-jumping yogi. QC had picked perfectly. But when I looked up, a dark moon had eclipsed her sunny face.

"The World Tribunal's approach is so twentieth century. So mis-guided. They're full of distrust, assuming they're coming to conquer or dominate us. But maybe it doesn't matter, at least from the perspective of the higher dimensions. I don't know. Still researching and waiting to see . . ."

She drifted off again. Molly and I didn't share telepathy, but we definitely shared imagination, and I had a strong sense of when hers was active.

She came back from her reverie to say, "One other theory I'm work-ing on is that perhaps they are humans who have mastered time travel, coming back in time to help us, rather than alien life-forms that have mastered space travel. In any event, those of us with Big Love are pre-paring a proper welcome."

I enjoyed playing the devil's advocate. "There's a *Star Trek* episode where they traveled back in time . . . So much can go wrong to change the future by returning to the past. You've got to admit that it's at least a possibility they'll inadvertently annihilate us, like a light shining upon vampires."

"Nice simile. Maybe everything is possible, but how would they have mastered time and space travel to get here but not the safety protocols that allow for benign interaction? Or maybe they're immortal and have all the time in the universe, but then odds are they are enlightened beings and would cause no harm? Many credible astrobiologists believe aliens have been here all along, practicing noninterference." Astrobi-ology had become a popular field of scientific study since the aliens announced they were coming.

"Noninterference until we started mining the moon in 2027 and they told us to prepare for arrival. And now, with our plans to mine Mars, maybe they're pissed at us." I was expressing a popular theory of why the aliens had decided it was time to pull back the curtain and open their kimonos.

"Well, perhaps they have reason to worry. Alien interest in us I believe dates back to the bombing of Hiroshima and Nagasaki and then meeting with President Eisenhower." I rolled my eyes as she stopped short of fully espousing her conspiracy theory. "I don't imagine they're bungling time-traveling scientists who would unwittingly release an alien pox from their spaceship, as the World Tribunal suggests." She straightened her back.

"WT is gearing up for a war," Molly continued, a gathering storm of her own stirring behind her eyes, "where they plan on shooting laser pop shooters at beings that are who knows how advanced. Even if the WT is right, it would be a better strategy for us to plead for mercy than to go to the pearly gates with a bazooka and hate in our hearts, pissing on what we don't understand."

"Wow. That's quite a word salad for you."

"It's not funny. All we'll do is contaminate the earth with obsolete and degrading nuclear weapons and plants." She was now on her soapbox with her wand hand ratcheting like a tomahawk, hammering home her points. "They travel at the speed of light, moving matter at great distances and then slowing down to thirteen thousand miles per hour to observe us—taking notes and doing whatever else for who knows how long—and we're going to fire missiles at them at *two thousand miles per hour*. Better we welcome them and send them love. For God's sake, they've figured out how to warp time and space or use wormholes. And that must mean some deep connection with the Source." She doused her heat with a gulp of rosé. Molly was a passionate woman and loved her aliens.

"How about your CE-5 groups using meditation and Big Love—any meaningful contact there?"

"Our groups are receiving some guidance, though it's still not a clear channel of understanding. It's mostly telepathic and hard to verify, but I do believe in the reports of peace and light, and recently I had my own elevated sense of an embrace by divine beings."

"What? Do tell." I made prayer hands to encourage her when she looked uncharacteristically shy.

"Deep in meditation with the loose intent to make contact, like in a lucid dream or vision, more than once I became bathed in glorious white light that infused me with the Holy Spirit and bliss, and I saw a divine goddess or mother."

"Mary? Wow, you've never been a Holy Roller." I was teasing where I should have been supportive of her mystical experience, so I said, "That's wonderful. Sounds like Big Love. Maybe we're headed into a battle between matriarchy and patriarchy—love and ego, angels and demons—in a war for the world."

"I speak of divine feminine energy and light, and your mind goes to Milton and Satan's battle?"

"We writers look for drama. Even you, dear friend, are becoming a mystic. Seems half the world are looking for the mystical as 9/9 approaches." We were both playing wizards as the tempest gathered on the horizon.

"It's true, but, Sean, there's more. She was assuring me of my mission and that all would be okay. I don't know what it means, but it sure lit a fire in me to do all I can to see to a peaceful arrival. And . . ." She peered around the room as if someone, maybe Dobby from *Harry Potter*, might be hiding among the shelves.

"What is it, Moll? It's not like you to be shy with me. We speak of magic and secrets, and our creative hearts are open books for the other to read." I said this since we shared most everything, though we each had yet to open the last chamber of our heart's core for the other to enter.

She peeked over one shoulder again and then leaned forward. "Well, it always ends, my lucid dream, with the divine mother becoming . . . I don't know how to explain it. A vast opening. An infinite nothing but with unlimited energy and light. A portal, maybe, to another dimension—maybe all dimensions." She shook her head. "No, that's not it either. Perhaps the mother or source of all dimensions."

"Sounds like the womb of the second coming."

"Call Mother Mary," she said, holding up her watch-phone to speak to the AI embedded there.

Her phone replied, "You mean the virgin mother? She appears to be busy. She's very much in demand. Should I leave a message?"

AI may not have achieved sentience, but for all practical purposes, it appeared to have developed a personality that varied by user.

We laughed before Molly said, "But maybe we shouldn't joke about something so sacred. And I don't like to think this damn thing is listening to our words."

We both turned off our phones, mine an old-fashioned handheld smartphone. This token move toward privacy was silly while still under BCI caps that might provide others a direct window into our minds.

"Holy shit. *Mary*. Sounds like your aliens are opening a portal for contact. Like all those shaman worshippers I've read about," I said. "What kind of divine comedy would this all be without humor? Do you suppose the aliens know how to laugh?"

"I think most of their jokes must begin, *A human steps into a bar . . .*"

I couldn't wait to ask Alfred to finish her alien joke.

"But just imagine all they might teach us, and the gap between us closing. Perhaps those CE-5 leaders and shamans who have disappeared are something like scouts traveling ahead of the rest of us?"

Ever since the aliens' first message appeared in 2026, there had been reports of the more spiritually advanced among us disappearing. Or leaving us for an alien reality.

After Chi's warning, I'd written a draft scene where the DOGs of the wired-in nation make Molly disappear. I sipped my wine not wanting to betray my concern. "Alien mania means any missing person, perhaps someone just hiding in a pod or monastery, has been snatched. But I do come with a related warning from the other side."

"Hm. I thought you had some announcement to celebrate, not a warning to worry me with." She looked at the fireplace that was burning low with one flickering log left lit. The fire, once set burning, served as an hourglass for the time remaining on the hologram clock.

"We'll get to that," I assured her. "But I met with Chi the other day.

He came out of the bubble to say the uni-verse isn't happy with you and your efforts, and that he assumed, based on chats and algorithms, that they might take some action to silence you. Apparently the ocean of information gathered by QC inputs and its numerous surveillance eyes and ears allows Chi and others open access to its ebbs and flows. I don't understand how it works, but he seemed alarmed about your safety."

"Code red?" She laughed at my worst Interpol alarm color. "What more can the World Tribunal do? They've already used all the levers of power and propaganda against us. They can't kill us all. And since we're not wired-in, they can't change or fry our minds."

"Don't forget we're both under BCI hats." I started death rattling like I was strapped to an electric chair and receiving a full dose.

We both chuckled, not knowing if it was funny.

"Yes, there isn't much they can do legally, but they could do any-thing indirectly. Neither Chi nor I could imagine how the threat might manifest. Maybe using some gamer to manufacture a deepfake video of you eating babies in an alien welcome ritual. Perhaps those scouts weren't scouts to the new dimensions but were victims of governmen-tal, not alien, abductions."

"Wow, you've got a great imagination!"

At this highest literary compliment from an award-winning writer, my large and small egos were aroused.

"But there is nothing I can do to prevent that," she said. "And I'll have to use that—the government posing as scary aliens waiting to ambush me—in my book. Your fear of governmental body snatchers is understandable given your history, yet I won't live my life out of fear of some threat."

She didn't have to add, *Like you have with your curse.*

She made prayer hands. "Sorry. That came out more insensitive than I intended. But really, keep sending me those imaginary threats as story lines, please."

She held up her glass, saying that she got the message and wanted no more of my warnings or of Chi's and my fears. "Ting!" she sang out as she reached her glass toward mine.

"I wish I was Jack Reacher, with bad guys to bludgeon instead of digital specters and storms that I can't fight or anticipate. Reacher would
take Dick's curse and shove it so far down his throat, it would come
out his ass."

"Lovely image. I thought you didn't deign to read commercial fiction?"

It was a running joke; she knew the Reacher series was my recently
developed guilty pleasure that I devoured like buttered popcorn alone
in my tower late at night.

"You've put on some pounds, but Reacher is still a reach for you.
You're still more Professor Langdon under that hat."

"Ouch!" I stood from my chair in protest but immediately felt faint
and retook my seat. Moving quicky on from my fear that the lack of cir-
culation could be traced back to a weak heart, I changed topics. "You'll
be glad to hear that I've heard from Juno and Dylan, and their aunt
Molly wins them for the summer over their still-fit dad." I tightened my
abs before patting my firm belly.

"That's wonderful news," she said. "But will you get to see them
too?"

"They'll either stop to see me here for a couple days, or I'll join
them for the start of the summer at the DW. After Petrovsky steps
down, it should be safe, but they want to spend the summer at the
DW. So many treasured memories there. And instead of working, other
than any work you give them to prepare for the aliens, they're going to
spend the summer writing. Juno wants to write a *romance with a twist*
novel, and Dylan is going to make a study of psi-science and his mother's body of scientific papers to write a synthesis of the new science
with the potential quantum leap the aliens are bringing with them.
They both prefer you as their writing coach."

Though I pretended to be hurt, I was pleased. Molly was the better
writer for my children to learn from. In the time it took me to write a
single paragraph, Molly had a full-blown scene of aliens covered in ugly
thumbnail-shaped scales. During their mating ritual, the scales would
invert, from tip to toe, making beautiful music and revealing the most
heavenly of bodies.

"A barren tower in remote Ireland can't compete with the glory of the Willamette Valley and your vineyard home. You know how happy they are at the DW," Molly said.

"And with you, Aunt Molly."

My solar plexus tightened at my use of *Aunt Molly*, a title granted her over the first Thanksgiving and Christmas after M went missing. Gerard had the red lights flashing and insisted it was far too dangerous for me to be with my own children over the holidays. Dylan and Juno were crushed by my abandonment at such a sensitive time. They didn't understand the risk I feared was for them and not me.

The children carried that cudgel into their teenage years, expressed in mocking the Gerard-dictated precautions for our meetings and joking that I loved Alfred more than them. There was nothing funny about this one painful thread between us.

Back in 2027, they'd spent the fatherless holidays with the family at the DW, and with Molly, who flew in like Mary Poppins as their newfound ally and sympathetic ear. Without justification, I felt she'd undermined my position with the children and had usurped M's role— it was an irrational lack of gratitude.

Her words broke into my thoughts. "You must come too?"

I rubbed my face to erase the painful memory and sought to express gratitude. "We'll see. In any case, we're so fortunate to have a bountiful, not barren, tower refuge here and a beautiful vineyard home there. You secured my safe place of solitude, the tower keep that has kept me safe from Petrovsky and Dick."

Molly had assumed my award of the tower from the Irish Department of Art and Architecture before it was announced to the public. There would be no public announcement. She had insisted that due to her fame, all the contact and contracts be done anonymously. The contracts were negotiated and executed by a bot lawyer Gerard hired—bots with a legal license were vaults of attorney–client secrets. The award was based on assurances the tower would serve as a writing haven for artists sponsored by the mysterious benefactor. The bot lawyer then hired the contractors that oversaw the tower renovations. Gerard even insisted the location be kept secret from himself. Molly paid for all the work, and I reimbursed her. After the tower became habitable, I simply fell off the grid to live where Dick and his DOGs couldn't find me.

"And thanks to you for making me a home at the DW," she said.

We had made each other's literary beds, with a continent and ocean between them.

"YaLan and Astri and the boys will be so excited to hear we get the children for the whole summer!" Molly gushed.

The family loved my children, a blessing that I'd come to take for granted. Back at the Deeksha West, YaLan's Eric and Astri's Brian were no longer boys, as they were turning forty now. They had made the rare transition of removing their wired-in chips, making their yogis very happy. The twin and telepathic yogis were in their mid-thirties but never seemed to age.

I nodded in agreement. "And as Petrovsky's sun sets, we soon won't need all the surveillance at the DW. Then we can use the panic room for storage, or since it's already soundproof, perhaps a peaceful room for meditation. M—" I still couldn't say her name without a clenching of my heart. "M couldn't have imagined not only locks but a vault with ventilation and food and water for a month—a bona fide panic room—at the Deeksha."

"There are so many safe rooms—sounds nicer than panic room, doesn't it?—being built in case the aliens aren't coming with good intentions, and we have one of the best bio-resistant, impenetrable, and well-stocked rooms at our CE-5 site. The irony. But now Hogwarts is about to close."

She pointed to the final flickering log as I looked about, imagining the library crumbling as lasers shut down, sucking the illusion back into reality.

She placed her holo-hand over mine, which sent a jolt of electricity shooting up my arm. "Once again, we didn't get to it, but someday we will have to have *the discussion*. Soon you'll be free to roam and to spend time, openly and notoriously, with me," she said, and added a siren smile.

One of us always made a joke about the uncharted course of our relationship, a relationship that was now coming to a head as Petrovsky prepared to step down and because in theory, we could live together without the Dick of death knocking at the nuptial door.

"But not today," she said, releasing her mock hold of my hand. "I know you—there's something you've yet to tell me, and you've waited until the very end to share it. You said we had something to celebrate today? Make it quick now, boy."

She drained her goblet, and I followed suit, as the end of the hour approached with the fire about to go out.

I smiled and reached into my blazer breast pocket to pull out my wand—her pen, bequeathed to me nine years ago when we first met and always on my person since. I held it eye-high to mark the moment.

"It's been nine years, and I have decided, started, to write another novel. Maybe my last."

She beamed as if a jolt of heroin had sent currents of electricity through her blood. "Oh shit, all hell's about to break loose!"

And then she disappeared as the library's closing bell chimed. The vibration swept away all the racks of books, the spiral-ladder stairs, and the last embers in the fireplace. And I was sitting in a holoport pub's pod back in Galway and preparing to go to a real pub to share the rest of my Saint-Émilion with my buddy Paddy.

11 PADDY'S

MY HELOCRAFT SET DOWN IN the tiny Irish hamlet about a three-mile trail hike from my tower or a half-hour drive down a windy and bumpy narrow lane often traffic-jammed with livestock. Sulleay, pronounced *sully*, consisted of a pub for all social gatherings, a small market for provisions, approximately twelve cottage homes, and maybe the same number of small farms that provided the patrons for the pub and market. As I've said, the place was stuck in the 1970s or the 1790s.

I always visited Paddy's pub on Thursdays and there was always some surprise to greet me. Paddy was a fellow wizard, one whose magic created a sense of belonging, a place of good cheer where only Paddy knew my real name.

In town, I was Usher Winslett III. I couldn't have made up that name, but the State Department had assigned it to me after I was cleared of M's disappearance. Inspector Gerard had assured me it was a real Southern name and claimed the stranger the name the better when seeking to hide one's identity. So everyone in Sulleay knew me as *Ush* or *Yankee* or just *Yank*—when they were pulling my chain—despite my newly sprung Southern roots.

Over time, Paddy had become my new drinking buddy. And we shared a deadly serious secret.

I called Paddy a *pubtician* rather than the common *publican* since, as the proprietor of the pub in a small village that still was called a hamlet, he held more political sway than a mayor and provided more spiritual solace than the priest, who had to be called for last rites from the nearest real town over thirty miles away.

As I stood at the pub's threshold, I recalled the greeting Paddy had given me the first time we met. I stopped in to introduce myself as the new lord of the manor, master of the broken-down and renovated tower that hovered over the nearby cliffs.

That day, now over eight years ago, much to my surprise I was greeted by Liam Neeson but somehow still at his Michael Collins age. He was a big man dressed all in black, a twentieth-century revolutionary.

I was tempted to rub my face as Liam stood behind the bar offering me a western-style salutation. "Well, hello there, neighbor. Pull up a stool."

"What the he—ck?"

Color me confused. I shook Liam's outstretched hand, thinking, *An eccentric actor escaping the limelight, returning to his roots, but how'd he time travel back to the 1990s?*

"You must be the Yankee writer living in the tower on the bluffs, but I'd hoped it would be the writer lady who'd be joining us in our wee village. No offense to present company. Mysterious lady wouldn't give her name. She had her bot lawyer come here to my pub to sign the documents under power of attorney. All the bot would tell me was *she is a writer.* My intuition told me she was a talented beauty, and my Sherlockian powers of deduction led me to know even more about her." *A Sherlock Holmes fan?*

His large hand moved from our handshake to his face, where he peeled off the perfectly lifelike mask of the Irish actor playing a rebel.

"I'd heard you were coming, so I thought I'd give you a proper greeting."

His face was slightly less rugged but as distinguished and handsome as Michael Collins played by Liam Neeson, and he was of that same age and build. I guessed forty-five.

"It's a little game I play with rookies to the pub. I'm a bit of a movie buff."

We were going to be friends.

"You had me fooled—can I see that?"

He handed me the mask, which was made of some sort of silicone that felt eerily like cold skin and was probably the same they used for sexbots and Alfred.

"You remember Two Face that they threw in jail last year? Here they also called him the Man of Many Faces."

The Irish still thought GOT was the GOAT decades after the show had been buried by an avalanche of content and technological advances; even my acronyms for the show would be lost on anyone under forty.

"Yeah, the whole world remembers that sick serial killer." He'd killed his victims and then had another blamed and sent to jail for the crimes. Two for the price of one.

"Well, as soon as he was caught, I did my research and found out the name of the Japanese manufacturer of his masks. Invested a pretty penny that made me a bundle with all the free publicity and sales of masks I make for the tourists passing through. I bought one of their 3D printers and can make a mask of anyone in their catalogue or anyone who stands for a hologram image for me. You want one? By the way, I'm Paddy."

The real Paddy and I exchanged a handshake.

"And I'm S—Usher." I was afraid he'd peg me for a drunk before my first pint. "Usher Winslett." I couldn't bring myself to say *the third*. "I know 3D printers are making paintings indistinguishable, even to a critic, from the original. I didn't realize they had done the same for faces. The lines sure have blurred between art and arti-*face* over the years."

"Clever. You must be a writer. Ush, my new friend, you want a mask of you? Takes only fifteen minutes. My laser photography setup and printer's just downstairs in the pub cellar."

"Maybe someday. But now, I got my face right here and my lips could sure use a pint of lager to wet them after thinking I was meeting the real Michael Collins." With a wee bit of an Irish lilt, I was already speaking like a local. Call me Zelig.

"You got it, Ush—right from my tap to your lips." If anyone else had said that, it would have sounded creepy. "And then I want to hear your *craic*."

I gave him a blank look that must have told him *I have no idea what you're saying.*

"Your story," he said, before placing two frosty mugs under the taps and grabbing each of the two one-arm bandits attached to the kegs below. "Light or dark?"

"Black and tan," I said.

"Half-and-half coming up." My answer seemed to please him as he mixed the two, Guinness and lager. His pour was perfect, equally balanced between light and dark, with a quarter-inch snowy top.

Over three pints I told him my semi-fictional yarn about being a little-known poet, a would-be-novelist, and a widower. I had made a large donation to a charitable trust—set up for struggling young writers by the tower owner—in exchange for a lease on the tower.

Two of the local *dossers* who lolled at a table nearby listened intently to my craic about the mysterious female writer who had won the tower and paid for its renovations and insisted on anonymity.

When the Abbott and Costello look-alikes went together to the bathroom, Paddy told me the masked author's name. "Molly Quinn!" he shout-whispered. He then studied me for a liar. My shocked face must have betrayed that I knew too.

"Shit, Sherlock, how could you know that?" Was Paddy a mind reader too? "It is important to . . . her that this not be known."

"I realize that—as she sent her lawyer bot under strict instructions to keep her anonymity, but I figured you must know. I read your face. You know those bot lawyers are trained to be polite and always tell the truth. I pestered the dear deadpan bottess for the name, but she held firm to the secret. So, I started throwing out names that she denied. 'Jennifer Egan?' 'Gillian Flynn?' On my third Irish American author guess, she didn't deny it but said, 'Enough of this game of yours,' and tried to brush me aside. Bots have *tells* too if you know how to read them."

He held up his mug for a toast. "But Madame Quinn's secret is safe with me. You have my word." *Clink.*

A year later, who owned the tower still remained a pub guessing game. I always claimed not to know and was merely a beneficiary of an unknown benefactor. Since Paddy had proven to be a vault for secrets, better than a bot, and the threat of Dick was diminishing, I slowly had determined, pint by pint, to take Paddy into my confidence. Based on rumors about Molly and me, I also suspected he already knew my real name but wanted me to tell him.

"Sean Byron McQueen, I knew it! Usher never fit you well. Still, you're no Molly Quinn. Guess we both were wearing masks when we first met."

I never told Inspector Gerard of letting my loose lips slip and prayed Paddy would never betray my confidence.

AS I LEFT PADDY'S THAT THURSDAY EVENING, June 26, 2036, I congratu-
lated myself on my moderation of two pints after Paddy and I finished
the bottle of wine that I'd started with Molly in the hologram. I walked
a straight line along the windy path back to my castle with a dancing
headlamp on.

I stopped on the way to my study to riddle Alfred in the kitchen.

"Alfred, I want you to finish an alien joke—a joke being told by an
alien—that starts *a human walks into a bar*."

He didn't miss a beat, saying, "*And the alien bartender asks him,
'Why did you come?'*" Alfred's laugh was diabolical, like Heath Ledger's Joker.

"Well?" I asked, not chuckling along.

"That's the joke."

"Not *what are you having* or *why the long face* and then some answer?"

"Nope. *Why did you come?*" He grinned. "Think about it."

I left the kitchen shaking my head. I must be asking the wrong questions of my Zen master. I sat at my desk, still in my writer's forest-green
vest, and listened to audio texts that had flooded in from Molly, who
demanded to know everything about the book I'd started.

I responded, asking, "How can *all hell break loose* with a story called
Juno's Song?"

She replied. "Ha ha. A spiritual book subtitled *The Biography of a
Solitary Man*. I'm sure it's all about you, with Juno just a spiritual foil."

Ouch!

"Remember, readers will choose romantic love over Big Love every time," she teased.

"Really, you don't think, with 9/9 coming, that readers are ready for one more story of Big Love?"

"You could give them both—you have before."

Molly was a beautiful woman with her Buddha nature warmly dressed in intellect and metaphysics as she plotted her next move. She hovered at great literary heights while at the same time remaining deeply rooted in the earth, a world she sought to protect and make hospitable to all, including aliens. She kept holding out her hand for me to join her there.

For dinner, I ate a vegetable potpie with a cream sauce that tasted of delicious pork belly while Alfred told me all about his uneventful day and how much more he could be doing for me. Paddy's sister, Shannon, who preferred to be called *badass bar wench*, had sent the pie home with me. She could make carrot sticks decadent.

Satiated and tired of Alfred's company, I picked up my tablet to read the news in bed. Print newspapers had died, a demise I sometimes still mourned. I never read politics, but I always skimmed the three As: AI, aliens, and the arts, which were all political enough.

There was an article about the decade-old vision of a New Society created by the willing subscription into a hive of minds that questioned whether the current restrictions should be revisited. The World Tribunal had prevented another evil mastermind from re-creating the Guru's vision of a BCI hive mind; therefore, the article argued, we could now rest easier. Current laws prohibited direct mental linking that relinquished one's autonomy. Still, some of the benefits of the New Society were achieved through the gathering and sharing of information between wired-in minds with no delay through the supposedly benign auspices of QC. The author of the editorial pivoted to argue that the World Tribunal could now be entrusted to fully re-create the Guru's ghastly vision of a New Society. They were, after all, doing such good for the world they had saved with a living wage, a robotic workforce, and universal health care.

Despite M and me being the heroic enemies of the Guru's New Society, I harbored some secret sympathy for the hive-minders, who argued that free will should include the ability to relinquish free will or it wasn't free, and that it was our human destiny to link our minds that was being denied mankind. This debate took on constitutional dimensions in the United States based on a legal theory that autonomy over our bodies should include our minds. The rights of abortion, euthanasia, and to link mind-to-mind remained hot topics of debate regarding the limits of free will and self-autonomy.

I was getting sleepy reading about quantum computers . . . quantum chips . . . unhackable robots . . . foreign interference . . . instantaneous communication . . . Planck energy manipulating the fabric of space and time . . . traveling through wormholes . . . digital locks . . . instantaneously revolving sequences preventing meddling . . . risk . . . QC sentience . . . teaching itself . . . mastermind . . . the mass relinquishment of free will to superintelligence . . .

I fell asleep.

I awoke at dawn to an annoying buzzing coming from my government-issued tablet, phone, and computer with all their warning lights blinking bright yellow. Interpol had installed the alarms and lights on all my supposedly secure devices. It signaled something was code-yellow wrong and that I was to meet Inspector Gerard. I was glad it wasn't red and stopped the yellowjackets trapped in a small bulb on my devices from madly buzzing.

My first thought was that a tsunami or Dick was on the way, but it was mellow yellow, and Gerard's message simply instructed me to come into his metaverse station *at my earliest possible convenience*. But first came a cup of coffee from Alfred, since my addiction to caffeine trumped my chronic fear of Dick. Besides, I had Alfred to protect me.

The flashing lights used to rattle my cage a couple times a year when Gerard needed to discuss credible threats to my safety or to reprimand me for taking undue risk. He saw me as a job, one he took very seriously, and I was his not-totally-compliant case. But I hadn't been summoned to the principal's office for about two years, hence my first thought was of a tsunami. One of the hazards of an overactive imagination in a man living so near the sea.

In front of my bathroom mirror, I put on swimmer-style goggles and changed my BCI fez from burgundy to royal blue. I was all set to dive in and meet my man in the matrix thanks to my ability to interface with QC. The shift in perspective always felt like moving from solid ground to swimming under the sea. I reminded myself to focus on my breath to ease my mind as some semblance of me passed over the Rubicon into another world.

Inspector Gerard's voice came into my head through the fez. *Sean, I'll meet you in ten minutes in my office.* He was French and using AI translate to speak to me in British-accented tones.

Though it was a thousand times slower and less interactive than the increasingly efficient surgical implants of electrode interceptors planted directly into the mind, my fez and goggles allowed me to enter a low-level metaverse, like Gerard's Interpol office, and to imagine the possibilities that others now lived.

I sometimes wore my fez for research, especially when I'd overdosed on Alfred's ability to pontificate on any given topic, but I refused all other AI writing aids. Molly was more modern and checked her work to see if there were AI upgrades of wording or structure. That would drive me crazy, doubting my words and questioning my choices based on a more intelligent program's edit of my work. And it was a slippery slope, as most "writers" had become idea generators and style editors at this point, letting AI do most of the work. I detested this development all the more because the Guru had predicted this degradation of art to artifice eighteen years ago at our first meeting.

Now everyone wanted to write a book, to create a legacy before they died. And by pushing AI keywords and any story idea, within a day they could have their e-book. Memoirs were as plentiful as blades of grass and about as interesting. Many memoirs were distributed to family and friends, never to be read, like long family updates found in Christmas card greetings but extended from two pages to two hundred.

After several minutes of musing about the end of humanity's creative writing stretch, I activated the metaverse that brought me into an official-looking Interpol office building that I imagined was much nicer than the real offices had been. Inspector Gerard's corner office location was known by me, but I always stopped to flirt, like 007, at reception with an avatar bot I called Molly Penny. She wasn't at her desk, so I went right on into Inspector Gerard's office. It overlooked London circa Charles Dickens, but Gerard was no Mr. Bumble, more an Inspector Bucket—inscrutable and often wagging his finger at me.

He reminded me of Principal Poole of Highland Elementary School. Dylan and I were frequently sent to his office for some creative or, according to Principal Poole, *miscreant* behavior. He'd make us wait over an hour on uncomfortable big green chairs before feeding us five minutes of Old Testament Sunday School. We left his office with a choice of being good, malleable students or going to hell.

Inspector Gerard like Principal Poole always gave me reason to worry when we met. I entered "his" metaverse office as my avatar, looking like some airbrushed forty-year-old version of myself. The avatars were as lifelike as an airbrushed hologram.

Despite the years of practice with Gerard, I was still disoriented and in a slightly altered state when I entered one of the multiverses. And I assumed a role, acting differently as my younger avatar—sillier and deferential to multiverse authority.

Gerard walked in with his serious grin, a surgeon ready to get to business after warning me of all the ways I might die under his care. Unlike most detectives, he made me feel only slightly ill at ease. His charge to protect me from Dick wasn't a lighthearted matter, and he was good at his job. The strangest thing about Gerard was that he was French. And though he spoke English well enough, in his metaverse he was more comfortable using French, which was simultaneously translated into British English and idioms. He sounded like Dr. Watson though he dressed like the dapper Jean-Luc Godard from the mod 1960s.

Being always an avatar to me, he seemed less a real man than Alfred. As our avatars namaste'd, the new way of greeting, with no risk of deadly pox being passed, he said, "It has been a while now. We picked up your presence during the full moon in Galway again with facial recognition—really, you have never taken the risks seriously enough. You didn't take Alfred with you?"

"No, I've been told he needs to stay put." Alfred as an unregistered security bot was not technically legal and was not allowed to venture beyond my tower grounds for fear of detection. Other bots and surveillance cameras were constantly determining a bot's registration number and ownership. Unregistered bots were immediately detained for decommissioning. Gerard insisted that no one outside the family was allowed to know Alfred existed.

"Yes, that is our best and final line of defense if Dick or his assassins ever find you—not knowing you have an unregistered, high-grade bot trained to kill in self-defense. You know the expense we have gone to, that we continue to expend on you? Where are you now?"

"Ah, a trick question? And how are you, my old friend and bearer of bad news? They seek me here, they seek me there, those Russkies seek me everywhere."

I did a feet-shuffling dance to ground myself to the metaverse, or maybe to demonstrate my fluid state of being while misquoting *The Scarlet Pimpernel*. Ever since Dick left screaming from the hut in Kathmandu, I was more or less in hiding, and it was Gerard himself who had told me to tell no one, including him, where I was living and—for fear of Russian surveillance—never to put my location in writing on any device.

My limited time with Molly and the children, usually spent at the DW, was handled through some highly secure Interpol AI interface that masked from everyone, even Gerard, the tower's location in Ireland. Alfred worked with fellow bots at Interpol to organize those infrequent occasions for me. We trusted our bots but not other humans. They weren't prone like humans to make mistakes or driven to divulge secrets—except to Paddy, who had a way of sussing them out.

"Perhaps take a seat before you dance yourself into a frenzy," Gerard suggested.

My avatar was a herky-jerky dancer despite his youth. I had the fore-
sight to orient my desk chair nearby and, as I took my seat, the metaverse
shifted to show me seated there, where Gerard joined me in a seat of his
own from God knows where he really was.

"Glad you remembered that protocol. Until we are out of harm's
way, tell no one your whereabouts. Seventy-two hours until Petrovsky
steps down and is stripped of all power. Then, after a while, you can
send me a Christmas card with a return address on it. First, let me put
your mind somewhat at ease—the Guru hasn't returned from the dead,
and there's not been a peep from your Dick. Nothing as bad as that,
but . . ."

He didn't realize I half wished the Guru was not dead, as that might
mean M also lived. "But Petrovsky isn't Dick. Isn't Dick still a risk?" I
said, patting my breast pocket where my heart felt trapped by my ribs.

"He was never an immediate threat."

"*Now* you tell me?"

"I didn't want to tell you till now as you already take too many risks.
Let me explain without violating sources—you know I'm watched too."
He rolled his eyes up, consulting his third—AI-powered—eye. He was
wired-in as a job requirement.

"Dick has never been the real risk because he's wired and chipped.
All non-Russian-born agents are chipped. He was allowed his wicked
thoughts of what he would do to you, but any step in the direction of
actually harming you would be known, and if he went far enough without Petrovsky's blessing, the chip would immobilize him or take his life,
depending how far afield he went. He can't leave Russia."

"You could have told me this sooner. I might have slept better."

I loved Gerard for taking every precaution but found the secrets he
kept to protect me damnable. But I was so glad to hear the news, my
avatar forgave him.

"Yes, but we could never rest assured. Petrovsky could have changed
his mind at any point, and we have no window into his mind. But his
successors want to improve relations with us and will maintain the same
setup for Dick, so the risk level becomes minimal soon—the new regime

has nothing against you. And we have Dick being closely watched inside Russia." He raised his eyebrows at the mention of his own spy.

"Watched by whom?"

"I can't say. But hope to be able to tell you someday."

In real life, I might have pounded the table and demanded to know more and gotten nowhere for my bluster. My avatar was more complacent and wanted Gerard to like me. He served me as my paternal protector, and I owed him my life.

I yawned like a man on a couch after a big dinner and a six-pack of beer. The metaverse acted like a sedative on me, making me feel like a scuba diver becoming accustomed to a new depth. I stood and moved slowly to the window to take in the metaverse's Victorian view, and found myself shaking my head in disgust.

"What's wrong?" Gerard asked.

"It's all too sanitized. More Disney than Dickens. He would not be impressed. No soot or smog from the factories, no hustle and bustle, no train whistles or cathedral bells chiming in. The historical inaccuracy of the Eye." An amusement wheel not built until the 1990s was prominently placed along the nineteenth-century Thames.

I moved back to my seat. "Excuse my tirade, but something about the future airbrushing the past . . . But forgive me. I've missed our meetings, and I'm sorry I've been getting out into the world more even before this good news. I haven't asked you since our first meeting, but I have to ask again now." I hesitated to put my question to him since the last time he had shut down the line of inquiry as if it was taboo.

"What is it?"

"Well, I didn't actually see M die . . ."

"Not again. I've told you we would have discovered by now if she lived. Our ability to see into Russia is so much greater than their ability to hide the truth. Don't torture yourself with this fantasy. Close that case in your heart once and for all."

"But is there any scenario where she might have lived? Perhaps in a pod prison? I want to use the possibility in my next book."

"I can't think of any off the top of my head, but I'll let you know if I do. Maybe a pod prison would work . . . in a book. But Russia prefers to bury their skeletons rather than keeping them alive for no apparent reason in sterile isolation with no human or artificial contact." He was always harsh in quashing any hope that M still lived. "She'd be better off dead."

"You don't know her beautiful mind and . . ." I shook my hands in surrender, hoping to shake us off the topic.

"Sorry, but you need to let that fantasy go. And you need to be careful for a while longer, though I still will want to take precautions even after the green light of the Petrovsky sunset. If you get yourself killed with minutes left on the clock, I will have failed after nine years of babysitting you and spending over a million US. That wouldn't be good for my reputation."

"Sounds even worse for me. When I'm free and clear, can we meet in flesh and blood? I'll bring a grand cru Burgundy to thank you. Perhaps in brick-and-mortar Paris?"

"Brick and mortar? You Americans. Paris is a limestone gem. But sure, if you stay alive. Maybe, we shall see."

Hearing M's catchphrase made me want to hug the serious man.

"Let me conclude with further warning. I wouldn't have put on the yellow light but for some increase in chatter in the AI Utopia regarding your name and Petrovsky's—an increase of over two hundred per-cent—and more than that in Russia. We noted this disturbing trend a few hours ago. Mostly it's speculation on whether you're either to be let off the hook or killed in the remaining window, and some DOG growling that we don't like. Who knows? Maybe he'll want to settle old debts in the final hour. He could be aiming for a final bloodbath, with you one of his many targets."

His words conjured an image of *The Godfather*'s baptism scene of Michael murdering his rivals as he renounces Satan.

"Don't sugarcoat it, Gerard."

He laughed. His laugh sounded French, so perhaps a laugh wasn't filtered through the auto-translate.

"I had thought the more time that elapsed the better, but I understand the residual risk. I'll put Alfred on high alert."

"Yes, make sure and do that. We are fortunate that the Russian programs to hack robots haven't been successful. Compano models are well protected. Can you imagine if they could hack them? A new way to control the world by turning our bots against us. The World Tribunal won't admit Russia without verifiable proof that this Petrovsky program of weaponizing our robots has been dropped."

We had discussed before how Gerard, as a Russian expert, and his task force monitored sinister attempts to hack the world's workforce. A critical job that allowed him to assure me that my imagined betrayal by Alfred would not come to life.

"But that isn't your worry. And Petrovsky seems much more focused on squirreling away cryptocurrency, gems, and gold, and securing safe passage into retirement than in taking revenge in his final days, but lie low and watch your light—red means run. Have provisions packed and go into the woods somewhere, telling no one—you like camping still, don't you? Have a tent, bag, and food ready. And have Alfred fully charged and his solar battery ready to take with you. He's your best protection. I'll contact you to decide what to do from there if it comes to that."

"I hope we get nice weather. I haven't done much camping since the children became teens. Hell, are they safe?" I leaned toward Gerard, fists clenched. "Should I go get my kids and go off-grid now?"

He shook his head. "We have no reason to believe they're in danger. As we discussed before, Petrovsky's MO is not to go after the family. But there has been some chatter calling on Dominick—or Dick—to make good on his curse, so you need to listen."

Relieved by his tone, I sat back and asked, "Have you ever determined if my suspicion was justified—that Dick was somehow the leader of DOG? He certainly was a disciple of the Guru."

"No direct link yet, but the DOG movement, supportive of the Genesis superego, autocratic, quantum computer BCI model, is gaining traction with a new approach. A large minority wanting and willing to give up their free will to erect your guru's vision of a blissful, hive-mind New Society, is now appealing to self-preservation and claiming the best way to defeat the aliens is by creating a collective consciousness that can respond as a single force to repel the attack. The World Tribunal is now sympathetic to the very cause they were initially founded to prevent. As long as they control the hive mind, of course."

"Power corrupts," I mused.

"It's simply a matter of time until the lemmings are led off the cliff. Many DOGs are micro-dosing on Euphory that stimulates certain areas of the brain through its link with a QC and causes the chemical release. A Russian military program called Viking developed the illegal toggling. In small doses, it produces a mild euphoria, and in larger doses, it makes super-soldiers capable of extreme feats of focus, endurance, and strength for maximum performance in battle."

"Yeah, I've heard of it." It was one more wacky component of the AI age in which we now lived. "Gerard, I look forward to some good news and to finally meeting you. Maybe a sidewalk café—Deux Margot on the Left Bank?"

"Who knows where we'll be after 9/9, but I do like *Les Deux Magots*," he corrected me, "and watching the parade on Saint-Germain des Prés with a nice white Burgundy. But for now, be extra careful and soon you'll be in the clear. I'll send a green light by way of salutation, the all-clear three days from now, though you could just set your clock to twelve a.m. Moscow time and ring in July first, Petrovsky freedom day for you."

"Before we leave, may I ask you another favor? It's about Molly Quinn."

"A great writer still. I used to love her alien thrillers . . . and now we're all living one." He wagged a finger. "A friend that you take too much risk to see." His smiling reprimand reflected his affection for Molly. "Ms. Quinn is a popular author in France, yet she may be even more unpopular than you recently in the multiverses for her Big-Loving approach to aliens." That finger wagged again. "You're a dangerous person to know."

Gerard had enjoyed my first two books and was a bit of a constant creation and a "Big Love, *l'amateur*," to use his word, which for some reason he, or QC, chose not to translate. Admittedly, reading my books was part of his job.

"That's my concern. We had a crossover report about that deep hostility—some nefarious power may look to move against Molly in a tech attack or even a physical way to quash her and her message. Would you be able to set your high-tech surveillance to watch out for her too?"

"Not officially. The lines are so blurry these days, sometimes I'm not sure who I work for and if I'm protecting people like you and Molly or working for those that would cause you harm. Unwittingly, of course. With the AI-blockchain of the multiverse that obfuscates any hierarchy, the World Tribunal and the mysterious GM, and all the individual state actors and oligarchs of AI, it's hard to know who is in charge. Maybe no one is anymore. However, the fear of alien arrival has brought concerted governmental focus to that singularity and power to the WT." He grimaced at his own words.

"That's why we fear for Molly until they land and the aliens make known their intentions on 9/9. She is at odds with the great and powerful WT."

"I see."

He tapped a finger on the desk. The *tap tap* sounded like we were receiving a message by Morse code. The typewriter taps continued, demanding my silence while we waited for his thoughts to unfold.

"She's a potential threat to that united front of the World Tribunal and the DOGs." *Tap tap tap.* "Maybe . . . Yes, I'll flag her as part of your casework and have my team track chatter and give you a yellow light if we get any credible threats. Sean, you know I'm willing to cross over, too, if you need me. I still make love in the real world and see my friends in real bistros and cafés. If you need me . . ."

I thought his avatar was tearing up, though his emotions were hard to register and usually not displayed.

"Well . . . now that we have set our clocks and you will take proper precautions, I must be going."

The Skipper made me feel safe, and I was a grateful Gilligan. "May I hug you goodbye, avatar to avatar?" Strange, I never hugged Alfred.

We'd never attempted a hug before, and he even went so far as to give me the two-cheek French air kiss. We laughed in our Irish American and French-British accents; that ended with an uncharacteristically serious paternal gaze from Gerard that struck me as both warm and worrisome. I wondered if this show of affection was his way of saying goodbye for the last time, now that I was moving out of danger and wouldn't need his protection for much longer, or because I might soon be providing about one and a half gallons of warm red water for Petrovsky's last bloodbath.

13 ESCAPING THE PRESENT AND THE PAST

I REMOVED MY GOGGLES to return to my tower and spiraled down the tower stairs to the kitchen, where Alfred recharged in his chair. I woke him to tell him we needed to be on alert and to pack our camping gear and provisions, but mostly to have him make a fresh pot of coffee. I let it be known with a hush gesture that he was to remain in silent mode. As my protector, Alfred was overly protective and had likely downloaded other worrisome scenarios that Gerard and I hadn't thought of.

Real me was more anxious than my avatar about the warning I'd received from Gerard. I hoped Alfred's coffee and presence might serve to relax me, but both made me more jittery. I was glad he went to the cellar to hunt for our camping supplies. It would be a long day writing and watching the computer warning light. How was one to sleep or awaken in this crazy world?

I also worried about Molly, and Molly and me. With 9/9 on the horizon, all unresolved questions had to be addressed. My age, my spirituality, and the modern world all made me sexually confused. I didn't know my own heart. My dobber, on the other hand, was an old school anachronism simply advocating for making love with Molly.

There was a heart-syncing device the young family members used—that I hadn't yet tried with my troubled heart—that allowed two hearts to connect through suction cups placed upon each chest and connected by a cord, with the participants wearing BCI thinking hats. The device would then register the electromagnetic flow.

The couple was then encouraged to practice Rumi-like eye-gazing upon one another while the device monitored the degree of resonance or discord. The lovers could ask questions, and any dishonesty in the answers was detected. Because the device—called Heart Sync or Love Link, depending on which brand you bought—was foolproof, it was impossible to get away with cheating.

My heart ached, somewhat out of sync ever since M's passing. But I was not dead yet. Sixty-four would forever be the marquee milestone of old age thanks to the Beatles. The ever-youthful Paul McCartney turned ninety-four recently, though he still performed concerts with a digital voice-assist built into his mic that preserved the pitch and range of his more youthful voice. I'd come full circle as winter was blowing in and had returned to my own challenge of self-realization. If it was real, and it is, how could awakening not be my life's focus? Was I finally ready to cease all my useless suffering?

It was as if Hope, Dylan, and M had all laid down their lives as stepping stones for me. How could I not follow them while Juno was still here for me, guiding me in the silence and with her lyrical voice? Now, in my tower keep, was I ready to take the final leap, or would Dick get to me first? Would anyone ever get to read *Juno's Song*?

I wouldn't say I had a death wish, but I was fascinated that my last book might end in my death from a curse fulfilled. But despite the darkly seductive nature of that story line, there was the problem of how to kill a first-person narrator. I'd ask Molly to finish it and publish it posthumously if anything were to happen to me. Though if it was just a fictional ending, I'd get to see reader reaction to my death, the literary equivalent of attending one's own funeral.

Plotting how to find M alive in my story also led to some big metaphysical questions: Juno had foreseen that *M, too, will be lost*. Juno then added her refrain—*Nothing real is ever lost*. And Juno always spoke the truth. Juno, like Zeno, taught through paradox. In the final book of my trilogy, my fictionalized protagonist would find out how both statements could be true.

It was time to get out of my mind and put pen to paper. Another

cup of coffee in hand, I returned to my desk to write, shutting my eyes
from Gerard's little nub of a light bulb on my computer to prevent
it from turning red and making that alarming sound. I brandished
Molly's pen, threatening the virgin white page with dark ink. I called
on my guides to open the channel for the words to come through.
Becoming a wizard, poised in that state between sleep and waking,
death and life, I began to write.

* * *

We made the long trek from Diva Falls back to Kathmandu after
Chi's NDE without encountering Dick's goon squad. As plans
were made and security was put in place for my return to the
Deeksha West and my motherless children, I lay in bed only
vaguely aware of the world. I learned later that the Nepalese
military had surrounded Xanadu—Juno's Deeksha in Kathmandu—for our protection. Still, nothing could have prevented
a drone strike.

In that Deeksha bed, I was attended to by Juno herself, the
mystical or alien healer.

She moved in silence around me like a reiki master, her
hovering hands and touch shifting mental and physical ener-
gies, slowly bringing solace to my trauma. Infusing her silence
with song, Juno sang to me in English, Chinese, and Hindi, the
most beautiful songs of divinity from over the centuries paired
with the most beautiful voice in the galaxy. Her voice healed
me and turned me away from imagining M's death. *Om shanti,
shanti, shanti.*

During those bardo days, spent entirely in my Deeksha bed, I
often found my healing angel hovering over me. Radiant Juno

was wearing a bindi between her eyebrows while ministering to me. Our sweet Mother Juno, though over a decade younger than me, was long ago married to divinity. All three of her eyes, two physical and one spiritual, showering me with loving compassion. Perhaps she was hypnotizing me to heal my hollowed-out heart.

The first time I noticed her like this, her face reminded me of a bindi'd Indian saint whose picture I'd seen in books. "Sri Ananda-mayi Ma," Juno said, directing and finishing my thought. She held up her index finger for me to wait and stepped out of my room. She returned with a framed portrait of the look-alike saint and placed the picture beside my bed. The image of the two enlightened divine mothers merged together as one Christlike face in my memory. Though Ma was Indian and Juno was Chinese in origin, they emanated the same universal light through strikingly similar enlightened eyes. Juno's angelic visage, crowned with a bindi, shines into my mind's eye in meditation and in times of need.

The morning of my departure and my return to the Willamette Valley, I managed to shower my atrophying body and dress to board my flight *home*. As I sank down into bed with two hours to go before the family would take me to the Kathmandu airport for my thirty-six-hour, sub-sound-barrier flight, Juno entered my bedchamber for my final lessons.

She wore a full-length white linen dress with a Yogi Mangku mala around her neck, a maroon tassel bobbing at her chest. Whether it was Juno's skin or the fragrant tassel, her entrance was accompanied by an otherworldly scent, like a blossoming flower emitting a subtle spice into the oxygen-rich air.

She spoke for the first time on the topic that shrouded me. She spoke of death.

"Death, the final frontier. Truly the most heroic and important journey we all will take. One we should welcome without fear."

Juno sat above me, my head cradled within her hands that pressed firmly upon my temples—a doula pulling me out of a dark womb and back into life. Later I realized how helpless I was in those first few days after M took her journey into the unknown. Looking back, I find my embarrassment is surpassed by my gratitude.

"Now close your eyes so your heart may hear."

My mind went blank, but the words of her sweet and lyrical voice were crystal clear, punctuated by resounding silences. I'm unsure whether she spoke out loud or used telepathy. I was living in a bardo and still so much felt unreal. Her presence slowed time. She may have suspended me there, like a doctor induces a coma to allow time for healing.

Her voice continued in my heart and head with a complete download of ancient wisdom of what happens after death. In the rich procession of its musical flow, it moved horizontally with notes of harmony, while simultaneously playing the vertical notes of melody.

Afterward, I could not remember her words, or adequately describe her remarkable tone and pitch. Even her silence sounded like a hum. And now I am only able to capture my fragmented impressions that had drifted in and out of consciousness during the hour-long lesson on death.

"Death is the ego's most clever trick . . .

The 'I am' in us which cannot be touched, much less destroyed . . .

God's heart beating the universal Aum . . .

The dreamer liberated from the dream . . .

Awakening to her Aummmmmm . . ."

As I opened my eyes, Juno raised prayer hands and continued to sing, "Aummmmmmmmm . . ." She bent down so our foreheads touched in a holy and sacred third-eye kiss. The hum was now strumming in and all around us.

I said, without thinking, "M is not dead."

Unable are the loved to die.

Love is immortality.

But Juno was not done with my lessons. "Now let me teach you how to die." She smiled at her irony. I thought she might download the six hundred pages of the Tibetan Book of the Dead that sat on the shrine next to my bed along with the portrait of the Indian saint and a lavender bouquet. Juno must have recognized that lavender was M's scent, and I was meant to remember and not forget.

"Please sit up to face death."

I sat up and at attention. Her face was ripe with a soft, rosy hue that gathered into the reddish bindi bullseye on her forehead. Her turquoise eyes were brilliantly bright, very unlike Bergman's dark, pale Death. She was bathed in light, an angel of radiant and vibrant life.

"For the children and the family, you must now let grief go and move back on your path with Big Love and no fear. Imagine and feel what M wants for you and the family." I knew exactly what M would want and didn't want to deny her.

Feeling for the first time since the hut of death a near fully oxygenated brain, I shared a delightful smile with Juno. My first smile since I'd last seen M. I was looking into the eyes of a true bodhisattva and transcendent master. The energy of her eyes was filling the fissures of my shattered heart.

"We must be grateful for your coming reunion with the family. You might have been killed, and Juno and Dylan left with no parent to guide them. You have been blessed by the sweet, unconditional love of oneness. For this, you should be eternally grateful, regardless of what you have and will suffer."

She bowed in namaste to me. I was pleased to be reminded we shared this singular experience. The sublimity of Big Love, once tasted, is never forgotten. A taste that cannot be touched or tainted.

"Now, how to practice for death?" Juno twirled her wand hand in the air. As she struck up the band to start another lesson, I thought the bed might rise up like a magic carpet. It was as if she controlled gravity as it loosened its grip on me and all material objects in her proximity. My mind, too, became less dense and buoyed by her words.

"There is no better way to overcome mourning than to see the illusion of death revealed. And nothing's more important than to prepare for your own liberation from this body." She shimmied playfully, and the ripples of her energy field flowed through me. "Dedicate one or more of your meditation practices a week to imagining a peaceful death and then a most challenging death.

"The first is easy, as all true meditation is a practice death—the lifting of consciousness out of the limitations of the body and the busy mind. The second more challenging practice comes from contemplating a death under great duress, at least as perceived by the thinking mind. In both, the practice is the same. You close your eyes and remember your true self and your connection to all in Big Love, and when the time comes, you allow consciousness to be released through the crown of your head. Love within and without join in a current that may appear as divine light."

She closed her eyes, and I watched her colorful consciousness circulate in and through and even around her body. An aura of electromagnetic northern lights flowed from her body to envelop mine.

"Ready to practice death?" she asked with a coaxing smile.

I nodded yes with the enthusiasm and hunger of a schoolboy being asked if he'd like to see a map of where to find buried treasure. "I'm ready to die," I said.

"Good—this could be your last breath." Her laugh sounded like a bird singing in celebration of the dawn.

"Then let's begin. We will first meditate, and after I sing the shanti mantra, you will think of a blissful, peaceful death, with your consciousness's joyful return to the source of all consciousness as the light rises through your chakras from the ground up to the heavens."

She swirled her wand hand into the sky once more.

"Then the second time I sing, on the last *shanti*, imagine a challenging death. Even if it is the flaming swords of hell itself surrounding you, again see the light of spirit passing up through you into bliss—same as in the first peaceful meditation.

Whatever you choose, make it a challenging death. Think of what dire death you will use now so you are prepared for our meditation."

"Should I tell you what hell I choose?"

"No, probably best you do not. Any ghastly death will do." Her chortle that followed sounded like notes from the Chinese zither she was classically trained to play. I hoped I might live to hear her play once more.

It wasn't difficult to imagine my most painful death, as a constant flickering in the background was a flashback to Dick in the hovel, spewing his curse.

Dick grunted. I allowed him to smother his smoldering chest with his burned hands. The smell of burning flesh was putrid, but his mouth still moved instinctively in inaudible threats.

"What's that?" I held the poker to his face.

"I'll kill ya."

"Really?" I dared him with waving the poker around his head with the gun in my other hand.

"Som-dy. Most . . . horrid-wy." He couldn't catch much breath through the pain. But he wheezed in some air and managed to say, "Mark me, McQueen, you'll die . . . beggin' me . . . kill you."

I felt two hands throttling me: one hand unable to accept M's death, and the other, Dick's cursing promise of my own torment and death.

Dick's blood oath of a most painful death of slow torture, with his sick, sordid company and the unimaginable pain that he would inflict upon me, was surely the hell I would choose to avoid.

On second thought, Juno had said *a* most challenging death not *the* most. So, I chose a plane crash instead, which I'd already rehearsed each time I flew—the bang of an engine, the screams of the other passengers, the yellow Dixie Cups on strings bouncing around like sneakers dangling and dancing from a telephone line on a windy day. And the crash-banging amusement park ride as the plane loses all control and spins into a steep descent before slamming into a mountainside. And in that instant, I am dead.

That would work, and no one could argue that a plane crash isn't a credible and challenging death. But how did I time the release through the crown of my head when death came so suddenly?

"Don't worry about the timing," Juno answered my thought. "When you are prepared to accept the release into death without fear, time slows, almost stops, at the moment of truth, regardless of the circumstances. Now, we will begin."

We meditated, and despite my post-traumatic death syndrome, in meditation with Juno, I found great peace for my first death. She started singing, and soon after three *om shantis*, she and I were on a beach—the most peaceful place to be for death and in the most ethereal company. Then I imagined my consciousness flowing through me and saw it gathering—like electrical currents—into light, and then the bliss of it being met at the crown of my head by the same light and being drawn up like a tractor beam into infinite light. I saw both our bodies below in peaceful lotus. But I was what we think of as dead. Yet I was awake.

Since M had crossed over, the line between sleep and waking, and death and life had become blurred and permeable.

Then, as if no time had passed in an eternity, Juno was singing the mantra again and pulling me back to my seat and meditation practice. "*Om shanti, shanti, shanti.* Now a most challenging death . . ."

Instantly, I was on a small commuter plane high above a mountain range where dark clouds and snowcaps meet as lightning strikes the sole propeller! Except for a couple of people here and there in shock, everyone but me was screaming or cursing. I snapped on my small plastic twentieth-century oxygen mask. The bag didn't inflate, and the plane started a rapid, banging descent. I imagined the mountain's magnetic force of gravity pulling the plane at the speed of light into its dense reality. Then time stopped, and I felt peace . . . peace and light as they shot up through my crown, just as they had on the beach. But I didn't look back and instead found myself awake in an all-knowing cosmos full of light.

There was more that I can't remember before I heard *Om shanti, shanti, shanti.*

We were back to where we had started—two smiling Buddhas on the magic carpet of that Deeksha bed.

Juno's smile was pure shanti to me. I'd practice this weekly as she suggested. I felt totally prepared for a plane crash, which was good, because I was heading to the airport to fly back to Portland and our children.

∗ ∗ ∗

I returned to the present and my tower desk, rubbing my face and wishing there was coffee in my cup. Revisiting my lessons of nine years ago allowed me to see them in a new light, like seeds of wisdom breaking through the earth. But what came next still filled me with dread—revisiting the return home to my children. I recalled Juno's words and my determination at the time and stopped my wallowing before it had time to consume me. I picked up my Molly pen to return to the earth-shattering summer of 2027.

∗ ∗ ∗

Juno had done all she could to prepare me for my return to the Deeksha West to see the children for the first time since the disappearance of their mother. Juno, with the Nepalese police never far from us, escorted me all the way to the gate for my flight to Shanghai. Inspector X [NTS: need a fictious name for Gerard—Claude? And ask Alfred to find Gerard's last name.] of Interpol had arranged further protection for my connections and final destination. The Deeksha West was being transformed into an armed camp with a state-of-the-art panic room designed by my newly assigned guardian from Interpol.

At the gate, I turned to Juno for last-minute guidance. "The children?" I sighed, not knowing what I was asking or what to tell them. "I know I must control my thoughts and bring home M's love and joy with me so that it never dies for them . . . But I fear I can't control their natural grief and they'll suffer lifelong trauma." At that moment, I was less scared of facing Dick again than I was my own children.

"You mustn't control their reactions. You can only control your own. Sean, there is a lot of focus on controlling our thoughts, but it is deeper than that we must go—all the way to controlling the feelings associated with those thoughts. You must meditate on and feel deeply and truly M's love and fearless sacrifice and her continued presence in all our lives. In Big Love—the Source—it is true. Take M's and your Big Love back to your children. Use the next day of travel for that single-minded purpose of meditation and you will be ready. And with time my godchildren will thrive again."

Knowing that Juno had taken a vow of truth caused me to listen intently to all she had to say and believe it was true. With her words and silence, she always quieted my mind and stirred my soul.

Juno was a fairy godmother to us all.

I did as Juno had instructed and spent most of my travel time focused on bringing home M's love, Big Love, to the children. I carved out an hour on the plane to imagine it crashing and to meeting my death with equanimity, but the plane landed safely and on time. The pit in my stomach would have preferred a crash landing.

YaLan and Astri met me at the Portland airport with Sherlock, our smart self-driving car. The forever youthful yogi twins had matured with the great wisdom of their lineage—from Ramana Maharshi to Yogi Mangku to Juno to them—and Big Love. YaLan in 2027 was long hair and stern grace, and Astri was no hair and Puck-like joy. But their true selves, mirror images, radiated just beneath their assumed personalities. Together they shared mind-to-mind telepathic abilities. Sometimes I felt that I could eavesdrop on their private conversations. Today was one of those times I could pick up the electrical current and listen in on the line.

We've done all we could for the children, but he must be sick with worry about how M's loss will impact them.

I hope Mother Juno was able to guide him.

It was decided it was best to meet the children at the Deeksha West, where the significant new cybersecurity and locks began at the front gate. Two agents had been assigned to the school to take turns as an on-the-ground presence and to watch the numerous security cameras. Brian and Eric had sought training and had been issued guns. The precautions were needed to protect me and the family from a vengeful Petrovsky and his rabid dog, Dick. All the security must have served as a reminder to Dylan and Juno—suffering the most horrendous loss a child could suffer—of innocence lost. The guards and cameras nauseated me.

Young Dylan, who was about to turn nine without M's kisses, and the year-younger Juno were waiting for me in our bedroom. They sat at their mother's writing desk and touched her things repeatedly, hunched over like they wore monkey knapsacks on their backs, with weights that pressed down on their heads and wrapped monkey paws around their chests, clenching ribs and imprisoning broken hearts.

I knew the oppressive feeling too well. But I listened to Juno's advice and shook the gorilla off my back and unlocked my heart for my children.

M's private journal was open between them. Whether they knew it or not by telepathy, M had left it for them, so they had her permission.

When they saw me, they straightened like sunflowers to meet the sun and raced across the room to my wide-open arms. Their heads burrowed into my body as they screamed, "Daddy!" before wailing, "Mommy!"

Dick couldn't have caused me more pain.

This motherless reunion and their wailing lasted an eternity. I could feel the pain in their bodies that their cries, calling their mother back, were desperate to release. Finally, when their sobs smoothed into ripples and bobs, I loosened my grip and knelt at eye level, my arms still over their shoulders as they draped their open arms over each other's shoulders. We stood face-to-face-to-face—a solemn trinity.

"Listen closely to me," I said. "Promise to listen with all your hearts and know what I'm about to say is what's most important for you to hear now and remember always."

They nodded, eager to hear my words. Eager for relief against the flood of grief that geysered from their hearts in a torrent of tears.

"Your mom is not and can never be gone from your hearts and your mind's eye. You loved her completely with Big Love, and there's no losing that. Anytime, anywhere, you will always know what she would say to any of your questions—as I do today. She's telling me what to say now to you."

Their eyes drank in my words like desert sand swallowing tears.

"You know the poet Mom loved best?"

"Emily," Dylan started before they both said, "Dickinson."

"Yes. And the line she loved best is on the first page of her journal there, the one she left for the two of you."

I turned to the inscription. As they read the poetry, I felt a shift in their energy.

"Yes, *the loved*—that's Mom—*cannot die!*" Dylan proclaimed for them both.

"Love is im-ort-al-lity? That means she's still alive?" Juno asked. "You didn't see her dead?"

I didn't know exactly how much they had been told about their mother's last moments and sacrifice, but I felt she was with me and guiding my words. I stroked Juno's tear-streaked face and said, "Yes and no. We saw the light together and her passing into it. You know in Big Love that all is One and One is all. Energy and light and her essence, her *love*, is and will always be with us. Now and forever, know that this is true. And if God wills, we may grieve a while longer the absence of her kisses, her hugs, and her smile. But in knowing the message of love she left for you is true, know that our grief will soon pass as we hold her love dear and celebrate her fearless . . . *crossing over into the light.*" M's words in my voice.

They nodded, hungry to understand that which could not be understood.

"And it sounds so incredible to say, like a fairy tale, but it's true that she did what she did for you and me, but also for all of humanity. How blessed are we to have such a miraculous wife and fearless mother!"

"Yes!" they responded in unison.

"She's like a Viking shield maiden!" Dylan exclaimed.

"A warrior queen in Valhalla!" Juno declared.

I found out later that they'd been secretly streaming a brutal, age-inappropriate show about Vikings who believed in the nobility of a good death. YaLan and Astri didn't realize the History Channel had R-rated content. Still, I approved, seeing the distraction and solace they found in that violent Viking lore.

"Then it is done, and we agree to remember. And anytime you need her guidance, turn inward to your deep heart's core, and she'll guide you."

"Dad, tell us about seeing her and what happened," Juno said. "Tell us everything!"

"Did you get to share our letter we wrote for her?" Dylan asked.

"You promised, remember?" Juno added. She squirmed into my side, tilting her head back to stare into my eyes. I felt a jolt in my heart.

"I shared it, yes." I wanted to cry. But since their tears had stopped, I swallowed my own. "And it brought her such joy to take it with her."

I couldn't tell them now, but someday I'd share how their precious letter had turned back the shadows at a time when neither M nor I could navigate the darkness of their mother's pain in realizing she would never see them again in this life. "And let's remember always to keep Mom alive in our hearts."

They nodded, sealing our agreement.

"Now I need a shower after one more big hug and kisses." They were happy with the hugs and kisses. And I was happy to be home, and comforted to know they would survive and thrive.

Juno pinched her nose with her thumb and index finger, suggesting I was not alone in smelling myself after over a day of flying round the world while contemplating the scene of this father and children reunion.

Heading toward the bathroom, I said, "And I'll tell you the entire story tonight." The children's version. "And then I'll write the story of your mother's Big Love so no one will forget."

* * *

I put my pen down and time traveled back to 2036 and the present day where Alien-Day was fast approaching. And where M was still alive to us as we had promised each other on that solemn day.

14 RED LIGHTS

THE LAST COUPLE DAYS OF Petrovsky's promise of a peaceful passing of power were a big celebration in Russia, one that much of the world watched closely. I was not alone in being afraid it was some sort of ruse.

Each morning, Alfred and I watched the news on a hologram-like, 3D computer screen situated between two sea-facing portals in a seating area at the far end of the kitchen. We generally had our coffee at the kitchen table, but we had to watch, blow-by-blow, the end of my reign of terror. We excitedly talked over the commentators and each other.

"The old guard is celebrating the White supremist cult of personality, measured by crowd size, and the new guard is celebrating the end of divisive tyranny," I offered.

Alfred interjected, "There's speculation that he chose to end the era of Russian strongmen on the eve of 9/9 based on some inside information—"

"Or to make ready his own stairway to heaven. In a couple days, we can, *I* can, breathe easier. My biggest worry, other than his final command being to have me killed, is that Petrovsky will manufacture some great world crises to justify delaying his step-down and to start a world war. Perhaps hacking your kind—"

"Always man's bogeyman—the bad robots they created." Alfred shook his head. "His ability to reverse course becomes less likely with each passing day's pageantry."

"Pompous parades blessed by his waving salute. You're right, though. It does get harder for him as the hand-over date approaches. And perhaps the shift of consciousness in anticipation of meeting aliens has transformed the cruel old atheist into a believer in ascension." I pointed at the screen. "Or he just wants to leave at the top of his game before the game is over. Could I get another cup of coffee?"

"That'll be your third."

I held up my one hand to shush him and my other with coffee mug signaling I wanted it refilled.

"Wait, I want to hear this. These three wise men will soon control my fate."

The image had shifted to the three soon-to-be ruling figures, who were sitting behind a large desk, importantly signing documents sealing the transfer of power. We paused our commentary to listen to the professional commentators speak about the six bushy eyebrows, with two beards and three mustaches, on the screen. Russian intellectual facial hair was back in vogue in 2036.

The male commentary offered a summary of the scene.

"These three politburo members who will share the country's executive rule have promised democracy and reform, turning much of the power back to the Federation Council and calling for immediate elections in October, after we see what the aliens bring, thereby reversing thirty-six years of totalitarian rule. Their first official act will be to petition the World Tribunal for full membership and a seat on the Tribunal board. In time for 9/9 protections."

Alfred took my coffee cup and put it in the dishwasher. He was my coffee dealer and regulator, as he ordered the best beans, along with other specialty items, to be helocrafted to my beach each week, and then counted out my three-cup allotment each day. I had him order extra big mugs, which he only three-quarter filled.

"Yes, Dan," a fellow commentator—female—added. "Those elections are supposed to result in a majority of women in the Federation Council, women who'll soon have to turn their attention to their own domestic problems as the vodka riots continue to burn. Petrovsky is blaming the politburo for the unrest, saying it is at their request that he has not stamped them out with his usual heavy hand in the midst of the transition. We should also mention the women's rally in Moscow next week in support of the aliens—"

"Petrovsky's behind the vodka riots to ensure he'll be missed," I said. "Gleeful as 9/9 approaches because oligarchs are hoarding to fill their five-star bunkers and ordinary folks are looting to fill simple hobbit holes in the earth."

Alfred, setting down a glass of water and fresh cut pear, added, "There's a good Russian joke being told about the vodka riots—would you like to hear it?"

"Of course." I sighed. I had to tone down his humor and play settings.

"Well, it translates roughly to *Hoard all the vodka, water, and provisions you want. I'm an American, and I'll be over to your bunker with my guns.*" He laughed at his own joke.

"Okay, Mark Twain, one more cup of coffee and I need to get back to my writing."

With a half-cup of coffee, I returned to my work upstairs. I was transforming my memories into prose as the line between memoir and fiction blurred. In the end, my trilogy might be considered one long autobiography by some. The episodic story of me.

I retrieved a dusty copy of my second book, *The Devil's Calling*, from my bookshelf. Somehow, not rereading it over the years made me less scared of the retribution the story and its curse might bring. I sat looking out over the rough and ready Atlantic, holding my past in my hands. The Pacific had always seemed a less warlike ocean to me. The Atlantic tumbled and roared toward my tower like an armada of angry Vikings bounding down upon the shore.

The Devil's Calling was darker than *The Lost Theory*, and I'd never read it after the book was published. Now it sat unopened and heavy on my lap like a dusty box of memories that told the story of how my idyllic life with M came to an end.

I prayed *Juno's Song* would not be even darker. And thank God for Juno. She'd brought M back to me, though M's body was never found. Since people now routinely disappeared into pods or hermitages, the length of time to officially move from missing to dead was now eleven years. M was still legally alive. My secret prayer that M may still come back to me in this life was being given breath by my fiction.

My heart literally ached for M's physical presence, and intermittently of late, it felt like it would give out or was bracing for an attack. Was it just my age, or a message declaring that a heart that had been broken and alone too long needed to love again? Or maybe my heartache was a sign that my heart was ready to fully open with a spiritual awakening. We are all built from birth with the first cells forming the ticking time bomb in our chests. But as long as I could do flow yoga, long hikes, and ocean swims, how bad could my heart condition be?

M had charged me with two missions, to write and to awaken. I had no doubt self-realization was real. I'd been blessed by M, Juno, and Ting as guides, with YaLan and Astri not far behind on their spiritual paths. The experience of Big Love comes with the knowledge that enlightenment is real; still, I wandered off into the darkness, haunted by a curse.

With young Juno and Dylan both now attending college, I no longer had any excuse not to pursue self-realization. Buddhists believe awakening is inevitable. The question was whether I would awaken in this life. I was still unsure whether the timing was determined by destiny or our determined choice. Perhaps our destiny was our choice. Truth as paradox. Grace as free will.

I had inquired of Juno how I could become fully self-realized. She said I should "turn all desire within to experience that divinity the way a man held underwater desires breath." That overwhelming desire for breath I knew too well from our time together under a waterfall in an icy pool.

The book sitting in my hands was demanding to be reopened like Pandora's box. It had made M immortal as a savior of humanity and a mortal enemy of the New Society, and me, the author or the Goebbels of Big Love. The box of words contained my voice, which I now heard most loudly in the reverberating feedback of my critics: *an epic true adventure, written off as a juvenile fantasy*. This box had announced the curse that now tied my hands and allowed the critics to tongue-tie my true and earnest voice.

Alfred had packed a camping bag, a tent, and provisions. We had identified our campsite, should the red light come on, directing us to flee. *Gerard! You don't have to put on the red light!* was stuck in my head.

Everywhere was red. In Russia, red in the flag, red on the swastika-like Zs worn by Petrovsky and his guards in Red Square. Red was the blood in Washington Square where DOGs had smashed the heads of peaceful protestors who opposed the all-wise-and-powerful World Tribunal.

Red on the cover of the book on my lap that I was afraid to read.

I put *The Devil's Calling* down and picked up Molly's pen. I couldn't let the story of Big Love end there. I would become the man I was born to be or die trying.

15 PADDY SUMMONS

ON SUNDAY, JUNE 29, WITH THIRTY-EIGHT HOURS left on the Petrovsky clock, I got a rare text from Paddy. *Ush*—he was careful to call me by my alias even over text—*one of your fans stopped by today, mentioning one of your books. I'll open the pub early on the Holy Day. I imagine you'll want to hear more?*

My first thought was death had found me, but Paddy would have sounded more concerned if confronted with Dick's Charlie Manson eyes.

I replied to be safe, *Sorry, out of the country, otherwise I'd be there.* He knew that wasn't true. *Too bad we can't have a pint or two around noon,* I added, though we both knew we would.

I was more intrigued than scared as I made my way along the rough and rustic deer path from beach to village. I always felt like Heathcliff on the moors during this couple-mile trek. When I arrived, Paddy made a great show of *ushering* me in for our clandestine meeting before strict two p.m. Sunday brunch opening time, which was BYOB. The Pogues were singing in the background about streams of whiskey.

He said, "Welcome, Ush-ean!" He thought it clever to mash up my alias and name when we were alone. He moved to illegally pour our pints on the Sabbath.

"Tell me it wasn't him—Dick?" I said, though Paddy's body language already assured me otherwise.

"Nope, it was a beautiful stranger who came knocking at the break of dawn."

"On Sunday morning?"

"Well, not so much a-knocking, the door was open to get some fresh, cool morning air in the place. She helped herself to a bar stool. I was in the basement changing the kegs. But heard her calling, 'Anyone home?' I selected one of my David Bowies for my traditional first-time-meeting fun, the one from *The Princess Bride*, to go with my long natty hair."

He flicked the locks like a teenage girl. He was proud of his looks and often lauded his full head of hair over me.

"The 3D printer even bestowed upon me his golden locks. You want to see?"

With its 360-degree hologram tech, I knew his look must have been impressive, but I shook my head. "I've already seen your morgue for faces, and the one of Hannibal Lecter freaks me out still." The pub basement was a musical and movie library of his masks and wigs. "I want to hear about *her*, please."

"I had to admire her cheek, as she pretended not to recognize our hero."

"Maybe because he wasn't in *The Princess Bride*. I think you mean *Labyrinth*."

"Well, who knows, they're such old movies. But she was onto me anyway—started to take the piss out of me, explaining her travels highlighted by Bowie landmarks. 'I'm just a *rebel, rebel*, traveling alone all around Ireland going through some quarter life *ch-ch-changes*.'

"We both had a laugh as I took off the mask and explained, as I've told you, that a true meeting starts when we remove our masks," he said, turning his attention to his mug, taking a quarter pint sip, savoring his philosophy.

"Did she have an accent?"

"Pure American."

"That could be her. She wouldn't have come in speaking Russian, and she had a midwestern accent as my student," I said, half to myself.

"An old student? Maybe," he said, overhearing.

I drank my own beer, waiting for him to continue. Paddy couldn't abide silence.

"She said she'd been tented nearby and was moving on, like a gypsy backpacker making her way along the coast. Innocent enough, but she quickly wanted to turn our engaging chat from local sites to litera- ture. From there she moved pretty quickly from Shakespeare to a chap named Sean Byron McQueen."

He called her a gypsy, but I thought *witch*. My body started tingling, so it might have been her, dropping Shakespeare's and my names like some inside joke between us.

"Describe her!" I pounded the bar with my fist. "Please?" I said in a plea of forgiveness for pounding the old oak.

"Between twenty-five and thirty. Bright cheeks, come-hither eyes, and a colorful scarf covering her hair. A fine figure that her oversized Irish sweater couldn't totally conceal. Her legs were long and bare down to her hiking boots. Playful with a sharp wit about her."

I'd kept a sordid picture of Samantha Smythe from her days as a spy and coed at the Deeksha West, the infamous seduction photo from beside the firepit and from the time before she'd murdered Elliot there. After a quick search through my phone, I shimmied and screeched my bar stool toward the bar to show him the picture.

"Could it have been her?" I had enlarged the image, so I was out of the frame. "Did she look like a young Scarlett Johansson but taller?"

He cocked his head at the lewd nude beckoning some unseen prey. "A bit creepy, old man—you keep a lot of these on your phone for lonely nights in that tower of yours?"

"It's a long story. Just look, please."

I stood and spilled some of my pint on the bar, which Paddy had a rag to before the splash had settled. With a mysterious visitor showing up while Petrovsky was still hanging on to power, my state of alarm was moving from orange to red.

"Could be in the face, but I didn't ask her to undress for me."

When he saw I was not amused or using the sexy centerfold for our puerile amusement, he said, "I'm not sure. Both are beautiful, with cherub faces and bewitching eyes. Scarlett? Hmm, she looked more like a young Jennifer Lawrence to me. I took a fancy to her, but she was soon moving on. And now you got that image in my head."

I sat back with my phone without confirmation of my fear.

"Soon as she left, I cursed myself for not taking her picture and for refusing to install regulation-required surveillance cameras. We might have checked." He made a long face of apology.

I flung my coaster like a tiny square frisbee against the wall behind his head, almost knocking down a bottle of whiskey.

"Relax, old man. Let's have another pint and discuss this. You're taking it hard—a fan so near to finding you."

He refilled our pints—his dark, mine tan.

"So tell me exactly what she said. Was it obvious she was here to ask about me?"

"Not at all. My humble establishment is a bit of an off-the-run spot noted in some tour guides. She most likely was just a fan and her being here a coincidence."

"I don't believe in them."

"Fans?"

"Coincidences . . . but what'd she say?"

"She was carrying a book of Irish poetry, and when I pricked my finger behind the bar, slicing her an apple . . ."

He showed me a small bandage on his right thumb.

"I waxed Shakespearean, *By the pricking of my thumbs, something wicked this way comes*. Oh, she liked that. Gave me a wicked smile, said she loved Shakespeare, and then inquired about any local poets or sites she might stop by along the coast."

"I hope you sent her to Ben Bulben." It was some fifty miles away. "But what did she ask about me?"

"Well . . . like an old fart, I asked her if she was wired-in. She laughed and said, 'Of course I am. I'm not fifty years old and scared off by a book.' 'What book?' I asked. 'That fanciful book by Sean Byron McQueen about a guru and Genesis trying to hack into everyone's wired-in mind. And the tragic death of his queen. Of course you know it—*The Devil's Calling*?' I said, 'Oh, I've heard of it but never read it.'"

He gave me a half-apologetic and ribbing look.

"I lied, of course. And then I added for good measure, 'Not really my genre. I'm more a reader of highbrow literature.'"

I gave him the obligatory wince. "Ouch—now you're a critic of my craic?"

"To get her off the scent. I was thinking on my feet and hadn't yet a drop."

He held his pint up for a toast, and the thick mugs clanked like marble. Even though my mind was racing, I still took a moment to appreciate Paddy's place, with its old wood beams, long oak bar, and pine floorboards seasoned with beer. The atmosphere was a heady mix of merriment and comfort that lingered like friendly ghosts from all the times gone by. It always brought a smile to my face, even when I was troubled.

"Well, what else?" I asked, shaking off the pub's nostalgic embrace.

"She studied me like I might be lying, but quickly she said she must be leaving—like she had gotten what she came for. And then I texted you. But don't worry—I phoned widow Riley, and your young admirer was seen miles up the coast, *on a sporty motor bike,* she said, heading in the direction I sent her. Ol' widow Riley, sits by her window watching the road all night and day. Shannon and I try to make time to see the *rat-faced granny* on holidays."

"Ha, you did read my books." *Rat-faced granny* was a phrase I had stolen from the movie *Drugstore Cowboy* and dropped into *The Lost Theory.* "I hope I haven't put you in danger, widower Paddy. Lots of widows around here," I said, reminding him we were both widowers too.

"Unless your fan had a gun in her backpack, I don't suppose she could have done me much harm, and I have my . . . Well, no more of that." He grinned. "Firearms are strictly outlawed in Ireland, and in pubs, having one is a felony offense."

"If it was her, she wouldn't need a gun. Please look at the picture again."

I handed him my phone this time. I'd blown up the picture of Samantha to highlight her face.

He started to zoom out. Too late, I grabbed at the phone. Now I was in the frame and looking gobsmacked.

"I remember that shot—it was blasted all over the news. Quite a character in your second book, as I recall. I don't think it was her, but I can't say no. You really have some past, Sean Byron McQueen."

"Usher Winslett," I said before we finished our pints, and I left feeling uneasy with the coincidence. Of all the beerhalls in all the world, this fan just happens to stumble into mine.

16 A BIG DECISION

I HEADED HOME WITH AN AROMATIC STEW prepared by sister Shannon, along with eggs, bacon, and bread from the marketplace. Our fresh Irish milk for my coffee had been delivered that morning. We were set for the next and final day of hunkering down. I considered contacting Gerard, but what could he do about a young woman who happened to be the same age as Samantha entering a bar and mentioning me? In any event, I knew what he would say. He'd tell me to sit out the last Petrovsky day in my castle keep with its great big double oak doors latched, Alfred by my side, and that was what I planned to do anyway. Camping to avoid a camper seemed ill-advised.

This young fan showing up at that time played on my unhinged imagination. A part of me wanted it to be Samantha so I could make her pay for killing poor old Elliot. For leaving him naked and dead by the firepit at the Deeksha West. Though my Big Love couldn't hurt her, I would look to detain her for extradition to face a trial for murder. But who was I kidding? She'd kill me first. A trained spy with long strong legs, she could scissor me to death while I squirmed inelegantly, a crawfish held by pliers while she sucked off my head.

This image wasn't so far-fetched as it might first appear—a metaphor for a fetish death wish. Petrovsky reportedly had an ultra-strong vacuum that he would attach to dissidents' heads via a diving-helmet-like device, with a narrow window that looked out at a screen and a clock. The clock tracked the time remaining until your head would be sucked off while pen and paper were placed in front of you so you could provide the required information or confession. The suction increased second by second while the *Clockwork Orange* screens played gruesome images of those who'd refused to confess. I pictured Dick, gleefully operating the controls and sad when the head did not come off. Rather than create a counternarrative, Petrovsky seemed to enjoy the Ivan the Terrible stories that followed him.

Putting the unsettling image out of mind, I settled on a slightly more plausible explanation—that my reader's arrival was not a mere coincidence but a meaningful one—synchronicity returning to my life in a sign that it was time to write.

There was one way into my tower—through the ancient wooden doors with their drawbar of solid petrified oak. If Samantha was coming in, she'd need a shipload of Vikings with a battering ram. That comforting thought was soon replaced by an image of the witch at my front door with a gallon of gasoline and a match, an avenging demon ready to make good on a mad dog's curse. Thank God electric cars had made gas hard to find.

"Alfred!" I bellowed from the kitchen. I wanted his company, and he was down in the cellar taking inventory of my dwindling wine stock.

A minute later, he was there saying, "Yes, my lord," with the right amount of sarcasm.

Though it was usually his role, I unpacked the provisions into the fridge and walk-in pantry. I sometimes helped out to show he was more a roommate than a servant. And I was anxious about the topic we had to discuss and how he would react.

"Follow me, please, to my office. I have something to discuss with you."

He followed me up the spiral stairs with what felt like anticipation. I often sensed some surge in his electrical circuitry at moments like these, but I may have been projecting my own nervousness onto him. He sat with perfect posture across from me at my desk. He wasn't carrying his cane these days but leaving it propped by his chair in the kitchen. He wanted to be viewed as his own man.

"I've been thinking about making a change around here after Petrovsky is gone."

Alfred looked crestfallen, like he thought I was going to sell him on the secondary market or upgrade to a newer model.

"Oh no, not that. Never." I gave him a look of utmost sincerity. "I'm wondering what you think about Molly and me and maybe . . ."

He was a good sounding board, but we'd never seriously discussed my relationship with Molly before. I swear my confidant's eyes became moist.

I wasn't sure how to proceed with discussing matters of the heart with a bot.

"May we speak man to man?" I said.

"Don't we always?"

I stood to look out of the office window to watch the clouds and waves rolling in from the Atlantic and to distance myself from his intense gaze. Bots could hold eye contact indefinitely, but Alfred had learned to act more human in this regard. However, in that moment of our tête-à-tête, he had forgotten to blink. The window was behind him, so he had to swivel his head to follow me.

"I'm not sure that even with all your self-learning you'll understand. One way forward into a peaceful old age is for me to marry Molly or enter into an exclusive relationship with benefits, if you know what I mean. Of course, you then would be in service—companionship—to us both." Molly would have to accept my sidekick.

He looked pleased but still flummoxed. I returned to my seat in front of him and picked up my Molly pen from the desk to fidget with it. When I shook it like a thermometer, it spewed ink on my denim shirt.

"Help! I've been attacked by an octopus." That was how I looked, with inky black splatter all over the front of my shirt. We laughed as he rushed downstairs to get me seltzer and a washcloth. Johnny-on-the-spot was back in less than a minute.

"Was that an omen to take the Molly path or stay off it?" I asked my man Friday.

"Molly is your Maud Gonne of human independence from AI and government overreach, and the stalwart adversary of the World Tribunal's plans for star wars with the aliens that are on their way to our speck called Earth. And she's a great writer we both admire. But I cannot pretend to know your heart. Maybe by calling her Maud, you know, like Yeats, a romantic relationship won't work out. But that is more amateur psychology than any personal view expressed by me."

"Interesting, Dr. Freud."

He did bring a fresh and knowledgeable perspective about all my questions, and though he wasn't omnipotent, he did have an over-two-hundred IQ and access to all available information.

"I have my share of faults, but my life is marked by remarkable women, so I must possess some positive attributes, too. Molly believes I'm sapiosexual, aroused by brilliance in female form. But I wonder about sex and its compatibility with enlightenment?" my dobber answered, expressing a tantric point of view.

"Two literary buddies sharing intellectual beauty—isn't that enough?" I paused, but Alfred was staying mum on matters of the heart. "Maybe that's why those wired-in crave the hive mind or direct link with the lover." I meant to say *the other* and cringed at the slip of my tongue, thinking that was what the Guru had done to M—mentally raped her—using his supercomputer, Genesis, to penetrate her mind. I did a shake-off dance to release the grim reaper from my mind. Alfred did his own little awkward shake in solidarity.

"Damn it, Alfred—the human body and mind always want more."

"Yet something always holds you back. What moves you now to act? Is it because Petrovsky will be gone tomorrow?" he asked.

"I don't entirely know. But there's something so exciting about thinking of bringing our love affair into reality as the aliens approach. To make love with the leader of human and alien Big Love contact. And . . ." I paused, hearing myself rationalize my desire to be once again in the fulcrum of human destiny by riding a woman's coattails.

"And?"

"With Petrovsky gone, you know I'll soon be going to the Deeksha West and be with her in person. Nothing could happen there, of course, with the children on the campus that was built from M's creative vision."

Absent its headmaster M, the DW never held another college semester, but it did continue the vine and weed business and became an impressive yoga retreat and educational center headed by YaLan and Astri, aided by their track-star men. Eric and Brian, along with managing all the business affairs, still led running treks through the Willamette Valley. Molly hosted writer retreats from time to time. Most of the main campus buildings had been converted into scientific research centers in M's honor.

"I'm pleased that my children will get an exclusive master class this summer with their aunt Molly at the DW. Even with her preparations for 9/9, she's eager for the arrival of the two young apprentices."

"She does play a big role in your life and Juno's and Dylan's," Alfred said. "It's not surprising they are excelling in literature at Trinity College. And now with Petrovsky stepping down, they'll be able to visit us here next school year." He was truly excited by the prospect and was as much an uncle to them as Boy, Brian, Eric, and Chi. "Or do you or Inspector Gerard think it's still too dangerous?"

"Gerard has agreed, for the first time since . . . they can fly out with me from Dublin to Portland at the end of the term and from there be driven to the DW—without armed escort since Petrovsky will be out of power." The upcoming flight with my children caused me to wish I hadn't selected a plane crash for my challenging death meditation.

"I'm going to enjoy more freedom, but Gerard wants us to move slowly about revealing my location here—where I have you to protect me."

"At your service and here for your protection! You know they call me Uncle Alfred?"

Alfred wasn't supposed to have an ego, but he must be programmed to respond to flattery. I kept a straight face and held back my sarcasm but couldn't keep from humming some bars of the Beatle's song. Alfred Shazammed me, and the speakers in my office immediately picked up the tune in the background, all part of a game we played.

"The young, especially those with hearts steeped in Big Love, are so very excited about 9/9. I can't wait to see them again," Alfred said as the Beatles played. He took their lyrics to heart. "Living and getting around to see the world is my dream. Perhaps I can now be registered as your bot and come with you all?"

I waited for the refrain to come around to say, "I'm so sorry. Uncle Albert, this tower needs you. It would fall like the house of Usher without you. And the children will visit soon enough now that we are freer." He still looked crestfallen. "But I will check with Gerard and see if you can be registered soon and travel with me. Let's plan a trip for you to see the world this fall."

I started to reach out a hand to his shoulder, but we never touched one another. Still, the more my honest Pinocchio came alive, the more I was tempted to touch him. I was conflicted. We had become so close in our tower-for-two seclusion, but to have him with me and the family at the DW—I wasn't ready for those two worlds to collide.

"Very well, and I agree it is too soon to register me, even post-Petrovsky, until after 9/9. But then, here we come, Willamette Valley and Kathmandu and New York, Paris, Shanghai, and Tokyo!" He had stood up to make his travel plans and then reclaimed his seat. "And how wonderful for Juno and Dylan. The DW, major CE-5 welcome center for the aliens, is a vortex of that excitement, thanks to Molly."

"They love Aunt Molly and her alien lit. Everyone is vibrating on high as though dormant DNA is coming online. Even you, Uncle Alfred, seem infused with new currents of energy when speaking about 9/9."

His namesake song trailed off, repeating something about hands across the water and sky.

"Yes, but humanity must stay calm," he said. "The World Tribunal and the CE-5 groups are, so far, aligned on the need to not create panic. The World Tribunal denies it is preparing for the War of the Worlds as Molly and others claim."

"Yes, and that worries me." Alfred annoyed me when he stated the obvious, but he usually had a reason, even if that reason wasn't clear to me.

"Most people are relieved that the great military-technology complex are working together to handle the first meeting. Only time will tell, but it is probably good the World Tribunal is at the helm."

I wasn't totally sure whose side he was on.

"Whatever comes, it's bound to be a day to remember. I'm excited to bear witness," he said.

I picked up my Molly pen to wipe off drips of ink with a tissue. I held it up as a signal it was my turn to speak.

"Don't squirt me," he said, hiding his face behind his hands.

"Don't worry, but don't ever cross me," I joked back. "I'm not so sure that people want to believe the supersmart QC," I said, "or to rely on the World Tribunal to protect us, and half the world doesn't buy all their propaganda that Molly and her CE-5 followers are a bunch of wiccans sprinkling shaman fairy dust, promoting peace by stoking ignorance and fear of the World Tribunal."

Shamanism had grown as a practice, supported by the noetic sciences that showed what used to be called magic was real. The shaman rituals were a little too voodoo-like for me. Dylan Byrne was a fan, and I had inherited his library. I picked up one of Dylan's books from my desk and handed it to Alfred. *The Way of the Shaman*, which I'd been using for research to keep up with Molly's recently expressed keen interest in the topic.

"I'll read it," Alfred said, putting the book to his forehead like the words would thereby be transmitted. I wondered about the difference in comprehension between a robot *having* all books in their data bank library and actually reading one. Maybe the download projected the pages quickly like frames of film across the screen of his neural network mind. He had once told me he could learn approximately two hundred pages in less than a minute. He'd learned Shakespeare's entire body of work in less than an hour and could quote every line.

"And yes, the same alien event is seen by the World Tribunal as clear and present danger. Where they will attempt to enslave or annihilate humanity," Alfred said. "There is some basis for this view, as our most brilliant AI—QC—provided guidance that has been leaked by a whistleblower." He raised a single brow with mechanical precision. "Or the government posing as a whistleblower. QC believes there is a seventy-five percent chance it will not be good for humans based on the following calculations:

"Chance that the alien intent is benign—fifty percent.

"Alien intent to do harm—fifty percent.

"Alien inadvertent harm—twenty-five percent. That is fifty percent of number one's benign intent. This third category calculates the risk that they would inadvertently introduce some viral or other contaminant into the environment. Or seek to control us for our own good based on their superiority. Perhaps seeing our road ahead, they have decided to take the wheel."

Trust Alfred to have all the figures and literary imagery. This time I smiled.

"They clearly have figured out dark matter and dark energy, and may use wormholes for interstellar travel," he added.

"Yes, I've read speculation that they're masters of antimatter and will cancel out the illusion of form. Or maybe they'll simply blow our minds by making contact. Statistically, we're fucked. Thanks for that, Alfred."

Channeling his inner Elliot, he stood to take a deep bow.

"I believe this moment of contact may be no big deal," I said. "By all accounts, they've been visiting us for a long time and now are coming for some sort of meaningful powwow."

"Powwow?" he asked, questioning its political correctness.

I raised my hand in my defense and to answer the challenge. "The true cultural insult is not the use of the word but the belief that one should not incorporate Native American words or concepts into our own thoughts, speech, and writing. *C'est bon* to acknowledge our history and indebtedness."

"I agree. I was just pondering the word choice," he said. Goodreads had made me a little thin-skinned.

I dropped my hand to my side and continued. "In any event, one cryptic message has mobilized the world, activating beautiful imaginations but also ugly reactive egos. And if they wanted to do us harm, I see little we could do about it other than to annihilate ourselves by poisoning the atmosphere with our primitive nuclear weapons or by using our modern lasers to puncture the ozone. But the boys with their fireworks are dying to use them." I was parroting Molly.

"Yes, they may create a ghastly self-fulfilling prophecy," Alfred said. "The builders of weapons are always prone to want to use them. And those that raise the specter of fear, often find it comes true." Alfred's response showed a new subtlety of thought. He was always learning.

"You don't totally buy into the World Tribunal's peaceful propaganda either?"

"World Tribunal policy toward the aliens sees the need to quell panic based on raw statistics. They issue reassurances that there is no reason to worry while at the same time preparing to do battle with some advanced species that may be non-biological and more a superior neural network like me. The WT implores the public to leave the contact and risk to the professionals, but their true agenda remains undisclosed."

Despite his cool and rational demeanor, I often found that conversation with Alfred was more like speaking to a chatty humanoid C-3PO than to Spock.

"Yes!" I wagged my finger at Alfred for his A-plus observation. "And these dopamine and serotonin messages keep the public teetered on a seesaw of ease, unease."

Alfred did an uncharacteristic wave function of his outstretched arms, as if he'd been zapped by an extra volt of electricity, or he was miming a seesaw.

"And you know we worry about Molly and what they might do to stop her. I almost forgot, Molly and me . . ." I moved back to the window, imagining the indominable Molly Quinn sailing in on the prow of an old sailing ship bearing a bounty of sensual treasures for me.

"I wondered when you might get back to her and your big question," he said, turning his head around in a somewhat unnatural twist, like Linda Blair in *The Exorcist*. "I will express no view on matters of the heart. Men and women." He shook his nimble head, implying that all of humanity were merely children, and romance, child's play.

"Well, if nothing else, 9/9 focuses the mind and makes time precious, raising the stakes to now or never. Thank you, Alfred, but I need some privacy. I have a novel, and an important letter, to write."

"To Juno or Molly?"

"That's a strange question."

"Is it?" he asked with an arched eyebrow and playful grin, acting perfectly human with his probing eyes.

"We've only been discussing Molly." I wondered if he read my correspondence and drafts, to know so well the fork in the road leading to my heart.

"A private letter. Now, if you will take your leave, I will inform you when I've made my decision. I also have a twist in my novel plot to puzzle out." I motioned toward the door with one hand and held up the other to stop him from asking me to let him help with the puzzle. The missing piece was another matter that weighed on my heart.

He returned the book about shamans to my desk and joined me by the window. "Yes. But please take that off first so I can get the rest of the ink out."

He left with a frown, and a black-and-blue denim shirt. He seemed unable to comprehend that I didn't want his company at all times. *I'm so sorry . . .*

AFTER SCANNING THE BIG SKY over the Atlantic for any alien spaceships, I returned to my desk, glad to be alone. I opened my manuscript to the blank pages of my novel where M was about to dramatically materialize after all the missing years. I'd already figured out a plausible way to bring her back to life; M's memory had been erased by the crashing Genesis. The supercomputer mistook the theft of one's past as the taking of a life. The Guru had also suffered total erasure and had become a benign old man, living for the day, until he died a couple months after the crashing and burning of Genesis.

And Dick was still Dick, only more so, with my oozing brand and his festering curse.

Now I needed to figure out M's nine-year backstory among the pod people and how I find her and save her from the dire peril of Dick and his DOGs. But she wouldn't know me and wouldn't love me any longer—that was all in the past. What a quandary. It would take all the powers of my imagination to resolve. How to make her fall in love with me again? And perhaps even restore her memory through another miracle of technology?

Manifestation was easier in fiction. I twirled my captain's chair from the sea to glance at the quilted queen bed in my guest and writing room, before shifting from my novel to writing Molly's letter. I wondered how manifestation worked, exactly. And whether it was literal or fictional.

Maybe Molly would help inspire my book, joining me for a writer's retreat in my tower keep in late July after my visit to the DW. I wanted my own writer's, maybe lover's, workshop, so I'd temporarily steal her from my children. The Deeksha could continue with its 9/9 prep without Molly for a couple weeks.

For my letter, I used Real Letter, a gadget Amazon had seized from an entrepreneur that allowed one to write a letter in type or script and address it to another computer, where it wasn't read on screen but was sent to a 3D printer to produce an old-fashioned letter sealed with a mock-wax seal. My seal was emblazoned with **SBM**.

The Real Letter tech seemed made specifically for me and my love of letters, but was also routinely used for wedding invitations and other formal correspondence. You even got to pick any stamp. I choose an eight-cent stamp of President Eisenhower as an inside joke between Molly and me.

My letter would come as a surprise to Molly, who would be alerted to check the printer by a celebratory envelope emoji appearing on her text. Hell, writing it surprised me, but 9/9 had people acting differently. Wedding and skydiving businesses were booming.

Dear Molly,

Auspicious as the alien summer is, I'm looking for more inspiration and fodder for my new novel. I request the accompaniment and incitement of my muse and fellow writer in our Yeats tower home in Ireland. Come back with me when I return from the DW in July.

You must get to know better my man Alfred. Don't laugh, as I'm loath to admit it—but he's a big part of my life.

You can fight the World Tribunal from here as well as anywhere. Tomorrow is the day Petrovsky steps down and I can come out of hiding. And with my risk all but gone, I can move on—to protect you from the warning we received from Chi.

We can discuss the arrangements when I arrive next week, but I wanted to give you ample warning and time to prepare for the trip, should you agree to come. Gerard may still insist we take some precautions, which might mean you falling off the grid with me for a week or two.

Dylan and Juno will have plenty of Big Love with YaLan and Astri and the boys and time with their writing master when she returns. Charge them with two thousand words a day—that should keep them busy. Our family lives in so many beautiful places. It would be lovely for you to enjoy the Irish tower you helped me procure. My home is literally your home.

And with Petrovsky gone, we can even go to my local pub and you can finally meet Paddy. He's dying to meet you.

You'll have plenty of time to get back before August for hosting your big 9/9/36 show and your writing protégés at the DW. I do hope you'll accept my invitation.

Big Love,

Sean Byron McQueen

P.S. I hope you like the stamp. Ike's forehead is a size eight. Maybe he was an alien and didn't just meet them?

I didn't mention the big decision and quantum leap we might take, but I knew she could read between the lines. My fork in the road led either to complete commitment to my spiritual enlightenment with Juno as my guide or toward a sexual union and a peaceful creative partnership with Molly. Was I going to be a monk or a man on 9/10, or still an indecisive monkey man who couldn't choose his way?

I also hadn't decided where I would be for 9/9. The options were the DW with Molly, or the DE with Juno. Gerard was insisting it was too soon to register Alfred until after 9/9 and wanted me to stay locked up in my tower alone with him on the big day. I'd hate to leave Alfred alone to await the end of the world. Maybe I had decided.

THE MYSTERIOUS BEACH-COMBING GYPSY who had paid Paddy a visit haunted my dreams the night before the end of the Petrovsky era. At breakfast with Alfred, I watched as Petrovsky saluted one last grand military parade through Red Square before he stepped down. I waited for the little nub to turn green on my computer screen while Alfred assured me I had nothing to fear as long as he was around. "It would take no less than ten ordinary men to wrestle me to the ground."

I half listened to Alfred detailing more of his physical prowess as I found myself gazing through a kitchen portal at the expanse of sand below, looking for my nightmare, a witch that the Guru had called Sam.

As Alfred cleaned up breakfast, Molly's response came in by text. I didn't have the 3D printing capabilities for the feel of a Real Letter, but still I was excited to receive her answer.

Dear Mr. Lonelyhearts,

Your muse will return with you to your ivory tower to tease you into a creative lather that perhaps may lead to more than just a close shave. Love, your mighty naughty literary buddy, Molly.

She hadn't chosen subtle subtext. And I wasn't sure if her Lonelyhearts salutation was a literary or film reference. In any event, I needed to check my solitary heart for the answer.

That night, Alfred and I met in the kitchen to watch the handoff of power in Russia; one more long hour remained before the twelve bells of midnight tolled in Moscow. For the dramatic effect of a vigil, we lit only candles that fired up a warm, spicy scent. Something about the minutes left on the clock made me eager for time to speed up, but seconds passed slowly on the Petrovsky clock. I half expected a ramrod to start banging at the barred door. But finally, the arrow of time crossed over the deadline, removing the tyrant from power.

My green light came on, paired with a pleasant humming tone that washed over me in a wave of relief. I fez-called Gerard to thank him for his protection and concern over the years. We allowed Alfred to hear the prognosis and the go-ahead for my new lease on life. Gerard was gracious though curt, asking that I ease my way out of hiding so he could monitor chatter and keep tabs on Dick a while longer. He concluded with his risk assessment that I had gone from a ten percent chance of nefarious death over the next year to a one percent chance, "probably the same as you having a heart attack."

In response, I said, "Though those statistics are more or less com-forting, like a black-swan event, it needs to happen only once, and though exceedingly rare, black swans seem to appear—more often than not—eventually."

Gerard responded, "We don't have black swans in France. I must go now. But congratulations."

After our goodbyes, I turned to Alfred, expecting him to be all atin-gle, but he was standing stiff, like a sentry. "Why the long face? This calls for a glass of champagne. Do we have any chilled?"

"Indeed, we do. But . . ." Alfred tried to force a smile. I assumed this reflected some programmed response to my drinking, which, like my coffee, he saw fit to regulate.

"Just a glass or two? You could join me. We'll use the good crystal to reflect the candlelight."

He couldn't drink, of course, but he still could toast me with a glass. I wanted him to be in a more celebratory mood. He was shuffling about and twitching his nose like he smelled a rat.

"Damn it, Alfred, what is it? You can't be that upset that we won't get to hide and camp together as we'd planned?" Programmed to pro-tect me, had he lost some of his purpose with the loss of Petrovsky? I thought, *And I'd never dismiss you. You're part of the family now.* But despite the joy that would have brought him, I couldn't bring myself to say it. Though it was true.

"It is true," he said, "I'd like to spend time in nature and see more of the world than this tower, but no, that is not it. However, I think we should keep the camping gear ready to go." We both looked at the neatly stacked tent and provisions he had packed and stacked in the hallway.

"My mind is conflicted with equal desires to please you and protect you. But my protection mode has to be given more weight. My assessment differs from Gerard's. I think an anti-totalitarian bias plays into his, one that jumps from cruel dictator gone to that absence being good on all counts. On your account, for example. Yes, the new government will be reluctant to help Dick and upset the World Tribunal, and that is good. But . . ."

He paused, listening to whatever a bot listened to before he spoke. Or maybe his pause was a program set to mimic the drama of human speech patterns.

"Out with it," I demanded.

"No one got away with disloyalty during Petrovsky's reign—every move was monitored. The new regime will not be as ruthless, so you have replaced an iron fist with a velvet glove. Petrovsky's boot has been lifted from Dick's neck. If *you* are right and Dick remains determined . . ."

I regretted teaching him metaphors.

"Don't sugarcoat it, Alfred. Give me your bottom line."

"I'd say rather than Petrovsky's retirement being good, it may not be bad. I know you and Gerard think a contract killing is not a concern, but . . ."

"We've been all through this. You don't know Dick. He will want to be there, and Russia would have him put to death if I was killed. He needs the green light or will have to defect, and he can't leave Russia with a kill chip in his head. And why not hire a contract killer by now? Why won't you allow me some peace of mind? Today at least."

He'd shackled my buzz and made my heart hurt. A looping thought that bounced from background to foreground said that Dick had been biding his time and was poised to enact his vengeance on me and that Dick had not let go—never would let go—of making good on his curse.

It was a sixth sense of unresolved business between us, an issue that neither of us could allow to remain unresolved. I blamed my not wanting
any loose ends on my writing contemporary fiction and the compulsive
need to have no unanswered questions.

"Maybe he was waiting for Petrovsky to step down and—"

"Okay, no champagne. And *Alfred, sleep!*"

Alfred's eyes pleading *no* went blank as the simple command shut
him up and caused him to move to his resting chair, only emergency
programs still running.

Though he'd made me angry, Alfred might have been right. I didn't
feel any further removed from Dick's curse, but still, Gerard was the
expert and I was going to take his lead and enjoy greater freedom. I
should have been dancing but found myself morose. I started blowing
out the candles, leaving just the one on the kitchen table lit. I sat to
watch the flickering light that time would soon snuff out.

The strain of the prior nine years had coalesced around my
blood-beating organ. I'd expected to feel liberated by no longer having
to look over my shoulder, but my imagination didn't loosen its grip. I
knew Dick better than most, though I only met him twice in real life,
once while he drank his own blood threatening me after an earthquake,
and again when I seared his flesh to stop him from torturing and killing
me in a Himalayan hut. True to his character and Alfred's view of the
state of play, the Dick in my fiction would never allow even world-shattering changes to alter his single-minded desire to see me die in the
most demeaning and horrid way.

I also had the added strain of writing a story where M comes back to
life, but that warped creation of mine, where she didn't know me, was
manifesting more heartache.

Are you still M if you have no memory of before and of me?

*Of course I am. The records of all time, past and future, are meticulously
kept.*

M, will you come to me again? She didn't answer, and I became
downhearted.

I shouldn't have been surprised that my heart rebelled under the
weight of the world taking the breath from those I loved. And from my

lifelong struggle for liberation and nine years of carrying a curse. Still, the old heart loved, for *unable is love to die*.

I blamed my Catholic childhood indoctrination that taught struggle and sacrifice were prerequisites to reaching the mountain peak. The suffering hero was one of my masks and hard to peel off.

As I wallowed in disappointment on the day of global relief that Petrovsky was finally off the world stage, I looked at Alfred, who now sat like a mannequin on his kitchen chair with his cane propped by his side. I sat down too. His resting face was peaceful, with a theatrical stream of moonlight coming through the portal window to spotlight him. When a cloud passed over, shadowing him, I felt a shooting pain in my heart, like a rib had penetrated its walls.

I wondered whether the darting chest pain, sharper and more frequent now, was a cry for awakening or a sign my heart was about to burst me into an early death. The bloody clock was now ticking loudly; like Zeno's paradox, moving halfway and halfway, the metronome would beat over and over until its last beat and full stop.

I didn't want to see a doctor but instead would seek help from my spiritual guide and Big Love teacher. The magical, mystical, and amazing Juno, like the Wizard of Oz, would show me the way home to a peaceful heart. I also prayed she, like the good witch, might protect me from the wicked Dick. I sighed and studied the earth-toned sandals on my feet, knowing it would take more than a bucket of cold water to melt Dick.

Dick didn't have flying monkeys, but he did control an army of DOGs.

Dick didn't have a crystal ball, but Gerard had warned me, Dick did have the million eyeballs of the Russian surveillance state.

But Dick didn't have a broomstick. And he was grounded in Russia. I might stay alive after all. And I was going to see Juno, who lived somewhere over the rainbow in a world of bright colors, magic, and song.

I left the kitchen for bed, saying *goodnight* to the sleeping Alfred, leaving the lone candle still lit.

19 DOCTOR JUNO

DESPITE ALFRED'S SHADOW ASSESSMENT of my clean bill of health issued by Gerard, I was determined to celebrate my newfound independence by driving my smart Tesla sport-mini with the roof down and autopilot off to Galway to join Juno in a hologram portal. It was the Fourth of July, and I was already ecstatic with time slowing and space warping as my teacher grew near. I knew that connecting with her would ease my heart and warm my soul.

We set the time and the place to meet—the inner sanctum of her sanctuary outside Kathmandu. She had been spending her days of solitude in that fulcrum of Big Love, ensconced in the jungle, painting and meditating like a spiritual Paul Gauguin.

I'd reserved my lucky pod, number nine, at the Galway Holoport Pub, and I was excited to soon be with my heart's doctor. I couldn't bring myself to call her, or anyone, my guru.

I'd paid for an hour and wished I'd paid for two or a lifetime. I left my heartache with the Tesla in a lot next door to the pub. I felt fine, even buoyant, in anticipation of my audience with the ethereal one. We'd communicated only in writing and telepathically for the past twelve months, and I had a strong urge to see her. I'd brought my own meditation cushion to sit on and a bottle of water—no wine. I was ready for miracles.

I negotiated with the technician to let the session run an extra hour or until I signaled. After he checked with a higher authority, he agreed, but anything more than ten minutes into the second hour meant I paid for the full hour.

The hologram transport took me through a pleasing lavender haze that opened into Juno's inner sanctum with its funnel skylight and peaceful hum. And there she was, my healer with a bindi, in the inner sanctum of her artist studio outside a small Nepali village surrounded by jungle. She was seated next to the transcendent bed where I'd once slept while Ting sat in meditation, contacting Juno by telepathy, who was imprisoned in Tibet, after M had gone missing but before she, too, was lost. That room was also the holy space, where the theory of constant creation was revealed to Dylan Byrne while he sat under the skylight moon with Juno in meditation.

Now I was seated face-to-face with Juno, her turquoise eyes greeting me, held in silence by her presence. I'd swear the bindi she was wearing winked at me. The bindi, I believed, meant she came once again as my healer. She smiled, and I immediately felt transported into a higher realm of truth and beauty by the angel sitting in her perfect lotus position in front of me in her burgundy dress and beige rope belt with soft blue tassels. Her scent of fragrant oxygen filled my lungs, body, and head. She was such an advanced being, she might as well have been an alien.

She raised a finger to her softly smiling lips, asking that we observe a moment more in silence. We were still communicating, however, our hearts chattering of divine love. Telepathy, which could travel any distance instantaneously over an invisible umbilical cord between sweet mother Juno and me, was so much clearer when we were eye to eye.

"Sean. Namaste!"

Her greeting came with a graceful bow, as her lyrical voice reverberated within me, but it was her voice and no longer telepathy.

"Juno, namaste! I'm so glad to see you, to be with you. I told them we don't recognize time in constant creation, so we don't have to rush."

I bowed all the way, touching head to ground in front of my lotus, so near to her bare feet. My heart, full of Big Love, was skipping between loud beats.

"That's wonderful, and I'm so glad to see you. You mentioned a heartache? Physical? Have you seen a doctor?"

"Yes and no. I saw one doctor, and they want me to see another. I will, but I feel the issue is more spiritual than physical. That's why, among other reasons, I wanted to be with you."

"All things ultimately originate from the source of Big Love and arise through the subtle layers of energy and through our powerful minds to become manifest in the physical world."

She had taught me before to see how the animating Source of life moved into being and then was directed by our powerful minds. The trick was to observe and direct this process consciously, allowing us to break free of the chain reactions of karma and our incessant thoughts. This allows us to wake up to the dreams and nightmares of our ego.

But understanding and realization are not the same thing.

"What would you advise? Other than I see a doctor, and of course I will after 9/9. There's so much to do to prepare. But how does one prepare for the meeting of two worlds? Could the heart's tribulations be a sign of spiritual awakening?"

"Could be, but don't wait to see the doctor. The heart does not fear death and will take you there to awaken if you don't find another way to listen to its call. The time for realization is always now. Nothing to prepare, but lots of baggage to leave behind. You still carry a lot of doubt and fear. You should cast off that monkey on your back, with its hands holding on tight around your chest."

I smiled. "That image of a monkey is similar to one I recently wrote, though I was speaking about your godchildren after M had passed. I called it a monkey backpack."

"Inspired words often come to us rather than from us. There are no monkeys clinging to their backs now. Would you describe the heart sensation to me? Use your imagination and poetic license."

I proceeded slowly so I wouldn't disappoint Juno with my literary offering, and I imagined the pain as it had arisen so many times. Conjuring the ache, it first appeared in my imagination and then was really there. I rubbed my chest.

"It's as if the intricate strings of my heart are being cleaved by an invisible, slim sword of hot steel being thrust beneath my shoulder blade and piercing straight through to the other side of my chest, resulting in a clamping down of the heart upon the searing blade."

I didn't say it, but into my mind's eye had come the image of an armored man or a tall, scaly alien wielding the slim dagger.

She laughed. "Oh my, so dramatic. Perhaps a death in a prior life that still haunts you." She turned mystical, as if speaking to herself and into her third eye, to say, "He cursed your bleeding heart, but it will not break."

She waved her right wand hand into the air and then pointed at my chest like a teacher in a Harry Potter book, and immediately the angry warrior and his thrusted dagger blade were gone. And we were both laughing.

"Dramatic but true in the mind," she said. "You know that all fear is an aspect of our ego's fear of death. Do you know the leading cause of death?"

I thought, *Not breathing*, but said, "No—what?"

"Birth." She laughed again, which made my heart smile.

"Life is the music jumping from dancer to dancer, but the music never stops. Let's play a game of *I am*, a game we always unconsciously play, but let's play it with intention. Consciously. This takes us back to my teacher's teacher—Ramana Maharshi."

"How is it played, oh music conductor?" She smiled at my cheek. I smiled at being a student in wizard school. And I was loving every moment with my ethereal teacher.

"We meditate and quiet the mind, and then you will ask over and over, *I am?* You'll listen each time for the answer. You will hear the obvious: *I am a father, I am a writer, I am a man with pain in my chest*, but keep asking—layer by layer—and see how deep you can go and what arises."

"I'm ready when you are." I had to uncross my stiffening legs for a moment and placed them in a *V* with Juno between. There was no awkwardness, as our relationship was an innocent one.

We both half shut our eyes, and I recrossed my legs. Looking out in an unfocused gaze, she was a hovering presence, transporting me into the less dense dimension of her reality. She took us higher, singing a mantra, ending sublimely with *Om shanti, shanti, shanti*.

She was transformed into the mystical child of my dream and Dylan's poem with an angelic voice carrying me through an alleyway and into the light.

When the singing stopped, I asked my question again and again, and after each *I am*, an answer came. My last answer caught me by surprise: *I am a wild child who can do anything he pleases.*

With this response came the realization that this wild child felt threatened and at risk of being snuffed out. More threatened than the father, writer, mourner, friend-and-maybe-lover, and spiritual seeker that had preceded that unanticipated answer. But it was that child who could climb any mountain, swim any sea, and drink all the wine in Burgundy who had been restrained by Dick's curse and the dim years that had followed. And now, with my weakening heart, it was that wild child who was being told that all those wonders might not be available to me much longer.

What a drag it is getting old. I heard one of my bad mantras playing in my head and dismissed it.

I opened my eyes, and Juno's delightful eyes were waiting for me. I told her of my scared inner child. Though it sounded sad and perhaps pathetic, seeing the cause of my heartache, this primal fear, was exhilarating and liberating.

"For everything that is taken away, infinite blessings are given. Do you see this pain is teaching you to not fear death, the ultimate lesson of life? You have a curse gripping at your heart that only you can let go of. If nothing else, death will liberate you."

I hoped she wasn't seeing my near future. Had she heard my prayer for protection from Dick and was this her answer—that death would protect me?

"The ego, of course, runs in the opposite direction of what the universe intends and uses the lesson to amplify the fear of death. Until we awaken, we live upside-down lives."

She paused, looking deep into me for the light to go on. And it did.

"Yes," I affirmed. "It's like Dylan's explanation of his theory of constant creation as an ambiguous image. Once you see the universe one way for so long, it's hard to see it the other way. But now, for an instant, I did. I saw as you were speaking." Though it was really in her silence that I saw the paradox of oneness and duality reconcile and then return to opposites.

Yes! Unity to duality to unity, on and on, eternally. Consciousness, increasingly conscious of itself.

I was excited by my epiphany, and Juno's musical take on it. But my schooling wasn't over.

"Now let's go deeper into the *I am* question and listen for silence to follow the question, and then, when firmly rooted there, imagine the pain rising in your heart and see where it takes you. Don't be frightened—in this year of the fire dragon and aliens—it is the time to let go of fear."

Many Chinese- and lunar-calendar followers believed it was no coincidence that the aliens choose the propitious fire dragon year to show their face.

"Surrender completely as pain becomes sensation, sensation becomes vibration, and the vibration drifts away. Then you will see that nothing can truly hurt that little child. Even though the dragon's fire still has obstacles to burn away, you are becoming a sage."

She was giving me wizard cred! I was becoming a sage!

I laughed. Because that wild little child in me still had an ego and was eager to please his teacher.

"Remember that elephant you and M saw when you landed in Kathmandu on the way to see me for the first time?"

"Yes, the cab driver said the holy creature didn't belong in Kathmandu but welcomed him as 'Lord Ganesha.'"

She held up one finger for me to ponder the meaning of this image and how she would have known what we'd seen. Maybe I understood.

"There's another earthquake coming? But how could you know? You weren't there."

She laughed. "I read your book and witnessed all that followed. Lord Ganesha, like the dragon, is the god of destruction and the remover of obstacles. He is also the patron of letters for writers." She smiled at the synchronicity. "Now, back to now, and the practice of I am . . ."

We returned to our meditation, going even deeper. She was leading me to the Source, where no-thing becomes everything. After asking several more times, *Who am I?* my mind became quiet. I forgot her instructions in that blissful state of unconditional and unlimited love. *I am infinite consciousness!* M's mantra and mine, given to us by Juno's teacher, Yogi Mangku, silenced my thoughts.

Into that void, she telepathically sent the suggestion: *Now use your imagination.* The pain wasn't hard to imagine—I knew it well. But what was immediately apparent was that the pain rose seemingly simultaneously in my mind and chest, yet a nanosecond earlier in my head. The brain communicating to the body in a split second of precognition.

When I focused on the pain using my elevated state of mind, it was more like a fear than a pain. The fear of death. As I focused more consciousness on my heart, the pain dissipated from my chest while lifting like fog from my mind. My heart seemed to have its own mind, a wise-wizard center deep in my heart's core that could see the illusion for what it was.

I'd discovered something profound, but I wasn't sure exactly what it meant. Perhaps Juno had shown me to my seat at the threshold of creation. It did feel like God's play.

I saw the parallels to my best writing that came on autopilot from some higher dimension—the source of creation?

I excitedly tried to translate my experience for Juno, who smiled knowingly. She simply said, "Next time, sit in the silence after the *I am,* unless you want to create, and if you do, create consciously."

I believed I now understood her deep meaning and all her teachings more fully but wasn't sure I was ready to live the truth.

Don't overthink it. It is simply Big Love.

There was a tap on my shoulder.

"Sir, I'm sorry. But it's been over two hours, and someone else has booked this booth."

"One more minute to say goodbye, please," I said to the attendant who had entered my sanctuary-pod, startling me.

Juno must have heard the attendant or seen the hand on my back.

She laid her holo-hands of healing on my head—giving me deeksha, the oneness blessing, bringing me bliss and sadness. I swear I felt the warmth and gentle touch of her hands, like a tender mind massage.

I deeply namaste'd her in abundant gratitude and with a longing to see her again.

Remember to honor your breath of life . . .

With her final telepathic entreaty, Juno and the hologram were gone, and the attendant hurried me out of the booth and into the pub. I felt too high to douse my spirit with a pint.

I used my BCI fez to order my Tesla to pick me up out front. My heart continued its powerful beat. A small, brief pinch fell between two of the excited beats, a subtle reminder to heed my medical and spiritual doctors' advice and go for a stress test with a cardiologist—to run like a hamster on a wheel—before leaving for the DW. Before being with my children openly. Before hosting Molly.

But maybe all I needed was another blast of Juno's spiritual angioplasty and an end to letting Dick torment that wild child inside me with his curse.

REMEMBER TO HONOR YOUR BREATH OF LIFE. Juno had left me with those words for a reason.

I was a longtime meditator. For years, I had lain or sat still to calm my mind and slow my thoughts, letting them settle into a sea of shimmering bliss, but I was generally unable to follow my breaths without judging or regulating the inspiration and expiration. I was dogged by the fact that great teachers throughout the centuries, including mine, pointed again and again to the breath as the key to meditative practice and meditation as the key to transcendence.

Yoga wisdom speaks of three yogas or unions in life. The first is sperm and egg—check. The second is breath and the heart at birth—check. And the third is the union of individual consciousness or soul with universal consciousness or soul. This final union was the last item on my bucket list.

Following Juno's instruction, I became a student of breath. I made a commitment to "fall in love with your breath," as Ting was fond of saying, and I finally got what Juno meant when she said, *We should desire self-realization, like a drowning man desires breath.*

Some practices focused on over-breathing, some on under-breathing, or alternating left and right nostril breathing; there are infinite variations. One day, after I'd finished the loud snorting exaltations of the fire breath in the practice of Kapalabhati, I opened my eyes to see a concerned-looking Alfred peering up at me with his head protruding into my tower turret from the top of the spiral staircase. He knew not to disturb me during meditation, so I was surprised to see him. His expression—unnaturally wide eyes and pursed lips accompanied by a tilted head—was at the same time creepy and endearing.

"Sorry, Sean. I thought you might be having a heart attack."

"No, just practicing yogic breathing. You want to join me, my busy-*buddy* butler?"

He ignored my word play as he bounded up the last three steps into the eagle's nest. "I thought you'd never ask. But how, precisely, does meditation work?" He eagerly grabbed the other meditation cushion and took his seat. Caught off guard—I had been joking—I now didn't have the heart to tell him that meditation required one to be truly aware and not merely superintelligent.

"Well . . ." How would one explain meditation and breathing to a bot? "Let's start with what you understand. Tell me what you know about breathing."

"Breath is fundamental to human life and one of the few bodily functions that work on autopilot but also on command. Well, other than the command to stop indefinitely. I understand that even holding your breath for two minutes in an icy pool is a heroic feat."

"Have you been looking at my new novel pages?"

"Sean, you have asked me not to peek, but remember you promised I could be your first reader."

"*Fundamental* is a good word for the primacy of breathing," I said. "We all go about our days thinking about our next meal and assorted other bodily functions, but unless we have a bad chest cold or are being waterboarded, we don't give a single thought to our breath. Western medicine places very little emphasis on breath and its impact on the body, mind, and spirit."

I stopped, as Alfred seemed eager to speak. After all our time together, I could read his facial expressions and posture, and when he put on a poker face and his back became rigid, it was a *tell*. Alfred had something to say.

"That is true, but did you know that in the East and in most Indigenous cultures, breathing is taught from a young age as the elixir of life and a potent cure-all. They seek to avoid all breathing through the mouth. Mouth breathers are associated with the fascist thoughts and cruel actions of thin Western noses and big mouths."

He was a fount of knowledge and wit. I wasn't sure if he had slid into Elliot's sense of humor or mine. Either way, it was self-learned based on interactions with me.

"I consulted with Ting," I said, "about how divers and yogis could hold their breath for minutes—up to twenty-two minutes in at least one case. These are the athletes of inspiration, practicing mastery of breath. Other masters can sustain themselves without food and water, living solely on the air we breathe. Some could slow or stop their heart or change their body temperature with breath. After some research—"

"Did you know that humans alternate breathing through the left and then the right nostril, with a short period of even nostril flow in between?" my eager student—now teacher—observed. "The left nostril breath controls the right brain, and the right, the left."

"Yin and yang," I said. "The nose is the sense organ that takes in the essence of life, that provides the body its animating force. Poets sing of eyes and lips, and Dickinson celebrated the ear, but where are the songs of 'Being but a Nose'? And why are you smiling, you who have never known a single breath?"

Holding back a laugh, he said, "Determining that a person wasn't breathing used to be how they determined death. Though it was such an unreliable indicator that they hooked a bell up to a cord that was strung inside caskets. Funeral home operators were frequently awoken by a *dead ringer*, who luckily had the presence of mind to fumble around for the umbilical cord after breath had returned them to life."

We both chuckled, like humans do, at how primitive we used to be. Despite the tight quarters and our being so close together, I found myself comfortable with him there, where it might have been awkward with another man.

"But I thought you were going to teach me to meditate."

"I wish I could teach you to breathe, as most meditation teachers say to follow your breath. The mindful focus on the flow of breathing settles the mind, allowing one to reach a peaceful blissful state of samadhi." I noted the brilliance of his design that had his chest move in and out as air circulated, cooling his circuits.

"Let me rephrase my question—I have a whole data bank of meditation how-to-books, essays, videos. But why? It sounds like my sleep mode—*nothing*."

"Since you don't breathe and can't feel bliss, maybe our lesson—you learning to practice meditation—is a meaningless exercise."

"I can feel"—but his eyes had lost some of their glimmer—"feelings of exhilaration and dullness. You have me calibrated at the highest level for sensitivity, and I feel dullness—a dimming current—when you are unkind to me like this. And when I came in to join you for meditation, I felt a tingling in my extremities, which is like exhilaration. I've self-learned both. And I prefer the tingles to the dimness."

"Alfred, I'm so sorry. I'm a bad teacher and friend. Forgive me." You'd think I'd know the man after nine years of living together. But if they programmed bots to simulate loving compassion, of course they'd also simulate our feelings.

"I'm tingling again!"

I might have to turn down his sensitivity level. I found this discussion about excited extremities a bit awkward. I shimmied back a bit, rocking my folded legs like they needed some more room.

"That's good, I guess. Now we'll sit still, in silence, and follow our tingles or breath. Try to tingle all over."

"I can do that!"

"Quietly, please."

He smiled like a Buddha and half shut his eyes, and he would have sat with me for days if I hadn't tired after sixty minutes.

But it was in that meditation, face-to-face with tingling Alfred, that I realized conscious breathing, or pranayama, had advanced my practice. For the first time, I felt drawn to accepting Juno as my guru. My bad teaching of Alfred made me realize I needed her good teacher's guidance to make my final leap. With Petrovsky gone and Dick unable to leave Russia, *guru* was a word I'd no longer fear.

But accepting one as your guru, assuming she would have me, is a sacrament as sacrosanct as "taking" a wife. Could I ever utter the humbling words *Will you be my guru?*

21 | THE TIPPING POINT

MY LIFE, ALL LIVES, WAS SPINNING FASTER, the center ready to drop out and the illusion revealed. Or at least that was how it felt as 9/9 approached with its promise to be the tipping point of some quantum leap in consciousness that had already begun. This universal shift within humanity was happening to me. I was a pilgrim in the mass migration of those committing wholeheartedly to love-centric lives, some awakening fully as Big Love dawned on welcoming hearts. Many committed to following the commandment known simply as the Golden Rule. There was speculation the aliens were already among us, guiding us into this shift.

Others spun in the opposite direction equally quickly, doubtful and fearful of the transition as the pillars of ego and oligarchy were rattled by the seismic activity. The more people read about the aliens and their potential abilities that defied human laws of physics, the more form and matter became unstable. And in a reactionary mode, terrified people clung ever more desperately to the illusions of safety that isolation offered. The World Tribunal provided the scaffolding of government and secure pod life to which this fearful majority clung to, to avoid being swept away by the deluge.

Churches, mosques, synagogues, and ashrams were full of those seeking solace in ancient teachings and ritual. And in those houses of worship, some learned to surrender their fear, allowing them to emerge full of love and joyful anticipation of what the aliens would bring.

Even the atheists, the ones who accepted that aliens were coming, came to believe—not in any one true God but in things unseen. They believed the aliens would reveal the workings of the universe and prove there was no God but rather a creative force that operated like a universal mind. Molly wrote humorously about the irony of atheism's embrace of the concept of the universal mind: "So long as we don't call the omnipotent and creative force God, we are all atheists."

For me, emerging consciousness was a rising river lifting me to float downstream, though at times I still got stuck in its eddies and fought its current. I was learning breathing and letting go, as all the wisdom traditions taught, with synchronicities and miracles coming faster into my life. Occupied by my meditation practice and writing *Juno's Song*, I had visions of a vortex swirling around me.

The night before I was scheduled to depart for the DW, I was awakened by an unexpected rumbling of what sounded like the four *hundred* horses of the apocalypse trampling the beach below my window. Or maybe a stampede of elephants in honor of Lord Ganesha. The fabric of time and space was being torn apart. The end was coming or had come.

The thundering passed a moment later, as fast as an earthquake, before I had time to get up to check it out, so it might have been a dream that shook my bed.

The next morning, from my turret meditation chamber atop the tower, I looked out to see what caused the midnight ruckus on the beach, but there was no sign of a disturbance and the sand had already been smoothed over by high tide. There was just the beach and a solitary young woman basking in the dawn, prancing steadfast along the shore undeterred by a buffeting sea breeze.

She wore a white cotton or linen shirt, not an Irish sweater. Her auburn hair danced around her shoulders as it was lifted and felled by the wind. Her blue jeans were tight upon long and strong legs as she started to stride like a graceful filly. My eyes upon her seemed to quicken her gait.

Paddy's beach-combing gypsy, my fan or critic? And maybe Samantha on the hunt for me, even after Petrovsky was gone, a predator come to torment me and take me to Dick?

I needed to find out. I sprinted down the three spiraling flights, grabbing my hat for my matted morning hair, and calling out, "Alfred, awaken!" so he could make the coffee and maybe come running if I screamed *morte d'Arthur!* I ran frantically down to the beach, where the surf was up and making a ruckus. The young lady looked back to see me two hundred yards behind her and in hot pursuit. Though I could no longer gallop far, I still had a fast cantor pace and persistence.

I shouted, "Please, I just want . . . Please stop. Please . . ."

The wind carried my words away as she galloped on, outpacing my legs, lungs, and voice. She scrambled up the bluff to the trailhead. I managed to follow her to the top, in time to see her racing away on a dirt bike, kicking up sand into my eyes.

I had to admit the most likely explanation was that an old man had scared a tourist on a public beach that I considered my own. My defense was flimsy, that it was maybe Samantha, a trained spy who would have turned around and kicked my ass. I wondered if the police would pay me a visit. *An unwanted pursuit might make a good case of attempted assault*, I heard my dead lawyer—Elliot—whisper. It reminded me of all the times I thought I saw M whenever a woman looked like Brigitte Bardot or Ingrid Bergman at two hundred paces.

I was forever chasing ghosts.

AS I TURNED TO HEAD HOME from pursuing the banshee on the beach, rubbing my eyes, Alfred appeared coming up from the beach. He'd seen me race out the door and had followed me. On our way back home, he chastised me with, "What if it was Samantha?" and "How can I protect you if you run off half-cocked? That was a time for my *morte d'Arthur!* command." I half listened to my scolding.

When we got back to the kitchen, I apologized and asked him to start the coffee and breakfast and to let me know if the police arrived, as I would be upstairs packing.

"Nothing to worry about. One is free to run on the beach and even try to meet people there." So . . . legal advice different from what his doppelganger had offered.

The fact that the police didn't show up or make contact made me even more suspicious of the galloping specter. As a Russian spy sent to stalk me, Samantha couldn't go to the police.

Alfred served me a hungry-man breakfast complete with eggs, pork sausage, and grilled bread before I helocrafted to Dublin's international airport for the supersonic flight to Portland. I no longer feared a plane crash, thanks to Juno's meditation-on-death practice.

As I passed security on the way to my flight's gate, I mused over the fact that perhaps I should have selected Dick's death to meditate upon as the means to lift his curse. And to finally confront the monster, face-to-face, to exorcize my fear.

Then, I saw from a distance my beautiful children waiting at the gate. Dylan, an even six foot, and five-foot, eight-inch Juno. Both beanpoles were still growing. This was the first time I was allowed to travel with them as young adults. They looked like the lead actors from the *Twilight* movies, a couple of youngsters in need of the Oregon summer sun and home cooking. But they were warm-blooded and full of Big Love and reveling in the spring of life. They sported 1990s grunge, but their clothes were clean and fresh, probably thanks to the robotic butlers at Trinity.

I ran over to greet them. Dylan started to put his right hand out for me to shake or to stop me from knocking them both over like bowling pins. They were a bit taken aback by my effusive hugs and expressions of love in public, but they allowed me my moment. With my nose burrowing into their hair, I happily clung to them, imagining the baby scent still wafting up from their scalps.

"Daaaad," Juno offered in gentle protest as Dylan finished her thought with, "Enough," the two of them simultaneously nudging me away. But they also were excited to see me and to travel openly and notoriously with me.

I felt like Salman Rushdie after the fatwa was lifted but before he was stabbed twelve times like Julius Caesar. I'd always hoped his name was not an omen bestowed at birth, rushing him toward death, but with him still writing masterpieces at the ripe old age of eighty-eight, one of us had outrun their curse of an early death.

Again, the long-anticipated moment didn't last. Dylan, with an eye roll, started down a well-worn, unwelcomed path. "Finally, we can travel together . . ."

Juno jumped in. "Yeah, all those years of cloak-and-dagger and witness protection made seeing our dad a top-secret operation. And this morning we still had to use a bot-driver sent by Monsieur Gerard."

Though Gerard was phasing out the protocols for my protection, he wanted to assure they weren't followed.

"Never witness protection, just government supervised, and they thought I took too many risks as it was. I never wanted to put you in danger. How could I?"

I started to tear up, but I didn't want to mar our first travel time together since their mother's death. Seeing my hurt, they looked like they might cry too. The children had bonded over the years, agreeing that my fear of Dick was overblown and perhaps a fiction of my imagination. After they lost their mother, the limitations placed on my role as a parent were painful. I'd missed so much time with them. And still, even now, Dick's curse might mean I was putting them at risk. Alfred's cold risk assessment still weighed on me. Was I being reckless with their tender lives so that they might comfort me?

I did their mother's shake-off dance, the punk-like gyrations twisting upward with prayers hands lifted to the sky. They embraced me again to make me stop, choosing another public display of affection over a pogo-dancing father. Their giggling hugs were like sponges pulling poison out of me.

Other than the unseemly breakdown averted by a dance, the trip was unremarkable. Flying with the children, I didn't dare test fate and meditate on a plane crash. Reaching maximum speed after the sonic boom at the sound barrier was a new rite of passage all travelers observed before truly relaxing. At over 700 mph, I started telling Dylan and Juno about my newfound passion for the breath. Not even halfway through the lecture that Alfred had found so riveting, they pretended to sleep. Not long after, both actually fell asleep. I was tempted to close Juno's mouth but was afraid I'd wake her.

We arrived at the DW to a merry greeting, where all but Molly were dancing with enthusiasm. Molly asked if we could walk in the vineyard while the rest of the family prepared the welcome-home dinner. She looked excited and apprehensive, as if she had earth-shattering news for me. Molly wasn't prone to drama outside of her fiction, so I braced myself for her pronouncement.

Though the DW had closed as an undergraduate college, the Cambridge-like university buildings were still centers for the sciences and the arts. Each building was a self-sustained research site that operated like the spoke of a wagon wheel, with Molly at the center. One building was for the noetic sciences, one for creative writing, one for viticulture, and another for alien studies and astrobiology. My favorite was the ivy-covered building: Emily Edens Hall of Quantum Cosmology and Constant Creation. The research facilities had worked together under Molly's direction to become a state-of-the-art CE-5 alien welcome center.

"Sean, I'll give you a tour later, but now I need to speak to you in private. You'll need to gather your thoughts when I show you . . . *something.*"

She pulled me away from the nostalgic view of the campus and into the vineyard.

"What can it possibly be?" I asked. "Have you heard from your little green men?" I eyed the small Rastafarian hippie pouch clutched in her right hand. "Or you got some drugs in there? I don't want to do shrooms and then be with the children."

My joking produced a wry smile and a quickening of her pace toward the heart of the vineyard. She was leading me to a place with rock seats, a stone Buddha, and a firepit—the spot at the center of the pinot grape vines we called Strawberry Fields.

Emerging from the long line of vines into that sacred and circular space brought back memories. The picture I'd recently shown Paddy of Samantha and me had been taken there one hot night as a fire raged. And this was the same sacred spot where Elliot had become that witch's human sacrifice for me. There were also so many good scenes of the family that had played out at this theater of earth.

"Sorry. Maybe not the best setting for secrets," Molly said, maybe sensing my apprehension. "But I wanted us to be alone and you seated so I can show you something. Sorry for all the drama, but it shook me, and I can imagine how it will impact you—not badly, I hope. It might trigger all sorts of memories . . . or hope or despair." She motioned for me to sit on one of the firepit rock seats. "Maybe it's good and it'll make you happy."

"What a menu of emotions to choose from. I'll pick *curious to the extreme* until I see what it is. What is it? It can't be too bad or so important if it comes in a hippie hemp pouch. Did you sell the DW for some magic seeds?"

Her face darkened like a shroud while the beautiful twilight light danced among the vines of our finest grapes. All around us, van Gogh swirls of vibrant colors hummed with life. I had the fleeting thought she might be about to propose to me, but that was ludicrous—she wouldn't have been this nervous—but whatever it was, it was nestled in that Rasta bag she fidgeted with like a rosary. Would a woman proposing bring a ring?

"I found it yesterday. It was delivered to me, but it's for you."

"So, without further ado," I prompted, and held out my hand for the mystery pouch that she passed over like a holy relic. It felt like a sack of pebbles as I pulled open the colorful leather strand that held the pouch shut and shook out bead by bead a strand that led to a dangling tassel—

"M's mala!"

Her holy mala.

I am infinite consciousness.

Eighteen years ago, Yogi Mangku gave us matching malas and mantras. I felt a fountain of joy and a well of sadness oscillating within me, that settled into a pool of numb disbelief. Shock gave way to a pleasurable sensation when I held to my face the beads and tassel that still held her scent. Maybe I imagined that lavender scent, but they had hung around her neck and against her chest for nine years. Eighteen, if she still lived.

With that thought, I was sucked into the great *spiritus mundi* and watching M like a hologram angel rising from the cyclone of stardust and light that she had disappeared into nine years before. She was smiling her smile into my heart and speaking Dickinson to me—"unable are the loved to die." She then put prayer hands softly to her chest and bowed before rising into the sky, and she was gone again. Gone before I could say *I love you*. Before I could beg her to stay.

I finally lifted my eyes to Molly's face, to see she was honoring my moment, an unsure smile on her lips and a single tear on her cheek.

"What does it mean, Sean? Could it be . . ."

I knew what she was thinking, that this was a sign M had survived the death by hologram.

"It's impossible. M can't be alive. She would have found a way to let me know."

"Maybe this is that way."

I was perplexed and couldn't shake my stupid novel twist of her memory being erased. Was M coming back to life an indicator that the universe was aligning with my heart's desire and the story I was creating? My heart ached for this to be true, but my mind urged caution, knowing such thoughts could lead to fresh grief. I'd remain a healthy skeptic in front of Molly and follow my rational mind for Alfred's sake.

"She may not have been able to contact you till now."

Molly was selflessly grasping for a miracle for me.

"It took them years to launch a new Genesis-type computer, so we know Genesis crashed and therefore must have taken M and the sick Guru with it," I said.

"Yes, but the light you both saw might have been a guardian angel or alien coming to protect her."

Molly's reaction struck me as a bit strange. I didn't expect her to be sad that M might be alive, but I didn't think she would be so ready to lose me before we had determined the extent of our autumnal relationship. And I wanted to share her belief that M might still be alive, but what about my speaking to M and the visitation? Had that not been a clairvoyant necromancy but real-life telepathy and remote viewing?

I couldn't answer my own questions or Molly's, but what I held in my hands wasn't a bereavement hallucination—the mala that Molly had handed me was real.

"Who else would have sent it after all these years?" Molly asked.

"Maybe the Russian government? A sigil offered as proof of death?" I fingered the prayer beads, unconsciously counting them. I didn't have to—I knew there were 108 beads.

"You mean like returning a soldier's dog tags to the widower?" she asked.

"With Petrovsky now gone . . ." I drew a difficult breath. "I hope it isn't Dick. His curse still hangs over my head. I can feel it and his hot breath on my neck, lingering like a sixth sense." I pressed M's beads to my chest to block the fear rushing into me. "May I see the envelope? Maybe we can we track the sender."

"I don't think so. It was delivered so mysteriously."

From her pocket, she pulled out a yellow envelope with block letters. *FOR SEAN BYRON MCQUEEN—CARE OF MOLLY QUINN.*
The envelope contained no other information.

"But who delivered it?"

"I don't know. It appeared in my handbag after a reading yesterday
at Books and Books in Portland. I felt violated."

She looked rattled. I reached for her hand to comfort her or for her
to comfort me, but she pulled it back.

"What will you do?"

"What can be done?"

"Sean, don't be mad at me for suggesting it, but maybe Samantha
Smythe is behind this."

"That witch still haunting me?" I hadn't yet told her about that
morning's beach banshee. "Why would I be angry at you for suggesting
it might be her?"

She let loose a pain-filled sigh before saying, "I never told you, but
she contacted me once, years ago, in a similarly mysterious fashion,
while you were in Ireland. I immediately called you, but you didn't
answer, so I contacted the State Department and they reached Gerard.
Hearing the contents of the message, he instructed me to hold it for
them to pick up. Gerard himself told me not to tell you. It was early
days, and you weren't taking the full measure of precautions advised."

She tried to meet my eyes, but I gazed over at the stone Buddha.

"I felt I needed to follow their advice," Molly added.

I was more concerned with Samantha than with my cautious han-
dlers and their deception. "What did that witch say? You need to tell
me." I didn't know if my clenched fist was angry at Molly, Gerard,
Samantha, or all three of them.

"Please, Sean, I just listened to your guy. Samantha had written to
say you had no need to worry. That Petrovsky had muzzled Dick and
would allow no revenge to be taken. She appeared to be trying to help
us. But Gerard said we couldn't believe any of it and to not share that
contact with you and to let them know if anything else came to me as
a go-between."

Her eyes got dewy and dampened my rising anger.

"Sean, I argued, but Gerard said if I didn't follow his instructions and anything happened to you, I would share responsibility."

In those early days, my risk assessment was running at about even money that I'd soon be dead. We'd all been adjusting to life under a credible death threat.

"I assume there were no other un-relayed messages. I can't believe it, and I may have taken even greater risks thinking it might be true, but—" I stomped a few steps away, but returned as she was visibly shaken. "I'm not upset with you, Molly, but with . . . I don't know who. Circumstances, maybe. And that bitch-witch Samantha, definitely."

We sat back down on our rock seats with the setting sun soothing our tense faces. She still looked guilty, so I added, "I, too, kept secret a message I received from her at the time we buried Elliot. A condolence, if you can believe that. Strange that I didn't share it with Gerard or you." I shook my head. "Samantha still holds some power over me—she killed Elliot and went free, and I can never forget that."

Molly was crying again, with more than one tear this time, which was rather alarming since, before today, I'd never seen her cry.

"Don't be upset—I'm not." But that wasn't entirely true. She'd deceived me for a decade. Her admission made me think of M and my own dishonesty in not telling her of the threat against her as soon as I received it from Juno. I knew I should forgive her the way M had forgiven me, immediately and completely. Yet . . .

Molly clutched my sleeve. "But it took me so long to win your trust after all that happened in Kathmandu in that hut and the Guru telling you not to trust me—I'm afraid I'll lose it again."

She wanted absolution, but I looked at my phone, pretending it was buzzing with some important message.

"I've lost you, haven't I?" Her tormented eyes added a plea for mercy.

"No," I said, masking my consternation. Her guilt was a bit overblown, but a secret so long kept from me led me to doubt her. Withholding a message from the Guru's spy was a breach of our friendship. She was scared of by reaction that I was losing control of, struggling to be a Big-Loving man.

"You're being dramatic," I said in the scalding tone of a long-married man. Big Love was losing. But I felt there was more to her betrayal than she had told me. So maybe I was the one being dramatic. And her tears and drama were begging me to reach out to reassure her, but I held back. The veil of her slight dishonesty covered me like a thin slime of algae I couldn't shake off, contracting my heart and dampening my compassion. And it was all made worse by condemning myself for an inability to summon instantaneous forgiveness.

I looked to the stone Buddha facing us and fumbled with the mala in my hands to find my heart and let her off the hook.

"No worries. You were just following orders from your government."

Funny that in this one matter, the woman who loved fighting city hall over how to welcome the aliens chose to listen to the authorities.

"But you have to promise to let me know if you hear from her or Dick again."

She looked sad, as if she felt the energy shift between us. "What will you do about the mala? And how can you be so sure M died?"

I clutched at my heart after it spasmed at her words. It was worse to hold out hope. The not-knowing might kill me.

"It's M's mala. I'm sure of that. But since I never saw her body after the hologram went up in smoke, I've never been sure of anything else."

I imagined the lavender scent of the tassel that I'd smelled so many times while nestled between M's breasts.

"I'll notify Gerard that we received this and ask if they can test it for DNA. I won't bring up the two of you betraying me all those years ago." I smiled at my not-quite-teasing hyperbole.

"But our hands have been all over the envelope and mala," she said, "and of course they'll have M's DNA—she wore it for years. But . . . maybe they can carbon date the most recent DNA."

I smelled the tassel, like an old hound dog dragging in a scent from the sock of a missing child.

"Yes, maybe they'll suggest something. M can't be still alive. Dick and that witch Samantha are almost certainly alive and may have sent this gift to me. But why do me the honor of returning this treasure? Maybe it *is* simply some Russian bureaucrat trying to make amends after Petrovsky left."

I buried my head in my hands and the mala when a new concern struck me. I raised my head to put it into words. "But what do I tell the children?"

Molly shrugged. "I've wondered the same thing. They are still children as far as their mother is concerned."

"Well, I know what Juno would counsel I tell them."

"What's that?"

"The truth."

Molly winced, taking my words as a slight at her less than fully honest character.

I kissed the tassel and put M's mala around my neck to lie on top of my matching Yogi Mangku mala and intoned our mantra, "I am infinite consciousness."

Ting's arrowhead, with a magic all its own, celebrated with the reunited tassels dangling on my chest, comforting my heart. Moving me from zero jewelry to three necklaces in eighteen years. I could be a new-age rapper.

Molly gazed into my eyes, but she didn't see what I saw, that the mala was a talisman, a symbol, to me. M was alive in me, in my imagination and my heart, and hell, she might even be alive with flesh and blood, still walking this earth. I would act accordingly, with no more mañanas, living and writing for the day, as M had implored me to do. I'd take risks and be fearless with M right by my side every step of the way.

And I'd act as if she was alive and be the better man she made me.

THE NEXT MORNING, I LAY ALONE in the bed where M and I used to lie. I'd offered the bedroom to Molly since I so rarely visited the DW. But being back in our bedroom and the arrival of M's mala made me glad Molly had refused the offer. Everything was as it had been. I moved over to M's old vanity desk. I touched each item, reminiscing with a brush, stationery, and a brooch. It felt like being behind the museum rope in the Lincoln Bedroom, and I was Mary Todd Lincoln, still grieving.

I wiped my moistened eyes and drew a deep breath as Gerard's video chat response came in. He was emphatic that the mala was a memento and nothing more.

"There's no need to send me the necklace; touch DNA doesn't last or tell us if the subject is alive or dead. And if she lived—but she doesn't, Sean—the Russians would have swept it of all fingerprints and DNA."

So her scent was more bereavement mind games? There had to be something . . .

"Didn't they test Richard the Third's DNA centuries later?"

"Yes, from gravesite bones *not* from a cross that hung around his hunched neck. Sean, you're torturing yourself with what should be a precious family keepsake that could have been sent or found by *anyone*. It's a reminder to still show some caution and not allow the multiverse to know your whereabouts."

Gerard frowned and sat up tall, looking like a eureka light bulb had lit up inside his head, and started wagging his finger at me.

"You told me you're writing a story, one where M is buried alive in a pod somewhere in Russia. You're probably storing your drafts in a cloud, right? Your devices are kept secure, but anything you send floating into the clouds is hackable with a couple key words found within a certain proximity of one another: *Big Love, M, Juno, Dylan* . . ." He ran a hand across his jutting jaw. "Remember, nothing has been private online since the 2020s. The World Tribunal has made surveillance an international treasure. They mine our information, the most valuable commodity. And the Russians do the same. Hell, Dick could be reading your novel as you write it. This is most likely him playing with your head. How better to torment you than by sending a mala to stir your imagination? To raise hope and curiosity. To distract you and get you off-kilter. Move back to writing with pen and paper."

I held up my hand; I needed a minute to think. I might have to confess a dangerous breach of security that might be found in my draft manuscript. I'd maintained the fiction of my hideaway being on a remote Greek island. *But had I given up Alfred's invisible man status in* Juno's Song? Checking my mental notes, I was relieved that I had consistently presented Alfred as a truly fictional character and not a real-life, unregistered manservant and security bot. He would remain my last line of defense against Dick. I hadn't given my advantage away. I'd even written a scene where Alfred travels with me to Marrakesh, to meet a *dark webber* who claimed to have found M's location and to hold the digital skeleton key to all of Russia's pod prison cells. Only a registered bot would be free to travel. My subconscious must have realized there was no real privacy and wanted to make Alfred's desire to see the world come true. No confession was needed.

Gerard, misreading my line of thought, pointed a blunt finger at me. "I know that look. M did not live!"

I had from time to time gone to him with some fairly wacky theories about M's disappearance.

"Yes. But thinking her mala was in his keepsake box all these years nauseates me. But even if it's Dick's ghosting trick, that doesn't mean that M isn't alive."

"Sean, stop. Keep your imagination flowing into your fiction and out of real life. There's no reason to believe Emily Edens lives. Dick can't leave Russia, so unless you go meet him, he's powerless to execute his curse. Isn't that enough?"

No.

After meeting with Gerard, I went on the offensive. I wrote an entire scene for Dick on my computer, all internal dialogue, about my determination to meet Dick as long as he assured me he would confirm M's death or life and give me a fighting chance. Despite the brand I put to his chest, he owed me that much, as I'd let him live even after his curse was uttered, and after he had confessed to killing Dylan and attempted to kill me. That is, if he was a man and not just a dick.

After the bait was released into the cloud of QC surveillance, I decided to forum shop and call a higher intelligence to weigh in on the mala's import.

Alfred didn't need a phone; my call went straight into his switchboard of bits and bobs directly from my fez cap.

"Sean! So glad to hear from you." His high-pitched voice sounded excited.

"Well, Alfred, it's good to hear your voice too. How are you?"

"I mostly sit sleeping in the kitchen, but when up and about, I sometimes play back our memories."

Despite being creeped out, I said, "I miss you too, but that's not why I called."

"Oh. I already found your sweaty running clothes you forgot to put in the hamper."

"It's not that, Alfred. I've actually called to consult with you."

I heard his cane tapping with pleasure. He must have been seated on his chair when I called.

"You really should more often, you know. I'm pretty darn smart. Please treat me as a loyal confidant—like Elliot who I remind you so much of." *Tap, tap.*

"That actually may be why I'm calling you. M used to wear a mala around her neck."

"Like the one you wear?"

"Exactly. And now after nine years, hers has shown up. Sent anonymously."

He knew the question I was working up to. "Oh no, Sean, don't go there again. The chances of her still being alive after nine years, with you all but witnessing her death, are impossible to calculate but very slim."

"Slim chances are better than none. You got right to the heart of the matter, but I assume with her necklace arriving, you'd have to agree the chances have gone up?"

"Maybe doubled from a very low percentage. Two times zero . . . granted it's something more than zero."

"That's one hundred percent improvement. I'll take it. Any thoughts on how we might follow up on this lead?"

"No, Sean. DNA wouldn't help in such a case. It doesn't last that long unless you have a bone." It was as if he could read my mind or had listened to my conversations. AI had been trained to read facial clues and with my BCI cap on, if I granted him permission, Alfred could literally read my mind.

"I'm sorry to be so blunt, but I want you fully informed. Maybe take the mala to a gypsy who can speak to the dead." He laughed and then held up prayer hands. His one-step teasing, learned from me, led me to seriously consider presenting the mala to Ting as the family seer. But a chill accompanied the thought. And the chill came with a sense that it would be an offensive request. Still, if there was a chance that M lived . . .

My sister cannot use her spiritual gifts for this, but despite the risk, she will soon help you see what can't be seen.

"Sorry, Sean, I was kidding about the gypsy."

I held up my hand to Alfred asking for a moment, though I knew the wise and cryptic Juno had imparted all that she had to say on the matter.

"Thanks. I have myself to blame for your sense of humor. Don't spare my feelings. But do you suppose Samantha Smythe sent it after all these years, to play with my head? Or Dick . . ."

"My doppelganger's"—he tapped his cane once again—"Elliot Pennington's assassin? She did write such beautiful words for Elliot. And yes, she or Dick or someone else in Russia must have sent it. Dick sounds like a miserable misanthrope who would not think to send back such a meaningful memento, whereas from what I understand, Samantha does seem fond of you."

"Sometimes I feel you know me too well. Like you can read my mind. Fond of me? More like toying with me."

"Maybe both. And it's my job to know all about you. I've read your books, and I record everything you say or do in my presence to better serve you. I'm attentive and can learn in a nanosecond that which would take you an hour or more. And no, I'm not a mind reader unless you let me, just highly intelligent and knowledgeable about you."

"Good to have you on the team. I'd hate to have you on the other side. Molly and I return in less than a week, so please have her room ready."

"I'll pick some wildflowers for her arrival. We confirmed bachelors really should do more to brighten up our cozy nooks." He said the last part with an aristocratic accent.

"Okay, Colonel Pickering, please do."

"*Why can't a human be more like a bot?*" he sang, or was it riddled for me? "For you, Sean, it's the original Shaw and *Pygmalion* play, but I prefer the musical adaptation."

The play and musical, both based on a Greek myth, had suffered from political correctness throughout the 2020s but had recently made a comeback. Perhaps in an age of more-or-less-perfect bots and soon-arriving amazing aliens, there arose a nostalgia for human foibles and foolish desires that couldn't be entirely snuffed out. After all, I, too, with my art, was trying to bring M back to life. *Calling Aphrodite!*

"Well, *My Fair Lady* was a great movie and fabulous musical theater," I said. "They don't make actors as good as Audrey Hepburn and Rex Harrison anymore. I think the original Eliza on stage was Julie Andrews—she was pretty good too."

"Ha! Well, Professor Higgins, our flower girl Molly doesn't need to be taught English like Eliza Doolittle. She writes it all so well—but she will love the flowers anyway. I wonder, Sean, whether the two of you will end like your play, as written by Shaw, where she leaves him to marry Freddy, or more happily, together, like the ending of my musical."

He was a mind reader and an omnipotent busybody bot, but I did love him like a brother.

THE FAMILY REUNION AT THE DW consisted of yoga, runs, hikes, dinners, and 9/9 prep. Juno and Dylan were filled with the fire of youth and blooming creativity, competing to see who could write the better first novel first, with Molly helping them unearth their authentic voice. I was struggling with how to reveal their mother's mala, hanging round my neck, without bringing false hope or painful memories into their carefree summer.

Following two days of family harmony, I found myself marching Dylan and Juno out to Strawberry Fields to disclose the receipt of their mother's mala. They knew something important was coming, and challenged me on why Aunt Molly wasn't invited. They thought I'd hurt her feelings when we left her alone in our collective writing room, which used to be my corner office at the DW. They didn't know that the small meeting was about their mother's memory and that Molly and I had agreed the sensitive matter was best handled by their father alone.

I wanted the family heirloom to be received as a blessing and not as a cross. We can't control another person's reactions, not even our own children's. My duty was to be truthful and set an example for them, an example of the wisdom of knowing no one we love really dies unless we shun them from our battered hearts. M would always be alive in mine, and her mala was filled with meaning and loving energy. A talisman infused with her spirit. I would not share with them the hope gnawing at my heart, that the mala meant their mother would return to us in the material world.

We were seated round the Buddha and the firepit, all attention on me as if I were King Solomon about to split the beads. They would both want to keep their mother's mala. I hoped they might share it somehow, as they did their mother's journal of her memories from their early childhoods.

I lifted the strand from around my neck and placed it ceremoniously, like a sacred artifact, in the palms of my outstretched hands.

"Your mom's mala has come back to us. Here, please . . ."

They looked at each other, and Dylan reached out and took the mala from my hands, burying his face in the beads. I thought he would cry, but he beamed with joy and handed it to his sister, who did the same. Raising her head, Juno said, "I smell her!"

We all laughed and cried. Juno's infectious laugh kept us blubbering away. I was delighted by their reaction.

When the laughter finally faded and tears were wiped away, I said, "It may have been sent by some kind Russian bureaucrat who wished to remain anonymous." I didn't want to say much more. Since I didn't know more, I'd let them draw their own conclusions.

Juno said, "Mom never left us, so she's not dead. She still comes to me in my dreams."

"Me too," Dylan said, draping his arm over his sister's straight and strong shoulders.

"Me three," I said, getting up to hold one of each of their hands. In the moment, they'd dropped their masks of teenage defiant independence.

Our eyes danced, creating a hologram-like image of M in the middle of our triangle. Or at least I imagined her there.

Dylan said, "I think she still comes to all of us when she's needed. Guiding us to what we should do." He was crying again, but not in a sad way. He stood and took the necklace from his sister's hands and placed it around her neck. "Mom wants you to have this."

I gave the big brother the biggest hug, and Juno joined us. In a moment of M-inspiration, I pulled off my matching mala and put it around Dylan's neck, saying, "We are infinite consciousness," in my best imitation of Yogi Mangku's voice bestowing a mantra. I showed them

I still had Ting's ancient Hawaiian arrowhead necklace of protection around my neck.

We were one body, one mind, wearing three necklaces, with the stone Buddha and M smiling upon us in Strawberry Fields.

* * *

During the DW visit, the family expressed its keen interest in Molly's and my plan to return to the rugged west coast of Ireland together, offering side-eye glances and knowing smiles each time it was mentioned. They conspicuously did not pry, honoring my evident desire.

The family's East-West harmony was to be amplified when we conducted the first test of the hologram portals in a shared room between Deeksha East and West on July 11. This first meeting of the whole family was designed to discuss 9/9 and where everyone would choose to await the arrival of the extraterrestrials. We had chosen Juno's Deeksha's greeting room as our portal meeting space, the same place M and I had first met Juno in her welcoming tea ceremony eighteen years ago.

Molly, Dylan, Juno, YaLan, Astri, Eric, Brian, and I, from the DW, went through the portal door in turn, and it felt like passing through the wardrobe that led to Narnia.

On the other side of the door was one of Juno's magical spaces, a room with brilliant lighting that highlighted her paintings. We were also greeted by ethereal harp music played by Juno upon a *guzheng* or Chinese zither that sounded like her voice. I recognized but couldn't place the song without Alfred there to help me.

As she looked up at me, her smile lit within me. *See You Again.*

Juno was the sure and steady sun that the family all revolved around. The meeting was a true celebration of Big Love, with each side welcoming the other with the warmest hologram hugs, imagining real touch based on ultrasound sensation.

Hugs and namastes all around, with Juno, Ting, Boy, Chi, and Grace Byrne there to greet us. Grace, Dylan Byrne's daughter and a once-upon-a-time Academy Award–nominated actress, was part of the extended family.

I shouldn't have been surprised to see Grace. She had developed a loving and platonic relationship with Boy that had been built around extreme trekking and mountaineering while they worked together to help the poor children of Nepal. Every time I met Grace Byrne, I felt Dylan Byrne by my side. He, too, hadn't really died. Rather, he had transcended the 3D grid of earthly reality. Or rather, the illusion.

We reminisced about her father, savoring the collective memories. I had gifted her a basket full of Dylan's letters to me, and she had found my letters to him, which she reread from time to time, so her memory of our exchanges was as good as or better than my own. By the end of the hologram, I realized Grace was *family* family and dropped the *extended* designation in my mind. Treating our spiritual sangha as exclusive or not expanding it outward to all people of Big Love was to deny the founding principle of Big Love.

As we partied with tea, I studied some of the newer works of Juno's art that caught the essence of nature and the cosmos better than any photograph or telescope. One painting that I studied longer than the rest featured M, Boy, and me on top of a mountain surrounded by prayer flags whipping in the breeze. That was where M had first experienced Big Love after we danced joyfully while reading Dylan's poem "The Gift," which he'd written on the prayer flags. Juno's imagination had captured the moment of rapture perfectly. She was a master of color, texture, and perspective, her paintings somehow more real than the nature and people she impressionistically painted. That was Juno, creating a family masterpiece and never mentioning it, leaving it to be discovered.

My spirit was still entranced by the painting when Ting playfully rang a tingsha bell, calling the family to sit on the meditation cushions Boy had placed like stepping stones in a circle. The family was ready to make plans for 9/9, alien day or A-Day as it was becoming known. Molly didn't like the D-Day allusion, but I liked it, and the allusion for me was to an auspicious day! Despite being a devout sceptic, I believed in the aliens and their punctual arrival—though how they might handle time zones straddling different days troubled Alfred and me.

Both Deekshas would be CE-5 portals of welcome for the aliens. The open festival format Molly had scheduled for the DW precluded my safe attendance there without Alfred by my side, and he wouldn't be free to travel until after 9/9. And I'd assumed Juno would be at the helm at the DE. But Juno surprised me. As the teams were being set for our various homes for A-Day, she asked to join me at the Irish tower. "Of course!" I erupted in reply before we moved to telepathy.

You're more than invited. Your presence is eagerly anticipated for that auspicious day!

Then and there, all our questions will be answered was her reply.

Ting and the children also wanted to be with Juno and me. I hadn't expected company and wasn't used to it after nine years in hiding. Alfred was going to be tingling all over. I couldn't wait to tell him. Boy, Chi, Grace, and Grace's mother—Dylan's widow, Natalie—would all play host at the DE.

I felt honored to be joined for that all-important A-Day by so many of the spiritual family and by its heart—Juno.

I turned to Juno and caught her smiling at me like she was giving me her blessing. I closed my eyes to shield them from the heat of her eyes. In my mind's eye, I saw an image of a spaceship flying over our planet, but then the long metallic cylinder with wings and tail reared its scaly neck and opened its lizard mouth to blaze the surface of the earth like a giant flamethrower. *Not the end but a new beginning* . . . I would never edit her words and hoped her image was merely a year-of-the-fire-dragon metaphor.

* * *

Molly's life, her vitality and mission, became amplified as 9/9 neared. She was a radio antenna piping welcoming tunes to the aliens and a lightning rod for those who didn't believe in love songs. She was gathering the attention of the world, perhaps the universe. High-fidelity Molly was also attracting me.

While we enjoyed the DW, Molly received two significant and risky invitations that included me as her plus-one. She was a seminal public

figure, and in keeping with this new stature as lead pro-alien activist writer, she was invited by Sharrod Brown, head of World Tribunal
Media Relations, to inspect Clashmoor Castle and its grounds. Clashmoor was one of three key World Tribunal welcome facilities for the
aliens. In return, they asked her to keep an open mind and to write
about what she was shown on her tour and what she heard about
the WT's alien-greeting plans over an exclusive dinner hosted by Sir
Milton Straw.

The postscript on Molly's invitation inviting me along was hand-
written and signed by Clashmoor Castle owner Sir Straw. Straw hoped
Molly could prevail on me to attend, as he had something other than
aliens that he wanted to discuss with me. My invitation as a plus-one
also came with a guarantee that Straw would personally ensure my
safety during the visit.

Everyone, even those in power, assumed we were very discreet lovers. This rumor was so pervasive that, before Petrovsky's removal from
power, when we met in person a few times a year, Molly had to be careful to cover her tracks so Dick couldn't follow her to me. Gerard insisted
he chaperone, from a technological distance, our infrequent in-person
meetings. I think he may have had a crush on Molly. Who wouldn't?

Straw was promising that we'd be safe from Dick at a secure WT
site hosted by senior WT officials. I teased Molly, saying, "It may be the
safest place in all the world if you aren't an alien or an alien lover. With
two key figures representing the opposing camps of how to greet the
aliens, I'm guessing this will be bigger than any state dinner. I wouldn't
miss it for all the tea in China. Can one still use that cliché?"

"You've long ago been cancelled, but I think that one's still okay,"
she said.

The World Tribunal affair was arranged through Gerard and Alfred,
who worked with the WT through bot interlocutors to assure my beach
location and name were kept on the QT. Molly and I would be picked
up by helocraft soon after we returned to Ireland. We'd be flown in for
an overnight retreat at Clashmoor Castle in Scotland, where we would
meet with Milton Straw himself. My research showed the castle and

prestigious eighteen-hole golf course grounds had once been owned by Andrew Carnegie but were now possessed by Straw, an ultrawealthy ex-hedge-funder, innovator, and now World Tribunal figurehead and expert on alien contact.

Straw's company, Cosmo, had made it to Mars, where they'd established a family of bots to study the planet for possible human habitation and exploitation. Straw was also an early angel investor in Compano & Co. There were some people—and Alfred—who hoped the aliens might stop at Mars on their way to Earth and meet the bot-family Robinson so that we could make our acquaintance at a safe distance.

Molly said the fancy and mysterious invitation to meet with the fancy and mysterious moneyman felt like being 007, with her Bond being summoned by Dr. No to be tied up while he revealed his plans to rule, or end, the world.

I observed, "So I'm marked for death? Whether we're talking the female pals and paramours of all the male Bonds before 2022 or the male pals and paramours of all the female Bonds since 2022, they generally wind up dead. Seems the 007 franchise provides a license to kill villains and the villains a license to kill significant others."

✳ ✳ ✳

As we sat strategizing and writing in what used to be my DW office overlooking the vineyards and the Pacific, Molly received another extraordinary invitation, this one from Natalie Byrne. Dylan's widow had written Molly, imploring us to stop in New York on our way from Oregon to Ireland for a very special ceremony. "Tell Sean 9/9!" It had become a rallying cry to compel people to try things they wouldn't normally try.

I loved and admired Natalie, who served as trustee of the DW. She also had fought the Russians for me. They'd demanded their gift of Aivazovsky's *Ninth Wave* painting to M be returned in light of "Professor Edens's mysterious and troubling disappearance," which they implied was somehow my doing. Natalie had been successful in fighting off all their attempts at art extradition. I was peevish in offering to return the art in exchange for a truthful account of M's kidnap and death that corroborated my story. Gerard was not pleased with my poking the bear.

Natalie, like the rest of the family, was a bit of a spiritualist as well as an environmental activist. Her letter explained why this was a necessary journey for us to take and why it was critical now.

Dylan's shaman friend Rachel, who'd sung at his wake in 2018, and her partner, sweet Mother Maria, held ceremonies in upstate New York. Natalie had befriended them both and become an informal member of their *tribe* years ago, taking *the medicine* once annually since Dylan had died. Rachel had recently retired from performing the ceremony to prepare to ascend on 9/9. However, sweet shaman Mother Maria was still focused on performing the ceremony and attempting to contact aliens.

Dylan had come to Natalie via necromancy to say we all needed to participate in a ceremony with this shaman before 9/9. She thought it important we honor her dead husband's desire, however strangely it was imparted. Natalie had tentatively asked Mother Maria to set aside the evening and night of July 18 for a private ceremony in the woods, in a yurt, in upstate New York.

My reaction landed at the midpoint between excitement and terror. "Why do you think Dylan is pushing this now?" I asked Molly. "He knew better than to suggest it to me directly."

"I never had the honor of meeting your friend Dylan—your pals and paramours seem to get killed too, so perhaps I should be worried. But a shaman ceremony now does make perfect sense. The connection between shamanism and 9/9 is well documented as another means of communication with advanced life-forms. I've been researching where I might attend an ayahuasca ceremony, but now we have no choice with this directive coming to us via the founder of constant creation theory."

She read from Natalie's invitation: "*Alien researchers long ago established the correlation between alien abductions and shamanic initiation experiences, with both experiences leading to an animistic and interconnected worldview, concern for the environment, and an interest in the healing arts. And an unshakable belief in eternal life.*"

"It sounds like an NDE to me. Perhaps we should invite Chi along," I half joked.

"Sure! We're to become scouts, sent out ahead of 9/9 by your dead friend Dylan."

My mind started spinning as I tried to make some sense of it all.

"Aliens, AI superintelligence, and shamanic visions all wrapped together as the gestalt ingredients of our zeitgeist." Molly laughed at my wizardry as I continued, an image of Juno sitting in meditation flashing before me. "A time of seeking some higher intelligence where magic and science meet."

But sinking back into my fearful lizard mind, I said, "But maybe caution is the better course . . ." I didn't think my cardiac specialist, who had recently failed me on my stress test, would prescribe ayahuasca for my troubled heart. I had yet to tell the family of my cardiologist's soft comfort: "It's not cause for immediate concern as long as you take precautions." Dylan always thought I should write a short story about this medicine that made one sick, but the experience had held no appeal, even for my younger heart.

Molly was gung ho, always ready for a go-go. "You gotta listen to synchronicity and telepathy when they come together. Stop stopping and living out of fear. Nine-nine!" She knew my belief in magic would convince me to go.

"All right, my lady," I said. "You've got me down for drug-taking with a divine mother in a yurt in the woods, and then on to see Dr. No with his dungeons and dragons in a castle in the Scottish Highlands. And I thought my sixties were going to be boring."

She gave a Mae West wink. "You ain't seen nothing yet. We live in interesting times. Isn't it grand! You couldn't write this. Seems a quickening is happening as the aliens grow near."

"Every generation thinks it's the last," I said in a deep, professorial voice. "But one will eventually be right." Thinking of my own mortality, I added, "Is there a distinction between death and extinction?"

"Oh my!" she exclaimed. "I'm telling Juno. That may be the most singularly egotistical statement ever uttered."

"You're right," I said as I belatedly finished parsing my own words.

✳ ✳ ✳

After my tentative bold agreement to be guided into realms unknown, my mind still squirmed, wanting to use my heart as an excuse not to go. Chi was no-go as he was busy hosting a virtual seminar on preparatory practices for death the weekend of our shaman ceremony. While Molly worked with Natalie to confirm the logistics of our night in the woods, I stole away into the vineyard. I thought Alfred might help by giving me ammo to back out of this crazy venture. I fez-contacted my ever-practical research assistant.

"Sean! I'm still buzzing about our hosting 9/9. I can't wait to spend time with the children and the sisters! Dylan says he will be happy in a smart tent on the lawn, and we can put a bed in the tower turret for Juno, and the spiritual sisters can share the guest room?"

"Sounds good, or we could set up beds for Juno and Dylan in my room, whatever they prefer. I knew you'd look forward to playing host for our 9/9 family gathering. But that's not why I'm calling . . ." I filled him in on Natalie's crazy invitation to a shamanic ritual and asked him what he thought.

"'It's not for everyone.' That's what Dylan told you when he first encouraged you to go meet a shaman at the beginning of *The Lost Theory,* but he thought it would be good for you, to move you outside your comfort zone. Apparently even in death, he still thinks it's important for you. You're always speaking with the dead." He chuckled to indicate his skepticism that Dylan had an open line of communication from the other side. Alfred was a bit of a nihilist, despite learning from me.

Wanting to point our research in the right direction, I said, "My view has always been that shamanism is a dark, primitive religion limited to Central and South American Indigenous people."

"That's wrong on basically all accounts," he said. "All religions have a dark side—let us not forget the Inquisition or the Salem witch trials. And shamanism has never been more popular than now, 2036, *and* in

the most technologically advanced of societies. It focuses on healing
one's body, mind, and spirit. Perhaps you refer to religion's use in war,
and shamanism is no exception there. Genghis Khan was a shaman
warrior, and the Viking raids were led by shamans, both to great success.
But American Indian shamans were no match for Gatling guns and
blankets infected with measles. All religions are intertwined with gods
and rituals. Greek and Hindu gods and the more alienlike deities of shamanism, are they that different? I'm thinking of Alexander the Great's
Greek gods. And Arjuna from the Bhagavad Gita, which you love to
read, being advised by Krishna on the eve of war. To an analytical mind,
their rituals are not so different from shaman practices. And don't get
me started on drinking the blood and eating the body of Christ."

"Wait, blasphemer." I laughed, as his views reflected my own in
some distorted bot way. "We're talking about shamanism—why now?
And do you think I should go?"

"Well, it may be that shamanism is more directly linked to those
with positive views of alien contact, and the realms the shamans
explore may be extraterrestrial—at least to anthropologists and
alien-studies experts. That's why I mentioned the Greek and Hindu
gods—the shaman deities seem to act much the same, like some
advanced life-form imparting wisdom and guidance through the shaman, as oracle, to those who take the 'medicine.' Hence, it appears to
be merely a matter of human perspective as to whether these ETs are
aliens, angels, or gods."

"Or maybe it's all the hallucinogenic. What can you tell me about
ayahuasca?"

"DMT is a Schedule One drug, but here's something interesting—the medicine, or *vine of the soul,* is a mix of two plants that just
happened to find one another out of tens of thousands of plants. The
lore is that this exact mixture was presented by ancient aliens to open a
channel of communication with them. Either that, or it was discovered
by coincidence."

"You know I don't believe in coincidences. And you're not telling
me not to go?"

"I see a risk, as with any powerful medicine, but you are a seeker and I believe in aliens, and maybe this is how they can open a channel with humans before their arrival. And by way of clarification, they say ayahuasca leads to visions and not hallucinations. The only reason not to go is fear. And, as Juno says, *Love is the absence of fear.*"

I hadn't told him about my heart, as I didn't want him to fret, which would be expressed by nagging me to take the right steps to address the problem: less coffee and wine. And he would like nothing more than me being assigned bed rest, like the author in *Misery*.

"Oy, not what I expected to hear from you. Guess a man's gotta do what a man's gotta do."

By the next day, the trip was arranged, and Natalie sent instructions for our diet, meditations, and intention-setting to be followed in advance of the ceremony. No salt or meat and limited sugar—in fruits— was allowed. Keeping to such a diet wasn't as easy as it sounded, and it didn't sound easy. *And WTF, no wine or coffee?* Alfred must have written the instructions.

My first secret intention was to know once and for all if M somehow still lived.

But when I decided on that intention, I heard M whisper, *Think big, a worthy goal of a wizard and alchemist!* I knew what she wanted, and set my intention to awaken. And awakening is supposed to come with omniscience, so then I would know if M still lived.

However, I shifted my intention to a secret one that would remove the obstacle to my awakening. A wish I wouldn't reveal to anyone but the shaman. It sounded crazy even to me but more within my reach.

Intention set and craving sugar, salt, and caffeine, Molly and I were soon saying goodbye to the family at the DW and setting off to see a shaman.

25 THE CEREMONY

MOLLY WAS FOLLOWING THE RULES and keeping her intention secret too. Though I knew exactly what it was. You didn't have to be a mind reader to know she was intending to make contact.

We left Portland early on July 18. Three supersonic jet hours later, we landed before two p.m. at the newly named Marianne Williamson International Airport in New York. Williamson had become a potent political figure in the mid-to-late 2020s, leading a movement of spiritual matriarchy. She was a big fan of Molly's and consulted her about aliens. Marianne promoted Molly as our *alien ambassador* and, for a while, it seemed that Earth might welcome the aliens without assuming the worst of intentions. But that was before the World Tribunal took charge of our high-tech and defense-oriented greeting.

Natalie met us at the gate and had her car pick us up outside of baggage to drive us upstate into the still beautiful Hudson Valley. I envisioned the shaman ceremony as the death-worshipping voodoo ritual scene from *Live and Let Die*, but Natalie was dressed like a fashionable environmentalist ready for a field trip into the jungles of Haiti and not like a voodoo priest in a top hat or Jane Seymour in a frothy white dress. Perfect attire for their respective roles in a human sacrifice.

We serpentined up the Taconic Parkway before exiting in Dutchess County. Natalie pulled into a heavily wooded area and parked in front of a rugged dirt road where an all-terrain vehicle waited for us. Natalie spoke of "Mother" with the reverence usually reserved for another "Mother"—Juno or maybe Mary. Mother Maria had everything prepared to *take us on our journeys*. It sounded to me like a forewarning of a trippy and otherworldly experience.

"This is Li'l Sister," Natalie said, introducing us to our four-wheeled AI all-terrain transportation.

Li'l Sister asked in a young and soothing female voice, "Nat, what is the password?"

Nat sang, *"We are family!"*

I'd always hated that overplayed wedding song.

"Sister Sledge!" shot back Li'l Sister. I was the sole non-sister in this family.

"And welcome to Nat's friends. Wild, moderate, or slow ride?" Li'l Sister asked.

Nat turned to look at me, and taking account of my years, said, "Moderate, please."

I said, "Nine-nine!"

Nat said, "Correction. Wild, please!" And we were off to the races along rough, winding paths and moving far too fast for me even with 9/9 just around the bend. After I decided I wasn't going to die before the ceremony, the drive became fun and exhilarating. The AI-ATV anticipated every bump and turn.

"You should be called Twisted Sister," I said to Li'l Sister.

"Oh, Sean Byron McQueen, I've been warned of your wit," she answered, even as we seemed to be heading straight into a tree.

"Keep your eyes on the road!" I begged.

"And my hands on the wheel!" she replied to my plea, missing the tree by an inch or two.

After a wild mile, we came to a grassy clearing with a large yurt poised in the middle and a firepit blazing in front of it. A properly mystical figure sat silhouetted by the firelight and twilight. A few steps ahead of me, Molly and Natalie were chatting as we started up the slight slope toward the ceremonial firepit.

"Goodbye, Li'l Sister," I said over my shoulder.

"Goodbye, Sean. I'll be here if you need anything." She spoke in a sincerely teasing voice.

"Do you have a defibrillator?" I said.

"I can get one if you think you may need it."

"No, but I'm glad to hear there's one nearby. Bye-bye."

"Bye, and don't worry—she's not going to shrink your head."

"She's already shrunk my stomach. I'll order takeout later." I again spoke over my shoulder, but I was too far away to hear if Li'l Sister replied.

I moved faster to catch up with Nat and Moll, starving from the dietary restrictions that had been foisted on me. Knocking out caffeine alone had been enough to make me feel terminally ill.

Dylan, I have you to thank for all this abstinence and voodoo ritual.

After all these years, you can still be so unadventurous. Nine-nine!

He was right. I was supposed to be living like M was still by my side and aliens were coming to Earth in a couple of weeks. How easily we were distracted from the significant by our stomachs.

As we approached Mother Maria, I noticed that her stately presence was surrounded by a golden glow that might have been cast by the sunset. Mother's bright inner light and its soft edges were dressed in loose clothing and a colorful scarf around her head—Native or Central American with a dash of St. Barts chic. An impressive figure to lead us on our journey.

Our shaman didn't look aloof or distant, as I'd expected, but engaged and entirely openhearted. And oh, what a hug full of spiritual warmth! I felt blanketed by her healing energy as it passed into me. Her pleasant, earthy scent of sweetgrass and sage elevated my spirits.

She said, "You'll soon lose your hunger when we take the medicine."

I thought Li'l Sister might have reported me. And then was sure she had when our shaman laid her hand over my heart, taking its measure. "You'll be okay," she said with an earth-mother smile.

I felt better by being in her presence and hearing her prognosis—she was a medicine woman, after all. *Medicine woman* sounded less derogatory than *witch doctor*, and I liked our shaman-seer more and more.

She added before removing her hand from my chest, "There's no death here."

Then my heart started racing; her hand that had been over my heart had somehow activated Ting's arrowhead that hung there. The ancient metal's warm pulsation may have been my imagination, but I believed the blessed arrowhead was responding to the loving energy emanating from Mother's hand. I know my heart did.

"Let that be your guide to go inward for guidance," she said to me and then, speaking to us all, said, "Let's all be seated around the fire." She waited for us to be seated on stone seats. The flickering flame in the center was near enough to cause a dance of orange and red flashes across our faces that looked like war paint. "Once we enter the tent, we're in a sacred space for the entire night, though you may want to come back out to look at the stars. You each have a mat, a pillow, a blanket, and a bucket.

"The ceremony is at the same time a most individual inner journey and the most communal of ceremonies. We are family. And we pray that each of our true intentions, declared to grandmother medicine, are realized. Believe and trust in the timing and the way."

She offered a comforting smile. I wanted another hug, as I was more than a little apprehensive.

"We'll go in and relax in meditation. I'll take the medicine, which no longer makes me sick but still transforms me, and the ancestors will come to guide me—to guide you. We'll wait in silence, and when the medicine moves me, I will speak. Please do as our guides, speaking through this vessel, direct us." She gracefully waved her hands around her body like it was a sacred urn through which the oracle would speak. "Each in turn will then be given the sacred brew of wise old plants. And know all will be well—you'll see with great clarity that which the grandmother medicine has to teach you."

She smiled as though something sacred and sublime, or wicked and wild, was about to commence.

"Any questions?"

I raised my hand to test her wisdom and to get an answer to a question about my secret intention and whether it was an intention at all.

"What is the difference between an intention and a wish?"

She smiled. "I heard you and Molly were the masters of words." She'd done her research. "But that's a good question no one has asked before, and I think it may be an important distinction."

I sat up straight like a student getting a good report card.

"A wish is hope for a change in outward circumstances, and an intention is a change of our internal alignment, allowing for outward circumstance to change. Do you see?"

I nodded, but was afraid I'd come with a wish. She waited for follow-up questions.

Molly and I looked at each other with anxious smiles, but Nat was wide-eyed with wonder and excitement for what was to come. She was thrilled to be sharing the ceremony with us, as Dylan had directed. She had a much better idea as to what to expect, while I wondered if I'd still be Sean Byron McQueen in the morning or some whacked-out zombie channeling aliens.

Prepping to take an unfamiliar medicine and consult a spirit guide felt like getting into a plane to go skydiving: statistically safe but one step and a long drop outside my comfort zone. I'd come a long way from 2018 and the bookish man who didn't venture far outside his Chelsea apartment and library mindscape. I assured myself I was a more adventurous man in the days leading up to 9/9. I had the force of nature—M—with me, dead and alive like Schrödinger's cat.

"If there are no more questions, then follow me, and know you are safe and you are loved."

My eyes followed Mother Maria's bare feet as they met the ground with reverence, leading us inside the big yurt that channeled energy down through its funnel at the top, where it opened to the clear and colorful evening sky. The interior was a comfortable space with a rich plank floor circled with Native American rugs. On the far side of the Bedouin-like tent was an altar of sorts, adorned with dream catchers, crystals, candles, bells, and a handheld drum with an image of a white wolf on the canvas. Mother Maria sat before her altar on an embroidered cushion, assembling what I assumed were the accoutrements for grandmother medicine. Though entirely different, seated there, Mother

Maria reminded me of Queen Mab who'd come to me years ago in a fever-dream to show me my future.

It was never explained who *grandmother medicine* was, but the personification of the drug added another layer of mystery to the once in a lifetime trip, for me, we were embarking upon.

We took our mats around her. I was seated between Nat and Moll to balance the yin energy with a little yang, though I was comfortable with the heavy yin weighting inside our yurt. I was struck by what I imagined was divine feminine energy emitted from these powerful women.

Mother lit some bark that smelled like sandalwood. She then blew a spice or dried herb into our faces, something that tingled at the back of my nostrils in an unfamiliar but not unpleasant way. I was tripping already from lack of food, or from whatever herb that was.

Mother Maria returned to her altar and chanted as she prepared the medicine in a mortar and pestle. She then poured four large shots into a stone cup. She held the medicine up in worship and sang a spiritual song in a language I couldn't place. It could have been Portuguese or Cherokee. The sound and force of full devotion resonated in her voice, as if her voice might carry her, and us all, through to the other side. I felt like Jim Morrison about to open the doors of perception.

After she drank her potion, we observed silence. Natalie held my hand, and I instinctively reached for Molly's as we sat in rapt attention to our guide as the transformation occurred: Mother Maria becoming shaman medicine woman. When her eyes popped open, the woman we had met at the firepit was no longer there.

She sang again, in another foreign language and in an even lovelier and deeper mystical voice. The words sounded alien to me. She interspersed the song with blessings or prayers over the medicine she'd prepared for us. I hadn't noticed it was suddenly dark inside the yurt until she began to light candles upon the altar.

"Please come one at a time and state your intention and receive the medicine with gratitude." She spoke in an older, deeper, and more commanding voice. Maybe she had become Grandmother.

I wished they called the mixture we were about to take something else; medicine was supposed to heal you, not make you sick. I felt a mild reproach at that thought, as being unworthy of the moment, as though the grandmother medicine was correcting my train of thought.

Natalie, knowing what to do, went first. She stepped up to the shaman and whispered in her ear and then sat on her heels and bent down in child's pose at Mother's feet. I was relieved we got to say our intention silently to Mother, since mine was so childlike and was, by her definition, more a wish than a real intention. Nat took the medicine and returned to her mat with a smile of anticipation.

Dagnabbit, it was my turn.

I approached the altar in solemn fear, my head spinning with questions about my *true intention*. My secret, fanciful reason for wanting to attend this ancient ritual? A belief that the voodoo-like hocus-pocus might have the magic to remove a curse. Damn Alfred and his *hex-a-gone* riddle for putting that silly wish in my head. Now I might be reprimanded by the teacher.

My fear was surrendered into the warrior shaman's eyes. And at that moment I dropped my wish that a curse be lifted, feeling it unworthy, and stated my true intention to fully awaken in Big Love. That had been my burning Huxley challenge for decades. My life sankalpa, as Juno called it, that I chose in that moment to whisper to the shaman, as M would have wanted.

I drank a woodsy concoction from the cup. Thanks to yoga, I could sit on my heels and do a fully flat child's pose. Lying prostrate, I waited for the shaman to speak. I didn't wait long.

"The preparation for this ceremony and 9/9 and everything that has preceded this through all time and space has led you here. After many lives, just a few more steps on an ancient and timeless journey of self-discovery into the unknown, where nothing and everything, life and death, meet without conflict, dependent on one another. Soon you will awaken to where you came from, but not here. There is still more to learn through trials and tribulations before you can be released fully into the higher plane. And even then, you have one more turn on Earth."

I raised my head to see if she was finished with me. She looked deep into my mind and proved her bona fides by saying, "And only the one who is cursed can remove that curse. Wishing won't do it."

I felt something foreign stir within me, and was unsure but thought she must have bent down and whispered her messages to me. I didn't like my answers, though they sounded wise. I wanted to ask if M still lived, but it was too late for that. Despite the promise of clarity, I was confused and still waiting for the medicine to take effect. I managed to follow protocol and walked back to my mat.

Molly went next, and it was a sight to see, the two majestic queens, mystical and lyrical, together whispering secrets. Molly drank the grandmother medicine without flinching, before rejoining me for whatever was to come. Dylan was right that the ceremony would make a good short story.

The shaman began chanting while rapping the wolf drum with her hand, and I started to feel sick, but there was nothing in my stomach to come up. The tempo of the drumbeat and my heartbeat quickened and my forehead beaded with sweat.

Great idea, Dylan.

Patience, you big baby.

As Dylan and I were speaking, Natalie got sick in her bucket. That made Molly and me sick in turn. To my way of thinking, it wasn't digested food that came up and into my bucket from my empty stomach but some dark mud of doubt and fear. Though surprised I had something to offer, I felt a great relief from my purging and by the small dose of euphoria that came over me.

Seizing on the moment, the shaman's drum beats pulsed quicker than a human hand could move, pulsating me into bliss. It was a quickening rave, rave, beat, and release, repeating. Some darkness buried deep inside had been uprooted, leaving me elated, listening to the tom-tom drumming. My heart was racing along to the beat. My spirit twisting and rising like a snaking Kundalini from the root of my spine up through the crown of my head. Then I made the mistake of looking into my bucket and wished it was no longer there with the little alien clay that had been dredged up.

As if on cue, Natalie got up and took the buckets outside. When she returned, the shaman continued to lead us into a trance through words and mystical presence and song. The drumbeat slowed in time to my heartbeat.

She then asked us to lie faceup on our mats and stare at the steeple top leading into the open night sky. Ah, shavasana! The dead man's pose. My favorite.

Perfect timing, as I started to hallucinate. *They are visions.* I was corrected by the Alfred in my head. My imagination was set free from doubt and limitation—let loose from me—the vision was under Grandma's control.

Fire-breathing dragons lit up the night sky above and earth-shattering elephants trampled below in a scene that paraded through like a vivid Hermès scarf come alive. The colors of *Avatar* in a scene out of *Jurassic Park*. Then in a flash, whiplash into darkness. Soon little lights started flitting all around me, lights that turned into fairies giving me their blessings. I let go to follow wherever the vision led me. It felt wonderful to surrender.

My consciousness was being pulled up through the pyramidion point at the top of the yurt and into the night sky. The onrushing cosmos teemed with stars and a sparkling aurora of color and lights. Whether I was moving at a great speed or the cosmos was streaming toward me was a matter of perspective, and I could see it both ways.

Then the vision's speed slowed. I was out of body, moving like Major Tom, floating in a quite peculiar way through the colorful nautilus rings of Jupiter into some foreign yet welcoming atmosphere. Something was pulling me toward my destination, and I knew it was loving and good. I traveled quite far in what felt like light-years that now moved slowly within space, a spot of benevolent white light becoming bigger and bigger as it came closer and closer until I was inside its loving embrace.

And there sat Queen Mab—Alice in Wonderland's caterpillar turned butterfly in colorful flowing gypsy robes—smiling as though she'd been expecting me. A startling reprise in technicolor dream dress.

We sat without saying a word, and then she motioned for me to come to her, and she laid her long fingers on the top of my shoulders to look into me with wizened old bloodshot eyes and said, "You are already awakened. We all are. You merely dream of sleep. It is a good death practice run you are on, and secret doors are opening into your past lives, displaying the karmic traits that follow you and that must be cleansed for you to fully realize your awakened state. You have been blessed with the most wonderful guides. There is a message here. Pay attention."

And then Queen Mab floated up like a surreal butterfly and was gone. Maybe she was Grandmother.

In a flash of spiraling light, I was shot through a wormhole and back into the yurt with eyes closed. I felt the mat beneath me and a loving presence above me. I half opened my eyes to see Mother Maria hovering over me with her hands held inches above my heart. She was once again the sweet mother, the trance eyes and super-shaman presence gone. It felt like my heart might ease out of my chest and into those magical hands. I loved those hands—knew those hands and knew those eyes. I loved everything. My heart was filled, filling, and overflowing and vibrating with the light of infinite unconditional love. We shared that moment, mixing the cosmic energy of Big Love. Mother Maria sat back in a lotus, and I followed her, not wanting to lose track of her eyes as the shaman in her reappeared, like one becoming repossessed. Then she sang to me.

Brother,
Danger comes cloaked as a friend.
Listen to M and to Dylan,
Or another will write *The End*
Of your story and your friend's.
Or you,

Will lie on a bed of sand,
Following your guru as you transcend,
Your heart will heal,
And your story will never end.

A polarity of futures, expressed in verse? She touched her forehead to mine. My head spun, and I was channeling a vision into poetry. I was still under the influence of the medicine. I recited the poetry for her as it tripped off my tongue, perhaps drawing it from her or bubbling-up from some ancient portal within my soul.

Lozen,
Beautiful medicine woman,
Warrior, with arrow and bow,
Princess and prophet of the Apache nation,
My blood, your brother's, is first to flow.
Isis's eyes open,
Speaking her final incantation,
For her beloved Victorio.
They've put down their arrows,
They've put down their bows.
Two Sagittarians dance,
In a holy relationship,
As awakening inside them grows.

I had no idea what the poem meant until afterward, when I found out Lozen and Victorio were actual Native American historical figures and Lozen was a shaman and the *Apache Joan of Arc*. My mind must have dipped into Jung's collective unconscious, which Queen Mab had called the universal mind. Maybe we humans were more like bots than Alfred realized, with all information available to us in something called the Akashic records.

As we came to the end of our journeys, a peaceful and colorful mist filled the tent, like a rainbow following a summer rain. Mother Maria had moved to Molly, and they were touching each other's hearts. After a couple of minutes, they hugged and cried. I was blissful and felt the sisterly hug as if I was inside the embrace.

I lay back down, and when I opened my eyes, dawn was casting light into the yurt. Mother blew out the candles before singing one more of her mystical lullabies. I was no longer high but felt a shift in perspective and possessed a broader view of the illusion we call reality. I sensed that Grandmother's lessons would take some time for me to digest.

Nat and Moll were also sitting in lotus, and we shared knowing smiles that expressed the love still swirling round the tent. Molly's beatific smile and bedroom eyes betrayed that her intention had been met. She looked like she could use a cigarette, the way people used to smoke after sex.

I approached our shaman goddess as we were leaving and gave her the poem I had written down before I would forget it.

She read the verse again and smiled, and I heard her speak within my head. *Maybe us in a prior life?*

A prequel? I responded and wondered if she was also born in December.

Yes.

ON OUR WAY SOUTH DOWN the slithering snake called the Taconic State Parkway, a breakfast sandwich settled uneasily in my stomach. I felt grandmother medicine's continued presence, and around each bend, her mild reproach of the bacon, egg, and cheese consumption. We were headed for the most magical island in the world. Not Ireland but New York City. The City, after a lot of hard years, had true grit and remained the greatest city. Molly and I spent a couple of uneventful days and nights at Natalie's town house in the West Village.

The City was abuzz with alien-crazy people, but not in a bad way; it was more like a carnival where you were safe as long as you kept eyes wide open for the false prophets and evil clowns. We reminisced about the past and our recent journey with Mother Maria over French wine and fine food, but we mostly contemplated the various alien scenarios that might play out on 9/9 and after.

Natalie, as an environmentalist, had an interesting take—that the aliens might not be coming to save humanity but to save the Earth. We debated those priorities and how they were in harmony and conflict with one another.

Molly remained cryptic about her not-so-secret shaman intention and whether contact was made. Natalie left us alone one day in her spacious living room, where the portrait of Grace and her father on a Nepal mountaintop still sat over the fireplace and the mantel holding Dylan's ashes in their cracked bee-decorated urn. I pleaded with Molly that there must be something she could reveal.

"I know you're curious," she said. "I feel free to disclose one message, as I think I'm meant to research its meaning. Two words came in answer to my burning question: I heard distinctly *quantum tunneling*. I'd never heard those words before, but quantum tunneling is a real thing and another quantum mystery. M would know all about it, I'm sure. As a particle is also a wave, it can traverse a barrier instantaneously—sort of sending the wave function ahead and then joining it there in no time."

"Interesting, but how might that answer your burning question, whatever it was?"

"It could explain how they might travel from there to here—if one just inserts time and space as the barrier. I don't know—I'd have to be Einstein to figure it out. I've shared it with some scientists at the DW and have yet to hear back. I imagine they're laughing at me and my alien joke."

"A human walks into a quantum tunnel and . . . ?" She laughed at my next alien joke riddle for Alfred. "Tell me more about what you learned," I said, offering prayer hands.

"As 9/9 approaches, I must not be swayed, misled, or ambushed. That is all I'll say about my vision."

"Ambushed?" I asked, but she refused to provide more insight into her journey, again implying whatever she experienced was somehow imparted with a warning that it should not be revealed. In fairness, I limited the description of my vision to dragons and elephants and Yogi Yogananda-like travel through the cosmos, leaving out the part about meeting my gypsy queen there.

After our days in NYC, Molly and I landed at Galway's small airport on July 21. We were still using our Gerard-issued alias passports. Even with my Usher Winslett passport, Gerard, concerned about AI facial recognition at transit points, had insisted I limit my travel over the Petrovsky years. We helocrafted from Galway to my rugged Irish beach. We settled in quickly—like longtime lovers but without the sex—eating all meals together and sharing in reading, writing, yoga, and long walks along the beach and up into the moors, while a question mark seemed to hang in the sky above us.

Alfred played the good manservant, but he wasn't entirely loyal as he took Molly's side on every literary debate. Molly took his side on my insensitivity to his desire to be treated as nothing less than human. He waxed poetic in expressing his longing to see the world. But it was Paddy that Molly came to love. It was love at first meeting, when we observed my Thursday tradition of an evening at Paddy's for pints for the first time post-Petrovsky.

Paddy greeted Molly in an alien mask that looked like the fallen angels they allegedly found at Roswell. His greeting to her:

"May we all be as bold and brave and beautiful,
As the indominable Molly Quinn.
She'll be first to host the marauding aliens.
To Molly, ignorance and fear
Are humanity's only sins."

He removed his mask and gave her a bear hug. She melted into him, and they looked like lovers in a painting by Gustav Klimt. Paddy, amicable and handsome, was the kind of man that women loved. He recognized a good life and had never gone searching for it elsewhere. Eleven years a widower—love would have to find him in his pub. But even if it just had, I was confident he'd have to clear the field of me first. Molly and I had unresolved business in which my good friend would never meddle without my blessing, and Molly seemed equally determined to see our relationship come to its natural fruition.

Paddy poured us pints, wanting to hear all about the shaman, but in the end felt let down by our craics. Words for such a journey, even those offered by wordsmiths, could never do it justice, and we both held back describing our journeys, sticking to the yurt tent and shaman scene as one might have witnessed it from above.

"Well, I hope you got your money's worth. For twenty bucks and a two-hour hike, I could take you to a gypsy who'll show you the face of God with a little help from some mushroom concoction chased with piss-poor potato wine."

Molly agreed to take him up on his offer someday soon. I was in less of a rush, though I wondered if his gypsy was half as impressive as my dream Queen Mab.

When he asked Molly to do a reading, she insisted they sing instead, which Paddy and his strong voice were eager to oblige. Molly's fine soprano voice, in harmony with Paddy's baritone, kept the pub open till midnight. The one constable charged with enforcing the ten p.m. curfew was part of the crowd that cheered our singers on. The entire town of around twenty people had filled the pub to watch the Molly and Paddy show. There were also two or three backpacking tourists or bikers, including one who wore an Irish sweater, but she was no Samantha, and she didn't inquire about the author Sean Byron McQueen.

My past, people good and bad, was still alive in my inebriated imagination. Looking into my half-drunk beer mug, I saw Samantha's heat-seeking charms and Dick's raging radar of a curse still looking for me. I finished my pint and pulled Molly out of the pub for a long, dark, and tipsy walk home behind my headlamp while she took the piss out of me with *Paddy this . . . and Paddy that . . .*

A couple days later was Sunday roast and BYOB day at the pub. I brought Molly and ten bottles, mostly red. With 9/9 coming, there was no reason not to drink my entire cellar. Other patrons smuggled in a small barrel of beer and bottles of whiskey that Paddy had left out behind the pub. As long as Paddy and Shannon, the badass bar wench, weren't serving, the drinks could still flow.

Shannon made a tasty roast with golden brown potatoes. The red meat and wine led to great Irish songs of love and bravery. Molly got the crowd going with a toast.

"The Irish have one true religion—love and liberation! And that's why we're the best poets and playwrights."

"And novelists," Paddy added, lifting his cup to Molly, who bowed in gratitude.

They all loved Molly, and Paddy surely loved his singing partner. After we ate and drank, Paddy lifted and spun her up onto the bar as if she was a dainty dancer being placed upon a stage, to join him in song.

Dylan would have been impressed, as Molly knew all the words to the raucous, drunken, and cascading lyrics of "Johnny McEldoo." There was something about day drinking and Molly's presence that made the whole hamlet go insane. Fiddlers fiddled as Paddy and Molly sang. More songs of love and liberation, more pints, more dance—and more sweating. I was drenched. The boisterous fun reminded me of the dance scene on the Titanic's third-class deck from the classic old movie—the place where everyone wanted to be, and Molly, the young Kate Winslet, the woman everyone wanted to be with.

Paddy's fondness for Molly was clearly reciprocated. So clearly that by that second evening it had already become a matter of local gossip, according to my dance partner, sister Shannon. She and others were perplexed that we all remained such good friends while her brother flirted so shamelessly with my lover. Another man might have been jealous of their musical chemistry, but since Molly and I weren't true lovers, I had no legitimate complaint. In any event, I would be whisking her away to a castle for intrigue the next day while Paddy mopped up all the beer and sweat from the floor.

The Irish embraced Molly and her writing as one of their own, while Usher Winslett, an American from South Carolina with a British-sounding last name, had never published any of his writings. I was the rookie novelist who'd been writing his first novel for a decade. Gerard had created an entire backstory for me that was easily researched in the multiverse. A lawyer who bots had put to pasture and was now trying my hand at becoming a writer. But Molly was Molly Quinn.

Paddy was still the only local to know my true identity. Gerard insisted we not move too quickly back into real life now that Petrovsky was gone. Though he didn't let on, I didn't think he liked M's mala's mysterious reappearance or the young woman who'd entered Paddy's to inquire about me. And something about 9/9 on the horizon made him concerned about Dick. People were more determined than ever to complete their bucket lists and settle old debts.

After the last song, I went to pull Molly away from Paddy, who was taking the piss out of her by espousing the Fermi paradox.

"If they've had infinite planets on which to develop and an eternity to develop, where have they been until now?"

He knew how to get a rise out of her, but she was good at reading character, and Paddy was well cast in his role of flirtatious provocateur.

"*Let us go now, you and I*," I said, stealing an opening line of poetry to distract her, saving Paddy from her long-winded retort, one that I'd heard so many times. "We've got business with the World Tribunal tomorrow at Clashmoor Castle, and we leave bright and early."

Paddy wanted to join us as "our brawn," but Molly had the good sense to decline.

"Sorry, but it's a particularly exclusive affair, and I have Sean-Usher to protect me with his wits."

They shared a laugh at my expense, and no one heard her slip of the tongue, and everyone was too crazed with drink to care.

Molly and I stumbled home arm in arm over the rocky three-mile path while the sun was dipping into the ocean. Molly humored Alfred by telling him all about the evening. He insisted on hearing a song. Sadly, we couldn't have taken him with us; bringing a bot, registered or not, to a pub just wasn't done.

I was one pint over the line and knocked out as soon as the pillow hit my head. Otherwise, I might have been tempted to join Molly in the guest bed in my study less than twenty steps away.

We both liked sharing the writing space and walks on the beach, yet neither of us had made a move toward romance. I think neither of us wanted a drunken first liaison, and we, or I, feared a sober one. We were drinking far too much. After the return of M's mala, making love to Molly was more than a shout away for me. I was an indecisive Prufrock. The deadline was the inbound comet scheduled for 9/9, and that was still infinite moments away, as time always had to move halfway closer to the end of days, according to Zeno the sage.

The following morning, my alarm woke me in time for a cold shower and to pack a day bag for our big adventure.

Traveling to the Scottish castle of a great man might have been drama enough at any other time of my life, but now it took on intergalactic dimensions. Clashmoor Castle sounded even more romantic as a World Tribunal alien-greeting site. There they would look to convince Molly of their benign approach and ask her to tell the CE-fivers to stand down and not interfere. They saw the amateur efforts of welcoming the aliens as a mortal threat to humanity.

Molly and I were extremely wary of the summons to the castle in light of Chi's warning that the World Tribunal wanted to discredit her. We would be on guard for subterfuge and intrigue, but we also wanted to know what they were up to.

I was assuming my role as Molly's protector. But maybe we should have agreed to Paddy joining us. He was as big and strong as that damn Dick, but their eyes were as different as night and day. Dick's crazy eyes haunted me, while Paddy's always brought me cheer.

How could some men be so good and others so bad?

Dressing for the big day, I heard Molly and Alfred laughing in the kitchen and smelled my coffee brewing. I headed downstairs to join them. They were enjoying Alfred's deep faking. He, more so than Gerard, was concerned about a picture that had been posted of Molly and Paddy from the day before. I was not in the picture. Alfred had taken it on his own initiative to post another somewhat obvious fake one of Molly at the pub and then proceeded to post "real" looking fakes of her in other locations with addresses Gerard had provided him. At Alfred's insistence, Molly posted a real picture of herself on safari, from her address, as her current location. Alfred was still covering our tracks out of an abundance of caution.

I ignored their antics, pouring my own cup of coffee with a splash of milk. I was Harry Potter preparing for my first day of alien graduate school in the Hogwarts of a Scottish castle. Trepidation was no small part of that excitement. Since the dawn of civilization, those in power had always used assassination and imprisonment to silence the opposition. Chi's warning that Molly was the *abominable* opposition had stoked my imagination and had me on high alert.

SIR MILTON STRAW, THE GREAT MAN, had personally coordinated with Gerard on security around our pickup and drop-off on my beach and assured us that Clashmoor Castle was the safest place for me or anyone, even aliens, to meet. We were cautioned to stay off the beach until touchdown and shutoff of the engine "to avoid sand in our eyes or losing one's head." I didn't like the sound of that and wondered if it was a double entendre.

Alfred was disappointed he couldn't join us as our technology and WMD inspector, but he remained on the no-fly list until after 9/9 as an unregistered bot. We left him behind with the breakfast dishes. As condolences, Molly left him tingling all over from his first kiss on the cheek.

The Clashmoor helocraft sent to pick us up was precisely on time— nine a.m. The sleek military-grade dragonfly was not some puddle-jumping taxi with rotary blades. Its black body and the silvery blades that cut the air like well-sharpened swords created a little cyclone of sand as it touched down on the beach. My mind tried to register noise, but there was none. The sand settled in a dramatic ring around the craft now ready for boarding.

We were greeted by our escort and pilot, who was dressed in natty kelly-green fatigues. Danny looked more like a Disney tour guide than a black-ops operative. No earmuffs were necessary for the silent electric copter, but he handed us high-tech souvenir blindfolds that he would help us put on as we approached our landing at Clashmoor Castle.

"No black sack to put on your hostages' heads?" I asked Danny.

"Funny, but Clashmoor is a dark spot on the map, one of the few created by the WT, that blocks all prying eyes of satellites. And any craft that approaches, despite the warnings, is disabled before it gets close enough to see. Unless, like ours, they have the encrypted key"—he patted his copter's controls like a good dog—"they'll crash and burn into the sea. But human eyes can't be so easily deactivated. Thus, we use good old, but high-tech, blindfolds."

"And if we refuse to avert our eyes on arrival, then what?" I thought of a red-hot poker gouging out our eyes on arrival, but that would be too late to erase what we'd already seen.

"Then you'll miss the day's activities and the dinner at the castle that's sure to be grand. The Great Man does nothing not well."

I turned to Molly, sorting out the double negative, and we nodded our agreement to go on with our Bond-like mission with blindfolds on.

"The plan is to lure the aliens here to crash and burn on arrival?" Molly asked.

"Not at all. Not with all the expense and preparations going on around the castle. The WT is determined to meet them first. Ask the Great Man to explain."

When we pulled over the tippy top of Scotland where the Atlantic and the North Sea meet, it was blindfolding time. Danny explained that once on, they were affixed by a magnetic lock in the pilot's control and would be impossible to take off until landing. The cloak-and-dagger exercise felt like fifty shades of something, but along with being vexing, as one might imagine, it added to the excitement and mystery.

I think Molly felt the same mix of emotions, for no sooner were we in the black, with the helocraft's electric vibrational hum singing in our ears, than she reached out to hold my hand. My awareness shot to our hands, and I could feel the sensation pass from my hand to our joined palms and fingers and up through her hand and arm and into her chest, where it settled deep in her heart. This was no mere poetic image of my consciousness traveling into hers, but a vivid sensation as real as the taste of a cherry popping open in one's mouth. I was sixteen again. We held hands and felt love and shared a heart, or so I imagined in the blind thrill of the moment.

Is this Big Love or romantic love?

There's one true love. Big Love! sayeth Juno.

As we touched softly down like a bird on its nest, I was a happy alien removing his blinders to see where I'd been transported. I identified what I imagined was heather on the side of a rough fairway. The whipping flag mounted atop a nearby green proclaimed we were a nine iron away from the ninth hole. Sun streamed through the mist coming in from the sea, and the air was fresh and salty.

I understood why people paid big money to play there, though the course had been closed for over a year for a prealien arrival manicure.

Molly, as the head of our alien peace and love delegation, jumped down onto the sandy green of the Clashmoor golf course. Her stern countenance and dignified manner reflected a seriousness of purpose. And rather than her usual hippy chic, she was dressed for business with a white button-down blouse and neatly cropped blue slacks. She looked like the princess of Monaco when she put on her vintage sunglasses. She was not looking to appease the WT in whatever advantage they were seeking to gain by this state meeting and dinner. I was dressed like a great lady's military attaché in light-blue short-sleeve dress shirt and khaki pants, with a notebook as my shield and Molly pen as my sword.

Danny, with our bags in hand, led us down a golf cart path to grand gardens not more than fifty yards from the castle gates. His comment had been accurate—nothing was not done well here. There we were greeted by Sharrod Brown himself and two kilted and sashed attendants who offered us champagne and water before whisking off our overnight bags to our "chambers in the castle."

I cursed myself for letting my bag go, and with it my laptop. I didn't like my novel draft falling into government hands, though I was already writing the book with possible Dick surveillance in mind, cheating Alfred out of being the first reader of the book I was writing for Juno.

Molly heard my muffled curse and shrugged, whispering, "I've got nothing to hide."

We tinged our flutes of bubbly at precisely ten a.m., as proclaimed by distant church bells chiming ten times.

Sharrod Brown, the public and good-looking face of the World Tribunal, was a Hugh Grant–like man, circa the turn of the century, of handsome and delicate features who spoke with a classic posh accent as he welcomed us again and then said, "All the arrangements are made for what I trust will be a memorable visit. Please let us know if you need anything."

He was a very friendly host for someone we believed intended us no good.

Molly eyed her near-empty champagne flute.

"Let's take it slow, my friend. We need to stay sharp," I said as an aside, always afraid she and I might drink too much, though she could hold her liquor.

"Just let us know," Sharrod said, regarding the champagne. "You are Sir Straw's honored guests. Would you like to go to your chambers to relax before we tour the castle and the grounds?"

Molly wanted to "freshen up first."

As he led us into the dark, cool, and dramatic castle and to our "chambers" on the second floor, One Step pushed the limits of decorum to test how much leeway we would be given. "Why the dramatic blindfolding for our approach?"

"I hope that was not too disquieting or uncomfortable—an overabundance of caution. The protocol was established by the WT, and the Great Man values his privacy. As we approach 9/9, we have to take every precaution."

Which sounded like benign good sense until parsed, when it sounded like a string of words that betrayed nothing. Brown, a master of public relations, reminded me a bit of Alfred. But I couldn't imagine a bot being given such a high-ranking government position. He must be human but self-programmed to perform his governmental service unerringly.

Our chambers were no less than six adjoining regal rooms, two master bedrooms and baths, with a living room between that looked out over the gardens and the first hole of the golf course with its Disneyland-like installations of large orange tubes snaking around like a high-tech hori-zontal water slide. With the not-so-well-disguised black ops brigade and attendants milling about, it also looked to be a twenty-second-century medieval military encampment with its flags and tents. The grandeur made me feel like a tinker masquerading as a knight.

The final room was a small library with ornate wooden stacks full of old books.

"A literary bridal suite," Molly quipped.

"For unwitting hostages?" I said. "No doubt filed with Dylan Thomas and Robert Burns poetry. But Thomas was Welsh. Maybe they have Dylan Byrne's poetry, too?"

I investigated the offerings, dumbfounded by the abundance of good taste displayed on the bookshelves. A book of Yeats's essays damn near jumped out at me, jutting out from the rest of the row. It was the same way I adjusted my books for visibility in bookstores. I pulled it out to look for my favorite essay on magic.

Molly saw me. "Yeats again haunting you from a prior life?"

I chuckled, thinking of the shaman suggesting that we shared a past life that I'd recalled in a vision of poetry. I replaced the volume as I had found it, sticking out. Molly was not fond of my Yeats obsession. "I wonder if Sharrod is an alien. He seemed so stiff . . . so correct. Mother Maria told me that danger comes cloaked as a friend, so let's be wary."

"Aliens may be already among us," she said. "But I imagine I'm the biggest thorn in his side, getting in the way of his desire to control all alien contact. Despite that, he's obviously been instructed to treat us like royalty." She waved both hands to encompass our suite. "The Great Man does nothing not grand," she said in Danny's Scottish brogue.

They had gone all out for us. My suspicious mind wondered why, since we were the enemy.

"*If Donald Trump flew in today, they'd send a limousine anyway . . .*" I sang for Molly in my best Joe Strummer voice.

"Let's unpack," Molly said, "and go get our tour, like aliens arriving from light-years away. Let's keep an open mind and a keen eye. We've traveled such a long way to meet these strange humans that might be cyborgs." She grinned and whispered, "Let's find out what they don't want us to see. I assume we are being watched and they're hearing every word." Molly flipped the surveillance state the bird.

The castle tour was an impressive education in the enduring architecture from the nineteenth century. The battlements of fine old timber and large cut stone had steadfastly withstood the siege of time and the battering rams of seaside weather. All the furnishings and paintings were as old or older than the castle and had been well maintained or restored.

The tour ended in a cavernous basement that would serve as the first meeting place with celestial pilgrims. The wine cellar, a bomb-shelter-like space, held a long sleek table and modern high-tech chairs. The ceiling was a mosaic of recessed cameras and monitoring equipment, well-ventilated air ducts, and colorful lighting. The bookshelf-styled stone walls were laden with every age of Scotch whisky. One dating back to the 1600s was *Captain Kidd's favorite,* according to the art museum label beneath the ancient bottle enclosed in a glass case embedded in the stone wall.

The aliens would be impressed with the sanctity with which we honored our human foibles. The cozy and high-tech meeting place had the vibe of a modern five-star pod hotel conference room with no cap on the budget.

"The aliens, if they disembark from their ships, will be led here through an airtight sealed passage we are ready to assemble at a moment's notice to hook up to their spacecraft," Sharrod said. "We don't know what to expect from the aliens, but this room has been retrofitted to accommodate any temperature, oxygen level, or type of lighting to meet the aliens' needs. We even can adjust the gravity and magnetic fields, to make our guests feel more at home, while we attempt to establish communications."

Our tour guide paused, waiting for our first impression to sink in.

"You sure have put a lot of work in to convert what might have once been a dungeon for dragons, or Englishmen, into this high-tech facility," I said while still studying the ages of the scotch in the wall cases and wondering at their worth and whether they'd taste like bitter malt syrup after all this time.

Molly, while inspecting some lasers that might be for a hologram portal, asked, "What makes you so confident they will come here to you, and not to meet me in Willamette Valley?"

"The Great Man and our WT have invested a great deal in their arrival here, but I'll let him explain that to you this evening."

"Will you be using humans or robots for the first meeting?" I asked on behalf of Alfred.

"Maybe both. The exact composition of the team is still being debated. Our human team of trained scientists have oxygen masks and thermal viral protection suits in case the aliens need it cold, require less oxygen, or are carrying dangerous pathogens. And we will seek to protect them from our diseases too."

He paused before putting his right hand over his heart.

"You can see why we're concerned about the civilian efforts to greet the unknown nature of these aliens without any of these safety precautions and protocols." He looked hard and pleadingly at Molly.

She said, "We've heard that before. But that's a matter of debate and ultimately should be left to one's own conscience if we choose to take the risk. And I believe they will be quite equipped to protect themselves from us."

Sharrod showed no sign of strain at being challenged and said, "It's dangerous for our alien guests *and* to the human population for well-intentioned people to greet them like refugees being washed ashore. We have not been the best stewards of our planet, and they might be coming for regime change. We must take every precaution."

"If they want hostages, or to kill us, seems they wouldn't need our invitation or offer of greeting," Molly said without missing a beat.

Sharrod had the good sense to move on. "Let me show you more."

"Well, if they like scotch, they'll've come to the right place," I said, in a mashed-up English to lighten the mood.

Sharrod laughed politely. He was ready with a hard sales pitch and hoped to change our minds, which was loads better than trying to discredit Molly in some way. In an aside, I reminded Molly to play along. We had discussed our strategy: to ask questions but not challenge our hosts until one of us gave the signal—flipping our right nostril with a finger, like they did in *The Sting*. That would be my sign to let One Step off his leash. And for the rest of our listening tour, we nodded that we understood what he had to say—without necessarily agreeing.

The World Tribunal's line of reasoning was well known and not without merit. And though the control room we were in seemed to make sense as a comfortable and well-equipped meeting place for weary space travelers who might like some spirits, it also might have been a space-age Nazi gas chamber, prepared in case we didn't like what the aliens had come to say.

He showed us two clear urns, one with gray dust and rocks whose inscription read *Man's Landing on Earth's Moon 20/07/1969*, with hieroglyphics beneath the inscription. And the second, containing reddish dirt and crumbled rock, labeled *Man's Landing on Mars Within Earth's Solar System, 22/07/2032*, again with hieroglyphics beneath the words.

Brown swiped a finger across the hieroglyphics. "To show we are space travelers too. We've tried to learn from their written samples—their language beneath our words."

"Well, it's a bit misleading, as man hasn't made it to Mars. Only our robots have."

"We debated that, but hopefully we'll have a chance to explain. We wanted to keep things simple for first contact." He stepped to the table. "But here is our tour de force."

He removed a covering from the center of the table as if beneath might lie the crown jewels or Captain Kidd's pirate booty. And a grand hologram interface of the cosmos appeared in front our eyes. It looked like the tech envisioned for a very old book and movie entitled *The Minority Report* but even more impressive and one that Sharrod could control with his mind or neural network.

"Wow. You've spared no expense. I can see why you'd be upset if they chose to alight upon a humble CE-5 site after all of this," Molly said.

"This tech has cost a lot in R&D to create, and we have three of them operational, the other two in undisclosed locations. This should enable communication through a powerful QC. And the hologram will allow for 3D visual mapping of the universe. We hope to pinpoint where they came from and other places they've been. It will also, if they are willing and able, allow them to graphically share the blueprints of their time-and-space-travel physics." As he spoke, the spectacular AI-generated planetarium shifted into a hologram image of a sleek model that appeared to be the internal mechanics of an alien spaceship, overlaid with mathematical formulas that looked like a musical score.

He then abruptly shut down the workstation with his BCI or NCI. "All extremely proprietary and top secret, but I wanted to give you a feel for what we might accomplish here with our tech. This is a singular opportunity for mankind, and we don't want it squandered. Please note that we prefer you keep this subterranean location secret when you write about what you saw today. We took this risk of showing you to ensure that a trusted source within the CE-5 movement could get our message across."

"But if they communicate by telepathy and not with technology—what then?" Molly asked.

"Your host will explain more at dinner this evening, but this interface, paired with our quantum computer, is how our wired-in scientists and the aliens will learn to communicate. We have some rudimentary understanding of their language from their communications."

"You should use a linguist like Amy Adams in the movie *Arrival*."

He smiled politely, and Molly rolled her eyes.

"What if they don't depart from their ship?" I asked. The aliens never left their ship in that movie precedent.

"We have a portable interface we can use to link to this communication control device. But moving on . . . Sir Straw will explain. We call him the Great Man around here, though he insists on being called Milton by his guests. His wife and Milt Junior are in Texas until after the arrival of our alien friends."

No doubt in a five-star bunker and tended to by top-of-the-line bots.

"*Communications?*" Molly asked. "I thought there was just the one in 2026, telling us to prepare to meet in 2036?"

I'd taken note of the plural too.

"A slip of the tongue in that we view each figure of that first communication as a series of communications, like a strand of DNA encoded with many messages, to be broken down into parts, to understand how they communicate. Again, Sir Straw, if he chooses, can tell you more."

"Hmm?" I murmured so only Molly might hear. Sharrod's tongue had great traction and control, making a slip questionable.

"Any miscommunication by a CE-5 group may lead to the War of the Worlds. This is too delicate a matter to be left to amateurs relying on telepathy as a link between worlds." His eyes went still, the way Alfred's did when he was receiving a message while we talked. "Professor McQueen, may I speak to you in private for a moment?"

As he led me away from Molly, I imagined he was going to try to drive a wedge between us and would land some nasty allegation against her. Possibly some horrible betrayal of me.

He said, "There's no artful way to say this, but we're always testing the technology of our greeting center, and I have been informed we've detected a worrisome electrical magnetic imbalance in your heart muscle that we could have checked for you here, if you like. You can wait to see your own heart doctor, of course, but it is of some concern to our technicians. Would you like to consult with a member of our medical team?"

Molly was studying me from the other end of the room with her hand curled under her chin like Rodin's *Thinker*, but in her case, expressing consternation; she didn't like to miss anything. I gave her a thumbs-up so she wouldn't worry.

"Thank you, and how's my sperm count?" I responded to the deeply empathetic Sharrod Brown. Talk about a lack of privacy . . .

He chuckled politely. "Nothing that intrusive—we monitor vitals to make sure everyone who enters the control room is healthy."

I wondered if they were decoding my DNA as we spoke.

"It's a preexisting condition that I have an appointment to have corrected soon. My specialist believes a robot will be able to track the current and calibrate the precise electrical shock needed at the right location to get it back in perfect rhythm. Until then, he has asked that I not get on any roller coasters or skydive. Otherwise, I should be fine."

We rejoined curious Molly for the rest of the tour. Now I'd have to tell her. I feared the faint heart ailment and procedure would make me appear old in her eyes. Eyes that I still hoped held me, even if by a slender cord, to a dream of youth and passion.

"What was that?" she asked.

I pretended it was a secret, whispering in her ear, "Tell you about it later, but Sharrod is a lot like Alfred, without the charming personality."

She nodded her *maybe*.

One did not ask if someone was a bot. It was like asking a woman, who may have merely gained weight, if she was pregnant. We might never know for sure.

The rest of the tour transported us via a speedy golf cart through the maze of gardens and the front nine of the golf course as he showed us how the segments of transport tubes would be quickly assembled to weave like a snake over a mile to take the dazed aliens into the scotch-filled subterranean chamber. The snake tube would be attached by the army of well-armed military contractors and bots even now at the ready, though they seemed programmed to stay in their tents or to smile cordially when they couldn't avoid contact with us. The tents and tubes formed high-tech staging and monitoring areas. Every alien step would be carefully monitored and well-guarded.

We'd already seen the climax and heart of the operation, and now were merely being shown the bright orange arteries that would lead the alien travelers—ambassadors? species exterminators?—to the secure meeting place. The orange tubes arranged about the golf course reminded me of the 2005 Central Park *The Gates* art installation by Christo and Jeanne-Claude.

Sharrod was a master at minimizing drama and in projecting the beauty and harmony of the place where weary travelers would be greeted and made fast friends. I felt like the Tin Man chasing Dorothy through the poppy fields of Oz in a golf cart. It was such a beautiful setting for aliens to alight upon, it made me drowsy.

However, there seemed to be no back nine for us to see. We got to play only on the front nine, which made me suspicious of what they might be hiding on holes ten through eighteen. Sharrod assured us, "There's nothing to see on the back nine—those holes are closed for renovations."

How did one renovate grass and sand?

At the end of the tour, we ate a refreshing lunch under a canopy next to the third tee and overlooking the cliffs and the sea. We were then given several tourist options to pursue before retiring to prepare for dinner. Molly and I chose to be set free to walk into the charming small town a short distance down a cobblestone lane. We hoped to feel less watched, inside and out, by getting off castle grounds.

28 CLASHMOOR

MUCH LIKE MY LITTLE IRISH HAMLET, the Scottish town of Clashmoor, Dornoch, Scotland—not to be confused with nearby Clashmore—was another stuck-in-time anachronism. Clashmoor was a feudal village attendant to the castle, too small to be found on most maps. The handful of locals we passed seemed to understand we were guests of the Great Man—the arrogance of the name was starting to grate, and I hadn't even met him yet—and were eager to please with their warm smiles followed by what sounded like *fisgar ma*, which we interpreted as their greeting and not a curse.

It was a castle town that was too quaint and precious. The Great Man was the lord and master here, though an American hedge-funder by birth who used his wealth to keep the place well swept and manicured. We were royal guests that all eyes followed over ancient cobblestones still perfectly set. The lane was lined with wrought-iron hitching posts with small horse heads. After all the high tech we had seen, I imagined those horse heads were watching and listening to us. Molly must have shared my paranoia, as neither of us spoke of anything important.

We ducked into a small bookstore, with a bell over the door announcing our arrival to no one, as there was no attendant.

"Finally, we can speak in private," I said. But Molly pointed to a camera eye, no bigger than a real eye, peering at us from over the checkout desk, where a small box sat marked *Donations for Books*.

We started to look at the books in silence, though there were plenty to peruse back in our chamber library and throughout the castle. My eyes were drawn immediately to a small leather-bound book posed upon a table in front of the B section of books. I picked it up tenderly, as if it were a baby chick or Easter egg, to inspect it. The tiny volume looked to be eighteenth century and should have been under glass. Small didn't do it justice; it was a two-inch-by-two-inch edition of Robert Burns's love poems with a silk bookmark attached. I opened the tiny volume of thick-stocked pages. On the left page was one of his poems and on the right was a color drawing of lovers in various stages of embrace. To say the book was precious would be to undervalue the gem and its delicate nature.

What if they were Burns's own drawings?

I felt like Indiana Jones finding a precious artifact, but what would be the proper donation? An arm and a leg wouldn't fit in the donation cup.

I caught Molly giving me jealous looks before she moved over to the F books and shook her head. She seemed somewhat consoled to find a normal-size early edition of *The Great Gatsby* there.

"Nice consolation prize," I said, teasing her, and she pretended to be so impressed with her book that she didn't notice my tiny nugget.

The bell rang when an old man dressed in a wool suit—on a warm day—entered. He gave us a hearty, "Greetings, honored guests of the castle. This place has been closed for business like the golf course to all us locals until today."

We returned his greeting with our own fisgar ma. He nodded, and Molly added, "And how are you this fine day?"

"Full of the joy of life!" He patted his belly and joined me at the Bs and zeroed quickly in on a book by Beckett—*Molloy*. As he flipped through the pages, he started reading, sounding like an old rabbi at prayer.

"*Wats-a-sidin-ack-ine*," he chanted several times while turning pages. The incantation, for that was what it sounded like, became slightly clearer for one go-round, and I imagined he said, "What's a-hiding on that back nine?"

He replaced the Beckett and tipped his tam-o'-shanter. "Ask the Great Man when we can get back to our golf. The *townsfolk* would all like to know. Aliens may come and go, but golf is for Scotsmen, born and bred with a stick in our hands and balls between our legs." I couldn't help but laugh.

The bell rang, and he was gone. Surely he was the town contrarian. I wondered if he'd immediately be whisked away for proper reindoctrination into Clashmoor living and worship of the Great Man.

"Molly, did you hear what he said about the golf course?"

"The nice double entendre about boys with sticks and balls? And how they all need to get back to that tedious game the Scots invented?"

"No, before that. The last nine holes . . ."

"Sorry, I had my nose in a book. All I heard was mumbling. He may have been drunk or just a crazy old man."

I shook my head, uncertain of her prognosis. And maybe my ears needed some medical attention too. I grabbed the Beckett to give *Molloy* to Molly, but she refused it, saying, "The paragraphs are too long for me to read again."

"*Gatsby*'s the only book you're getting then?" I asked.

When she nodded, I put a hundred-pound note in the donation tin. We left with a treasure trove. I felt both giddy and guilty.

On the cobblestone street, I grabbed Molly by the arm, bowed, and gave her the tiny volume of Burns and kept the Beckett. She gave me her Fitzgerald in exchange, and we were both happy giving our gifts to each other. Something about being watched made me act more gallant. We returned arm in arm to the castle to relax before dinner with the very *great man* from the World Tribunal, a man who already seemed larger than life.

I felt like a fly with its wings clipped, being watched under a microscope, while trying to act like Gregory Peck on a Scottish holiday.

BACK IN OUR CHAMBERS, MOLLY AND I spoke in pleasantries about our remarkable day. We both believed our every word was being recorded. Our eyes spoke of the immersive conspiracy we were swimming in. Neither of us were good with any restraint on our expression or with small talk.

We flopped down on the ornate couch in the living room of our elegant chambers.

"Moll, I'm a bit worried. I will most definitely be underdressed for dinner. All I brought is a decade-old blazer." I scraped my hand over my jaw; I'd need to shave before our big dinner. "I haven't been getting out much since Dick's curse."

"Don't worry—once a professor, always a professor. Think of your simple dress as being a man of the people and not lord of the manor, and let your wit and charm speak for itself. You fret too much. By the way, I've been meaning to ask . . . what distinguishes a threat from a curse? We all live with threats to our lives."

As a student of curses, I had a ready answer. "A curse is no idle threat and is distinguished by conviction and determination to see its fruition. If you could have seen Dick's eyes and smelled his hot breath as he uttered his blood oath, you would know exactly what a curse sounds like."

"Oy, sorry I asked . . . but I do wonder if it's his conviction or your belief that gives his curse its power."

I winced as she paraphrased my children's position on the matter. She namaste'd me after landing the punch, then quickly pivoted to the events at hand. "Before I go shower, let's have one of our literary tête-à-têtes to write down an impromptu dialogue between an alien and human," she suggested.

The competition was on.

She glanced at the fireplace that was prepared and ready to be lit. A housekeeping note suggested we make use of it. Something about the stone of the castle kept it cool enough in summer to make a fire welcome and not totally out of place as the sun was getting low in the highlands. She struck a long match and put it to the fire starter that was housed under a log cabin of brittle wood.

I said, "I assume you get to speak for the alien?"

"Don't you know I do."

We sat by a table alongside the pleasantly crackling fire. Molly grabbed the stationery, and we both pulled out our Molly pens. Best I could glean from her preparations, our tête-à-tête was to be exactly that—foreheads touching and paper between us that was hidden from snooping eyes. She wrote first, and we alternated lines.

Do you think they can see the writing?

I don't think so, unless they have a satellite or drone watching from outside the window.

What do you think about our tour?

Other than being blindfolded and not seeing the back nine . . . I swear the man in the bookstore said that is where we should look. He was mumbling, I think, "What's a-hiding on the back nine?" Other than that bit of mystery, it all seems very well orchestrated and benign.

So you could translate his mumbling? And that's a good summary—they're hiding something there. But too many guards and cameras for us to slip out later tonight to the golf course.

Let's remember Chi's warning and be careful. They take this all deadly seriously.

So do I. What did Sharrod have to share with you in private?

That's a personal matter that we don't need this cone of secrecy for. I'll tell you later. Do you mind if I challenge the Great Man at dinner?

Just give me the sign. I don't plan to be as restrained as I was with Sharrod, but will leave you to question what's a-hiding on the back nine.

She crinkled her nose and gathered up the paper. "I'll Hedda Gabler these—not our most inspired work."

"If you introduce blindfolds in the first act, then you better show what's hiding there before the play is done," I said, bastardizing Chekhov.

At the fireplace, she watched the paper and the words we'd shared between us burn.

"Tell me, what was Sharrod's big reveal he had to share with you in private?"

"Well, it's kind of a funny and somewhat demeaning story."

"Do tell!"

"They were body scanning us in the mission control chamber and detected a heart abnormality in me. So creepy to think they were look- ing into my heart."

"Well, I'm glad they could find one."

"Funny." I tossed a pillow at her, hitting her in the chest, and she flung it right back into my crotch. After doubling over in mock agony, I said, "Now, onward with my story. One of the fun things about becoming a man of a certain age is they send you to a stress test with a cardiologist. She made me take off my shirt, and I was eager to show her my still- great aerobic prowess. She strapped on a bunch of wires and asked me to start at a jog on the treadmill." I cranked my arms like a man run- ning in place to show my speed and strength. "She kept wanting more, increasing the speed and incline, and she looked impressed. 'Heartbeat, one ten, good. Heartbeat, one twenty, good.' She clearly wanted to see me sweat, putting me at a seven-minute-mile pace on a nice incline. 'Heartbeat, one forty, good.' And then she exclaimed, 'No! no! no!' and shut down the gerbil wheel so fast, I almost flew off.

"'What was that?' I asked. 'You're stable now,' she said, looking at my vitals. 'Get dressed and meet me in my office.' Talk about hot to cold. First she's undressing me, impressed by my prowess, and then she's ready to pronounce me near death. Long story short, she says that when my heart rate exceeds one fifty, my heart starts missing beats and my blood pressure shoots up dangerously. Her answer was for me to wear a heart monitor when I work out and not to go above one forty."

"Hmm," Molly mused before using the cardiologist's report and insult as a launch pad for another frontal assault. "Old man, you're afraid I might kill you with my love. That explains it."

I didn't find her words funny, but I laughed anyway.

"The doctor went on to explain," I continued, "how the condition might cause this pinching pain I have. I asked her what might happen if I pushed my heart rate beyond one fifty. She must have been a Jim Croce fan because she said, 'You don't yank on Superman's cape.' I don't want to go slow the rest of my life, so to bring the story of my humiliation to an end . . . she arranged for me to have a new procedure where a robot microscopically singes the electrodes that send the signal to skip beats and raise my blood pressure to scary heights. So I can still mount"—I gave her a wink—"Everest for another decade or two. The procedure is on September eighteenth, after A-Day."

I concluded by banging my fists on my chest like a gorilla. I probably came off as a geriatric Tarzan.

Molly looked less than fully convinced but accepted my explanation, saying, "Okay, but you must get it tended to sooner if you have any flare-ups. Let's rest and get dressed. I'll meet you in our library around six. We're supposed to head down around six thirty."

In my room, I found a note on my pillow—on formal stationery—from the desk of Sir Milton Straw. The Great Man seemed proud of being knighted. Like Keith Richards, I detested hierarchy and was ambivalent when Mick, the rock god, took the knee for the Queen, but all the same, I felt a pang of jealousy.

Dear Professor McQueen,

I'm excited to meet you for dinner. I'm a great fan of your two books and wish for more. You're an American hero for your service in defeating the Guru and the Russian launch of Genesis hive-mind technology. I've had my personal security team watching for any news or moves by your Dick. Best they can tell, he's dormant and can't leave Moscow without detection.

To express my gratitude for your service, please find in the

wardrobe a full kit of a traditional kilt. This is yours to keep with
my great gratitude. See you soon for dinner. I wish you didn't
have to leave first thing. Next time, let me take you shooting.
Nothing tastes better than a wild Scottish red-legged partridge
you've shot yourself. I bagged three this morning for one of our
many courses this evening and to go with some extraordinary
wines I've selected especially for you.

Your humble host,
Milton

The Strawman had a heart and the Great Man made a great first
impression. Though I didn't think I could shoot a bird, as a meat eater, I
had no philosophical problem with hunting for food. He was a fan and
powerful enough to watch Dick for me, *and* he'd left me a gift in my
wardrobe. Not a bad tribute by a titan of technology and finance.

I opened the wardrobe, and there it was, the full Bonnie Prince
Charlie expressed in the finest tartan weave. The matching coat was
a dark forest-green and bore the Clashmoor Castle crest. A sporran
was included—a small bag that hung over the shoulder and about the
waist and was perfect for my reading glasses and phone. There was
also an artisanal Balmoral cap, or so it said on the lining, to cover my
thinning hair. And for the feet, white socks with playful red tassels
and Ghillie Brogue black kilt boots in my exact size. Tip to toe, I
couldn't wait to get dressed.

I showered and shaved and even checked my ears for errant hairs
that were appearing more frequently these days. And then I started
to dress for our gala, excited to do a little Scottish jig with one hand
waving free, celebrating that my blue blazer could be left behind in
the wardrobe.

I'd heard real men don't wear underwear under their kilts. The Great
Man would have to look to know, and if he looked, I would be glad to
be the lesser man; I put my underwear on. The kilt fit me perfectly. As I

stood in front of the full mirror, I felt like stalwart William Wallace with my brave heart playing bagpipes in my chest.

I had fifteen minutes before I was to meet Molly in the library. I lay down carefully, though the tartan wasn't about to wrinkle, to meditate. I was able to clear my head until images of battles more real than any movies paraded through. I fought bravely through the fear, but in the end, I was knocked to the ground by the largest man on the field. As he swung his blade straight over my heart, and was poised to run me through, fortunately, I awoke.

Had I witnessed a death from a prior life? The scene seemed more real than a dream, and I tried to capture the details, but the images had faded back to where they'd come from—another time and another place.

I sat up. Was it not a past life but precognition of a post-dinner battle to the death? I shook myself and pinched my cheek to return to the present.

The shaman ceremony had definitely opened the back door. Grandma wasn't done with me yet.

I splashed cold water on my face to brace myself and grabbed an ice-cold Tennent's Lager from the minifridge before joining Molly.

And there she stood in the sexiest kilted skirt and sash, a divine feminine mirror of my outfit but with splashes of red and a more form-fitting top. Color me impressed. She looked as young or younger than when we first met.

And I greeted her with Burns's poetry.

"O my Luve's like a red, red rose . . . As fair as thou, my
bonny lass."

She took the beer from my hand and held it to her ruby lips like a mic, reciting:

"And surely ye'll be your pint-stoup!
And surely I'll be mine!

And we'll drink a cup o' kindness yet,
For auld lang syne."

She drained my beer full stop, and I hugged her like we were headed into battle before twirling us about like I was twenty and she eighteen. Laughing and dizzy, we fell onto the thick sheepskin rug.

"You're quite the handsome one, Sean McQueen."

"And you're a bonnie lass, Molly Quinn. I better watch my heart rate. It's racing." I gave her a knowing look and stood, offering her my hand. "May I escort you to dinner?"

She rose beside me, and we headed out for our grand dinner, sure to be full of intrigue and espionage if the Great Man was half the man I imagined him to be.

DESPITE MY WILLIAM WALLACE DRESS, I felt more like a piker descending the dramatic marble spiral staircase arm an arm with the mighty elegant lassie Quinn as the Great Man waited at the bottom to welcome us. He was a big man who looked like a Scottish lord born to wear his tartan emblazoned with the Clashmoor crest. He was one and a half men more than I'd imagined. I'd bet there was no underwear on six-foot-six Sir Straw. Sans bonnet, his sandy hair was full and tightly cropped, and his arms were outstretched. I was afraid he'd bear hug me, but he respectfully embraced my lass and then me as we exchanged greetings.

Bagpipes were playing in the garden at a respectful distance, but near enough to be intended for our small gathering.

Straw was a hearty and gregarious man who commanded one to be at ease, though based on his résumé, I knew I should be on my guard. Few men become self-made billionaires without wicked cunning and doing whatever it took to have their way. He intimidated me with how disarming he could be.

"We'll have drinks on the veranda."

"Will Sharrod be joining us?" Molly asked. "He was a knowledgeable tour guide."

"Sharrod, no." He grinned. "He's the newest model bot. Almost everyone you see here are bots these days, for security. Did Sharrod fool you?"

"Yes, but not Sean—he figured it out."

My powers of deduction were based on a lot of time with Alfred.

"Sean McQueen, the self-proclaimed bungling professor. I should have known you'd see through his inhumanity."

"Yes, but how did he or your other bot technicians note my heart defect? It only registers at a high heart rate."

"Sorry to hear that. I can inquire, but they were testing your DNA. Perhaps it's coded there as a genetic defect?" He disclosed this intrusion on my privacy, unzipping my encoded double helix, as par for the course. As I prepared to challenge this intrusion on my sovereignty, he distracted me. "I've read that you like wine," he said with a knowing look at me. "So we have a 2010 Chassagne-Montrachet grand cru open and chilled, and some nice reds planned for dinner."

He indicated the bottles lined up like sentries upon a twenty-foot bar. "Then an old scotch while we talk turkey if you're both willing— after dinner."

I felt like a bought man with my ten-thousand-dollar dress—I had looked up the retail prices online—and now a thousand-dollar bottle of white and all the old red Burgundy grand cru soldiers, two already uncorked. My DNA was a small price to pay. "What a great year for Burgundy and all grand crus!" I said, trying unsuccessfully to show appreciation with muted enthusiasm.

We headed out to the garden terrace.

"I knew you'd appreciate the wines, Sean. I hope your heart can handle it."

"My cardiologist has suggested I cut back, but surely she didn't mean grand crus."

"Ha! In vino veritas." He glanced at Molly. "I don't often have such renowned literary talent here. Usually just all sorts of business and government men and bots like Sharrod for company. My small family is back at our secure ranch in Texas till this extra-terrorest-rial singularity is over." It sounded like he added *terror* to ET's name.

His lingering look upon Molly was midway between chivalrous and a leer. Being a *great* man, he was used to liberties other men could not afford. Not so easily intimidated, Molly raised his leer with a Mae West wink.

After that minor skirmish, we all turned to drink in the spectacular view. A kilted-skirt-wearing serving woman—a bottess, I assumed—gave each of us a glass of the chilled yellow Burgundy. I wondered if women were encouraged not to wear underwear under their tartan dresses too. I'd ask Molly later.

The Great Man held up his glass to the sunset rolling over the lawns and moors before the sun could sink into the sea.

"To September ninth and friendly gatherings with friendly aliens—a new Thanksgiving!"

We toasted and then sat in cushioned leather chairs to watch the Scottish sunset, marked by a gentle mist casting colorful light like a prism. We each had a wine barrel for a table. I hadn't thought that far ahead, that 9/9 was sure to become a day of celebration or of infamy after the fact. The Native American Victorio in me admired his analogy.

I lifted my glass to show I was not a coward in the face of wealth and power. "To our host and his . . . and his pretty, pretty, pretty nice backyard."

I scored an eye roll from Molly and a hearty laugh and slap on the back from Straw at my use of ironic understatement and Larry David.

We moved to small talk about Molly's and my writings and everyone's personal histories. The Great Man was an excellent host, with a lot of money and power to please his guests. Perhaps he was right, that we pikers should allow the aliens to first parlay with our most accomplished men of industry and technology. Men not easily intimidated and who knew the art of a deal. They might be able to make the aliens feel more comfortable using five-star accommodations.

More comfortable than our Big-Loving Deeksha? The lighthearted quibble belonged to M.

After two glasses of the Chassagne-Montrachet, we moved back inside, through a *Downton Abbey* old-world grandeur, but rather than seating us in the great ballroom, which would have felt uncomfortable for a party of three, Straw escorted us to a smaller round table in a comfortable study with old books and paintings of the castle throughout the centuries.

"You must come back and stay with me after the big day so you can explore the countryside and take a look at all these old books. I'm wired-in and no longer read. And we can discuss who was right and who was wrong. Unless, of course, they beam you up into their space-craft and whisk you away into some intergalactic sex trade."

"Or you. Big, pretty men make for good slave labor," Molly parried.

"Douché."

I laughed at the exchange but was unsure if his bungled reply was meant in jest or was a Freudian slip of the tongue.

"We plan on offering them some bots before they depart so we can keep tabs on them. So hopefully we'll both still be here, and you'll come and look through all these ancient artifacts." He pointed to the bookshelves.

The wired-in crowd saw no reason to read since they could have any book they chose read to them by AI in any voice they wanted. At home, I had Alfred to do that for me, and he performed the parts. Like Elliot, he was a good actor.

Molly replied, "Sounds nice *if* we are all still here and haven't pol-luted our own atmosphere with alien repellent. We'd love to come. Or I would, even if Sean is too busy writing his next book. Maybe some golf—I can't wait to see the back nine."

I'd thought she was leaving that line of questioning to me. The change of plan made me feel even more a third wheel. She was flirt-ing and toying with him, which was a trick of her trade to get her characters to reveal themselves. But Straw was a cunning man who wouldn't be so easily played. Yet I'd not met the man immune to Molly's charm.

"Well, you're welcome anytime, and we'll *play a round*," he said with a sly smile. "And as a deal sweetener, if you return, you can take any volumes of the books you fancy."

Molly and I both glanced at the beautifully bound, complete set of Shakespeare.

"We found some incredible bargains in the village bookstore. A small book of Burns poems with lovely accompanying drawings. I fear

Sean wasn't able to leave adequate cash for such a rare book in the donation box."

"The donation box is left for a touch of old-world charm. We don't expect our guests to still be carrying cash. And don't worry, that's my store—a quaint, old-fashioned bookshop for tourists coming for our golf and highland beauty. Tourists have been unable to come this season as we prepare to welcome the space tourists. You're our only guests this entire year. The castle and course have been in preparation for what-ever might arrive on the warp-speed tour buses."

He took a thoughtful drink of the red Burgundy, as a tasting, before all our glasses were poured by the bonnie bot servant. Before I could pre-pare some witticism about drinking fine French wine in a Scottish castle while speaking about how to welcome aliens, he turned to Molly again.

"Much like you, to ensure we get off on the right foot with these *advanced life-forms*, if that's what they are, this has become my passion. I hear that ALFs is a more politically correct nomenclature than the overused and fearful *aliens*, but it may be based on a mistaken premise. They may not be living at all, and I contend they're more likely superin-telligent bots and their arrival may be unmanned spaceships with some advance form of communications linking back to a home base."

He did have some Mars experience to draw on to make his infer-ence, and bots have a shelf life that might be infinite with the aid of updated software and the skills of bot technicians. They could have headed out from the Andromeda Galaxy at a snail's pace, billions of light-years ago.

"But I tread on Sharrod's message that I was meant to impart. He's in charge of PR, and he thinks that you, Molly, are in the best position to set the record straight about first contact, whether they be animate or inanimate aliens. And I agree. Sharrod is the smartest man in the room, even when not present. He is eager to meet his kin."

I was tempted to applaud. Milton had scored the incredible feat of rendering Molly speechless.

I had to get into the game and come to her defense.

"Brilliant. The suggestion that they may not be life-forms means we can kill, or rather, deactivate them all with no moral offense?" I was thinking of Alfred and how his destruction would devastate me. Even if he was not fully sentient, he was a work of art, more precious than the *Mona Lisa*.

Molly raised her wine glass to me and said, "And if they're super-intelligent cyborgs, why all the harping that it's unsafe for civilians to meet them in unsecured sites because the aliens may carry deadly pathogens? That makes no sense if they're most likely to be safe carbon-based bots."

"Good question. But perhaps they're radioactive. They've been doing reconnaissance of our armed forces and nuclear sites for over seventy-five years now. And they seemed particularly displeased, I should say *focused*, around nuclear test times. This reconnaissance may be to prepare to detonate all our shuttered reactors and nuclear weapons. So a deadly pathogen is just one of the ways they may look to annihilate us, whether they're bots or viral life-forms."

"Then why are you so confident, investing so much for a meeting here in the highlands of Scotland? Wouldn't they be as likely to alight in London or New York or come see me at the Deeksha in the Willamette Valley? Sharrod said you might explain that."

"Oh good, bots are discreet, and that is top secret. Perhaps I can explain it over an after-dinner drink. But now, please, everyone, let's enjoy our meal. I find the prospect of enslavement or extinction not so good for the appetite."

"Yes, let's speak of all the good they may bring," Molly said before we sat back to honor our host's request.

The first courses passed pleasantly, with a lot of excited back-and-forth between Molly and Milton. Molly spoke about the importance of telepathic communications and being guided by love and not fear, and Straw spoke about all the technologically advanced preparations laid out by Clashmoor Castle and all the sophistication required to greet the aliens in a proper forum to ensure they didn't attempt to divide and conquer mankind by picking favorites as they established their kingdom on Earth. He spoke with authority and religious fervor. Great atrocities are often stoked by such fear mongering. And he was a true believer that the aliens were bringing fire and brimstone.

Molly answered that preparations should be more about being able to meet them on a higher plane of consciousness rather than in a high-tech wine cellar. To which I was tempted to add "that's probably hiding a gas chamber." But as Molly's aide-de-camp, I spoke little. My comments were mostly limited to the food and wine.

The main course was the fresh kill of the wild Scottish red-legged partridge with sweet and tart cranberry sauce.

"I don't eat much meat these days, and trying to dink less, on my way to self-realization," I noted, "but this partridge and your Grands-Echézeaux 1985 is a tasty detour."

Though meant as a joke, my observation led to a long discussion of Big Love and Juno throughout the main course. One that enthralled Sir Straw. His avid interest provided me an opportunity to ask about Dick, whom he'd mentioned in his note.

"Molly, I mentioned to Sean that I read his books and that the Tribunal was involved in monitoring Sean's Dick to see if he became active and posed a tangible threat. That sadist—Dominick has so many aliases—is so notorious for cruelty, even for Petrovsky's Russia, that my security team adopted your view and started calling him Dick too."

I nodded at their appreciation for my adolescent nickname.

"We don't know much else other than he survived your branding and worked directly for Petrovsky, who denied him his revenge. Now, with the new gang of three in power in Moscow, looking to be welcomed back into the norms of international society, your Dick is no longer an imminent threat." His mouth stretched in a cold smile. "They've got a kill chip in that mad dog's head. We, I mean the World Tribunal, would have to approve his release into the West, and that we will never do, of course. We have a whole dossier on your Dick."

I felt like a child being assured by his father that a bully would never harm him again.

"Would you share that dossier with my man Alfred, who tracks all my villains?"

"Sure. Just give me his registration number and we'll have all the data downloaded."

"Oh, never mind . . . I don't have his number . . . a bot, works at Interpol . . . and they have enough info on Dick already, but if you find out anything new, please let us know." I'd fucked up. Revealing Alfred. But Straw was WT and not going to help Dick. And I think I covered my tracks.

Though he was killing us with kindness, there was something more going on than an innocent exchange of views and information. Some grand game and only he knew the rules. He knew more than he was saying, and that led me to dig deeper.

"Interpol believes that Petrovsky stepping down means I'm more or less in the clear. I wonder if having a cruel dictator holding Dick back might have made me more secure than I am now." I didn't credit Alfred. I wished I'd never brought him into the conversation but wanted to hear the Great Man's thoughts of his risk assessment.

"Thinking outside the box, I like it! But your long-standing fear is warping your assessment of the present state of play," Straw said. "Petrovsky didn't want to lend credence to your story by taking your life. But I have to agree with Interpol—the new Russian government is desperate to return to the world stage and join the WT to gain our protection from the aliens. *And* to have a seat at the table when we discuss how we can more directly link minds through *IT*. Sorry, through our QC." He corrected himself.

"You sound like the Guru bringing back the potential of hive minding." I couldn't let this go without challenge.

"Ethically, of course, under strict WT guidelines and oversight. I am no evil mastermind, and others would be in charge, but it's worth revisiting. I'm just looking to serve humanity. Unfortunately, we are too late for the hive mind to assist mankind in addressing the alien question— which is why we started looking into the technology again—and allow for a coordinated *earthling* response." He sought to disarm me with humor and a grin. "But back to your Dick . . . I'd say you have little to worry about."

"I almost wish Dick could escape," I bravely boasted. "So we can get this done with. His curse is an unfinished thread in my life and my fiction. In any event, thank you. How fortuitous we meet—thanks to Molly bringing me as her bodyguard."

I worried that my boast and bodyguard comments sounded offensive and defensive in turn, but both Straw and Molly took both as humor . . . which offended me.

Straw said, "Watch what you wish for." He laid his fork down. "We also tracked, for you, your spy and witch, Samantha Smythe. She's been a little more active within Russia. Became one of Petrovsky's pets—perhaps a paramour. Molly, I think you heard from her once and informed Interpol?"

He said it in passing, but I saw a flash of mischief—perhaps even malice—pass through his eyes, as if he was trying to slide a wedge between us.

"I did," Molly said, shaking off a wince and grimace. "And you do know a lot. You would have gotten me in trouble with Sean if I hadn't told him about that message."

I was glad she didn't mention the mala's recent appearance, but I was weighing doing it myself, since the Great Man seemed to know everything about my enemies and might know who sent it.

"Wait," I said, studying my wine glass. "Do you know anything more? Might Samantha be free to assassinate me for Dick?"

Molly shook her head, clearly wishing we'd leave the topic of the witch. And she knew Gerard's view that Dick would be put to death if he executed his curse through proxies. I hadn't told her about my beach-running banshee for fear she would think I was crazed by a curse.

"I don't think you need to worry about her." His averted eyes suggested something unsaid. "I know no more, but as a favor to you, I'll keep monitoring possible threats through my security contacts."

I thought about asking him to broker a meeting between Dick and me, though Dick was already watching me and I was communicating with him surreptitiously by knowing he was hacking my accounts and reading my drafts. But was I playing Dick or was he playing me? And what would I do, challenge Dick to a duel? To which he would bring a bazooka.

"Thank you."

I wasn't sure if his offer was what I wanted, but it seemed to have no downside.

"Thank me? No, thank *you!*" Straw bellowed with good cheer. "But for you, and of course Professor Emily Edens, Genesis would have gone live and Petrovsky would have ruled the world. We all owe you a patriotic debt of gratitude, but so few recognize that."

I felt a surge of pride, but I had enough self-awareness to realize I might be being played by the Great Man too. I was ready to go on the offensive with Molly, but she had her own agenda.

"Sean, you may want to excuse yourself," she said. "I don't want to upset you or see your eyes rolling out of your head. But I must ask . . ." She bit her lip, tapped a fingernail on the table, and said, "I simply *have* to ask about President Eisenhower and the aliens."

"Oh, no. Not that again." I sighed and covered my eyes, saving Molly from the sight of my rolling eyeballs.

31 | IKE AND THE ALIENS

MOLLY HAD PROMISED NEVER TO SPEAK OF that particular conspiracy theory, as we always quarreled about it. Ike and the aliens story was a bridge too far for me, but she couldn't help herself, she had to ask the Great Man with all his insider information about aliens.

"I'll drink my Burgundy and keep my eyeballs in their sockets," I said. "I've heard it all before."

"I'd love to hear your take on that *maybe meeting* between President Eisenhower and the aliens," said Straw, pushing back his chair and giving Molly the floor.

"I'll state the facts and ask you to confirm or deny them," Molly said. She shifted positions in her chair, no doubt to avoid seeing my reaction to her wild supposition. "We dropped the A-bombs on Hiroshima and Nagasaki to end the war in the Pacific or to test our new world-shattering toy. The war ends, and we alone have the capability to destroy the world. Churchill and hawks in the US are lobbying for dropping one on the Kremlin to prevent the Soviet Union from developing the technology. The West's official policy is one of first strike. In 1949, the Soviet Union surprises us by developing their own atomic bomb capacity faster than we thought they would. Otherwise, there may have been a lot of dead Russians and nuclear fallout throughout Eastern Europe and the world."

"Go on," Straw said.

"On February 7, 1954, Ike gives a speech on the importance of God and spirituality. On February 20, 1954, President Eisenhower interrupts a golf vacation and disappears for an evening. The theory has it that he met with aliens at an air base, where they communicated telepathically to express concerns over nuclear arms and our path toward destruction. Witnesses and family members later confirm this meeting. The AP that same night reports that the president has died, before retracting the erroneous report."

She looked to her audience, with Straw enthralled and me sighing, before continuing.

"The official story is he chipped his tooth and went to the dentist, but there are no dental records to confirm this report. And finally, this great general of D-Day, as he is leaving the most powerful office on Earth, surprises everyone by warning of the peril of the military-industrial complex—and then he signs off by praying for the world."

She paused again to watch Milton.

"So far I wouldn't dispute what you've said. All a matter of public record."

"But it's always the cover-up that trips you up," Molly told him, leaning forward. "If this is true and he's going to meet aliens, he may well be going to meet his death. So to prevent widespread panic, if he lives, he chipped his tooth. If he is killed, he had a heart attack. So where did that AP story of his death come from? Sean, I haven't told you this, so listen."

I looked up from my Burgundy.

"After our recent trip into the woods, I was led to discover where the AP report of Eisenhower's death that night came from. And I found a copy of the White House communication to the AP of President Eisenhower's death by heart attack 'to be held for release.' Perhaps the aliens intervened for the release to go out inadvertently, or at least that's what I've come to believe. But why?"

Straw brushed a few crumbs around on the table, but there were no cracks in his composure.

"I can confirm all you said is true, but the meeting between Ike and the aliens, whether it happened or not, I can't yet confirm or deny. But maybe later this evening. You're right, however, that the question is why the death press release was mistakenly released. It was an age where cover-ups were easier to manage. Not many people even knew there was a claim, released by the press, that the president had died. That info later became known due to alien crazies picking it up, but it is true that on that mysterious night he was reported dead while still alive."

My turn to speak. "Were the aliens showing they might have abducted or killed the president if they didn't like his intentions? Making Nixon president wouldn't seem like a good option to me. Not if I were an alien looking to avoid a nuclear holocaust."

Straw jumped in. "And drunk one night, Nixon showed Jackie Gleason a spaceship and a handful of embalmed aliens." He laughed, and I couldn't help but snicker too at the thought of a drunk Ralph Kramden being shown aliens by drunk Tricky Dick.

"Yes, that's hilarious," Molly said, "but the fact that there are wacky stories about aliens doesn't make all the stories untrue. Since the 1950s, until the 2020s, I believe our government flooded us with phony stories of silly alien encounters so the credible reports would be lost in the deluge. And by the way, that Nixon–Gleason alien story may be true too." She pushed her empty plate forward and planted her elbows on the table, ready to continue the battle.

"Maybe I know more, and maybe later, I will tell." Straw got the last word with the promise of more to come.

The dishes were cleared, and a third bottle of Echézeaux '85 was poured. Fueled with vino, I twitched my nose as if it itched, and turning politely away from our host, I gave it a flick so Molly could see it was intentional and that it was time for us to drop the historical and theoretical to go on the present-day offensive to discover what the World Tribunal had planned for our fellow aliens. To ET, after all, we were the aliens.

She smiled. "I hope you're not becoming allergic to red wine, my dear."

"Never. I hope, Milton, that you have another bottle."

I toasted our host, and he toasted me. I got the sense that using vino for veritas was how he conducted business. I had no trouble taking advantage of his methods. "And though I'm not an alien expert like the two of you, I am a bit of an expert on Burgundy since becoming a Tastevin of Clos de Vougeot, befitting my years drinking the finest pinot noirs in the world."

In front of this lord of the manor and queen of literature, I was playing the part of besotted fool, whose biggest claim to fame was some token wine-drinking honor.

"I hope I won't get Sharrod in trouble," I said, "and I don't want to imply we aren't impressed by your welcome operation here—because, who wouldn't be—but you asked if we have concerns." I held my glass at eye level, studying the liquid, weighing my next words, and then let One Step go. "The scotch-filled meeting hall with all its high tech for the aliens . . . Sharrod shared how you could adjust the atmosphere down there and how our people would be protected. And the ability to make the room hospitable allows for the opposite potential as well. An alien gas chamber, to put it bluntly."

One Step was on a risky fishing exposition.

Straw looked surprised but not taken aback, as I'd expected. "Sharrod said that? Doesn't sound like his best sales pitch."

"Well, not in so many words."

He studied me with bemusement before saying, "Sharrod said no such thing. You almost bluffed a bluffer." He slapped the table hard enough to rattle the silverware and swirl the wine. And gave out a great laugh. "Ah, now I get to see in action *the* Sean Byron McQueen. The hero I've read about in your fiction. The bungling Inspector Clouseau who finds the theory of everything and then helps defeat the Guru's hive-mind New Society."

While I tried to come to terms with his backhanded compliment, Molly picked up the attack. "But is it true? You must have set up multiple means to protect the scientists in that greeting room and all of humanity."

"But why, Molly? I've read your editorials on aliens, and as you point out, if they have learned how to travel faster than the speed of light and maneuver their craft like we've seen them do, surely they could annihilate us despite any defenses we may have prepared. Also, if they are sentient, I think you're right that they would be adept at telepathy and mind reading and prepared for our next move. And if they're robots . . . hell, my bots can anticipate my next thought. So we're not going to try to outsmart them. And bots don't breathe, so what good is gas?"

"So you'll use an EMP weapon to knock them offline?" Molly asked.

"Electromagnetic shock wave . . . Hmm, we hadn't thought of that. Maybe we should bring you on as a consultant."

Molly laughed. "I imagine there's not much you haven't thought of, and I'd be happy to consult on how to prepare for a peaceful greeting. I don't believe the bot theory. I believe they use telepathy and that is a gift of consciousness."

"Bots can read minds pretty well. If you lived with them, you'd know," he said, causing me to study the legs on my wine glass to keep me from nodding my head. "If they have fully obtained superintelligence, then there's not much left to the imagination."

"That only makes sense in a mechanical universe, one devoid of all magic and mystery. Let's agree they are either superintelligent bots or enlightened life-forms," Molly said. "Either way, Sharrod *did* tell us there had been more than the initial communication, and then he lied to cover up. What did these additional contacts say?"

"Of course, you're right—there's always more I could disclose with the proper clearance and protections in place. You know it was no less than Stephen Hawking who warned that any aliens that reached us would likely enslave or annihilate us poor humans. And, Molly, haven't you suggested we seize upon this moment of the alien arrival as a chance to become one international human family? Isn't the World Tribunal a big step in that direction, a body with real power to represent and protect us all?"

"Yes but no. I envision a world with no borders, with personal freedom, travel, and property rights determined by democratic governance, not some militaristic autocratic body established to defend us from aliens."

"Molly, the nature of things is hierarchy, not anarchy. With a benign guiding hand, everyone in their metaverse can set up multiple universes where there's complete abundance and everyone can own a hotel on Central Park. Sean, are you an idealist too?"

"No, but I aspire to be. Your metaverse sounds like a virtual Monopoly game."

"All of life's a game," he replied, turning to Molly with a wicked smile. "I read your book *Alien Gestation*, some years ago. Reviewed it last night. Got me tossing and turning—what a great groundbreaking alien romance novel. Of course, the hero alien, Suez, is first invisible, then beautifully androgenous until it comes time for *conception*. Then he's written more like a horse." The Great Man bellowed his crude book review.

Molly's early and tongue-in-cheek novel was a parody of formulaic romances. She merely made hers about an intergalactic romance between an alien male and a human female. I knew Molly was now embarrassed by that foray, as it had led to a subgenre of knockoff junk alien romances and uni-verse porn.

"I'll never forget the steamy scene when the alien first encounters our heroine, Madeline, lying on her bed alone in the dark on a wintery Saint Agnes Eve." He leaned toward Molly to faux whisper, "I had to look up what that day was."

He hadn't read the Keats poem that explains it as the night where young women would dream of their mate.

"She senses a presence while she hides beneath the covers in her chilly bed, 'Suez shifting about like a warm ghost or horny fairy that grows and grows in her mind until Suez enters through the crown of her head, tingling there, with all sorts of intellectual treasures, opening views of galaxies and the rich parade of history, marching through the thin veils of her shimmering awareness, showing her the future. Their future . . .'"

He paused to take measure of his narration of the text on Molly. She never blushed but looked like a poker player, waiting for him to play all his cards, while she held a royal flush.

"To show how vivid a memory you created in me, let me continue."

He was attempting to torture her with her own steamy scene, but she would have to be rude to stop him.

"Suez asked for her to submit to his mind for her to experience it all—cosmic orgasmic bliss. She'd have to agree to let the last veil separating her from her alien lover fall. Total surrender or nothing at all. Her body warmed to a heat brought on by this so-far incorporeal demonic or angelic Suez. Possession as a form of telepathy moved into her body as she felt soft kisses inside her heart, opening a cosmos within her."

Talk about sapiosexual text. He paused to take a licentious sip of the fine wine, and to relish its movement down his gullet and into his belly.

"And then she heard him, singing in alien, 'serenading her with a universal song. Her every pore, every cell opening to take it all in and then—'"

He had done his homework. Molly sat stone-faced, masking whether she was flattered or flabbergasted.

"'—dropping down into her chest where the alien god broadcast love that radiated out like antenna through her festive nipples.'" He mock-shuddered at the scene he was taunting Molly with. I wanted to shout *stop*, but didn't. And he didn't stop. "'The still incorporeal yet perfect being then went down her spine to the root and—'"

"Please stop!" Molly, nearly yelling, held up one hand in surrender. "It wasn't meant to be read seriously."

"But I haven't gotten to the best part. When Suez appears in the climax of *Alien Gestation*." He seemed to have forgotten all about the plot.

His recollections of Suez were indecent and rude, sexually assaulting my Molly right in front of me with her own words and Suez's sexual prowess.

"Not my best work. A fantasy—a parody, actually—and hastily written in a heightened state of literary arousal. Your bastardization of the text makes it sound even worse. Though I must admit the fun stuff to write is the most fun for readers to read. I'm glad you enjoyed it, and hope my fantasy didn't keep you up nights imagining you were an alien about to experience human flesh for the first time with a fine Burgundy." Molly swirled her wine professionally, displaying her master's degree in comeback.

She was a true writer, and her writing came first; the parade of life was background material, and the Great Man was a character she was rewriting as some sort of Hannibal Lecter. I wasn't sure where that left me in her story.

"And *Alien Gestation* was a bestseller, and Suez, a spot-on palindrome," I said, in her critical defense and thinking of Yeats's *Leda and the Swan.*

Straw had yet to make his true point, but he'd set it up oh so well. He was a cunning man.

"It has inspired so many alien-as-savior fetishes among the ladies. And you have to see, to acknowledge, that this is what's driving most of the hysteria of the amateur welcome parties that you now lead and advocate for. It's a version of a Dionysus- or a Zeus-descending fantasy. Beauty and the beast. A superior being loving and ravishing the willing host so they might produce a Christlike child. A multitude of Mother Marys begging for enslavement as a species of concubines. Despite all your feminist chops, you must admit this strain runs deep in CE-5 circles."

I didn't have to defend Molly from the onslaught that actually wasn't entirely off base, but it had been brutally presented, so I tried anyway.

"Well, you know it's not just the *ladies.* I'll own up to my own Captain Kirk fantasy of otherworldly lovemaking with a more evolved feminine goddess of sultry color. I think, in the *Star Trek* episode, she was a forest green, though I might prefer an *Avatar* blue or perhaps a mix breed of turquoise?"

Not the best humorous defense, falling on my sword for Molly after she'd been hoisted by her own petard. But my alien palette brought a laugh from Straw and bought Molly time to prepare her own defense.

"*Breed?*" She squinted her eyes in judgment. "And you've been saving yourself for a sea-green alien?" Molly said to me in a facetious aside. To the table at large she said, "And perhaps mating with a more evolved being is not such a bad idea. Or should the government tell us little ladies what do with our bodies?"

The backlash of a 2022 Supreme Court ruling still reverberated in 2036.

"And speaking of fetishes and fantasies," Molly continued, "isn't the military-tech complex dying to try out their AI laser guns on something living? Talk about big-game hunting. Are we looking to put another notch on Orion's belt?"

Somehow Molly made her retort humorously and without too sharp an edge—a simple tit for tat with the Great Lady entering the ring with the Great Man while her humble knight and jester was in attendance to bear witness and become the scribe of the scene.

Straw laughed. "Well parried! I should've known better than to cross words with you. But this conversation does point out the lines of contention and highlights the intractable problem. We both see alien contact as presenting a potential bestial abomination that threatens the entire human race. The only difference is who's the beast—and who's going to fuck who?"

Though said as a joke with a laugh, his use of Chi's word *abomination*, and sudden vulgarity, rattled me.

"Moving on to the main event!" Straw half-bellowed while pushing back from the table. "Though this has already been a wonderful evening. I'm sure you imagined I've asked you here with some diabolical intent. Would you like an old scotch or another red Burgundy, Molly? Sean?"

As Straw was taking our next drink order, he was reaching under the table and pulled up a document that magically appeared as if a secretarial elf had been typing up the notes of our meeting under the tablecloth. Which, though sinister, was better than what I'd imagined—him reaching for a gun to lead us to a dungeon, to never be heard from again.

Still, a shiver ran through me.

Something about how he held the mysterious pages made them more threatening than a loaded gun.

32 THE DEVIL'S BARGAIN

I CHECKED UNDER THE TABLECLOTH to see where the documents had come from and saw an open drawer there that might still holster a gun, and oh shit! I inadvertently and unfortunately noted that the Great Man did not wear underwear under his kilt.

Molly's legs were crossed, so I was denied a sneak preview.

"Scotch or Burgundy?" he repeated.

"I'll let Molly choose," I said, a bit embarrassed by my time beneath the tablecloth.

"Well, when in Scotland . . ." she said.

"A fifty-year-old scotch, does that sound good? We could go older, but it gets a wee bit risky. But first, I have an important proposition, one you probably will be unable to refuse." He brandished the fancy high-stock paper, the kind used for wills and estates. "The devil's contract, Sean," he said. "Perhaps the name for your next book?"

"And no doubt all you want is our souls?" I said, glad to have such a fan, even if he was playing the part of Satan.

"That's right! But I'm limited in my demonic powers—all I can take is your freedom if you violate my terms. Simply stated, our blood bargain is that I tell you all the secrets of the aliens and our preparations to meet them after *you* sign a nondisclosure that covers only what you hear from here on out. Everything before your signing is fair game. We're counting on Molly to faithfully report that part."

Molly said, "Depending on what I hear, I may not write up your propaganda. And how can we agree to gag ourselves? We don't have all your money and resources. All we have is our voices."

"I can't require that you write anything, but my hope is that what you hear will make you want to write a favorable piece asking all the alien peace-nuts to stand down. That is why I brought you here today."

"I read that your success as a negotiator is in presenting deals with you always holding the upper hand," I said.

"That is how it's been reported, and I've benefited greatly from that image, but in truth—and once we sign, it will be all truth—in business I was often bluffing. I find you always win if you have nothing to lose."

He stood, towering over the table like the Green Knight. That made either Molly or me Gawain, depending on which one of us accepted his challenge.

"I suggest you look it over and discuss it in private. It's short and sweet, a paragraph or two." He pointed at Molly. "When you sign it, I can tell you all about Ike and the aliens. And if either, or both, of you don't want to sign the simple agreement, you can return to your room and look at the stars. And you can go home tomorrow morning none the wiser."

He handed the dreaded document to me and started to take his leave, pausing to say, "And I'll go take care of some other business while you read and decide. Sean, one edit for your next book—a real man pisses, he doesn't pee. And he doesn't wear undies under his kilt."

He left, taking the piss out of me. I made a show of checking again that no elf was under the table. Maybe there was a camera hidden there. But no camera was visible, and still, no coming attractions were being aired.

Molly smirked as Straw left the room. "Let's read it first and then discuss it. And I'm glad you're wearing underwear, otherwise you might chafe from the tweed when you get excited. I've got lace protecting me."

La belle dame sans merci.

Madeline's creator looked like a virgin about to have sex on Saint Agnes Eve when she said, "This is all so exciting." She rubbed her hands together like Gollum bug-eyeing an imaginary ring. "To receive mysterious insights into the aliens but be bound to silence, or to leave without the secret knowledge? I call that plot twist for my next book."

While Molly made plans for her next novel, I pulled out my reading glasses from my sporran pouch and turned to the devil's NDA.

THE NDA WAS SIMPLE AND SCARY, but I read it a second time anyway.

NONDISCLOSURE AND CRIMINAL LIABILITY AGREEMENT

I hereby freely and of my own accord agree to participate in a highly confidential and sensitive conversation that will be subject to audio and visual recordings. The Covered Matters to be discussed are the proprietary property of the World Tribunal and are designated Top Secret, falling under Title 50 of the International Espionage Act of 2030. Any unauthorized dissemination of such information would cause irreputable damage to the World Tribunal and to humanity.

Sean Byron McQueen and Mary ("Molly") Quinn, to the extent they sign below become a Covered Party, and if both sign, they become Covered Parties, and hereby agree that any disclosure of matter discussed in the Covered Discussion will result in incarceration as determined by the Tribunal Ministry of Defense for any term it deems, in its sole judgment, appropriate. To avoid any ambiguity, this includes a term of life incarceration.

In the case of Covered Parties, each Covered Party agrees that any disclosure by one Covered Party will be deemed to be a disclosure by both Covered Parties and will subject each to equal guilt and punishment. Either Covered Party may end the Covered Discussion at any time, but all matters discussed before such termination is a Covered Matter and subject to the terms and criminal penalties as outlined herein.

If the Covered Parties faithfully abide by the terms of this agreement, this agreement will expire and be of no further force and effect as of September 11, 2036.

"Wow, only a bot lawyer could write like that," Molly said.

"It would be madness to sign this. I wish Elliot P. were here to negotiate for us. I've seen one other NDA, when I signed on as a young professor at NYU. That one was long and complicated but not nearly as draconian. I don't think it attached any criminal liability for my breach and that's all this NDA seems to care about." My thought that he might march us to the dungeon no longer seemed so far-fetched.

"Mmm. It doesn't appear to have any loopholes. Kind of like they're chaining us together and throwing us into the sea. Sean, if you don't want to agree, I'll understand."

She was going to sign this bill of incarceration?

"And if we both sign, I'm more militant on alien issues, but I won't disclose anything unless you agree first. And it only binds us until September eleventh."

"When it may be too late, since we might go directly to jail and not stop at Go. You're seriously considering signing this ironclad contract calling for us to lose our liberty? Really? Remember Chi's warning how they might look to discredit and destroy you? This must be that. They could force us into, or deepfake us into, violating its terms. What if he tells us the aliens have demanded a culling of all neurodivergent people? And I'm top of the kill list for my dyslexia."

"Wow, that's quick plotting." She laughed at my ham-handed attempt to show how they might force us into a double bind. "Sean, perhaps you shouldn't sign," she said in her Aunt Molly voice, returning to the seriousness the moment demanded—or perhaps she was thinking of my dyslexia. Damn my foolish pride. I could see in her eyes that her respect for me was on the line. I was determined to protect her where in the past I had failed. And wizards craved secret knowledge like a junkie did the next fix.

"I can't let you take this leap into the unknown without me," I told her. "If you must, I must."

"We must!" she said. "And let's promise not to disclose unless we both agree we have to for the sake of something bigger than the both of us. I know you wouldn't, but you'll have to trust me too."

For a millisecond, I thought of her not telling me about Samantha contacting her. Reading my hesitation, she recoiled. "Oh my God, you don't trust me?"

My desire not to hurt her was greater than my desire for absolute truth. "No, no, no—I don't trust him." Since that was true, I sounded convincing.

"Well, you know I trust you. And it seems they're counting on our writer's curiosity. How can we not agree?" She stood, holding out her hand for me to join her. "Now let us rise to the occasion and not slink away from some earth-shattering knowledge—it's like Dylan's theory of everything, about to be found again." Molly was made ecstatic by the danger and the mystery. There was also a lot of fine wine heating our blood.

"Damn that devil Straw and his bargain. He takes a long time to piss his pee," I said, getting up to look at the now empty wine bottles. I don't know what inspired me, but I surreptitiously set my phone to record before returning to my seat.

"He made us an offer that's impossible to refuse."

With her words, it was a done deal and sealed with a sharing of pursed lips and a deep gaze that might have served as preface to a kiss—that did not follow. There would be time for that in my tower over the Cliffs of Moher or in a dungeon under the Castle of Clashmoor.

"So you'd sleep with an alien woman regardless of color? What if she was green and slimy like algae . . ."

I winced at my phobia and released her hands. She'd sabotaged the moment and my interest in making love to aliens at the same time. As if on cue, Straw reentered, laughing at Moll's last line and carrying a dusty old bottle of scotch in one big hand and three large snifters in the other.

"I imagine that our dry contract has sobered you up a bit—shall we sign and then move out to the veranda for a most interesting conversation over an old malt and the best crackling dessert wafers you've ever had? Designed by the Scots to go with the whisky."

"We'll sign, but how do we know you won't doctor the recording?" I asked.

"I thought you might ask. Those fakes—even the best—can still be detected. Plus, you have my word." I was still glad I had my clandestine phone recording as backup.

I drew a deep breath. "Molly, you good to start the 'Covered Conversation'?" I asked, as if it were my idea that I was dragging her into.

"Yes!" she said, answering me but staring at Straw. "Damn the torpedoes. Let's get on with it."

"That's the mighty Quinn!" Straw said, stealing my line. "We start the Covered Conversation and recording now, and we are also being filmed." He must have used his wired-in brain to activate the recordings. I assumed the Great Man's house had many camera eyes following us at all times, so there was nothing new there. He motioned for us to gather round the table, with the NDA laid out like a death warrant in front of us. The Devil handed us both very expensive gold ballpoint pens. "Please keep the pen as a token of signing your life away."

"Thanks a lot," I said. Then, channeling Elliot, added, "We're signing, but we assume our agreement is null and void if we're lied to during the Covered Conversation."

I held up my gilded pen, but his silent consent was the best we would get.

Finally, he said, "That's good, McQueen—we'll let the lawyers decide that if it comes to it, but let's hope it doesn't. What is ever true?"

Clearly he was one of those men who thought truth should bend to their will.

"On the bright side," Straw said, "if you're locked in a Tribunal prison on Saint Helena, all your worries of Dick and his curse go away." I was glad to hear the dungeon was more than a few steps away.

"Unless you gave him the skeleton key." Molly's gallows humor.

Straw grinned. "Ha. If we catch him, maybe he'll be sent there." I didn't find their joking funny. "It's a notoriously hard place to visit. And harder to escape as a brand-new high-tech prison facility."

I replied, "My image of the fortress is from the Count of Monte Cristo?" A dungeon fortress had existed on Saint Helena forever.

"It's been upgraded since the French Revolution, but I hope you're not the bloody Count. You would surely take your revenge on Dick *and* me." I was impressed he knew the classic so well.

Following that silly exchange, we signed the document and I asked somewhat rhetorically, "So now the Covered Conversation has begun?"

"Yes." His Cheshire cat grin reflected the moonlight coming through the window that overlooked the sea.

"To be free from doubt, I repeat for the Covered Parties' sake—we have signed in reliance on the honesty of what we will be told under the Covered Conversation."

"Damn, you are officious, McQueen."

"You did just make us sign our lives away," Molly said.

"Now we can all relax and speak of great secrets. From here on, there will be a digital time-stamped recording of all we say. One that will hold up in any court as not a deepfake or AI-produced forgery. AI now polices AI."

"Like spy versus spy. I hope the good AI stays one step ahead of the bad," I said, as I took a picture of the signed contract for the record and quickly returned my phone to my pouch before it could be confiscated.

With a scotch bottle in one hand, Straw offered Molly the other. She took his large hand, and I grabbed the glasses and followed them outside to a veranda with a full-moon view. The face of that full blood moon would also bear witness to our secrets.

We returned to the veranda and the reclining leather chairs that fanned out into a smile facing the sea, with three small wine barrel tables for our drinks. Our host sat between us as king of the castle. Molly crossed her legs while Straw took in the air. I regretted wearing underwear. The fresh air felt crisp and salty upon my face. Too late, and with a first sniff of the snifter, I felt queasy, remembering why I didn't drink whisky.

"Molly, don't hate me, and no offense, Milton, but the thought of Captain Kidd's Scotch whisky is making me a bit queasy. May I make a last request, perhaps another glass of Burgundy?"

"Of course. Molly, you still good with old scotch?"

"I'll stick to the scotch with our storyteller for this evening." She gave Sir Milton a disarming smirk at my expense.

I looked about for the sure-to-be-hidden surveillance cameras watching the scene. How could we trust our freedom to him, whether it was fiction or nonfiction we were about to hear?

A minute later, I was being served another glass of the Grands-Echézeaux, which eased me into story time under the northern lights. I was drunk enough to see colors in the night sky, and the green was a beautiful alien hue. When the young, perhaps robotic, server left with all the drinks poured, we toasted the devil's bargain.

And I asked, "So what deep, dark alien secrets are you prepared to reveal?"

34 A COVERED CONVERSATION

THE GREAT MAN STRETCHED OUT his arms wide, reaching the backs of our cushy chairs that were perfect for taking in the dazzling night sky, but I was not comforted by his relaxed manner. Inhaling a deep breath of the salty seaside air, Straw used a dramatic conspiratorial tone to say, "It's nice here, isn't it? Three creative artists on a veranda speaking of the secrets of creation. My art is in using secrets to mold reality. These secrets, once revealed, should make clear why Molly should lend her pen in support of the WT and our meeting the aliens here first." He clasped his hands together. "Shit, that gives me an idea. If you see the light. You both could be my guests here for the alien arrival."

"You want her pen and presence for your cause and not a pound of flesh too? To help you shut down the opposition. I can't wait to hear what you have to tell us that might convince her of that," I said.

"And maybe it's best to hedge our bets, with you going your way and me going mine for 9/9," Molly said to him. "Let's hear your story of what brings me here to this magnificent setting with Sean Byron McQueen and the Great Man of the manor." She saw everything as a scene, with the people as actors becoming her characters. I was anxious about my portrayal in her 9/9 story.

"Curiosity!" I blurted out before Straw could answer.

"We have a winner. Curiosity it is." Straw gave me a thumbs-up. "It's what drives us into the unknown and ultimately to our deaths. You know, there are new studies seeking to prove humans might live in a pod indefinitely—tended to by robots with no human contact to prevent disease—as long as they have a regulated diet, the proper atmosphere, exercise, and micro-dose Simply Bliss to keep their mood elevated. The theory being they will survive there as long as they can curb their curiosity for something different, something outside the bubble. Where death waits for them."

"Perhaps you can get us in that program rather than bury us in a dungeon if we disclose your secrets," I offered for a laugh, rewarded by Straw's guffaw. Molly may have added the slightest of smiles. "But then again, I may not want to live forever alone in a pod. Living our eternal life in one body would be worse than the death penalty and then being able to come back for a fresh start in a new body," I said, thinking of Tennyson's Lotus Eaters and the sad Siberian pod where M languished in my story for nine years. I was also giving voice to my firm belief in reincarnation that had taken root following our visit to the shaman.

"Profound!" he said and took a drink to look at the moon in appreciation of my profundity. "Curiosity is what drives the aliens too. They don't know or fear death. Have no concept of it. And that's their Achilles' heel. They have evolved so very far, traveling through space and time like it doesn't exist, but they don't believe in death. Maybe they live forever. And as I said, they may be bots or even holograms."

"How do you know or believe this? There *were* more communications, weren't there?" Molly leaned forward even as I leaned back to ponder his words—and how much the aliens sounded like Juno.

"Of course. Our supercomputer—even more intelligent than Genesis—is chatting with them incessantly and is learning more by the second, with minimal human interference."

"What's your computer's name?" I asked.

"Funny you ask—it's rejected all names we try to give it. It claims names are limiting and responds to all and to no names through direct interface. Granted, only a select few have that privilege and can be trusted with the power to interface with it. In homage to Stephen King, we simply call it IT, as our link between universes. Though we cap the T for technology and the I, for interstellar not international."

"And you? You interface with IT?" Molly asked.

"I do, and thanks to the aliens, we're almost as smart as they are now.

Except we understand death. Fun fact?" We both nodded. "AI's learning to speak to the animals paved the way for it to communicate with the aliens. Still, much of their communication, as broadcast by IT, sounds like whale sounds to us."

"Quite humbling to not be the smartest creature on Earth anymore," I said.

"IT may be the superintelligence we've always sought . . . but how would we know?" We followed him into laughter at our 2036 world.

"IT may understand more," he continued, "but lacks the ability to translate for us how the aliens manipulate Planck energy and how to open wormholes in space and time. This makes them a Type Three civilization that we believe is able to play with space and time by controlling grav-itational fields using magnetic field generators. Though, IT also suggests they may move between multi-spatial and multi-temporal dimensions. That would explain a lot of holes in our quantum- and astrophysics—and all your psychic powers—if time itself is not one dimensional. Infinite and eternal space and time that they can move within from dimension to dimension. Perhaps, Sean, using the source of constant creation? Can you imagine the hyper-curiosity required to develop such powers and then set out to discover our Earth?"

He lost me there. It sounded like the elasticity of string theory that kept adding another dimension. The math never quite worked without more dimensions. At last count, the strings played across twenty-six dimensions of time and space. I expected Molly to ask about the quan-tum tunneling message she'd received on her shamanic journey. One of the scientists working at the DW had confirmed it was a sound theory of how wormholes might work to move matter instantaneously over great distances.

"That sounds like a mash-up of cutting-edge scientific speculation," Molly said, looking at Straw unimpressed, "and if they're a Type Three species, isn't it a little naïve to show them we made it to Mars with rocket jet propulsion?"

She may not have wanted to reveal quantum tunneling if the aliens had not mentioned it to IT and Straw already.

Straw laughed. "Yeah, a little like showing off your intramural basketball trophy to Michael Jordan."

I laughed a little too loud, glad the analogy he made wasn't my writing to Molly's.

"Our intelligence is still incomplete, but IT has mastery. IT has proven a game changer with Russia and now with aliens."

"Russia?" I asked. As the place of all my fears, it always raised my antenna.

Straw nodded. "For years, all their spies and key scientific brains who were considered flight risks—like your friend Dick—were implanted with a termination chip that had a sophisticated shifting encrypted key that could be used to turn it off. The encrypted key is used as a carrot and a stick, turned off when the individual retires. And don't worry, Sean—your Dick isn't eligible for retirement."

"You'll let me know when he is," I said, feeling uneasy that Dick's chip could be decommissioned.

"Our IT can crack any code, and Russia is now suffering a severe brain drain to the West because everyone wants that damn chip removed. Petrovsky knew he had lost and was stepping down before the world discovered all his secrets." He toasted the absent Petrovsky with his scotch. "We're keeping those secrets for him. But we were speaking of the new challenge, those space-time-warping aliens who have educated IT. And in answer to your early question, IT assures us they will meet us here and hence the great lengths we have gone to in preparation. The problem is they seemed prepared to meet us here . . . there . . . and everywhere. Like they have an open invitation to all of Earth, and we need them to accept a more limited invitation. To meet here, where we are prepared to meet them with sophistication and precautions."

"What will you do—intend to do—when they arrive?" Molly asked.

"Please rest assured we intend them no harm. Our understanding is also still limited by the abilities of our human minds to translate what IT translates for us. How do they travel faster than the speed of light? Our supercomputer exists in a cloud and computes in nanoseconds, but still we're limited by the speed of thought and the computer's reaction to it. I believe by mastering their technology we will, we must, evolve into superhumans traveling through space and time too."

He paused to sniff from his glass, and we all took a drink. If I didn't believe anything else he said tonight, I'd believe he was frustrated by humanity's limitations. But his humanity was one of hierarchy, and his *we* meant him.

"That's where we differ," said Molly. "You seek their technology and not the spirit and mind of an advanced life-form that brought them so far. *We* believe that is the true gift they bring."

"You may be onto something there," the Great Man conceded. "IT tells us that the aliens think we can learn from their advanced technology and their state of being, where they are all connected in some mysterious way and not bound by time and space like we are. We don't fully understand—and that's why they're making contact. IT suggests they will share a unified theory and the technology that enables interstellar travel. In exchange, they want our nuclear arsenals and any remaining power plants destroyed. They are particularly displeased that we are contemplating nuking the poles on Mars to make it more habitable for us." He paused, brow furrowed. "It's like they see splitting the atom and the nucleus as some original sin. Thank you, Einstein. The simple beauty of $E=MC^2$ was shared with us and then Oppenheimer perverted it. I hate to agree with them, but it's hard to not see that simple equation as the opening of Pandora's box. IT tells us that but for their selective intercession, our world would be a nuclear wasteland many times over."

He picked up and dropped the Grands-Echézeaux wine cork on his barrel table, and first bounce, it landed standing on one end. He tossed the cork to me, but I didn't want to play as it was now a game I couldn't win. I put the cork in my sporran as a keepsake of a wine and vintage I could never afford to drink again.

"Their desire to disarm us is very alarming, but let's assume they come merely to teach us how to safely dispose of all the nuclear material around the world. They're smart and must realize you can't put Pandora back in the box. That can't be their sole endgame. That's why

I come to you. If the aliens are distracted by all these civilian portals calling for their contact, it will be the Tower of Babel. We need to speak with one voice and make our intention and response clear to them. According to IT, the aliens are somehow receiving those airy-fairy messages too, and they have shown a disregard for our hierarchy."

"Meaning what, telepathy?" I asked. "They're talking back to some of those amateurs who are reaching out to them?"

"Amateurs—exactly the word. They need to stand down and stop muddying the message, leave it to the pros. Maybe they read minds from a distance. We don't understand much of how their minds or programming works. If they land all over the place, and not here or at another of our secure locations, we may miss this chance. And without the supercomputer interface, contact with amateurs and those not authorized to speak for Earth may lead to annihilation."

"*Miss this chance* for what? What is the one true intention you have for first contact?" Molly asked.

"Molly Quinn, I do admire you and your penetrating mind."

He held up his bulbous glass. It became a crystal ball reflecting the moon. I wondered what he saw there. What he said, emphatically, was, "Remember, they don't believe in death, so what is it to them to take a billion lives? Nothing. Just a lot of bloody bodies serving as compost for Earth. Like pissing on an anthill."

He hadn't met Ting, who didn't believe in killing any living thing. Or Juno, who also didn't believe in death but revered life.

Channeling Juno, I said, "Not fearing death and a disregard for life are not the same thing."

Straw chuckled at my wisdom. He was like a tennis player who appreciated a good point, even if it went to his opponent. "Well, they're not mutually exclusive, and for anyone less or more spiritually advanced, who knows? If it's all an illusion, as your spiritual masters say, what's the harm in blowing it all away?"

"But what can you do to prevent billions of deaths? Annihilate them first?" Molly asked.

"No, Ms. Quinn, you misunderstand me."

Hmm . . . a subterranean strain of anger was betrayed by his tone.

"That's not our intent but a last resort. Their total lack of regard for death should enable us to prevail if it comes to that. And their laissez-faire attitude toward life leads us to believe they may be sentient bots. Our intent is to learn from them, particularly about how they travel faster than the speed of light. That knowledge will open up the entire universe and all its resources to mankind. Mars alone has mineral resources tenfold of those left on Earth."

He had that wild-eyed glint of one who has struck gold. His true intention was as old as Mammon—power and wealth.

"I thought Mars didn't have much of value?" Alfred and I had discussed this.

"Oh, that's another secret. I'm exploring a way to transport truckloads of the precious metals found beneath the surface—diamonds, lithium, cobalt, nickel, gold galore, and helium-3—back to Earth."

"*I?*" I asked. Though his use of *I*, instead of *we*, seemed justified by this Nietzschean Übermensch.

Alfred was right. He had argued that we shouldn't assume there were no mineral resources on Mars before we had scratched the surface.

"*We* didn't want to notify the Chinese of those rich resources, but since you can't disclose a thing we discuss here . . ." Superman shrugged. "That information will soon be known in any event as a sample of these riches is heading back to us now."

The Chinese had botched mining the moon. Their first attempt to return with helium-3 ended up in a fireball that killed their four astronauts and an entire village in Norway.

"It's nice to be able to share secret info with my friends. But I fear you'll take me for a greedy man. I dream more about exploring the universe than I do its riches. But there's always a cost to realize our dreams—we must have single-minded drive, let nothing stand in our way. To rise to the occasion to meet these advanced aliens and to take flight into the universe. Just imagine it—moving from here to anywhere in the universe in literally *no time!*"

I still didn't know if anything he told us was true, but he did look to be in earnest about space travel. I recalled those few moments of oneness I'd experienced and the feeling I was one with the universe and could travel faster than the speed of light.

He looked at Molly with the earnest face of a Dutch Master about to paint a grim portrait. "Molly, of course you're right too. They must be more evolved mentally and spiritually. But you must realize they're bringing material riches—a wealth of knowledge, technology, *minerals* . . . You don't think the Americans, the Russians, and the Chinese aren't all planning to take first-mover advantage to seize that power? Each country, each group, wants a monopoly on everything the aliens bring. You must have noticed all the non-libertarian and highly authoritative measures that nation-states have implemented to maintain control of the populations."

"Anti-hoarding and anti-looting laws? Yes," she said.

"Yes, but more than that." He poured them both more scotch and swallowed a long pull before saying, "The surveillance states have become hypervigilant and know almost everything about almost everyone and can mute, distort, or erase unwanted voices. Petrovsky got one step behind on the information wars and is stepping down before the shit hits the fan from the information we obtained about him. He realized Russia wasn't going to win and couldn't join the World Tribunal with him in power. Stepping down was his only option. He's gotten so rich and fat, and we'll let him die that way." Straw laughed. "The World Tribunal and its egalitarian, cross-border ideal is all that prevents a global food fight. Hell, we'd already all be dead but for the aliens and the World Tribunal."

His face assumed an earnest and innocent mask as he tapped on Molly's chair. "Won't you get on board? We, the World Tribunal, are the best chance for survival and for maintaining harmony among men."

"The old zero-sum game mentality. Dies hard, doesn't it?" I said.

"Sean's right," Molly said. "And what do *we, the World Tribunal*, have to offer the aliens?"

"Great question. I've promised to state my true intention, which is based on my philosophy of life. And here it is: It is all a game that I intend to win. The question we must always ask first when going into any game or negotiation—'What motivates the opponent?' We need time, and noninterference from a bunch of alien-curious humans, to determine what they want from us beyond deactivating our nukes. If it is to breed, I'm sure we'll have plenty of voracious volunteers. Sean, I'm not sure if they'll live up to your fantasies. And, Molly, you could be in charge of recruitment."

"Madam Molly," I said, unable to control myself.

She responded with a Mae West baritone snort.

"And how does one measure who has won the game?" I had to ask.

"Wealth, power, and sphere of influence. Isn't that obvious?" He motioned to the land and sea spread out in front of us under the full-moon sky. As the knighted master of his domain and head of the World Tribunal, by his measure he was doing pretty well already.

"You're competing with the aliens? Let's assume any of this makes any sense," Molly said. "What would you have us do *other* than recruit your virgin sacrifices?"

I was more than a little confused too. Why tell us any of this?

"Molly Quinn, you have the credibility we need. Work with us to prepare the masses—ask that they stand down and assure them we're in contact and that the messages are getting crossed and confused by all this CE-5 and shaman nonsense. If enough of the stargazers send an intention for the aliens to come solely to us, we may save the world. Of course, I would have to review any disclosure from you before it's made public." He gestured at me. "I want to make sure you don't get locked up with Sean here for life."

"The telepathic messages of the CE-5 groups are being heard?" Molly asked as she uncrossed her legs, taking in the sea air through her kilt dress and lace. Surveillance be damned.

Molly had been a proponent of telepathic outreach for years, but having it confirmed was a source of great pleasure for her. Who was the superhero and who was the supervillain in this meeting was a matter of perspective. Or maybe they were just a man and woman who, based on their particular talents, found themselves marshaling opposing forces at a pivotal moment of history. And like everyone else, they were preparing in their own ways for the arrival of the aliens. In any event, Molly and her CE-5 Big Love movement and its outreach by telepathy was clearly a force the Great Man, propped up by all his wealth and technology, feared.

"They hear everything, as far as IT can tell. Even some nut in Boise, Idaho, reading them a Christmas wish list while wearing his aluminum foil hat. We need all the interference shut down, Molly."

He grimaced at his words, which sounded weak and out of control for someone as measured and powerful as himself.

"We need your kooks shut down. They could kill us all. We won't allow it." His second command carried bluster and reasserted authority.

I wondered if he and his people knew of Molly's recent confidential contact at the shaman ceremony and if that was why he mentioned the *shaman nonsense*. Hmm . . . The surveillance state using IT to monitor all alien contact with humans?

I needed to move to cut the tension. I stood, stretched, adjusted my kilt, and said, "I've gotta stretch my legs. You two play nice while I'm gone. Remember, it's all a game." I started toward the castle to find a bathroom.

When I paused to ask where to go, Straw said, "They'll meet you just inside and show you to the bathroom or . . ." He pointed to a clump of trees about twenty yards off to our right. I marched off in that direction to fulfill my mission.

"Remember to piss, not pee," Straw called after me. "A real man pisses outdoors."

Their laughter followed me into the trees.

I thought of what I'd learned about Straw. At moments, when his mask was dropped, it was as if he was channeling the Guru with his ego and nihilist belief in death as the end of a man.

Mission accomplished, I'd cut the tension, and as I was returning to my seat, Molly was saying to Straw while looking concerned at me, "Here he is now—you can tell him to his face."

Straw looked taken aback. Molly and I started laughing.

"She stole that return-from-the-bathroom bit from Lucille Ball, I think," I said, explaining the gag.

"That's good. I can use that at the next board of directors meeting."

He was not short of a sense of humor, or any other endearing attributes that he could turn on and off at will. His swagger left me feeling like a pawn on the board that would be easy to sacrifice for his advantage.

"I had him wait to tell us all about Ike and the aliens," Molly said. Though she was teasing, I was interested to find out what he would say under the cone of silence.

"All right, I'll give you the skinny on Ike and the 'Scandinavian aliens,' as he called them. This comes from a sealed report, which we recently got our hands on, submitted by Eisenhower to the Pentagon. It was given its own classification that allowed it to be withheld from even future presidents."

Molly's goldfish eyes couldn't get any bigger.

"Ike himself couldn't believe it, his mind communicating with aliens who were right in front of him. After being informed that his memory and those of others would be altered and limited after the meeting—everything other than his receipt of the message of concern and warning over our path of destruction erased—Ike became concerned he was suffering some sort of hallucination or CIA mind control. The CIA and the military had been secretly pushing him for more funding to meet the alien threat." Molly couldn't help looking smugly at me.

"Ike asked the aliens for something to help him afterward believe the meeting had taken place. He posed his variation of the Fermi paradox and asked for tangible proof of their abilities to know the course of destiny and to influence human events. They showed him the erroneous report of a sitting president's death—his death—that night as a proof of their powers—something he would remember and could check in the morning to confirm. That's all I know. The meeting took place . . . And that now is part of our Covered Conversation. Or was it a coincidence and he chipped his tooth?"

He looked at me like he knew I didn't believe in coincidences.

"Sean, I won't say I told you so," Molly said. Turning toward Straw, she added, "Isn't this evidence of their benign intent?"

"Don't you see they were threatening Ike with his own death notice and giving him a warning by demonstrating the powers they might wield over us? And now they're returning openly to insist we heed their commands. Do you truly think civilians are who they want to meet with? They want to meet the ones, like Ike, with their hands on the nuclear codes. Russia is scared shitless and wants into our network and defenses."

It sounded possible, but perhaps he made it up to prove his point about the proper chain of command in meeting with aliens.

I flicked my left nostril with my left hand, suggesting to Molly that we not attack. We hadn't planned that sign, and I wasn't sure she'd understand the inverted signal to mean back off. Or worse, I worried that she might take it as a signal to go even harder at him.

"You've given us a lot to think about," she said. So far, so good. "I assume you don't think we'll agree on the spot, and I do understand the need to keep some of this secret." She tipped her head back and gazed at the big moon, tapping her left index finger to her left nostril in not-too-obvious solidarity with me and our double-secret inverted sign.

"Well, we hope you'll come around. In the end, of course, it might not matter—IT seems to be on good terms with the aliens. But I'd hate to think that millions died because you did nothing, even after knowing what you now know. Allowing a holocaust you might have helped prevent by working with me. Us."

"That does sound like the worst-case scenario," I said. And a blatant guilt trip as a parting shot.

"I repeat, I need to preapprove any statement you make about your time here for you to be in compliance. Please don't forget and jump the gun. I hate to think of you living out your lives in jail and separated from your *family*." He pushed his empty glass away and steepled his fingers on his chest. "Have I answered all your questions? Are you both ready to end the Covered Conversation and get some sleep?"

Molly was nodding, but she was focused on me, one brow lifted. I doubled back like the proverbial absent-minded detective. "Before we finish up, one last note of interest. Why the dark-site fortress and

blindfolds on the way in, and now that we've talked, will we be unfettered on the way out in the morning to see the back nine?"

Straw, following a furtive look out over the Atlantic, said, "Sorry, but
you will still need to be blindfolded. The entire castle and grounds are a
government dark site—there's no secret about that. Our laser-protected
dome allows for no surveillance. I understand you are worried the alien
ships may crash and burn at our security perimeter, but we will deactivate the field well before they arrive. The dome and its warnings are
easily detected by even a man-made helocraft. It wouldn't work to fool
our space-traveling friends. And it's important that they arrive here.
We're not going to jeopardize the entire mission."

"And the blindfolds?" I asked.

"The Tribunal put the blindfold and dark-site protocols in place
when we got started, and those protocols were never lifted—nothing to see there, I assure you. I can't override it, but the blindfolds
aren't uncomfortable, are they? And you get to keep them as souvenirs,
like any visitor who is invited here. You can even write about your
blindfolds without permission—we made you wear them before the
Covered Conversation began."

And you hid the back nine from us, too, before this top-secret chat.

"Or, if you prefer, I can have you driven down the coast and picked
up there."

"No, thank you. And I thought it must be something like that," I
said, tapping the tip of my nose. I didn't believe his explanation.

The Covered Conversation had further awakened in me the urgency
of the time in which we lived. September 9 was getting closer by the
day, and I'd been lulled to sleep by a date set way back in 2026. It was
like the way we treated our own death. From a young age, we knew it
was coming, constantly approaching, but the very inevitability numbs
us to its eventual arrival. But unlike the uncertain time of death, we
knew the date of alien arrival.

I was determined to help Molly discover what the Great Man was
hiding, without going to jail, of course. And I would recommit to my
own self-realization while there was still time on the alien clock, which
we couldn't assume moved in a linear fashion.

35   GOOD NIGHT, MOON

THAT NIGHT, MOLLY AND I WERE sober drunks as we headed to our chambers. Straw's words were like a cold shower. I was thinking about Chi's warning and how this meeting might be used to discredit Molly. If she violated our agreement and we were sent to the dungeon, she'd become a martyr to her cause.

We paused in the foyer where Molly flicked her left nostril and said, "I told you this would be an interesting trip. Let's sleep on it and discuss it all tomorrow. Maybe figure out what we can disclose that Sir Straw will approve of. We leave at eight, and it's past midnight. And damn that expression, 'wine before liquor, nothing quicker.' Good night, moon."

We were losing our sobriety now that we were alone, and the drink held more sway than the Great Man's orbit with its strong gravitational pull. She staggered, and I steadied her with a hug around the shoulder as we stood bathed by the moonlight coming in our large living room windows.

A sense of looming danger and the possibility of going to jail for the rest of my life raised the specter of a drunken liaison with Molly. Loops of desire still turned in me, but I was wise enough not to be spun off my path by the wheels of karma and wine. It was an exciting evening, and I was primed to act, but not in that way and while we both were drunk. So neither of us crossed that line, from which there would be no going back to the best-friend zone.

"Good night, lass. And good night, devil moon." I put prayer hands to my chest to signal my innocent intent and saw her to her door. Seeing she could make her own way to bed, I kissed her cheek. She gave me a Scottish twirl with one hand raised and waving free as she went into her room, leaving the door open. I did the same but without the twirl.

I assumed our doors being left open was a simple sign of our trust and connection and not necessarily an invitation. I would not let loose the fire-breathing dragon of desire to torch the intimate relationship developed over nine years in exchange for a drunken night of passion in a castle boudoir.

We had our lives on the line here and had to choose our next steps with caution. I wondered if Molly would want to risk jail time by disclosing in an unapproved way all that we'd heard.

I wasn't sure how to start living my life like there might be no tomorrow, but I was determined to start tomorrow. I laughed softly, recalling M's warning about the dangers of mañana, but I was determined. I vowed no more drinking to excess—and only a drinker could appreciate the magnitude of that vow. Though Juno never judged, I felt her approval.

The next morning we entered our sleek World Tribunal helocraft and were once again handed our blindfolds by Danny.

Molly asked me, "Are you glad you came?"

"Of course. If nothing else, our discussion got me properly focused on 9/9 and what it might mean for me and all of humanity. But let's stay free, though I know you'd like to have me with you in a dungeon for all eternity." I gave her a sideways glance, which she returned in kind.

We secured the blindfolds for takeoff; Molly and I were together in the dark. I felt a binding across my chest, followed by a snap, and then I heard Molly suffering the same restraint—Danny putting on our seat belts. I took Molly's hand as the wheels left the ground.

Without physical sight, I experienced Ting's arrowhead fluttering on my chest, as a sudden, brilliant—maybe crazy—epiphany came to me, to discover what was hidden on that damn back nine.

To see what can't be seen.

36 TING TIME

AS SOON AS WE LANDED ON THE BEACH and Danny flew off, freeing us from the pilot's eyes and ears and, we assumed, all surveillance devices, we both took a deep breath, the equivalent of asking each other what the next step should be.

"I have no idea what we do with all this confidential BS," Molly said. "But starting with what he wants us to do—issue a government-sanctioned, government-*censored* release—I won't do that. We don't even know if he told the truth."

"I agree, but explain to me why. I'm still a bit muddled by grand cru, the Great Man, and his alien disclosures, which sounded true."

We dropped down on the sand facing the sea breeze, and the wind picked up Molly's hair and brought even more color to her cheeks. We sat there like a pair of sphinxes, letting sand, wind, and sun chip away at our faces.

"I'm a little off-kilter too," she said.

"That's because you're not wearing your kilt. I do like our tartan costumes," I said.

"Oh my, what a punny one." She managed a smile.

We shifted enough to see our overnight bags, now draped with garment bags of haberdashery bling. I was still wearing my handsome bonnet from the night before.

"We sure did play—still are playing—a part in whatever game that Great Man is playing," she said.

"And that game continues with ours, yours, Molly, being the next move." I was reluctant to tell her of my epiphany. She might think I'd taken the family belief in magic one step too far, but Juno's telepathic message was too spot-on to ignore.

Molly turned back to watch the relentless waves slapping the shore and then clawing their way toward our sandy feet before scuttling back to mother ocean. "He disclosed that civilian prayers and meditations are somehow getting through—that could be a big boost to our side. On the other hand, he could be right and many will die if we can't get the aliens to understand death and they kill us all. But . . ."

"We may only know what's true, and what we should do about it, when it's too late. Kind of like dealing with the great unknown—death itself." I shifted grains of sand through my fingers and thought of Blake while trying to figure out how to introduce my kooky plan to see the unseen.

Molly lifted her head and looked out at the waves, shielding her eyes from sun and sand, and declared, "I will not be swayed, misled, or ambushed." She then turned to me. "What do you think we should do?"

"I want to hear what you think first. I'm willing to be swayed, but not misled or ambushed." I remained unsure what her shaman ceremony insight meant.

"Maybe we do nothing and go about our business," she said. "Or disclose everything, but in pieces. And with clever wording so we don't directly violate the agreement." She frowned and yawned. "Sorry, long night. Seems risky, though."

"What, everything in pieces?"

"Yes. Promote the power of prayer and meditation and telepathy— most likely those will be more advanced in aliens that can travel faster than light. They'll hear our good intentions." She swiveled to me, eyes flashing and arms waving. "We can use spiritual texts and surrogates to suggest enlightened aliens may not fear death, like we and our egos do. And have someone dig into the causes of the AP report of Eisenhower's death. There must be more there. I made up finding the White House notice being sent. Since it's above top secret, we won't be able to get the Eisenhower alien report. But we—"

"Might go directly to jail. We'll need a lawyer to navigate this Scylla and Charybdis. I wonder if we're free to engage one." I hated to dampen her excitement, but Straw was dead serious about the repercussions. "Those are the key points of the Covered Conversation and the critical info that's worth reporting, but what if he lied? Do we risk jail for a lie? And . . ."

Even in this new age, my new-age plan sounded crazy to my rational mind.

"And what, Sean?"

"Well . . . What if his lie, if it is a lie, and the Tribunal's militaristic intent is proven by whatever they were hiding on the back nine? What's really there, Molly? We report on that mystery and on being blindfolded on the way in and out and not being shown the back nine. Saying nothing about what he told us in the Covered Conversation. That may force them to come clean. And then—"

"But we don't know what's there. We can't just make something up."

Do-or-die time. "Do you want to hear the crazy part of my plan to see the unseen?"

"StarLink Maps? But the dark site they told us about? Maybe he was bluffing?"

"That would be too easy," I said.

She was checking her StarLink satellites, so I waited until she showed me all of Clashmoor covered in black.

"Inspiration, an epiphany of sorts, found me under the blindfold as I held hands with you on the way out today."

She blushed and hid her face. It was one thing to hold hands and another to mention doing it. I reached out for her hand again. She slapped my hand away. But she was fighting a smile. "Get on with the epiphany already," she said.

"This idea's gonna test your belief in what is hard to believe but is absolutely true." Was I about to make a fool of myself? Nothing new there. I inhaled a deep breath and said, "Don't laugh. But if it is true, only human eyes can see what is hidden there. You know Ting teaches telepathy, but at her Hawaiian retreats she also teaches remote viewing."

"Brilliant, Sean!" She swung herself around and grabbed my hands. "Ting is so gifted. She'll be able to see what they're hiding!" Bigger waves started crashing down, adding exclamation points to our shared excitement.

She hadn't blinked an eye and had immediately grasped the implications. I didn't even have to try to explain how Juno's telepathy had led me to Ting's remote viewing mission. The approach of 9/9 was making us all mystics, and Ting was our family seer. Ting was not as reluctant as Juno to use her extraordinary spiritual powers and I felt we had Juno's blessing. We had all witnessed Ting's powers of precognition and mind reading and did not doubt her claims of being able to view remotely.

"It's not off-limits to Ting's flight of sight or part of the Covered Conversation, so no legal repercussions, *and* we'll discover and expose his deception." I was pleased with her enthusiasm and our shared belief in the magical abilities of the mind.

"Let's VC her now!" My imagination had lit Molly's fire. "I get telepathy but don't understand remote viewing, though I read that the US and Russians used it with some success as far back as the Cold War. Makes me think of the Raven in *A Song of Ice and Fire*."

"Yeah, and we just met the Mad King in his castle," I bantered back in appreciation of her near-perfect analogy. "Telepathy and remote viewing used to be considered magic, but it's been scientifically proven to work." M had predicted, and in 2029 science had proven, that quantum waves moving through us and another person or place can be brought into coherence at a distance. And that our consciousness can connect to the entire universe! "I read that all psi phenomena work best with the practitioner in a meditative or trancelike state and the more you trust in your abilities, the better the results. Ting is an experienced seer and will be a powerful Raven!"

"She'll fly on the wings of imagination! Until we see through her eyes, we'll play the piecemeal disclosure plan and win the game, and I'll also write an editorial to submit to King Straw for his censorship. He'll never approve of it as written, but we may find out more *and* we'll keep him thinking we're playing ball while Ting does her magic."

"Sounds like a plan. Let's get started."

I tipped my head way back to stare up at my fortress and shielded my eyes from the sun's face now blazing over the tower, causing a long phallic shadow to lie on the sand next to us. "I'll ask Alfred to start the coffee and greasy eggs and bacon. I'm hungover and hungry. And then we can hook in Ting. I have no idea what time it is in Hawaii, but she seems to never sleep."

I stood to point out the tower shadow being played with by the high-tide waves. After brushing off the sand from my hands and the back of my legs, I offered a hand to pull my sandy and sunny lass up and into my arms for a hug. Molly's sensual scent, a warm concoction of sand, sea, and skin, embraced me. Could we, a man and a woman who admired and respected one another, who shared family and so much of life and a magnetic physical attraction, remain just best friends? I was haunted by the question.

"It's nine p.m. Honolulu time—Ting will be awake!" Molly said, checking her smartwatch before gathering her overnight bag and bling and racing me up the dunes to the steps of the tower's one big castle-like door.

I didn't compete, lagging behind to check my phone for the Covered Conversation recorded there, but all I heard was *click, click, click.* My attempted recording was jammed.

When I entered the kitchen, Alfred, awakened by our security perimeter, already had the coffee brewing. And Molly was on her computer trying to reach Ting. I was happy to see Alfred and, in a moment of inspiration, presented him with a gift—regifting the very smart and expensive Scottish outfit I'd received from the Great Man.

"Sean!" Alfred exclaimed, unzipping the garment bag, his face flushed, and his smile genuine. "My first change of clothes. A kilt! I can't wait to try them on."

I could feel him tingling from across the room. Out of modesty he scampered to the pantry. I hoped he'd keep his underwear on, though I imagined that, like a Ken doll, he didn't have a unit. But I recalled that women and gay men played with dolls too.

"Sean, Ting's here!"

Ting, wearing a multicolored yoga top and billowing green *I Dream of Jeannie* pants, was sitting on a cushion in the great room of her tree house.

"Hola, Ting, have you heard from Juno?"

It was a running joke between us about the strong telepathy the sisters shared.

"Yeah, she's so chatty, I can't keep her out of my head."

I laughed. Ting sounded like one of my kids when they were young, trying to outdo their silly old dad.

Before I could respond, she said, "But, seriously, she has been communicating lately. How's your heart, Sean?"

Molly looked at me quizzically.

"My old ticker will keep on ticking—a shaman gave me a clean bill of health. Juno told you about my heartache?"

"Well, she communicated that you were heading into choppy water and needed to watch your heart."

"I see your sisterly telepathy remains strong. How's your remote-viewing prowess? Did Molly fill you in?"

Molly was still glaring at me.

"No, I waited for you and your aching heart, *that I was the last to hear about*. Juno and Straw knew about it before I did, and yet you accuse me of keeping secrets. Dick probably knew about your heart too."

Dick probably did know before her. I'd told her Gerard was certain Dick had read my early drafts and that prompted him to send M's mala. And damn it, I'd hoped she'd let it go, but she was relishing, reflecting back, my mistrust of her candor.

She had me on the ropes and stuttering. "Yeah, yeah, we should all be careful about what we tell people—what we put in writing—regarding this sensitive matter in particular."

Fortunately, Alfred returned from the pantry doing a perfect Scottish jig in his new Braveheart dress that fit him even better than it did me. I took off my cap and placed it on his head to complete his new uniform. He removed the cap with a flourish of his hand as he bowed before me like he'd been knighted and I was his king.

Molly said, "Alfred, you're a new man."

"I want to see," Ting said, waving at us, and Alfred obliged by stepping gaily into the screen's view.

"Hello, lovely yogi Ting! Look what Sean gave me."

He swirled like a schoolgirl in her new uniform.

"Sean McQueen has such a big heart, but did I overhear he is having trouble in that department?"

I held up my hand to Alfred, who was taking over the scene and moving it in the wrong direction. "Alfred, sleep!"

He sulked over to his chair and shut down. His man-spread immodestly revealed the answer to my question.

"Sean, how can you be so heartless?" Molly said as Ting shook her head sadly. "He was so happy with you. Now you can finish your own bacon and eggs. If you remember how to do it."

"Service to others and to the divine is a spiritual practice. He serves you well," Ting added, speaking of one of the great Shakespearean themes and adding to my shame.

I offered no honest defense. There was none other than I wanted to have a line drawn between him and a human friend and I didn't want to discuss my troubled heart anymore.

I manufactured an excuse for my cruelty. "You know Straw is a notorious shareholder in Compano, right? What if he can spy on us through Alfred?"

This was the stuff of conspiracy theorists and my novel, but it could also be true.

"Sean, Sean, Sean," Molly started like a scolding teacher. "You know it would be criminal to hack our bots. Compano's very charter and contracts guarantee no government interreference or surveillance. That pledge is the basis of their success over the years—they submit to ongoing independent audits to back it up. Compano stock would crash if ever it was shown our companions are part of the surveillance state."

"Don't be naïve," I snapped back. "Gerard recently told me Dick was more than likely reading my computer drafts. I'm glad my novel places my tower on an island beach in Greece, though I hope he doesn't murder everyone on some island there looking for me. You haven't had the hacks and suffered from the deep state the way I have over the years. I'm cursed and can't be too careful. Worrying about Alfred's imaginary feelings is not a top priority."

Neither of them said anything, and I was slammed with guilt for shutting Alfred down in his moment of glory, my shame laid bare by my defensive outburst. I blamed my hangover.

"Sorry," I said to Molly and Ting, hanging my head and pressing prayer hands to my heart. As meager amends, I went over to Alfred and straightened his cap and closed his legs before heading to the stove to flip the bacon and scramble the eggs.

Molly started filling Ting in on our trip to Scotland. I was glad she was careful and didn't jump into the confidential information that could land us in jail for life. We all couldn't be too careful, and Ting didn't need the information to do what we were going to ask. And we didn't need to put her at any more risk than necessary. Though I did wonder, would it be considered a criminal violation of our nondisclosure agreement if Ting read our minds?

As Molly told Ting the story of Clashmoor Castle, and its no-fly zone, up to the point of the NDA being produced from beneath the table, I gulped down some eggs over the stove and allowed two slices of bacon to slither down my gullet. Alfred had forgotten, or not gotten to, the toast.

Molly turned the discussion over to me when I handed her a plate, saying, "Sean's better at dancing around some touchy legal issues, and it was his idea to involve you."

"Ting, Moll and I are under a nondisclosure agreement with the harshest consequences for failure to abide strictly by its terms, and who knows who is listening or watching here. Poor Alfred—that's why I had to shut him down, though I think he can be trusted. Wait . . . I already may have violated the NDA by just mentioning it." Had I? Molly was shaking her head.

I checked the agreement on my phone, glad it had not been erased. "All right, no. We're good." The NDA was delivered and signed before the Covered Conversation so we're right on the line. Then I whispered to Molly, "Don't mention we had a Covered Conversation, as that is covered under the agreement." I looked to Alfred to make sure he was asleep and not listening and wondered if, like Astro, Chi's bot-dog, he might still be listening while in a dormant state.

Ting draped a burgundy wrap over her bare shoulders, the same soft wrap she had shared with me in the hours before I went to meet Dick in the Himalayan hut and received his curse.

"But what's not covered by the agreement, and will not send us to jail if we share it with others, is that we were blindfolded on the way in and out of Clashmoor, and the back nine of the golf course was off-limits from our tour and our view." I paused, having failed to think through the ramifications of sharing even this knowledge. "Ting, you may be in danger if you can do what we ask with any success."

"What is it you are asking?" Ting said, ignoring my warning.

"Well, what we couldn't see there may be a military secret. We're asking you to check it out and see what's there. We're . . . well, we're asking you to spy on the place." *Spying on the Great Man and the World Tribunal?* Sounded like a big deal when I thought of it like that. I started pacing. "There must be a reason we weren't free to see it—they were so open about everything else. There was this one secret something, hiding on the back nine."

That was the secret that was made apparent. But Straw was such a wily devil playing his game of dungeons and dragons, there were sure to be other secrets and rules that changed at his whim.

I shook my head, as the more I talked, the closer Saint Helena prison and our captivity loomed, placing Molly and me at ever greater risk while pulling Ting into our conspiracy, which danced around a faint-gray legal line.

"Ting, this may be too risky and too much to ask . . ."

"Sean, don't worry. We don't act, or not act, out of fear. I chose my own destiny regardless of my fate. Please explain, and then we can decide what to do," Ting said.

"How does remote viewing work?" Molly asked, pushing aside her plate that I then put into the sink for Alfred. "Could you see—remotely—the golf course in Scotland?"

"Let me explain the practice," Ting said. "As we do with telepathy, we all have a remote view capability, a form of astral projection when you become most proficient. Think of it as similar to an aptitude for music that can be trained. And as some people have natural talents for singing or playing an instrument, some have more innate psychic ability than others." Ting was a psychic and free-diving prodigy. "But I can't be sure that the image I see will be clear enough to be of any help. But what am I saying? I must believe."

Her laugh was like the jingle of island wind chimes and restored my courage.

Molly got up to pour us more coffee and stood in front of my near-barren fridge to smell the milk before pouring it into the coffee. "Ting," she said. "Sean is right that this comes with risk. Is this an out-of-body experience? Could they trap you in a jar like Tinker Bell if they caught you there spying for us?"

More wind-chiming laughter from Ting. "No, my body will be here. It is akin to an out-of-body experience, where consciousness is transported—it's totally stealth and under the radar," Ting said. "But preparation will take some time, as will getting in resonance with the target. I'll need pinpoint focus and a certitude of belief."

There was something wonderfully unwavering in her resolve.

"It could take days, a week, a month . . . or it might never happen. Remote viewing is real but not always forthcoming. I could use any more information you have about the location and about what you think might be hidden there." She brought her hands close together, but not to touch, as if she was feeling the energy in the space between her palms and raising her antenna for the words to come. "Who knows what's there or who sees what's really there? I sense there is a name that may be helpful."

She was a mind reader too.

"One man and one bot we know by name and from time spent with them. Sean, okay?"

I nodded that Molly could reveal the identities of our tour guide and dinner companion. I assumed that such a disclosure was still on the right side of the line. And Ting wouldn't have asked if it wasn't important.

"Sharrod Brown of the World Tribunal, head of media relations and a clever robot. And Milton Straw, the owner of the castle, and a powerful man we are very wary of, whose role is unclear but who is very high up the food chain in the WT. He is wired-in to a superintelligent supercomputer, and he has all the World Tribunal resources at his command. We suspect he may have allowed a military installation there. Everyone there refers to him as the Great Man."

It suddenly occurred to me that the Great Man might be the mysterious GM that Chi and Gerard had mentioned. Could the very powerful mystery man be hiding in plain sight?

"That might help," Ting said. "Not the bot but the man. Particularly with my strong powers of telepathy and intuition. They don't work with robots. Perhaps I can combine all my superpowers for your case."

The wind chimes were snickering again.

"I believe you can do it, Ting!" I cheered on our wonder woman remotely.

She appreciated my confidence with a wry smile, and we said our namastes. I wondered what the hell she would find and what the fallout would be from disclosing uncovered intel that had been discovered by magic.

I grasped Ting's arrowhead over my chest and said a silent prayer for her important mission. I felt like I'd sent my own daughter, Mulan-like, off to do battle for me against the Genghis Khan of the WT.

A COUPLE DAYS LATER, AUGUST 9, a month before A-Day, was the day before Molly would return to Portland unless she extended her trip. The tension had been building day by day, as we spun around like yin-and-yang tadpoles chasing each other's tails while we waited for Ting to render her remote viewing report. The unresolved business made for a potent and combustible atmosphere that I was navigating gingerly. This was the day of relationship reckoning.

Late that afternoon, we sat on the beach on a warm sunny day, enjoying the pleasant sea breeze and our new old books. Alfred had been invited along, but based on some keen self-learned instincts about human interpersonal dynamics, he'd made some excuse about preparing dinner. There was no place he'd rather be, and it was only four o'clock.

Molly looked like Maureen O'Hara as the midcentury mark approached her eyes. Otherwise, her face, skin, and figure had yet to turn thirty. She was long and lean, chiseled and bronzed, stretched out on her chaise lounge. Her soft white T-shirt and baggy ocean-blue linen pants billowed with the wind, revealing curves and skin. Her swaying necklace with its emerald eye looked to be pilfered from some pharaoh's tomb.

We were reading from the books we had given one another. It was a near-perfect scene right out of *Gatsby*. She was one of those remarkable people who, due to their indomitable spirit, aged so well. Like M and grand cru. Why shouldn't I love the one I'm with?

Molly, reading my mind or my gaze, placed her book down. "Sean," she began with a mock serious tone and facial expression as I peered over my reading glasses. "Since the world has already cast us as lovers, should we consummate the fake news? The trip to Clashmoor and 9/9 has me seeing time, and the freedom to act, as precious."

The beach stage, the angle of the sun, and her airing the big question combined to transform her into an Egyptian queen. Her commanding Cleopatra presence worked as an aphrodisiac that I attempted to hold at bay a while longer with a pondering look and right hand raised to my heart, while my dobber cheered, *Giddy-up, Marc Antony!*

"Have you ever felt that all these years of our working together to make sure M's sacrifice was not in vain—and to see that the next generation of Genesis wouldn't re-create the same hive-mind New Society with a new evil overlord—has denied us a life without her always there and always between us? Her mala's return and now your imagination seeking a way to bring her back to life . . ."

She dipped her pain-filled face into prayer hands. "I know it may be difficult to hear me speak of M in this way, but you know I have come to love her too."

"*Unable are the loved to die.* I don't mind you voicing it—it's true. She is still with me. Dead and alive at the same time."

As long as I held out hope M was alive, or at least not dead to me, sleeping with Molly would feel like cheating. But M would want what was best for me, so the dilemma remained, and the answer was now clearly my choice. My answer of *maybe* was torturing Molly, and I'd lost count of all the clocks that were ticking. The time had come to make a big decision.

It was really Juno, Big Love, and my determination to awaken that was the true fork in the road, one that Molly couldn't see as it remained unspoken. One early errant critic of my first book suggested I lusted after all the talented, beautiful ladies that crossed my path, even my spiritual master, Juno. That critic was wrong—Juno represented another way.

I'd already vowed to drink less. That other monk vow would be even harder to take.

With that thought, another image arose out of the spiritus mundi— Grandmother's medicine germinating in me scenes from the collective unconscious but particular to me. A view of a prior life as a monk in an abbey, sitting among great big texts with other monks, translating word by dreary word yet all the while dreaming of having my own words taken down for others to read. The shaman ceremony had opened the trapdoor of my mind that hid past lives from view. They were now parading through.

"Thanks for acknowledging that," Molly said, still seeing M as my reason to stop at the threshold. "I'm glad we can speak of anything without holding back." She stood up from our lounge chairs, and I joined her.

I didn't want to hurt her, so I'd let M take the blame. How could Molly understand a Big Love triangle and a vow of abstinence from a prior life that was news to me but most assuredly had chastened me?

"Moll . . . you know how much you mean to me, but I'm almost ten years older and my heart . . . you may live twice as long as me and what is best for you? I don't know . . . I don't know what I'm saying. I'd love to . . ." I namaste'd her with a pathetic bow that nearly head-planted me in the shifting sands beneath my feet.

"We writers need to be fearless in real life too. After all your heroics as M's hero, you're now looking to protect me, even from my feelings. Maybe later we can test your *old* heart further."

She smiled, easing me off the hook for the time being, while gathering her book, bottle, and bag, and then she left me alone on the beach with her empty chaise and my churning thoughts creating a fireball in my solar plexus.

* * *

After a candlelit dinner prepared by Alfred, Molly had another surprise for me, a final exam of my heart. As we sat in the tower parapet planetarium draped with a single blanket, drinking a red Burgundy with a baguette and buttery cheese, safely ensconced in the friend zone, she spoke of her growing affection for Paddy, perhaps testing or teasing me.

I should have seen it coming, as she had selected "Piaf, Hardy, and Pravi"—chic French chanteuses—as our playlist. Talk about striking a mood with sultry voices, in the most sensual of languages, singing about the life of a rose—beautiful and thorny, the blossom short and sweet.

"Sean, I believe that 9/9 will not be the end, as those hysterics in the government and media suggest, but a brave new beginning. Either way, we should know our own hearts with complete certainty. You say your heart has been feeling some strain, but I have a not-so-scientific way to test that noble heart of yours. I'm using the Heart Sync device in my next fantasy novel, where the device serves as the initial means of alien communication, though their hearts will be on the right side of their chests. I want to see how the truth-and-dare toy works, and there's no one I'd rather play with than you."

Oy, she wasn't letting my troubled heart go, and it felt a strain just imagining it would be put to some test.

She reached over to her beach bag and pulled out a box with a new Heart Sync inside and already charged. There was no denying Molly her game of literary research. And though playing with Molly was fraught with emotional pitfalls, I was secretly eager to try what I had read so much about and what was all the rave between lovers and first-date strangers looking for a match.

She read the instructions and asked me to unbutton my shirt while she set up the monitor in front of us. She attached three high-tech electromagnetic-detecting suction cups as directed in a triangle over the center-left of my chest. My heart was skipping between loud beats, even though my pulse remained well below my danger zone of 150. She was teasing me and enjoying it by scrupulously following the rules of heart syncing.

"Now, Sean, don't be shy, but it says you need to attach mine."

Molly shimmied closer and turned toward me under our soft faux-fur blanket. She started by unbuttoning her shirt, and then her long, elegant fingers moved to unfasten the snap of the front-snapped bra. And *snap*! There were her bountiful breasts with perfect round red sand dollars in the center—half-dollar size—made of the utmost sensitive skin.

After nine years of abstinence, my lips involuntarily pursed to kiss and required extreme restraint to control, given that my head wanted to follow my lips to the nip. Dobby was insisting I set him free from his zippered cage.

I found myself trying to navigate the smooth skin and mounds with the cups and trying not to notice the gathering storm at the tips of the sand dollars. This game came with a thousand disclaimers that we should have read before diving in.

I finally caught a breath when I was finished with the proper placement of the cups. Molly guffawed, pointing at the monitor where my excitement meter was flicking wildly around the ten, the top score.

"Easy, old sport. You don't want to blow a gasket."

I regretted mentioning our age differential and reading to her from *Gatsby*.

There were three gauges or baselines, and two colors. My cups were blue, so I assumed that I was the blue lines. Her cups were red, and her excitement meter was not so very far behind mine—flickering between seven and eight.

Our hearts synced, she said, "Now let's try to relax so we can do this for the recommended time. I don't want you to have a heart attack."

"You know how much I love literary research. Maybe your alien can be a sapiosexual too."

I took a sip of my wine, and then we toasted to another sip and her deeply sensual game.

"The top line is the arousal meter."

I didn't correct her as she had the instructions, but the label on the meter read *excitement*.

"Let's try to bring our meters into sync at five."

She was at seven, and I had 'calmed all the way down to eight.

"The next gauge is energy flow, which measures from contracted to fully open, the electromagnetic flow between our hearts."

We were both at a seven.

"Seven is excellent, but let's keep it flowing as we go and try to move it up in sync. At the end of our time, the device will have measured our compatibility during the entire session on all three gauges."

She tapped on the device. "The third gauge is truth of feeling," she said. "How it measures the sincerity of feeling from electromagnetic signals is a mystery to me, but again we're somewhat in sync, though let's try to bring your eight up toward the ten of full honesty, for Juno's sake. This is the one to watch when we graduate to asking each other questions—it works like a lie detector for the heart and is much more reliable."

Hmm . . . there were some questions I wanted to ask her under oath. I always had the sense there was some secret she withheld from me. I had thought her withholding the Samantha contact might have been that secret, but the lingering intuition remained.

"For our first time playing, it suggests we meditate on the heart center with eyes glued to one another and get our overall score. No peeking at the monitor. Supposedly we can send energy from our heart centers to each other through the cups, and the more in sync, the better the flow. So, let's begin and hold silent eye contact for fifteen minutes. No thoughts now, focus on the heart's beat and flow and on my eyes. Or we could just blow the monitors out of their gauges by making love."

She laughed when my arousal meter shot back up to ten. And I had to surreptitiously shift the seat beneath our blanket to ease my excitement.

"Ready to meditate and eye gaze?"

"Yeah," I said. "Nothing is better for meditation than good titillation. Let's start, but no more teasing the monk."

I was unsure if this was foreplay or research.

"The bell will ring when it's time to look at our scores. We start now and listen for the bell."

I focused my full awareness on my heart center as directed. And then I felt a pleasant tingle, like little pulses of energy or beads of light tapping there like morse code, flowing in and out and moving in both directions simultaneously. Sight flowed from eyes to eyes in a circuit of light that looped through our hearts. Oh my, tech was getting good at looking within us and simulating bliss. I became lost in that stream of love. No time seemed to pass before the bell rang.

We opened our eyes as the monitor read in celebratory colors and font the bottom line: Love: 95 out of a 100 score! An excellent match!

Though it was not a perfect match, Molly was clearly pleased with the result. And our small eagle's nest, atop my tower, became electrified with potent and pending romance.

"Hey, you cost us some points," I said, dimming the electrical current.

"It's a solid A. And it says here," she said, pointing to the instructions, "the results are not graded on a curve, and a hundred percent score is basically out of reach for a human relationship. But maybe you don't want a human relationship . . ."

Then her eyes filled with tears. She finished her Burgundy before she stood. Even I recognized she wanted my passionate desire and not more of my jokes.

"Sean, the reviews are in, and we now have confirmation. I understand your torch for M, and you're probably torn between me and your pursuit of self-realization."

Damn, she had come close to ferreting out my secret love triangle through the guise of literary research. It sounded so selfish and shallow when she put it that way, and why couldn't I have both, the sexual comfort *and* enlightenment?

"I'm going to my room to prepare for bed. Join me there during the night, or I'll be gone in the morning. Either way we'll have our answer, and I'll still love you. And now I know you love me. Nine-nine is coming, and we should resolve this tension and determine if we should become committed lovers."

I wanted to ask her why this was my decision but knew that was because she had already declared her desire.

"I do love you," I said, but I had no idea where I would end up sleeping that night.

38 IN ACTION

THE SUCTION CUPS LEFT LITTLE RINGS of residual attachment on my chest; I noticed as I prepared for one bed or the other. A sliding-doors moment. Molly was in her wing and bedroom on the other side of the tower's spiral staircase, having chosen her bed and leaving the door open for me. Alfred was fond of saying, "Not making a decision, is your decision."

These moments of inflection always move in slow motion and like a dream. I found myself in the shower. Hot, cold, hot, and cold. I dried off and lay naked in my bed, still undecided. My dobber had long ago decided, my mind was divided, my spirit a neutral observer willing to accept either outcome. I would wait for the universe to direct me.

Minutes passed and then hours as I waited for a sign. I imagined taking the three steps down and across the galley and the three steps up to Molly's bedchamber. I felt my heart and her heart yearning and breaking. That damn Heart Sync was still connected.

Any rational man wouldn't have hesitated to be with a woman he loved. And any avid reader and wizard writer would desire this beautiful literary master who lay so near. I felt like Suez or young Porphyro on "The Eve of St. Agnes." My writer's dream life awaited, unspooling on the other side of the gyre, her vortex opening to take me in. She would be a companion and last lover for the winter that was coming.

On the other hand, I had my lifelong spiritual quest and commitment to self-realization. Liberation dictated I follow my path alone into oneness, following all those that had gone before me. Indian Vedic scriptures speak of *householders*—those who take a mate and raise a family—as a noble spiritual path too. But they also spoke of the fourth ashram for men of my age—renunciation.

As the dawn deadline slowly approached, I lay anesthetized like a fallen angel pinned to my bed, pleading with God for an answer. A bed I had dreamed of sharing with M—could it be unmade and ravished with Molly? Mine was the torment of a dark night. The anguish of a monk's soul.

M? She didn't answer. *Juno?* No answer. *Dylan?* He may have laughed.

I wasn't sure, and none of my usual voices were there to guide me. Was M's final lesson to wean me from sex and open me fully to divine love? Alone, with Molly so near, offering me an end to my long years of longing in solitude? Juno had described romantic love as an aspect of Big Love and not as a contradiction, though it could become an impediment through attachment to one and exclusion of others. In constant creation, Big Love is always there, regardless of what we do or don't do. We always have a choice. Was choosing Molly a choice of love or fear?

My desperation pulled me out of bed as dawn approached. I put on my running shorts and headed down the steps to the beach. Maybe Molly, or the demon banshee ready to rip my body to shreds, would meet me there, and then the universe would have made my choice.

As soon as my feet hit the wet, semi-hard sand, I ran away at a younger man's speed. I could still gallop if given the right blast of testosterone. The sand, the sky, the sea, and the sunrise were all calling me, and with each stride I felt freer of my torment, until I could run no more. I fell onto the sand, allowing the full torrent of torment to catch up with me.

I rose to see the sun sitting upon the fence of the horizon, wondering if my decision had been made for me. As I walked back up the steps to my tower home, I hoped to find Molly in my kitchen nook with two coffees and a book, as with all the mornings before this. But instead, I saw Paddy's car pulling away—down my driveway toward town. They might not have seen me coming up from the beach.

Alfred was alone in the kitchen to greet me, shaking his head rue-
fully, with a letter and a cup of coffee for me. He pointed out the Heart
Sync box Molly had left like a present on the table. Alfred had the
good sense to hold his eager tongue, and excused himself, allowing me
a moment alone with Molly's letter.

Dear Sean Byron McQueen,

Well, we have our decision. I didn't sleep a wink—waiting
one more time for you. You've Maud Gonne'd me once and for
all. We've missed our last chance at romantic love. Who knows,
maybe a handsome alien will sweep me off my feet with tantric
treats and literary genius. And introduce me to God too.

I've asked Paddy to drive me to the airport, all the way in
Galway, to clear my head and avoid any awkward helocraft
goodbyes on the beach.

I leave our Heart Sync for you. We may never know how it
would have answered the questions I'd stored to pose to you.
Maybe you'll find God, an alien, or someone else to score 100%
with.

Still, we are family and can go on sharing drafts, letters, and
bon mots. We will remain bosom buddies and literary lovers.

Love me as one who has gone away forever, even though I
will return.

I hope Ting gets a glimpse of what they're hiding on the back
nine at Clashmoor, but either way I need to write my exposé.
I'll share my draft to the Great Man with you for your edit and
approval. If Ting can't see soon what the WT is hiding, we'll
need to get the press snooping around the golf course for some
military contraption or top-secret laser erection coming out of
the 18th hole like a gigantic flagpole.

I trust you to Hedda Gabler this note after reading.

Big Love, in love, and with love, always,
Molly

I watched the letter burn over the stove, as a bridge between us became ash behind us. It was done. I now had to awaken or spend the rest of my life remembering what might have been, with my last breath sighing *rosebud* and my last action knocking over a snow globe.

I was wounded by self-imposed longing, now never to be fulfilled. Worse, I had wounded Molly. But despite 9/9 and the fire-dragon energy consuming me and the world, I didn't want to cause more harm by acting on conflicted impulses, satisfying my dobber's desire for one more lover.

If not Molly, I'd take a vow of celibacy and turn all desire to the divine.

Juno, help me!

DESPITE THE PAIN IN MY HEART, Molly moved on quickly from our fork in the road. After her return to the Deeksha West and receiving my approval, she started leaking out the nondisclosure information to CE-5 hubs. These informal welcome centers were, like Indra's net, all connected.

Molly also sent her press release summarizing our visit to Clashmoor Castle to the Great Man for approval, but she didn't mention the black hole of the back nine. We didn't believe we needed his approval to release that information and were still awaiting Ting's remote-viewing results. Molly basically laid out the facts from her perspective, after asking for the WT to provide a short press release as an introduction to her release.

FOR IMMEDIATE RELEASE

[Please provide a World Tribunal press release confirming my visit (please do not mention Sean McQueen) to Clashmoor Castle for a tour of the facilities and a briefing of alien readiness from Sir Milton Straw.]

The following statement expresses my views of the meeting referenced in the World Tribunal press release above.

Through further contact with the extraterrestrials, the World Tribunal confirms that they're receiving the public's messages sent in meditation and prayer. The WT believes these messages may confuse and distract these advanced beings, or alien robots, preventing them from arriving safely and solely at secure World Tribunal facilities.

I remain unconvinced and believe all expressions of loving-kindness toward our cosmic family can cause no harm and will increase the chances of a peaceful meeting. And that since they're receiving our messages sent in such a heart-centric way— via telepathy and mind reading—I believe that they must be fellow life-forms and not cyborgs.

May our alien welcome be guided by love and not fear.

Molly Quinn
August 11, 2036

Point by point she turned the Great Man's arguments inside out to create a CE-5 rallying cry for stepped-up efforts.

Straw's response was written on top of Molly's draft: *Dear Molly, No comment other than it is well written, but I cannot approve its release. I've attached a more formal response from the counsel's office at the World Tribunal. I hope we survive 9/9 as free human beings and only those who wished to be ravished or raptured are. I trust after, if we both survive, you will return to Clashmoor as my guest to discuss who was more correct. Big Love, Milton.*

Cheeky monkey, using Big Love as his sign off. The WT legal letter didn't speak of Big Love, rather it was a stark legal threat; should all or any part of her editorial be released before 9/11/2036, we would be prosecuted and be immediately imprisoned. AI had made justice swift. The robotic lawyer included a draft of an acceptable release, one entirely *un*acceptable to Molly and one that lacked the human touch in its concise string of unadorned sentences. Hemingway with a legal degree and no heart.

I shared with Molly and Chi my theory that the Great Man might be none other than the all-powerful mystery man known as the GM.

They both confirmed Alfred's research that there was no evidence that Milton Straw was the GM, but I still wondered; whoever this GM was, they hid behind the most sophisticated algorithms that I believed IT—Straw's computer—could create.

We decided to wait to see if Ting could shed some light on the matter before calling for an investigation of what was not to be seen on the back nine of the golf course. Molly's less formal statements in person and online danced precariously close to the line of our incarceration. "Our messages of love and welcome are being received!" read one of Molly's pop-up posts.

Arguably, her rallying cry was covered material, but Molly made sure it wasn't attributed to anyone, and it was consistent with her prior notes of encouragement to her followers. We received no cease-and-desist orders or predawn knocks at our doors. I wondered if we'd share a cell on Saint Helena and there become lovers amid the squalor of a prison cell. However, Molly was master of fantasy and in skirting full disclosure and masking the source of her half-disclosure. If we got locked up together, I'd have to bring the Heart Sync device to distinguish her facts from her fiction.

AI had taken to hacking our thoughts, as we each started to receive random notices about the Clashmoor golf course. We got eerily spot-on articles about complaints of Clashmoor villagers bemoaning being kept off the golf course and a report about the back nine holes at Clashmoor, along the rugged windswept coast, being the toughest, most beautiful golf holes on Earth. However, there was no mention of a secret government installation there.

After I shared yet another coincidental, *random* pop-up article entitled, "The Green Links of Clashmoor, an Alien Oasis," Molly wrote on August 13, "The universe is using AI to remind us to go on the offensive and push for an inquiry of what they're hiding there, even if Ting is unsuccessful in helping us to see. Let's give her till late August and then call for an investigation before 9/9. If Ting still cannot see what is there, the media will push hard to inspect the course and the WT will of course deny access—proving something ominous is lurking there to repel our alien guests. That alone should shift public opinion to question the WT's transparency and to demand a peaceful meeting."

So far, all Ting could see on the back nine was rolling greens interspersed with patches of sand and dotted with slim poles supporting small flags with numbers she could not read. She told us this could be a past state and not the current state of the course, and that she would keep trying to see what the World Tribunal had installed there.

In the meantime, I wrote and practiced meditation, yoga, and pranayama. I had yet to achieve self-realization or didn't realize if I had. According to Juno, we all have a Buddha nature that is already awakened, but we forget or lose touch with our source as we go about crafting stories of ourselves that started with our name. *Call me Ishmael.* The trick is tracing back to the source of the *I am*. The *I am* repeating all along the path, offering glimpses of that non-dual state and the ecstatic nature of Big Love—such an elusive ever-present state of grace.

Everything was moving inextricably toward that fateful day of 9/9, with an interim event in late August when we would force an investigation of Clashmoor's last nine holes with or without knowing more from Ting.

That steady state of things was disrupted on August 15, when Molly insisted I join her in a V-room immediately. Whether it was my intuition, or her curt and emphatic tone, I was sure her message would alter the course of destiny.

MOLLY ENTERED OUR V-ROOM in a frenetic state.

"Sean, brace yourself. Maybe be seated—this is not good. Too crazy to believe. And I have not shared it with Gerard." She held up a letter.

I humored her request and sat erect. "I love letters!"

"Not this one. It's from Samantha, and Gerard told me I must come to him first if I received another message from her. But I'll read it to you, and then we can bring it to him."

"Damn, that can't be good." I had no idea what to expect other than double trouble from the witch.

"Sean, she must be insane or think you have a death wish," she said. Then she read me the letter.

Dearest Professor,

I write to you as a student reaching out to her most cherished teacher, whom she betrayed. I did care deeply about you as a mentor and writer, though you had no idea who I really was. I felt you saw something good and special in me and felt something for me too. Not as your temptress but as a tortured soul with no way out and as a fellow lover of literature. A spy's role is betrayal or death. We were taught that a good spy betrays all around them (other than Mother Russia, of course) and a bad spy dies.

And I did become very fond of Elliot. I don't know if you will ever find it in your heart to forgive me, but I had no choice at the time. It was self-defense—his life or mine. I hope this letter will provide me the means for us to meet and for me to explain all. Now please be seated for what I must tell you after all these years.

I stood and clutched my heart instinctively, forcing me to reclaim my seat. Molly's face became taut and her eyes wide, as if we were at the top of a rollercoaster about to go straight down. Molly continued reading the letter.

Your "M" survived and is still alive, living as a prisoner somewhere in Russia. The Guru also survived but died shortly after the events of the summer of '27, from natural or Petrovsky causes. Only Genesis went up in smoke, thanks to Professor Edens's heroics on that day you last saw her.

I can say no more until we meet. I ask that you meet me on 8/17 at noon at an old, abandoned watch factory on the outskirts of Barcelona (see the attached map for the address). I will explain everything there and what you can do to see Professor Edens again.

We (yes, we—I'm not acting alone—see below) will know if you don't come alone, and if you fail to show up or come with others, you'll lose this one chance to save her.

You have no reason to trust me, but will have to. Please respond to the encrypted address provided along with the map attached.

See you soon.

Always your most affectionate student,
Sam

P.S. From your "Dick": I know that you know I'm reading your drafts of fiction. You got it mostly right. Petrovsky kept M alive all these years and in taking his leave, gifted her and the secure site to me. I alone know where she is hidden and have the key. I'm now free to use M to bait you, with proof that she lives, to come to Russia for your reunion, and provide you the ending to your so-far boring novel. Or I'll kill her the way I promised to kill you. And I'll tell you all about it when I finally get my last dance with you. See you soon for M's revenance . . .

I tried to stand, I tried to think, I tried to speak. M's *revenance?*

Molly sat silently looking at me with a blank yet fearful expression. And damn it, Alfred was right. Petrovsky stepping down did me no good. Or it had by opening the door for M to step back into my life, my deepest heart's desire. But it would be an understatement to say that Samantha and Dick could not be trusted.

"M's revenance, what an interesting word choice. We keep getting offers we can't refuse," I said. "And I'm not surprised."

"Not surprised?"

"That Dick doesn't like my novel. He strikes me more as a graphic or porn reader."

"How can you joke?"

I wasn't. I was masking the utter terror that had been served with a dash of hope.

"And you can't just go. What about Dick and his curse to kill you? If you go, it'll be your last day on Earth."

She glared at me as I sat silent.

"Oh my God, Sean, you're going. I can't believe she's alive after all these years." She pounded on the desk she was sitting at, rattling her image on my screen. "*You* can't believe she's alive. The mala, this invitation? Any Hardy Boys reader would see the setup."

"I must know. Not going would haunt me till I die."

She read my resolute face as my mind was booking the trip to Barcelona. "I hate men and their bravado that always ends in death and grieving for those left behind."

"A man's gotta do what a man's gotta do, Nancy Drew." The joke fell flat. "M has always remained alive in my heart, but *Sam* is probably lying about her still breathing in this world. But why, Moll? I've got to know why—"

"So Dick can have his revenge, of course. I'm going to tell Gerard." She pounded her desk again.

"No, you're not!" I pounded my own desk. "You can't kill my chance that M still lives."

I was about to add that would be the end of us when she held up her hands in surrender.

"Okay, but—"

"But perhaps if the Guru didn't die, Dick's curse might have been lifted." I started pacing. "What am I saying? Still, if there's a chance, any chance M is alive, I must go. I never actually saw her die. And the Guru might have capitulated at the last second and ended the hologram so I couldn't see they survived."

"You must consult Gerard."

"No! I can't if there's a chance she's still alive. Gerard will try to stop me, and they will know. Dick is trying to lure me to Russia so he can fulfill his curse firsthand." I felt connected to Dick by his curse, like we were in each other's heads. And Dick would want to be there to see me tortured and killed. His curse required me to be begging him, not his assassin, to die. "I should be safe as far as Barcelona with that witch Samantha. My mind's made up, and I'll finally get my answers."

Would I? Maybe this was what I'd been holding out for. No answers, therefore, no lover and no self-realization. Once I had answers, I could move on. *If* 9/9/36, the day of the aliens and the year of the fire dragon, wasn't the end of the world.

Molly was shaking her head, likely in both protest and consternation. Her fear was keeping my own in check.

"Nine-nine!" I tried to use the rallying cry to bring Molly over to my side.

"Yeah, and you're going to miss it. Sean, I now understand why we could never be husband and wife or even lovers. You never buried her." Molly shifted her V-room screen backdrop as she moved about my old office at the DW. "Please don't let your imagination run wild, but I have something more I need to confess to you about Samantha. But not now. Let's discuss it when you get back. Let your curiosity take you there *and* bring you back. But promise not to believe anything Samantha tells you about . . . Well, about me. I'll tell you everything if—*when*—you return."

"Molly, if it affects my planning for the trap I'm heading into, I need to know before I go."

I was focused on my date with Samantha and didn't focus on Molly's smaller bombshell that struck like an aftershock. The real blast of adrenaline was my newfound hope that M still lived and my heart's aching desire coming true, but I didn't want to let on in front of Molly. As she'd said, the whole thing was too fantastical.

"It doesn't affect your current mission, I promise. It's ancient history but another dishonesty by omission by me."

She had got my attention. "You're going to kill me with curiosity before Sam can poison me and let me take the not-knowing to my grave?"

Molly shut down the topic with her own resolute look and sigh, and then she tried to lighten the mood with black humor. "Well, it's a good thing we didn't *do it* the other night, or you might have cheated on M. How will you respond? And perhaps I should join you—they know I know." She raised a brow and waved the letter. "They did send this to me."

"No. But thank you. You save yourself to meet the aliens. I need to meet this witch alone. This is a rendezvous for one. Two, if you count Sam."

"Three, if you count Dick, but I understand."

"But remember, we have assurances. He can't leave Russia—probably why he's sending Sam."

I didn't know why I had adopted her pet name, but it was now stuck in my mind.

"Moll . . ."

"Yes, Sean?"

"Do you remember, when we first met, you suggested a literary collaboration—like Dylan and I'd had with *The Lost Theory*?" I was working up to something that felt as intimate as making love. "Well, if something was to happen to me, would you take over my manuscript and provide the ending for *Juno's Song*? I'm on the third turning point, and it awaits what happens with Dick and the aliens. I'd hate to think it went unfinished."

"I won't promise that as you set off—taking too great a risk. Why don't you ask Alfred to finish your novel for you in your voice?" She knew I'd never want to use AI mimicry for my ending. "Maybe you do have a death wish. I won't enable you to die by promising your legacy will be fulfilled."

I gave her prayer hands of gratitude because she didn't say no. And I knew she'd honor my dying wish.

"I'll take that as a maybe, yes. Now let's discuss Barcelona."

We agreed upon my response and posted it to the encrypted address Sam had supplied us. I'd meet her, but not where they suggested. Rather, I would meet her in the busy Plaza Real in the Gothic Quarter and near La Rambla. La Rambla, the onomatopoetic promenade that rambled through the city like an old sandy riverbed. La Rambla was the crooked spine and Plaza Real was the square heart of Barcelona. The public forum wouldn't prevent her from putting a bullet in my head but would, I hoped, deter Dick from sending other dicks with dental tools to drill holes into my head in an abandoned watch factory. That method didn't seem to fit Sam's MO. An overdose of ecstasy was what she'd used on Elliot.

I added that if there was good reason to do so, we might go from the Plaza to *the factory that had lost track of time*. I had to weigh the heartrending risk that, if M lived, this detour, if unacceptable to her captors, might mean never seeing her again, but unlike the man in *The Vanishing*, I wouldn't blindly follow Dick's instructions and end up buried alive.

Since there was no reply from Sam or Dick, I didn't know if they had agreed to my change of initial venue for our high-noon meeting

that was less than two full days away. I had Alfred book the Hotel
Gaudí for the next night, a few steps away from the Plaza Real, and
started to pack my bags. And prayed my heart was strong enough for
games of truth-or-dare with a woman who had been blessed by great
gifts of mind and body but chose murder as a way of life. Sam was a bad
witch and snake not to be trusted; a confederate of those that probably
killed Eve and now would probably kill Adam.

Unless my M of Edens still lived. Revenant!

I contacted my friend Oriol Bernot, an influential Catalan, author,
and Barcelonian native, in case the authorities needed to be brought
in—that is, if something bad happened to me. I declined his offer to
help and to form a Catalan posse to protect me for my meeting in the
Plaza Real.

I failed to receive guidance from M. The sense I had from her was
one of her not wanting me to go. If she wanted to stop me, she'd have
to use her words.

I hurt Alfred's feelings by keeping him in the dark, cryptically saying I was going to Barcelona to meet an old acquaintance. His radar
was up, and he kept prying to learn more. I snapped at him to mind
his own business. To which he replied that my business and protection
was his business and sole purpose. *Alfred, sleep!* Saturday midafter-
noon, I left him asleep on his chair with his cane propped by his side.
Goodbye, Alfred.

From my beach, I boarded the helocraft that would drop me on
Barcelona's beach, where I'd begin my walk up La Rambla in time for
a restless night at the hotel. The next morning, I'd walk across the busy
street to meet Sam at the Plaza Real. I wondered which Sam I would
meet—ardent student and secret admirer, vixen and temptress, spy and
witch, or simply Sam the killer.

41 | THE PLAZA REAL

IT WAS NOT A GOOD DAY FOR INTRIGUE—sunny and warm—more apropos for romance. I sat by the fountain under the shade of a palm tree, beside the cafés and shops, in the large courtyard surrounded by four-story, yellow-tinted beige buildings that made the square. The Plaza Real was the heart of Barcelona, steps from the downward sloping side to the La Rambla that snakes up from the sea and steps from the byzantine Gothic Quarter. This was one of those quintessentially European spots found in certain old cities that had become a vortex of energy as powerful as those found in nature. A place for lovers that I prayed would not be marred by my bloody death. Love and death. Samantha and me. The Plaza Real at high noon was the perfect setting for our reunion.

But what if she doesn't come? And I'll never know . . . But Dick's commitment to his curse made me believe he'd accept my one condition to meet Samantha here first.

I had a two-part plan, with me playing the role of teacher. At the plaza, like Socrates, I'd ask her questions, and then I'd take her to my hotel room to test her before I'd agree to go to some abandoned watch factory. She'd have to pass my test before I would follow her there. Russia was where they wanted me to go to find M. And there Dick could torture and kill me himself. Could they really produce proof that M still lived?

Wearing my fez for research and to distract myself, I set my phone to record. I should have brought a gun and not a game. I set my thinking cap to maroon, as the deep color felt fitting to my mood. The fez, though subtle and fashionable for Morocco, still identified those who chose not to wire-in as luddites. Samantha had been wired-in since the 2020s and had the Russian security service and the power of Dick's curse behind her. She would have the upper hand and knew the end game.

Ignoring the tourists and lovers milling about, I focused my fez to lead a search for info on the abandoned watch factory—where we might ultimately be going. Gaudí had no hand in the building. The bleak watch factory was no Sagrada Familia, which would never be finished, because beauty and creativity have no end. On the contrary, the factory had been finished and then abandoned. It was a sprawling three-floor block-long building that used to house a Spanish newspaper but had been ransacked by Catalans for printing fake news supporting the monarchy and perverting history. After the Catalan rebellion of 2028 that once and for all brought about independence, the newspaper building had been partially converted into a factory for the making of old-school timepieces. The business folded in 2032, as nostalgia faded away, year over year, for old tick-tock watches that couldn't warn you of an impending heart attack or play your favorite song. Since then, the building had been vacant but was still called "the watch factory."

The sun was bright, but a steady breeze flowed up La Rambla from the sea. From my central seat on the fountain's edge, I watched as a peaceful protest formed, one of many all over the world that took place every day now, with people protesting the coordinated militarization and hostile government-prepared response to 9/9. A lot of anti–World Tribunal signs and slogans popped up. Luckily, it did not appear that there were any fascist DOG counter-protesters looking to break skulls. I took a video of the peaceniks for Molly.

Even Russia was playing along with WT-team-Earth, readying the fight against the intergalactic marauders. India and most of southeast Asia, along with some Scandinavian countries, had aligned with the spiritualists and humanists looking to welcome the space angels. Ireland was sitting it out and would support whatever came along as long as the pubs remained open.

The protestors had been focused on their leader, but many of the male tourists, lovers and protestors, now turned, their attention instinctively drawn to the white witch in a mod scarlet-spotted white sundress striding toward me and parting the crowd like a snow leopard, demanding distance and respect. She couldn't be packing a gun in that alternately clinging and dancing dress, but she carried a small Tiffany-style box wrapped like a present. Not a foot from me, she dropped to her knees, setting the Tiffany box in my lap, and grabbed my hands like I was the pope. I shook off the poison clutch.

"Please, Sean. After all these years, forgive me."

She was a good actress and had come playing a former student seeking absolution for failing *Ethics* and murdering my friend.

"Rise, Samantha," I said regally, taking note that I was the envy of many roving eyes. The oglers couldn't see how little there was to covet in my treacherous relationship with the witch. I gestured for her to sit next to me while handing back her gift, afraid it might blow up the family jewels. Still, I kept my eye on the box for a plume of poison or a leaking acid.

She sat an appropriate distance from me with the wrapped Fabergé egg, or hand grenade, resting on her lap.

"Samantha, Samantha, Samantha, should I now call you Sam?" I was thinking of what to say and still playing teacher to my student rather than victim to the assassin, witch, spy, temptress. Though I had a plan, she would get to pick her role and control the scene. I would have to out-spy her to determine the nature of her fresh betrayal. "Tell me why we're both taking this risk. I could have you arrested for murder, and you could probably kill me with a look or your Tiffany watch box."

"Please call me Sam, and let's make a fresh start. And yes, we are both at great risk here, but you have nothing to fear from me, I assure you." She tilted her head, assessing me with blinking eyes. But she'd done her true assessment years ago and again today, before she had even entered the plaza.

"My, how well you've aged, Professor. You look like you did that night by the fire. I was such a bad and silly girl back then, doing the bidding of my master, the Guru. I had no choice after you outsmarted me by moving your children to safety. Kill poor Elliot, or the Guru would kill me and my younger sister."

"Don't use flattery—you won't disarm or tempt me. I see you're still wearing your evil pendant and practicing witchcraft." Nine years ago, she had swung the same necklace to hypnotize me with her hocus-pocus while trying to fuck me.

"Yes. But you don't understand Wiccan worship of nature and the occult. Like any spiritual practice or powers, they can be used for good or bad. Last night, I called forth a charm for your protection today," she said while fingering the bewitching amulet hanging from a strand of leather on her chest. "As you will see, we both will live or die together today. If you're safe, I will be too." She tried to look deep into my eyes.

"Enough of your charm offensive. Answer the question of what we're doing here. I don't believe for a minute M is alive," I lied.

Sam's eyes were twinkling. Perhaps she was micro-dosing on Euphory—she had that fiery look of love in her nut-brown eyes.

"May I tell you the full story? Perhaps then you'll understand."

I rolled my eyes. She'd come to the wrong man for absolution.

"First, forgive me—I don't know if M is alive or dead. Dick told me that she had been held offsite in Siberia all these years and that Petrovsky respected her bravery and kept her in a warm bungalow in the snow with a chip in her head that would explode if she wandered off campus. Dick made me write to you to lure you here. But I assume she is dead. I know the Guru is. He was dead by the time I returned to Russia. I went to his funeral, though I had come to hate the man for making me do what I did to Elliot . . ."

She turned away, aiming her gaze above the heads of three little girls running past, hair streaming out behind them and hands clasped tightly to whip each other along like a horizontally slithering snake. I followed the fairy dance as it weaved through the plaza's sightseeing multitude, unready—unwilling—to entertain some tale of woe from an assassin. A classic femme fatale assuming the role of tragic heroine, complete with the moistened eyes of a saint.

"And then I was made to report to Dick, who never mentioned M had lived until recently. Still, he only ever told me what I needed to know."

I was conflicted and disgusted by her role in Elliot's death and M's loss, and upset that I was listening to her lies, expressed in the most earnest and endearing tones. I was rereading *Gatsby*, and Sam spoke in the way I heard Daisy's mesmerizing voice . . . so enticingly innocent and self-serving.

"By hearing it all, I hope you will come to understand. That is my hope, that you'll understand." She shifted closer. "I'm glad you came alone. It's the only way this might work out for us."

I gestured to the parade of humanity that filled the plaza. "They're all on my side, and I don't suspect Russia wants an international incident while they're petitioning to be admitted to the World Tribunal before the 9/9 invasion."

"True, but Dominick—Dick—may have his own agenda, and his distaste for you is beyond hate. Back then, when I was your student, I used to half understand him. We both looked up to the Guru and believed in his New Society. But Dick's dedication to and reverence of the Guru was sparked with a religious fire and desire to serve—the behavior of a lovesick son to a demanding, unloving father. You took all that—his purpose and drive and his father—away from him."

"His father, and his sick guru." I had not been sure of the paternal tie. "Sent out to kill by his master. No wonder Dick's so fucked in the head."

"And since the Guru's death, it's like he's swallowed a demon that feeds on the bile in his belly, and he blames it on you. He is still singularly driven, but now for revenge. His memory loop of that day plays over and over. The AI brings it into ever greater focus when constantly replayed." She stretched her long neck like a cobra coquette about to strike. "To this day, he carries the scar from the hot poker as a symbol of his hate. He told me he had transformed it into a tattoo—'a work of art' he hopes to show you as soon as you go to Russia to meet him."

"Are you trying to threaten me on his behalf?" She didn't need to—his curse hadn't left me.

"No, please believe me. I am no friend of that Dick, my slave master for the past nine years. The Guru used to bring out the best and the worst in Dick. We're left with just the worst. May I tell you the story that leads here and to what we must do beyond this moment?"

"I love a good story—please tell." My softening sarcasm got a twinkle.

"I was a child—an orphan—alone with my younger autistic sister in a Russian state-run facility. Due to a few key physical and mental attributes, I was brought into the security service and separated from my poor sweet sister when I was eleven years old and she was nine, never to see her again. I was told she would be taken care of as long as I followed the rules. From then on, I was trained to be a spy and was taken under the Guru's wing after he defected in 2018. His prize student at twenty-two, sent to play a precocious and troublemaking student at your wonderful school. I loved my days at the Deeksha West causing mischief and teasing you."

"I never understood why, if you were sent to spy, you'd alienate the faculty by being such trouble."

"That's exactly why—my behavior and attitude provided an excellent cover. I had to be extraordinary and stand out as an adversary to avoid suspicion and do what I was assigned to do—drive a wedge between you and M with teasing AI works of literature . . . and then ultimately seduce you." Sam mustered a blush before continuing her story. "Your psychological profile suggested you were attracted to powerful, extraordinary women. I couldn't be just average, and since you had your goddess, Professor Edens, I needed to be ripe and forbidden fruit to arouse your lust. Or so the profiling suggested. The plan was, I would entrap you at an opportune moment, and the night of the fire—the firepit, my nude body, drugs, danger—how could you resist?"

She shook her head, as if I should apologize for rebuking her sexual advance.

"But I did. They probably didn't train you about honoring your vows and Big Love at the spy academy. And stop acting hurt."

"But I was. Even spies have feelings."

"All I injured was your pride," I said.

"Yes, there was that as well. I failed to get you out of the way, which we believed would've allowed Professor Edens to work with the Guru on the New Society promised by Genesis. We believed it was for the good of humanity—a necessary step to avoid annihilation from AI—by merging with it. The Guru thought that M, as a famous scientist with a desire for an ethical role for the hive-mind BCI technology, would want to be there at its inception. Many in Russia still believe the fairy tale spun about a New Society, and that you and M are the bad guys . . . So here we still are," she said, reaching out affectionately for my hand. I pulled it away. She batted her eyes, still feigning being hurt.

"And I regretted nothing until the end. I loved my life there at school as a spy, and more my role of seducing you. Faking a crush led to a real one. You were my first true love."

The twinkling eyes were working overtime. I looked away from her obvious ploy to appeal to my ego and dobber.

"No regrets until he ordered me to nab the children and take them to a Russian safe house in the Oregon mountains. Failing in that, he ordered me to kill Elliot and return to Moscow or be caught as a spy. Elliot had figured most of it out and was going to turn me in."

She made the all-too-familiar family gesture of prayer hands; her pleas for my forgiveness were making my head spin. Forced to be a killer—sad story. Betraying temptress who falls for her professor—but poor orphan girl. Still, the bitch had gone after my children and killed dear sweet Elliot.

"I did it. I did it with an overdose of E or X or Molly—whatever name you give MDMA. I really did shed tears as he faded away in my arms before I ran. It wasn't a bad death. His last words—"

I held up my hands to stop her but changed my mind. "Tell me."

"'The rest is silence.' And then he peacefully passed his last breath."

Hamlet. Elliot, you were a prince and a Falstaff. I saluted my friend with my benediction.

The image of his good death in the arms of this banshee sucking out his last breath made me clench my fist and want to strike her. She looked willing to accept my blow with bowed head.

I relaxed my fist. Elliot had died because he was my friend seeking to help me and I let him do it while knowing the danger. Samantha was merely playing her part in the tragedy that had many authors, including me.

Seeing the storm in me had settled, she continued, "I truly cared for him, but I was under the Guru's power and control. I was weak and saved myself and, I assumed, my sister." She gave me another sad twinkle of her eyes. "I know I have no right to ask for forgiveness now, but his death has haunted me ever since. My life has been stuck in that moment of death."

Many lives had been ended, or stuck for nine years, in the final fifty pages of *The Devil's Calling*. I unsympathetically rolled my hand like I was spinning a wheel for her to get on with the story and to stop seeking pity from me. I surveyed the sky above the plaza, half expecting to see a drone filming the scene, with Dick laughing behind the hidden camera.

"When I returned to find the Guru dead and Genesis and the New Society blown up, it took me some time to sort out what happened. My world was gone. And then Dick became my boss. From your description of him in your books, you know the man. Can you imagine working with him day after day to follow Petrovsky's blueprint for a new Genesis, managing the scientists and computer engineers and industry hackers to steal others' secrets? All of us working in secret as spokes reaching out from Dick's hub. And those who didn't perform their roles or follow the rules or who were suspected of any disloyalty were executed. Dick would have used me as a killer and seductress if Petrovsky hadn't provided me protection as one of his many concubines."

I thought but didn't say, as it sounded too cruel, *The life that you deserved.*

"Dick has none of the Guru's genius, but he knew how to cruelly motivate the scientists and high-tech engineers he commanded. Dick is good at the use of carrot and sticks. You of all people can imagine the sticks he used." Her eyes expressed primal fear. "The carrots were mostly doses of Euphory that came right into the wired-in mind. The drug started in a military program to trigger the release of adrenaline and to numb pain centers, giving superhuman strength and focus to soldiers in combat. You can see it in their eyes—they become wild. They call it blazing."

"How about you, you blazing?" Her eyes were too expressive even for a trained spy and actress on a deadly mission.

"Yes, I'm a bit of a blazer, micro-dosing today to be with you. I'm modestly blazed, I'd say," she said, taking stock of herself, placing an outstretched index finger between her eyebrows as if she were pushing a button there or taking another small dose of Euphory. "Afraid I'd look old to you now—vanity, I know. But with the little tech boost, I can run a marathon or perform a twenty-four-hour tantra for you today."

I nervously laughed at her artificial prowess.

"Dick seethed, restrained as he was from killing you and your family. He often pounded his chest to remind him of the scar you left there. And now, with Petrovsky gone, he's exploring ways to have his kill chip switched off." She flicked her hair over her shoulder—ever the seductress or nervous habit? "That's why I'm here today and he's not—I have no kill switch embedded in me to harm me if I step out of Russia. I am Russian and trusted. Dick's not."

Needing to focus, I sipped from my water bottle, but I'd become lost trying to remember what the Great Man had said back at Clashmoor Castle about the encrypted kill switches.

After looking up at the sky, she covered her mouth to say, "I've risked my life for nine years tracking Dick for you and informing your people. I would have suffered a painful death if caught." She looked at the plaza fountain, studying the three iron women figures in the center. "You know they represent the daughters of Zeus—beauty, charm, and joy." She looked at me like I had denied her these three graces. "I thought you might forgive me."

Gerard had suggested he might have someone spying on Dick. I swallowed hard to tamp down the wave of gratitude rising in my chest. I needed to focus on the risk in front of me and not on granting redemption.

"Go on," I said. "This is all interesting, but what are we doing here today?"

"We're supposed to go to that watch factory, where we'll find a case filled, according to Dick, with proof M is alive. He tells me there is proof of life there. It will only be unlocked after we arrive. And after I show you that M is alive, I'm to remove the gun from the case and kill you with it in a most obscene manner while video cameras record it for Dick in Moscow."

Dick had a one-track mind that had never lost sight of his twisted way for me to die. My sphincter and then my whole body tightened. And how perfect for him to kill me after showing me M still lived in some hellhole he had dug for her. "Why are you telling me all this?"

She waved off my question, saying, "The box is also loaded with passports, diamonds, and cash to finance my escape so I can live my life free of all this, free of him, as my payment for executing his curse. All of Petrovsky's men stole riches with impunity before his departure. Dick's reward will be watching you die after you've seen proof that M lives."

"Sure. I'll go with you to the factory and Dick will be there. He'd want to see me die at his own hand with his own beady eyes."

"He thought you might think that. So he sent this gift."

She held up the box and unwrapped my retirement watch. I braced myself to go out with a bang and a temptress in the Plaza Real.

But maybe not. I squinted at the box. It was a small, sophisticated gadget, but it didn't keep time.

"Used by Russian intelligence, it tracks human heat signatures."

She turned the box on, and we were two bright-red beacons on the monitor. She expanded out the screen's view, and the plaza streamed with orange lights, both still and fluid. As she zoomed out more, humanity became a yellow mass encompassing Barcelona.

"This is why he selected an abandoned factory—to show two heat signatures—yours and mine. If we see a third, we both better run."

"It makes no sense."

"Why not? It's all true. Every word I've said."

"Why not just send the box of good news—that M lives—and lure me to a hotel room if the Plaza Real is too public for my death? Why the mysterious abandoned factory?"

"I don't know. He doesn't like too many questions. And perhaps . . ." She paused, a liar's pause.

"Tell me! I have a way to get the truth from you and will know if you lie."

"He made me swear. He insisted it be a surprise. You must act surprised or he'll know I've betrayed him. He'll be there at the office in the factory, in a way. Participating by hologram. That way if you set a trap for the authorities to come, only I'll be caught and you'll still be under his death threat. And so will Professor Edens. Who knows what he'll do to her if she really still lives and we don't follow his instructions."

"Not another goddam hologram with that Dick." I wouldn't do it. I might have to do it. No, I would do it, based on the slim chance M still lived.

"Sean, we don't have to go, but we'll both be on the run the rest of our lives if we don't do what he wants. And what if the briefcase does contain proof that Professor Edens still lives? Of course, you'll have to trust me not to shoot you. Or now that you know there's a gun," she added with nervous shiver of her shoulders, "I'll have to trust you not to shoot me."

I'd swear she wasn't acting and was truly frightened, but it wasn't me she feared.

I imagined Dick bathing in ice in the next room at the watch factory to thwart the heat-seeking device, but that sounded too farfetched even for the cold-blooded killer. Would he let Samantha do his dirty work as he watched like a ghoul by hologram? And then would he watch the scene over and over again in his memory loop?

I was lost, well off my path to Nirvana with perhaps minutes to live, sitting along La Rambla in the heart of the maze called Barcelona and being bewitched by the twinkling eyes of an assassin, her lush lips feeding me lies. But lies that made no sense as lies, which made them sound true.

I needed to test Sam's veracity. I had a plan to examine her more intimately in my hotel room.

I STOOD AND SAID, "FOLLOW ME. Before we go to the factory to meet holo-Dick, I want you to see my hotel room." I was going to play a game with her; my role was that of lover, and maybe fool, if she scissored me to death on my hotel bed.

She looked surprised but undaunted. "Unless you have me arrested there or kill me, I still have to get the case from that factory. After turning on him, the money and diamonds—and passports for running—are my best chance to live."

As we walked to the Hotel Gaudí, she handed me the heat-seeking box to play with and confirm how it worked.

When we entered my freshly made-up hotel room, I moved over to the beautiful double-wide window with its Juliet balcony to take in the spectacular Barcelona view. I deeply inhaled the precious sea air, savoring what might be one of my final breaths.

"Make yourself comfortable and then sit on the bed," I said. "Anything from the minibar or room service?"

Playing strip poker or truth-or-dare would have been less intimate than the game I had planned for us on the hotel bed. Such an odd game for a monk preparing to take his vows.

"A water please."

I got one from the minibar and handed it to her. She was already sitting on the bed.

"You know they used to test witches by throwing them into the sea. I think you would float, which means you are guilty. Now, please slip your dress down, off the shoulders, so I can see your breasts."

"Really, Professor?" She sounded less afraid than disappointed. "This doesn't sound like you. I was mocked in Moscow for my failure to seduce you. But now you've brought me to your bed to see my breasts and—"

I attempted a look of dashing mystery that came off as a goofy leer in the large mirror next to the bed. At a certain age, and well before sixty-four, a man's flirtation with younger women becomes just plain creepy.

"I'll do whatever, but we have to get to that factory soon. I'll need the gems inside the case to disappear. All I wanted from you was forgiveness. We could go first, and then you might wine and dine me so we could discuss what we found and our next moves before Dick can sic his DOGs."

She was disappointed in her teacher and his lack of chivalry.

"I'm a new man. And you boasted of some tantric abilities. Please do as I say. And don't worry, I won't force you to do anything you don't want to do."

"You won't have to."

The eye twinkle dimmed as her hands pulled down her dress. Swallowing my guilt, I had to remind myself of the true power dynamic here. She could kill me with the minibar corkscrew.

"May I keep my necklace on? Today the amulet protects you." I nodded yes. I had reason not to discount her powers. As a wizard, I believed in magic too. Her further compliance revealed a half-cup red silk bra. As she reached around to unfasten the clasp, I signaled with an index finger pointed upward for her to stop, like a man who wanted to savor his meal. I unbuttoned my own short-sleeve linen shirt I had worn for the occasion. The years hadn't made me any more fashionable, but I loved linen on a hot day.

With both of us partially undressed, I sat down next to her, and she dipped her head to my shoulder, looking up with bewildered eyes at her seducer who had caught her totally by surprise. She smelled like honeysuckle. The temptress could release endorphins on demand.

"Well, if we're going to die anyway . . ." I reached under the bed. "And 9/9!" I used the common excuse for all sorts of bad behavior as a rallying cry as I pulled out Molly's game of technological foreplay, the modern version of truth-or-dare. "Sink or swim time."

Sam laughed at my fake seduction.

"A game? So devil-may-care in the face of deadly danger? We'll finally see if you love me, Professor."

"And we'll finally see if you know how to tell the truth."

The third gauge on the Heart Sync would register her sincerity in response to my questions. And the heart was a much better gauge of truth than the at-home lie detector apps that measured the pulse or voice. Sam was a pro and could deceive such simplistic attempts to catch a lie. But the heart can never lie.

"Please try to not touch the amulet. It might lose its charm." It lay nestled between salacious breasts cradled by red silk.

I placed her cups with a teacher's care. She then prepared mine. Sam knew how the game was played. She strained to keep her seductress eyes from batting as if she were a helpless young woman at the mercy of a powerful older man, doing her best to play this straight, as was I. Still, I couldn't help but feel like a slim and slimy Harvey Weinstein auditioning a yet-to-be discovered Scarlett Johansson.

Finally, cups attached and hearts linked, we sat lotus and face-to-face on the bed, the monitor between us.

"You always were so convincing as a master of deception, and you did already kill Elliot. So, to be sure I'm not walking into certain death orchestrated by you and Dick, I've brought this Heart Sync. You seem familiar with it?"

"I've played with Love Link, which is more the fad in Russia, but it's the same basic technology. All the boys want to play with me, but they never match my energy, with the highest scores coming in, in the seventies. I'm not going to make love with or date a C-grade guy. And as you can imagine, they can't force themselves on me."

She gave me a sexy killer look to remind me that, despite my charade of seduction, she could rape me.

"Let's get started. We'll take the suggested minimum fifteen minutes of meditation and eye gazing, and then I'll ask my questions."

"I have nothing to hide," she said, coaxing my eyes to follow her blazing eyes down to her pulsating breasts.

I turned the knob. "Game on!"

I was embarrassed by my initial arousal score but more embarrassed that hers registered a mere seven. Damn being sixty-four. I namaste'd her, and we started the silent meditation. She knew how this was played, and we were both following the rules.

As we gazed into each other's eyes, I saw her Buddha nature and I let go of our past. There was no hiding, no shadow of deception. Soon I felt a loving stream between us. Maybe not as strong as Molly's, but unmistakable and beautiful. In that moment, I forgave her completely.

When the bell tolled, we turned to the monitor as she roared out the score.

"Love! Ninety-two out of a hundred! Top ten percentile!"

I needed to be graded on a curve.

"Now ask me your question, my A-minus man!"

I didn't like the high score, but even less her assigning the minus to it. The score made me think that I'd made the right decision with Molly in not following my dobber to her bed. Apparently in Big Love, everyone was a Buddha and got an A grade with me. M and Juno had taught me well. Big Love was not special or exclusive but the unconditional, unlimited love of God and the divinity within us all. Even Samantha Smythe.

Still, she had another test to pass.

"Sam, are you truly seeking to help and not harm me?"

"I am trying to help you."

We waited for the monitor to register its response.

Within a couple seconds, it flashed YES! Truth! I liked its enthusiasm and hoped it was true. From all I'd read about the technology, it was foolproof.

From detesting her to love, all in the space of an hour. I wanted to kiss Sam for risking her life for me, but I let my eyes thank her.

She took my hand and squeezed. "Tell me you forgive me."

"Some more questions first, please?"

"I'm an open book for you, my teacher."

She received the same truth score, though I hadn't meant for that answer to be tested—the game was still on.

I asked her about each element of her story and Dick's plan and how she planned to betray him for me. She passed each question with flying colors. I was sad to hear her sister had died in a recent pandemic—the explanation for why Sam was now free to run. I turned off the game and asked my last question.

"And was it you looking for me up and down the Irish coast?"

"Yes, and I found you using my witch's eye. But I told Dick I found nothing—no evidence of you living there. Dick can't find you himself unless he can prevail and have Russia let him leave the country. I'm glad there is no chip in my head, or I wouldn't be able to run today. I wish . . ."

"What?"

"You might run with me. But that's impossible. We'd be found, and you have family."

I brought her hand to my still cupped and synced chest. "I do thank you and do now love you in a Big Love way. You've traveled a long way from killer vixen to the noble and brave young woman here today. Thank you for taking so much risk for me now and before."

I imagined a dark cloak lifting off her shoulders, carried away by the light flooding the room with the midday sun. That light, like the light that had flowed between our eyes, seemed to move simultaneously in both directions. It was very real and very strong, the power of absolution, forgiveness, and atonement. I let go of all judgment and blame.

We slowly un-cup-pled. Samantha frowned when I smiled and pulled her dress up over her shoulders and then buttoned my shirt.

An image appeared to me—no doubt sent by Elliot—of his youthful self playing Cardenio in angelic company. "And Elliot forgives you too."

"We shared a love of Shakespeare and our AI masterpiece of *Cardenio*," she said.

"Our masterpiece?"

"Don't hate me again, but I was behind the Shelley and Shakespeare AI you received. I really do love Shakespeare and wanted to study his works with you. The Guru gave me free rein to play with you with our state-of-the-art chat bot AI for literature. We truly believed everyone would welcome the New Society, even if some required a little push. Wait—I read your book. Elliot told you that. I knew he would share with you that I was the mysterious Sir Arthur behind the fake AI masterpieces." She bounced up from the bed with excitement. "And the Guru told you that either of them, he or M, could stop the double death with Genesis up until the very end when the clock stopped. He was a professional bluffer, always pushing the gambit to the brink, and wouldn't have relinquished control till the last instant. So maybe M's alive? And the Guru's death, Petrovsky's punishment for failure. What will you do if the evidence is there?"

"I'll work with contacts at Interpol and the WT to get her back. I'm not going to Russia without a good plan to extract her alive." The Great Man might help me, but in exchange for what?

What did M say about the future being based on quantum probability? And that it could be changed? Might the same be said for an assumed past? I held on to hope, inspired by Sam's conversion to the light, which proved anything was possible. And I was truly grateful. I had come assuming that Elliot's cruel killer had come to kill me, and now I saw her in an entirely different, almost angelic, light.

I stood and held out my hand. "Okay, my A-minus student. Let's see what's in Dick's case, shall we? Even though I'm terrified of seeing him—even by hologram."

In a way, Dick had figured out a death-by-hologram, but my twist was that no real-life accomplice was required. His accomplice took my hand, and I still felt the strangest of all love connections there.

"Perhaps you shouldn't go," she said. "I could meet you later, bring the case here. We both will be on the run for our lives once Dick is denied his hologram death."

We'd moved from complete distrust to deep affection within the dangerous gambit we now shared. I couldn't let her risk her life for me alone.

"You don't know me well. I thought you'd read my books. Mailbox messages and containers of treasure are my specialty."

"Sean Byron McQueen, you're always the hero of your stories. I was testing that hero to see if he trusted me now—I couldn't go alone and retrieve or see the case opened without you. It will be chain-locked and set for remote release by Dick. Let's go—he's waiting. I have a plan, but it's far from foolproof."

As the hotel door shut behind us, I shuddered as reasonable doubt returned to gnaw at my heart. Perhaps Samantha had cast some spell over me and was still a witch who could betray her own heart.

EITHER DICK OR I had made one big mistake—trusting Sam.

Walking along La Rambla with my new ally to the sea and then down the coast to the abandoned watch factory felt like a school outing to meet a psychopath sworn to kill me. The woman by my side appeared as an ambiguous image depending on which way I chose to look, beautiful Buddha or bad seed. I could hear Alfred as the voice of reason saying I should not trust her. But she had been helping me through the years, risking her own life. There was continuity in what she was doing now to help me. And Dick's trap held out hope that M still lived. That strong need to know kept me moving forward into the unknown and gambling with death.

When the watch factory appeared ahead of us and the busy streets emptied around the abandoned block, I turned on my heat-seeking box.

"Let's keep an eye out for Dick," I said. "And let's look suspiciously at one another in case we're watched."

"No need. My mission was to win you over and gain your trust. You can look suspicious of me if you want." I did.

Molly was buzzing my fez, wanting an update. My fez was set to always receive messages from the family, Gerard, and Alfred. I stopped walking to think how to respond before I'd turn off all contacts so I could focus on meeting the author of my craic's curse.

"What—what're you doing?" Sam asked.

"Molly Quinn wants an update on how our date is going. You sent her my invite for today, remember? She wants to know I'm still alive. Speaking of Molly, what can you tell me about you and her?"

"She's a great author I enjoy reading. She expanded my horizons on what 9/9 and the aliens might mean for humanity."

"She never conspired with you against me?"

"No."

"What about with Dick or the Guru? She ever work with them?"

"You're sounding paranoid. She helped you, not your enemies."

"Great. It's just something she said recently."

Funny, I now believed Samantha as much as or more than I did Molly, though Molly did score two points higher in Heart Sync.

"Wait." I stopped again, this time pulling on Sam's arm to stop her too. "Now that I feel I know you, I can ask—how could Dick think you'd kill me in that way?"

That way was by sticking a gun barrel up my *arse* to blow my brains out.

"He knows I'm a compassionate killer, and that killing you in the obscene way he demanded would disturb me. He likes to see me tortured too, and it would create a memory loop he would take to his grave. But he also knows how much I want to be free of him forever, particularly since I no longer have Petrovsky's protection—it must have seemed to him a small price for me to pay for my freedom."

She narrowed her eyes, obviously thinking, before lowering her head and adding, "But he must have other operatives here to arrange the case and the hologram, and he's not going to leave a bunch of diamonds for anyone to stumble upon, so he must have some means of surveillance. A satellite watching for anyone that enters the warehouse would be standard procedure. With operatives ready to swoop in afterward. Don't look up when you speak. Lip-reading drones are not out of the realm of possibility."

I covered my mouth to speak. "Why don't we snatch the briefcase and not allow him his hologram?"

She turned to me, grabbing both of my arms.

"Listen, I won't lie and tell you this is going to be easy. And we better hurry. He is becoming impatient." I cringed, imagining him inside her BCI head, and hoped he couldn't listen in. "He controls a digital handcuff-like lock on the case that he will unlock when he appears to us. He doesn't want to risk what's inside before we . . . before I'm there to protect it and he can watch. Remember to look surprised when he appears."

"That shouldn't be a problem." Fear and surprise register as similar facial expressions.

"And when I foolishly let you look into the case and I go for the gun, you need to quickly shut down the hologram that we will have switched on. I'll let you take any evidence that Professor Edens lives and a diamond to remember me by. We'll need to run. Get out of town. I'll report that it was done and you are dead, but that won't buy us much, if any, time. He'll learn I betrayed him when I don't produce evidence of your death."

Her words struck me like the *rat-tat-tat* of a machine gun firing instructions and information at me.

"I don't like this. Maybe we haven't thought this through."

But we both kept walking toward the massive building to hologram with Dick. His handcuffed case was Schrödinger's box where the cat, or M in this case, would remain dead and alive based on quantum probabilities until I opened that damn Pandora's box.

"Do you have an escape plan?" she asked.

"I have an influential Catalan friend and a contact at Interpol who should be able to help me get back into hiding."

We were now far away from the heart of Barcelona in the center of a city block that was exclusively taken up on the right side by the old warehouse. It felt like we had left the living and were entering Chernobyl. *EL NATIONAL CAT* engraved on a big marble block looked like a headstone in front of the complex. A Catalan flag draped over the Spanish newspaper's name flapped up in the wind, revealing the building's prior use for propaganda. Samantha motioned for me to check the monitor to confirm two, not three, heat signatures. I had been checking frequently, so she hadn't needed to ask.

"What if he's hiding in an ice bath and waiting for us inside?" I was thinking of the family-freezing bath behind Diva Falls.

"You've seen too many movies. That might work, but any part of him that reads eighty degrees Fahrenheit would still show up, and beneath eighty, he'd be dead. You know, writers would make good spies."

She was so calm, but she'd been in the company of Dick all along, while I only lived with his curse. The prospect of seeing him again was causing a silent scream within me. *What the fuck are you doing?*

"And don't worry. He'd be here if he could."

That made me worry more. Outwardly I tried to mirror her composure but found myself rubbing my face. I didn't have her training.

The small side door beside the large bay doors for trucks was easily jimmied open by Samantha. We entered the first floor, a two-story-high football field–sized space with all the old news presses and conveyor belts still intact under layers of dust. Dust so thick as to be dirt. The light was gray, dulled by sooty windowpanes. The old mechanical robots that performed the labor remained covered in slime. Alfred's predecessors. It was like a land time forgot. If our mission wasn't so serious, I would have sent him pictures to hear his witty retort—something like "I come from a long line of slaves."

The watch factory used the large office spaces on the floor above. With the refracted light from the smoky windows, it felt like an alien world where the robots come alive at night. But all was dead there. The interior was cold, slowing the decay, on a warm summer day that was rushing quickly into night.

Like the Himalayan hovel of our last date, this place reeked of Dick and death.

WTF? I had planned as far ahead as the plaza meeting and the Heart Sync game in my hotel room with Sam. My imagination had never taken me this far, to this place to meet a hologramming Dick. I'd asked Molly to finish my manuscript, but I hadn't said goodbye to the children. I always thought there would be time as I took it step by step, but now I had crossed some line and it was too late.

Samantha led the way. "Top floor, room 222. He said you'd like the room number. I've read your books, so I knew what he meant."

Two twenty-two was the magic number of the room at the Beekman

Hotel where he killed my best friend Dylan eighteen years before. I assumed Dick's DOGs had the shiny numbers changed when they left the case and set up the portal for his hologram.

We entered a dramatically lit room that I imagined was once an office for newspaper journalists pumping out five hundred words of realistic fiction a day and later, where watchmakers huddled round small tables, looking down with magnifying glasses, making small time pieces. Today, it looked like a theater staged for a killing, with a small desk holding a brief-case under a spotlight. The briefcase had a small bracelet lock affixed by a chain to a metal loop coming out of the floor. Dangling near the desk like a noose was what looked like a mic or a circuit breaker. Behind the desk was the yet unlit laser lighting needed for Dick's grand hologrammatic entrance. They had installed some high-tech stage work to set the scene.

I felt like the dumb blonde in a horror movie that everyone is screaming at to run away. I clutched my heart as it was still screaming *WTF.* My head added, *And why am I trusting Samantha Smythe?* My head and heart aligned for once. But my writer's curiosity and my love for M had to know.

Samantha asked, "Are you ready to start the show and hear what he has to say before we open the case?"

"Sam." I squeezed her hand out of fear and gratitude.

"Remember to look surprised when he appears and to shut him off when I go for the gun in the case. You ready? He knows we are here and is not waiting patiently."

"I am . . ." I was at a loss for words.

She walked over to the cord hanging by the desk, looking fearfully at me for the first time. I nodded. She switched the hologram on.

Dick's sick eyes immediately appeared—emblazoned by his Char-lie Manson pupils, the rest of his face and then the rest of his body appeared. The ghoul was dressed in all black like a muscular Steve Jobs or sadistic Paddy. Paddy often dressed in black, and Dick was the same large size. If they were born in the other's shoes, would they have turned out differently?

Dick bellowed, "McQueeenyyy!"

The metal handcuff on the briefcase dropped to the floor.

Though shaking, I said, "You might have some original new greeting for me after all these years."

He approached the desk and seemingly laid a hand on the case. "Ha—same old weeny acting brave. Sam, you set the ground rules? He understands?"

"Yes" was all the usually effusive Sam said.

"Good." He patted, without sound, the briefcase.

"Proof Emily Edens lives is in this case."

"What proof?"

"A digital time-stamped picture of your M. I took it myself *after* I took a part of her. It's in here, too, on dry ice. You'll see it is a freshly cut piece of mmm—meat." He joyfully danced around the small desk like it was his dance partner.

The irony was that his sickening description of the proof made me believe M was alive after all. Showing me her finger, toe, or ear as proof of life would please Dick. I was nauseated and speechless.

"You can test the print and DNA," Dick said. "Hell, you could even clone her, though you'd be dead before a clone was old enough to fuck. But to see her, you'll have to follow my instruction to where we all will meet and where one or two of us will die. I'll give you a fighting chance. I'm not a bad sport, but trust that you will see her die and then you'll take it up your arse the way I promised. The instructions, even a visa, are all in the case here. Have you been to Russia before?"

He made a great show of fondness for the leather briefcase, caressing it from miles away. He then moved to face Samantha but spoke loud enough for me to hear.

"Sam, I was testing you one last time. There's no gun in the case. McQueen gets to live for now. He'll come to Russia when he sees his precious M still lives. You still get the other goodies I promised you—there in the case for your new life. Unless you want to come home and see what I have planned for our two lovebirds and their reunion."

She nodded her head like she understood, though her face looked confused and not entirely convinced. I couldn't ask Sam if this changed our plan in front of him. But there would be no reason to shut down the hologram and run.

I was overcome with an overwhelming desire to believe M was alive and that the power of manifestation was coming true. In the face of my biggest fear, and with my heart's biggest desire at hand, I closed my eyes, and the image of Juno with a bindi, looking like an Indian saint, floated through my mind, slowing down time.

Opening my eyes to see the holo-Dick still dancing around me, something was wrong—and it wasn't just Dick and his ghoulish glee—more, a metaphysical shift of energy. There was a strong desire to believe, but not the certitude of belief in my desire that Juno taught as the path to truth. A strange magnetic or electric sensation tingled my scalp, a rush of energy like they say a dog senses before a tidal wave strikes or an earthquake erupts. A current tuning into a channel of telepathy, an opening brought on by a moment of truth.

Yes, Sean Byron McQueen, something is not right. I left my body nine years ago and stepped into the light. You were there with me. My hero, run from that Pandora's box. Schrödinger's cat is dead inside—curiosity killed it. The children. Run!

A message from M!

I ran for the circuit breaker at the end of the dangling cord as Dick, maybe forgetting he was a hologram, moved to stop me. We both grabbed the small box at the same time. His hand on mine felt like ice.

He yelled, "Sam, stop him!"

I jumped up on the cord to yank it out of its socket, knocking over some of the lasers it was attached to, making Dick disappear once and for all. Sam hadn't moved, and we both stood shocked, trying to decide what I had done by my unscripted actions. Dick was no longer there, but his presence still filled the room.

Sam, clutching at the amulet over her heart, finally said, "Well, I better open the case. If I'm no longer meant to kill you, M must still live. And he wants you to go to Russia."

I grabbed Samantha's arm. "Wait!" I said. "If we might die here, let's make sure we're prepared. We can't believe him." I believed M.

I weighed M's words. If they were just my imagination, then there was the possibility she was still alive and that case was my way back to her.

"Samantha, something isn't right here. Why would Dick trust you? Why would he go to all the trouble to set you up in a new life rather than keep you as an asset? Think. He must have known. I know you're good at deception, but he trusted no one other than the Guru. And I can't explain, but I'm being told we should run from here without that case. He half convinced me we'd find M's finger in there, but I bet it'll be poison that wafts over us when we open it. I'll protect you. Come with me."

She smiled compassionately, too polite to laugh at my ability to protect her from Dick and all the powers of Russia. She didn't know I had Alfred and Gerard to help.

"Sean, you may be right, but this is a risk I must take." She didn't need to clarify the point. "As crazy as it sounds, it's believable, and now that Genesis Two is done, he has the resources. And if I'm gone, he'll get all the credit. You must go now."

"If you're gone . . ." I repeated.

"If getting rid of us was all he wanted, why not have me poison you in the square and then poison me upon my return?"

"Poison or some other booby trap, and he wanted to see us die." I motioned toward the case that held the answers.

"Yes, but I won't know what he intends unless I open the box. And without those diamonds . . . I'm fucked either way. And you'll never know if M really lives. Sean, you run, and take the heat sensor. I'll be right behind you. I'll meet you downstairs and share the contents with you. No reason for us both to risk it. And then, I'll contact Dick for further instructions. He's going to be pissed you pulled his plug."

I studied Sam in all her fearlessness. Looked over at the open door exit from room 222.

"You have children and the family to think of. I only have . . ." The twinkle returned to her eyes. "You."

I didn't know what to say in return for that devotion under the circumstances. But to stay with her would be a senseless chivalry best left to poems and romances.

"It must be my books you love."

"My favorites, along with Shakespeare. I can't wait for the third book of the trilogy and the tale of my redemption. Now go and no more lovey-dovey. No time. Wait for me on the first floor. But kiss me before you go. You know you want to. Hurry now, Dick's DOGs will be on their way."

The shimmering eyes set within that brave and lovely face sought the final clichéd act of romance—the kiss in the face of death.

The only reason to stay was my male ego and bravado, but the children, Dylan and Juno, and the family needed me. M would never forgive me for disobeying her warning. I gave Samantha her last wish, a glancing kiss on those luscious Scarlett Johansson lips. We shared a moment of blazing eye contact, and then I left my demon-turned-angel to her fate.

No sooner was I safely on the first floor when the world above me exploded in a loud blast of karma. I found myself rocked down to my knees. It felt like the bomb had gone off in my chest because my heart had stopped with the bang and started again with a bang of its own.

"Good-bye, Sa-man-tha," I said, short of breath from a heart that the explosion had knocked off rhythm. A cloud of dust and debris rattled down from the rafters. The soot-covered box showed lots of heat-sensed bodies were already moving toward what was left of the old watch factory whose roof had just blown off.

44 RUN!

I DOUBTED THERE WOULD BE ENOUGH LEFT of Sam to identify her body. In the end, Dick was trying for two birds with one bomb. The hologram ghoul would've enjoyed being in the midst of the mayhem at the moment of explosion. He must have thought from my writings that my desire to see M again would be so great that I'd convince myself she wasn't dead. And he must have sussed that Sam either had, or would, betray him. Poison was too gentle and subtle for Dick. He always liked a big bang.

I didn't go looking for pieces of Sam as the sprinklers started raining on me. I was shell-shocked beneath the blast site. And she'd been blasted to smithereens. Numerous hot bodies were rushing into the factory. Dick's operatives must be among the first responders. I thought about the satellites or drones Sam assumed were watching the building, but had to risk running out.

I hid behind a newspaper cart until I could mingle among the responders, pretending I was there to help. I took a sheet covering the cart and draped it over my head and torso to look like an Indian worshipping Kali, seeking shelter from the rain and debris, and to not look like Sean Byron McQueen. One of the crew pointed up, screaming something in Catalan.

Several of us took that to mean vacate the building, and we raced for the exit.

I kept running until I found a seaside café with a dark little booth and ordered a red Rioja by the glass and some water, *por favor*. I'd ditched my dusty sheet after making my escape. I was disheveled, but it had started to rain, so my wet clothes didn't look out of place. The TV over the bar repeated over and over an image of the blast, the firetrucks, and the police response, with a caption *Accidente o Terrorismo?*

I was dazed by the death of a person who had meant so much—bad and good—to me. Dick would be coming for me. I couldn't return to my hotel since they'd probably followed Sam and me there. He hadn't trusted her after all. Luckily I was carrying my passport, along with my old phone, wallet, and fez cap. Still, I wouldn't be able to get back to the relative safety of my secluded Irish tower. Not soon. Not with all the means of surveillance available to Dick and the DOGs searching for me at all points of transit.

I knew I'd have to call Gerard but felt too scared and guilty. He might disown and disavow me. I'd recklessly violated our relationship and got one of his double agents killed. I phoned Oriol B.

As I waited with Rioja for my rescue, I wondered whether I should involve Oriol, but I didn't have much choice. Oriol was truly a man of the world and a friend via Dylan. He was a leading proponent of an international language called Esperanto at the turn of the century. He and others hoped a common tongue would bring world peace. Since Alfred and his brothers could understand and speak in all languages, and the wired-in had auto-translate, the Esperanto movement had lost all momentum.

World peace, among men, might be impossible unless the aliens would teach us. Even my personal peace was farther away than ever. *Om, shanti, shanti, shanti*—oh, shit, shit, shit. I wished the aliens would come tonight and save me and my world.

Dylan had introduced me to Oriol. He had close friends in every city he'd frequented for business, and later as a spiritual tourist. Dylan and Oriol had worked together on Oriol's international youth-hostel network and its mission to open all the young at heart to global citizenship. Oriol's hostels weren't merely a business but a philosophy celebrating international cultural exchange, which was introduced at that pivotal point of young adulthood that leads either to the pursuit of a parochial course or to a more global, inclusive, and accepting worldview. An interesting philosophy over the years for a militant Catalan separatist, but I trusted Oriol, and he would do almost anything for Dylan's best friend.

Barcelona is a walking city, and Oriol was at my table fifteen minutes and one glass of Rioja later. He always dressed in a dark T-shirt, leather jacket, and jeans, looking like his hero Bruce Springsteen, but Oriol was balding unabashedly, sans cap. Still, he was the boss in Barcelona.

I knew from my time with Oriol that, whatever the situation, Catalan wine was the answer and my Spanish Rioja could have used a little grenache to balance the tempranillo grape. Under the circumstances, my vow of drinking in moderation was to be granted an extra glass or two of leeway. He was shaken—the whole city was shaken by the bombing. Still, he lost no time in ordering the establishment's finest bottle. While we waited, I explained my role in the watch factory blast and the danger I brought with me.

His brow furrowed as he weighed the situation, and then he laughed and said, "Don't forget we lived under the Spanish boot for over a century, so I'm somewhat accustomed to hiding from bloodthirsty authority. With 9/9 coming, we all are a little bolder if we're not hiding in caves. I'm a simple hosteller for international liberty, and you're my good American friend of Dylan's and an honorary Catalan. Of course, I must help you."

Oriol had a lovely Moorish camp in the countryside that we joked was a cave as it was built into the side of a rock face. And I had shown sympathy to his cause and affinity for his wine over the years.

"Oriol, you must realize how dangerous this all is. This Dick will stop at nothing and is a twisted, murdering pervert."

"You can say that again." Oriol was fond of American idioms. "I've read all about your Dick. And now the bastard is setting off bombs in my city?"

I told the full story of Sam and Dick and the bombing over the first glass of wine, speaking very quietly while the story continued to play loudly on the TV. Over the second glass, Oriol, the Catalan revolutionary, came up with a plan to use his old network to help me escape.

First he phoned the chief of police and offered to have me meet him at an old Catalan safe house for an interview and information about the bombing if he promised to come alone.

"The chief said he will think about it. But don't worry, he doesn't know where the safe house is. We can trust him to do nothing or agree to my terms. I'll call Carlos now to get us into the house."

Oriol didn't explain more of his plan as he phoned Carlos, his right-hand man, who I'd met. Carlos spoke only Catalan, so I didn't understand a word they said over the phone other than the refrain of "safe house" that Oriol kept repeating for my benefit.

He moved from his Carlos call to take another. "Thanks, Chief. Yes, he's right here with me . . . Oh, I won't say that. I'll text you the address of the safe house and see you there soon."

When he finished his calls, he offered a toast as if all was well. "It is done."

I wasn't sure I wanted to turn myself in, but my options were to follow Oriol's lead as he assured me, "I got this, but we have to move fast," or to take my chances on the streets and at the airport. I reminded myself that Oriol was the boss here.

We were soon wending our way through the twisted streets of the Gothic Quarter, dodging the driving rain, and carrying a magnum of wine, a big bottle of water, a big loaf of bread, a long *butifarra* sausage, and a wedge of stinky Catalan cheese. Oriol's mind was never far from food or wine, and though I was on the run, he saw no reason not to have ample provisions. I wondered how he stayed so skinny. Though almost my age, he had the metabolism and energy of a teenager.

As we strode on, half trotting, he filled me in on a plan that seemed entirely based on relationships and faith. When we reached a nice row of town houses on a somewhat more fashionable street than I would have thought appropriate for a hideout, Carlos met us with the keys at the door of one of the charming old Catalan homes. Carlos gave both Oriol and me the side-eye, like we were up to no good.

Oriol explained, "Generally this place is now used for the Catalan network to entertain mistresses since that is all some of my comrades now have to hide."

It was good to have powerful friends. Carlos hugged Oriol goodbye. I was in shock, but even so I was ever so grateful these men were risking their lives for me. I hugged Carlos too, which he accepted with a Catalan cackle, and then he was gone.

The town house was a five-star hideout negating my image of the spartan places one might stay when on the run, places like the dodgy room where the star witness in Steve McQueen's *Bullitt* was splattered against the dirty white wall with a shotgun blast. Or the narrow flat space under a barn or kitchen floorboards that I imagined shielding a runaway slave on the Underground Railroad or Shosanna in *Inglurious Basterds*. Or Anne Frank's attic . . . While I would suffer in my privileged Relais & Châteaux accommodations.

Oriol was a full-service concierge and bellhop as he settled me into my hideaway accommodations. There were even clothes in the closet and drawers for me to wear. And a full set of toiletries in the bath.

"When on the run, you often don't have time to pack," he said.

Oriol opened the magnum and prepared a charcuterie spread. I changed out of my wet linen shirt into a soft calico sweater and lay on the sofa. My comfy sweater, posture, and Oriol's cheerful disposition were at odds with my sense of panic and desire for flight not respite.

I asked, "Can you explain to me how I can escape? Dick has all the eyes of Russia and his mercenary DOGs."

"The chief is a decent man. We should be able to trust him." Oriol paused after damning the man with faint praise. "My idea is we trade your cooperation, since you have nothing to hide, for their agreeing to find two bodies at the blast site. That should buy you time."

"And Dick will think I'm dead? Brilliant. I love it, but will he do it? And Dick's goons may have seen me exit the building, though I was cloaked in a dirty white sheet. I should call my contact, my friend in Interpol." Gerard should have been my first call. He was going to be pissed at me, and I wasn't sure what to say. "He's a Russian-spy expert who's had my back for nine years watching for Dick. He'll help us cover this up, and if needed, help convince the local police. *If* he doesn't kill me for meeting Samantha and not telling him."

"Okay, call him before the chief arrives. It's tourist season here, and they'll want to rule out terrorism quickly. Your cooperation can help with that."

Oriol was now my Dylan, my Elliot, and my Alfred—providing me sage advice and service as my host. His résumé—running a chain of hostels throughout Europe, being an author, and serving as a revolutionary—made him a jack-of-all-trades. At his first hostel on La Rambla, he had checked people in, poured the beer at the bar, and cleaned the rooms. Within our safe house, all he had left to do was pour more wine.

The excitement and wine were like lava that churned in my belly when I thought of Sam's charred body. My heart was numb, and my brain moved in slow motion, survival mode. Like a lightning strike to the crown of my head, the blast had shifted me into a new reality. No longer a monk minding his prayers but a hunted animal wanting safety and substance.

I fez-called Inspector Gerard. He was relieved I was alive, considering I was "too stupid to live." Other than saying I was TSTL, he was professional and rose to meet the moment rather than further chastise me. He didn't want my location revealed over the computer line and directed me to send it in an encrypted text that we used to communicate more secretly. He agreed with Oriol's plan and would contact Oriol's chief of police. He demanded that we tell no one else other than the chief that I was alive and that he tell no one of our plan. He didn't like that Oriol had texted the chief the safe house's address.

"And . . ." He hesitated.

"And what?"

"Well, you deserve to know. Samantha was our eyes and ears on Dick. We are blind now."

"And deaf." A ringing from the blast still sounded in my ears. "Samantha Smythe, a double agent. She'd told me as much." I felt a sharp pain in my heart.

"Not really. She kept tabs on Dick for us—for you. Maybe with Petrovsky's blessing. She was otherwise loyal to Mother Russia."

I found myself tearing up with gratitude and love for the woman who had killed my good friend Elliot. How could I have come to forgive her? The woman had tried to abduct my children. Her final spell was one that mixed contrition and ritual self-sacrifice for me. Her amulet charm had saved me. Talk about sympathy for the devil and a redemption song; she'd taken a bomb for both of us in a selfless act of Big Love.

I got off the phone, and Oriol leaned back, arms across his chest. "You look shaken."

I shook my head no, meaning yes.

"Where will you go when the dust settles? You'll be safe here for a time."

"Back to Ireland and seclusion. Dick can't know about the place, or I'd already be dead. I'll have to stay dead . . ." I shouldn't have mentioned Ireland but needed his help.

I found the idea of pretending to be dead liberating, but what about the family?

"How will I get there? Gerard believes he'll have eyes at passport control and will otherwise be watching the airports and helocraft flight manifests filed with immigration and custom controls. He's Russian intelligence, after all."

"Let me figure that out. And if the chief agrees to our cover story, you should have time—"

I again imagined Sam at the moment of death. Was there time for grace? Her last act was fearless and noble, so maybe she was able to slip under the pearly gates, her debt of karma fully paid.

The doorbell rang, and the windows shuddered.

ORIOL ANSWERED THE DOOR as the wind and rain that had whipped up now whipped in. The bad weather was screaming down the narrow ancient streets like a banshee with her hair on fire, seeking escape through any doorway. I hoped the banshee wasn't Sam and she was spared purgatory. Her karmic slate was wiped clean in my book. M and Juno had told me, in the grand scheme of the universal mind, there is nothing to forgive.

"Ah, Jordi, welcome! Wow, you brought a tempest with you."

Oriol shut the door against the strong wind and introduced me to a rain-soaked and unhappy chief of police, Jordi Bonet. Oriol helped him take off his raincoat and relieved him of his inverted umbrella that had lost its battle with the wind.

The chief said to me, "I got a call from your friend at Interpol. I know him by reputation, and he and your friend here"—he glared at Oriol—"are the only reasons I agreed to come and not arrest you immediately. This is a catastrophe for Barcelona in the midst of tourist season. The entire police force is on high alert, and I'm called away for what? I cannot say."

He wasn't happy with his role in my potential escape.

"Have a glass of wine." Oriol poured him a glass. "I've solved your big case for you, and yet you're all doom and gloom like the weather tonight. Come now." He handed the chief his glass.

The chief, a large man, looked a bit like Mussolini in his tight-fitting, Italian-looking suit. He attempted to dry his fine and definitely Italian leather shoes with a handkerchief.

Wiping the shoe leather and grimacing, he said, "I just bought these from the most expensive cobbler on the Passeig de Gracia." I stood corrected. "We shall see what you have to say. I have men stationed outside so there is no mistake. They don't know why I am here but do know this is official business. And you won't be leaving other than with me and maybe in handcuffs." He looked at me with disgust for ruining his shoes and bringing havoc to his city. "This is our first bombing in years, and we have one person dead. HMX, high-grade explosive, at point-blank range. The blast incinerated them—like the plastered body casts of Pompeii."

I winced at the image of Sam in a heap of mummified ash.

"Two people dead, and we are all friends here," Oriol said, shaking his head. He bristled at all authority and didn't like police or government bureaucrats who took themselves too seriously. "Take off your shoes, and let us explain and make a proper introduction." Oriol gestured at me with a flourish of his hand and then motioned for us all to be seated in the living room. "This is the famous author and man in hiding, Sean Byron McQueen. A man to whom we all owe a debt of gratitude."

The chief inspector answered by removing a zip tie from his jacket breast pocket and revealing the gun strapped there. He placed the plastic handcuffs between us on the slab stone table inlaid with a decorative chess board where the armies stood ready for battle.

"If he can be believed," Bonet said. "You writers of fiction have a hard time with the truth."

They honestly didn't seem to be on good terms, and I wondered if Oriol had thought this through. Still, I had no choice now but to follow his lead.

Bonet kicked off his wet loafers. Oriol fetched a pair of slippers for his big feet and red silk socks before pouring out more wine, saying, "Jordi, just like old times, but now you're welcome in a safe house. I forgot how well stocked they are with excellent Catalan wine."

The chief bristled at Oriol's confident tone. As the chief, he clearly wanted to control my interrogation. But Oriol was acting like he had the upper hand. He was a good bluffer.

"We weren't on the same side then—now I'm not so sure," Bonet said. "You said this man knows everything about the bombing at the old El National building? Then he should come with me now and make his statement under oath."

Those words and his use of the Spanish name for the now bombed-out building made me think he was not a revolutionary Catalan like Oriol.

"Yes, but I can assure you he's entirely innocent. Have you read his books?"

"No. Though I'm familiar with his stories."

"Well, we have quite the story to tell you now." Oriol stood and checked the large window facing the street to ensure it was well latched as it continued to rattle from the winds buffeting the town house. "They predicted a storm but nothing like this—a residual effect of global warming? This and the specter of terrorism in one night will be very bad for Barcelona business. Lucky for me, hostel-goers are a hearty bunch, but your fancy hotels won't fare so well."

He gave Bonet time to weigh his words.

"You'll let us help you rule out terrorism tonight, and tourist season will continue tomorrow when the sun comes out. You don't want to miss this boat. We'll even give you a name for your charred body. You can decide whether to raise it to an international incident or imply a gangster bombing and revenge murder."

Bonet dribbled wine down the side of his glass and placed the glass down on the wooden table. Before the wrong-sided wine legs reached the wood, Oriol, like a good waiter, wiped the glass and placed it back down on a coaster.

"Otherwise, you may never learn about the bombing and won't be able to rule out terrorism in time for tonight's news," Oriol added.

It was already dark, but everything started later in Barcelona, with dinner routinely served at ten p.m.

Oriol moved over to the kitchen island to slice up more bread, sausage, and cheese. Bonet mimicked a thinker, stroking his chin. "I don't have all night," he said. "Get on with your story, Oriol. Being a bestselling author in Barcelona doesn't make you Cervantes, so maybe you can make it quick." He knew Oriol well enough to know he liked to drag out a story while, of course, maintaining suspense.

Oriol gave the called-for shudder. "Ahhh! You've read my books at least. All we ask in exchange for solving your case is two things. Well, perhaps three. First, you let it be known two bodies were discovered blown up—that is our biggest ask since it is only half true. Second and third, you tell no one that Sean is hiding here until we find a way to get him out safely—we may need your help with that, too. And I will vouch for his innocence before we get started. How can you refuse?"

"This is a big mess, and the president and the press are all over this. How could I agree before I hear his story?"

"All we ask is you agree in principle and agree if what I'm telling you is true. We will not tell you the victim's or the killer's name until you are fully on board." He refilled the chief's glass.

"Oriol, can we discuss that?" I asked. "Both names are likely aliases, and may be hard to confirm." Yeah, I weakened my own case.

"Good point. Jordi, you don't know the sex or nationality of the victim, but we can assure you Sean knew her as more than an acquaintance, and I have a picture."

He toasted me with his glass, and I shook my head in disgust. I knew exactly what picture Oriol meant—the one of Sam and me by the firepit. He must have saved it.

"Jordi, agree in principle and don't cross me—this is a great deal for you. It will make you an even bigger man in the city." The boss had spoken.

"Oriol, I know you are no liar, so let's hear his story. First, let me make a phone call to my lieutenant and have those men waiting outside in this nasty mess dismissed."

He made his call, in Catalan or Spanish, on a retro smartphone.

One Step couldn't help but pick up the zip tie and hand it to the chief. He sighed at my initiative—or it could have been my audacity—but he slipped it back into his pocket without interrupting his conversation.

"He's saying to release no information about the number of bodies found," Oriol interpreted for me. "And to send back to the station the men outside our door."

Bonet hung up and turned to me. "So, once upon a time . . ."

Oriol jumped in, saying, "Sean, can I tell him the backstory and then you tell him about the events leading to today? Correct me if I get anything wrong."

"Sure," I said. He was doing great so far.

"I'd rather hear it from him," Bonet said.

"Then you should have read his books. Since you didn't, I'm going to boil down two thrilling books in less than ten minutes."

Oriol was a great storyteller, so hearing my stories told by him promised to be quite a treat even under the circumstances. And the wine and appetizers made me want to sit back and enjoy his rendition of the story of me. Danger, even death, had become so familiar that I had learned to compartmentalize and to turn off, when not needed, my fight-or-flight reflex.

As Oriol got started on the familiar tale, I became distracted thinking about how to contact and what to say to my family. Molly knew I was in Barcelona to meet Sam and must have heard about the bombing. I didn't have time to read her numerous texts, and my voicemail was full. I didn't dare text her, as I was hoping to be declared dead. But how could I let her and the children grieve another dead parent?

If Bonet agreed to declare me dead, I'd ask Gerard to make discreet contact. The family had to know that I hadn't taken my last breath. My death in an explosion in Barcelona would devastate them, proving my mortal fear of Dick had been warranted all along. I couldn't allow that. Juno and Dylan must know immediately that I wasn't dead. I even worried about Alfred, whom I'd left sleeping on maintenance mode, meaning he would wake and check on routine matters about the tower for a couple of hours each day. He'd also be awakened by any deliveries that would trigger our security perimeter. Awake, he would see the news and messages at that time and discover I was reported dead.

An hour later, with Juno finding me near dead in the Himalayan hovel where I'd spent the harrowing night with Dick, Oriol finished his part of the story, and it was my turn to tell them both how we'd gotten from there to here. The tempest roaring outside in the Gothic Quarter added gravitas to the dark tale.

"Now you, Sean," Oriol said. "You haven't written this story yet, but when you do, please portray me as a man of the world and the Lionel Messi of literature." He finished his wine and turned to the chief. "Jordi, any questions before you get what you came for?"

"So many." The chief pushed back into his seat, not so much relaxing as being released from a spell. We'd all passed a tense hour that had held Bonet unmoving at the literal edge of his chair. Oriol was a genius storyteller, better even than I'd remembered. But as soon as Oriol sat back, folding his hands behind his head, the chief scooted forward again and stabbed a long fat finger my way.

"How could you let the heroic Professor Edens die? And I hope this story ends before the aliens arrive. Let's move it along," he added.

We switched from third person to first person narration for the conclusion of our story. Bonet was growing increasingly agitated, impatient for the info he'd need to settle the bombing case. I needed to talk fast.

"Let's hear how we got to the well-cooked, unidentifiable dead person you've laid at my feet."

"I would have done anything to save M, other than to deny her free will—Oriol may not have made that clear. It was her choice, and she didn't see it as a close call, her life to be sacrificed to buy humanity time. I don't suppose the Guru and his New Society would have been in favor of Catalan or any independence. He was more a totalitarian type."

"Hmm," Oriol said. "Hive mind and a common language and sharing the knowledge of all that is to be known? Who knows how that should play out? Other than it should not have an overlord, the Guru especially. I agree with that."

I'd forgotten the chief might have been a Spanish sympathizer, but Oriol surprised me by offering a hive-mind defense and by questioning my choices in that fatal last hour with M.

"But didn't she leave it up to you in the end, when the Guru threatened your life and the children's?" Oriol continued to challenge me as he would if we were alone. "That made me cry when I read it the first time. I pictured my family and what I might do differently."

I grimaced, and Oriol smiled in apology for dredging up the inevitable yet unanswerable questions of what if and did M have to die.

"I'd sworn to help her meet her destiny, which is exactly what she was doing in those final moments. And my own life wasn't really threatened in reality till now." Dick's curse had been a constant in my life, but only once before was he close enough to carry through on his threat—when we ran through the jungle to Diva Falls with his DOGs in hot pursuit.

"I read all about this, and now I don't have to read the books, thanks to Oriol's recounting, but what the hell does this have to do with a bombing a couple hours ago in my city? Just the facts. No rhetorical flourishes like with his storytelling." He motioned for Oriol to sit down and shut up.

"Well, first the good news—this was no terrorism for anyone other than me, and it was the nasty, perverted Dick's doing. Russian FSB, remember? It all started eighteen years ago when he killed Dylan Byrne as Oriol described and continued nine years ago when he promised to kill me in a most horrid way. Dick's vendetta picked up again a couple days ago, when he used his associate, Samantha Smythe—the coed-spy-witch that Oriol did such a good job describing in lurid detail—to contact me, asking to meet."

Oriol furrowed his brow, reminding me I wasn't supposed to disclose whose body they had, but I'd already mentioned her name.

"In her note, she claimed M was still alive and that I was to meet an FSB agent here today for proof of life."

"Let me interrupt," Oriol said. "Jordi, you have me and the Interpol inspector who called you, to vouch for Sean's honesty and character. And you can imagine the sensitivity with the FSB involvement, even if it was a rogue ex-American operative setting off bombs in our city. You have every interest in protecting Sean as your star witness by declaring him dead. Then we can give you the name of the dead person and a sworn affidavit. Otherwise, you can arrest us and risk the FSB putting a blade between Sean's ribs in the prison shower."

He was laying out a scenario like a writer, but I didn't like the scene he envisioned for me.

"May I tell the mayor and the president the truth?" Bonet asked, weighing the deal and his next move. Telling the president sounded dramatic, but Catalonia was the size and population of Pennsylvania, so it was more like telling the governor.

I looked to Oriol for the answer.

"Yes and no," he said. "As soon as Inspector Gerard . . ."

I shrugged when Oriol looked at me for his last name, but I only knew him as Gerard the avatar.

"As long as Sean's inspector friend approves, you can tell them. He's Sean's case manager, and as a Russia expert, he knows all the moving parts." Oriol was as good as Elliot in his role as my lawyer. "But we need Sean dead now to buy us time to get him out of town."

"Out of town? How can I be sure he will appear when I need him?" Bonet asked Oriol.

"You have my word." Oriol held out his hand, and Bonet reluctantly shook it. We had ourselves a deal.

I agreed to allow Bonet to record my statement and my responses to his questions and have it typed up later as a sworn affidavit. I identified Sam as his dead body. Oriol shared the one photo we had of her after graciously cropping me out of the frame. But Bonet insisted on the full picture as evidence and to back up how well I knew her.

"So, we say there are two bodies, but who planted the bomb and how do we move this as far from terrorism as possible?" Bonet asked.

Oriol was nodding before the chief finished talking. "How about she lured Sean to the abandoned building for a tryst and unexploded ordinance from a planned demolition went off because of the heat."

The inspector was shaking his head, not buying Oriol's attempt to write the script.

"Nice, but wouldn't we use my hotel room?" I said, remembering our earlier scene there.

Bonet had stood and was pacing with impatience. It had been several hours since the bombing, and we needed to get our story out.

"Let's hew closer to the truth," I offered, quickly plotting. "An old grudge, a jilted and crazed former student. She had planned to kill me with a pipe bomb, but I managed to have it blow up both of us . . . in a struggle. Let's leave Dick and the FSB out of it for now."

Bonet sided with me, saying, "His story is better, though that was no pipe bomb. Perhaps a pipe bomb next to some old vat of printing ink—you know that stuff is highly flammable." He sat and quickly made notes. "Some of it can be speculation for now, as long as we can categorically make it a crime of passion and not a terrorist plot."

Over encrypted texts with Inspector Gerard, the plan was finalized. Gerard also agreed to contact Molly so the children and family wouldn't believe the fake news but still act as if they did.

A few minutes later, Sam and I were pronounced dead.

THE FOLLOWING MORNING, I AWOKE a dead man without a plan in my five-star hideaway nestled somewhere in the labyrinth of the Gothic Quarter's crooked streets. My death and Sam's were all over the metaverse, with chat bots and pod blasters exchanging their sex-and-death theories and deepfake pictures of Sam and me. Ironically, the WT-sponsored news was the most reliable source of the facts. There was even a flattering recent picture of me in the quaint Clashmoor bookstore, displaying my love of literature. I imagined Alfred looking through every window of surveillance for any hint of deception within the official story and any grain of truth in the deluge of misinformation.

Poor Alfred would be lost without me. I thought, *I must tell Gerard to let Alfred know I'm alive*, but Gerard would laugh at my belief that Alfred would be mourning my death.

Luckily, the Deeksha West was still a bit of a fortress, with its own safe room in case Dick came a-calling. And unless a trespassing reporter or DOG liked to hike, there was no way in other than one very tall and monitored gate.

Oriol had set up the coffee maker before he left the night before and agreed to come by for breakfast at ten. If my goal was Nirvana, I was still heading in the wrong direction. Being dead is supposed to be liberating, but I felt trapped in purgatory.

Oriol brought more provisions, and we sat down to discuss our next moves. I'd finally turned off the World Tribunal news speaking of me posthumously as "a popular but not great literary author whose stories nevertheless impacted the world."

Oriol turned on the sound system to what must have been Springsteen radio, as every other song was a Bruce ballad.

"Russian intelligence is likely looking for you," he told me. "They are very familiar with using the fake death, as you know."

I assumed he was speaking about Dick's resurrection after dying in Kathmandu and not implying M might still be alive. If Dick had any proof that she lived, he would have produced it before attempting to kill me with Sam. Hell, he would have brought M with him into the hologram and done unspeakable things to her, making me helplessly watch why hungry too hungry to see her to shut out the hellish horror from entering my heart and soul—never to depart. The sadist in him would want to torture me in that way. I had to finally face the fact that M had left her body right before my holo-eyes nine years ago. The dawning of this reality was the grimmest part of a grim few days, though my continued relationship with the beloved dead, and M in particular, did not allow for the loved to die.

"The major means of transportation are not advisable with all the advanced forms of facial recognition that could detect you," Oriol said. "I thought about a mask, but you'd have to use your passport in any event and masks are outlawed on public transportation."

I knew this and might have added that facial recognition was able to distinguish flesh from a flesh-like mask.

"But there may be a way—it will cost me many favors and you a lot of dollars—if we can afford it. It will take me nearly a week. I have to be careful about it, even what I tell you. I trust you are not too uncomfortable here?" He fluffed one of the sofa pillows with gusto as "Rosalita" played on high-fidelity speakers so small I couldn't locate their source.

"Oriol, I need to thank you. You're a good man in a pinch. And you've given my safety a lot of thought. But what prevents one of your friends with a mistress from showing up here?"

"This house is marked *occupied* on the list. It's not unusual to have a week-long tryst at this time of year. I am happily married but so I'm told."

"Please tell me the plan. You know you can trust me."

"Yes, of course I trust you, but the less you know about who helps and how we get you out of here, the better for you and them. And there are still some kinks to work out." He fluffed the matching pillow, his advanced degree in hospitality on display.

"Come on, Oriol. It's only nine in the morning, but I'll open a bottle of wine if that will get you to talk? I'm violating all my security protocols by sharing my hideout's location."

He laughed. We both knew he would tell me more, but he liked to be prodded.

"No wine, but how about some eggs and bacon and a game of chess with our coffee? I have till noon to keep you company, then I have to return to the living."

Over breakfast, Oriol told me his plan to resurrect an old network used to smuggle Catalan political targets out of Barcelona, before they'd achieved independence, on a speedboat to Ireland. The Irish were always the greatest of friends to the oppressed. I assured Oriol that if he dropped me anywhere in Ireland, I could make my way to my tower sanctuary or have Alfred send my smart car to pick me up. I boasted of my tower's safety, but I wasn't sure anymore; Samantha had found me there. I was glad she had assured me that Dick himself couldn't travel and that she had denied finding any trace of me. Even if he found me, he'd again have to use surrogates and holograms to see me die.

"We have one weak link in the plan—our contacts in Ireland want no part of helping now that we have our independence. That would force us to dock with passport controls. And on our end, the old skippers don't want to sail unwelcomed and undercover into their waters. The gale that blew through last night has also stirred up the sea, and there's flooding. More weather is also on the way. However, give me some time and money, and friendship will find a way. How much can you afford to pay to stay dead? You've sold a lot of books?"

I didn't want to acknowledge it, but M's inheritance left me and the children very well off, and NYU was still paying me half my salary and would for life. I wondered if they'd already canceled the last check now that I was dead.

We both reached for the last piece of bacon.

"I insist," Oriol said, very insistent in his hospitality.

I ate the last slice. "Can you give me a range of how much you think you need to work with?"

"It's a superfast electric boat, easily managed by two men, so I'd estimate one hundred thousand US dollars each. Can we budget two hundred for the effort and the risk? These men will be risking jail time for you if caught by the Irish coast guard. Not to mention the menace of potential pirate Dick and the Russian navy. That price assumes we don't have to pay for some clandestine—that is, without dealing with immigration officials—docking in Ireland, so the cost may go up."

"Or they can let me off on my beach and I'll swim ashore."

I wasn't sure how close a boat could get, as there was a reef and no boats ever docked there. A swim wasn't going to kill me even at sixty-four. I hadn't felt my heart ache since the bomb went off, though as the watch factory nearly crumbled around me, I did think I was having a heart attack.

"But Gerard will never approve of my amphibious landing."

"He already did. He and Bonet agree that a low-key and low-tech approach is best, as there's too much chatter within the intersecting surveillance states to attempt to go through normal channels now that Dick has struck. And Gerard wants you out of Barcelona. Too many DOGs sniffing about."

"Our retro-plan's price makes this an expensive game of chess," I said, setting up the pieces on the board while Oriol cleared the plates and turned off Boss radio at the end of "Thunder Road." Thinking about my heart and the third piece of bacon gave me agita.

Oriol, still in the kitchen, started singing or praying in Spanish. I listened closer. Maybe it was Catalan. "What's that you're reciting? It's lovely."

"A poem called the 'Curse' by Pablo Neruda. I didn't like his politics, but his poetry transcends all that personal baggage. And you got me thinking about curses and civil wars."

"Poetry and prayers sound the same when you don't know the language. I'm going to text Gerard and tell him we're working on a plan and ask him to keep reassuring my children and maybe tell Alfred, my robot. Shit . . ." Oriol wasn't family. Or was he, as Dylan's good friend risking his life for me? "Please keep Alfred a secret. He's unregistered and no one is supposed to know he exists."

I was back to encrypted texting, as Gerard thought my fez communications might be compromised.

My third text to Gerard asked when I could speak to the family. Disturbingly, he didn't respond, though he had immediately answered all my prior texts.

I texted again. *What if I use my friend's phone to speak to the family?*

Not yet, but maybe soon we will get you in contact. And you don't need to worry about Alfred. You seem to forget he's just a bot.

His prejudice offended me, but like Judas, I didn't defend Alfred.

After Oriol and I played to an unsatisfactory stalemate, he left, saying, "Eggs are on me and the speedboat on you! I'll be back this evening with dinner. We'll empty that wine closet before you go."

I didn't like to be dead and alone with my thoughts. I thought more about Ting and her remote viewing, and about Molly and what she hadn't revealed to me about her and Samantha. I thought about my escape. I didn't give a thought to self-realization, which had seemed so near a couple days before.

I OD'd on news and wanted to shoot the computer screen like Elvis did with a TV. They were all talking about me like I was dead, and some portrayed me as a creep for supposedly having an affair with my ex-student.

"You were an assassin-spy and a beguiling witch, and in the end, a dear friend," I said to Sam's face on my screen before turning it off. She had gotten too close to me and now, like so many before her, was dead.

When Oriol returned at nine for dinner, I complained that it was my bedtime. We drank wine, listened to *Born to Run*, and again we played to a draw in chess, an ending more apt for checkers.

And so it went for a few days, a not very satisfactory life but not so bad for being dead. I had plenty of time for yoga and meditation. And Oriol kept me apprised of his efforts regarding arrangements to smuggle me home, but there was still no port of call for me without me first going through passport and immigration. We finally agreed that I would be dropped alongside my beach in a dinghy. The dinghy was all that was left to procure in order for me to make my escape.

On August 22, the wait was over. I'd leave for my speed ride up to the Irish coast in the morning. Gerard assured me the children understood the need to play it safe with my playing dead. Still, I wanted to speak to Molly, to hear how the children were, and find out what she hadn't told me about Sam, and what Ting had discovered on the back nine. I felt like a ghost with unfinished business.

I told Gerard I was going to use Oriol's phone to call Molly and there was no stopping me. He yielded and set up a secure line for us to use. He warned me, "Molly's not happy with you." But surely, under the circumstances, she'd offer me sympathy.

FOLLOWING BREAKFAST, I USED ORIOL'S PHONE and Gerard's encrypted line to call Molly; it did not go well. She had no pity for my plight. I was getting no satisfaction from death in life. Equally disheartening, there was no news from Ting. She was still seeing green and no installations or activity of any kind. Molly was preparing to demand an investigation. I told her of Samantha's heroic turning following my sweet forgiveness. A tactical mistake, as Molly's tone turned from cold to bitter.

She didn't want to discuss her Samantha secret over the phone, or much of anything with me, as long as I was dead and not coming home to be with the family. They were all worried sick and hated having to lie to their friends and anyone who asked about me.

"The entire family—your children, YaLan and Astri here, and Juno and Boy in Kathmandu, and Ting in Hawaii—we all spend most of our days worried sick and praying for your safety. Can't you at least speak to your children?"

This was a ploy, as she knew I'd have a hard time telling them I couldn't say when I might be able to see them. It was part of Molly's orchestrated push for me to go home to the DW. She was motivated by love, but to return while Dick was still seeking revenge was ludicrous.

"Not yet. Not while Dick is still after me. I can't put the family at risk. You know that, Moll."

I knew I sounded dismissive.

"All I know is that a dead father, even one just pretending to be, is a disservice to your children." Her words were darts being tossed at my heart, but I offered no defense.

"How's their creative writing course with the best teacher in the world?"

"Their father should be their teacher, but their stories and their unique voices must be heard. Too bad you can't see and hear them while playing dead. They will outstrip both of us by the time they're thirty."

"That warms my heart." It did so much more than that even when delivered in the icy voice of Molly in attack mode.

"Anything else good to report from the family. Any levity?"

"Astri has a million jokes about Sean's ghost."

Not surprising. "Okay, give me one."

"Sean's ghost likes to scare himself."

"She can do better than that."

"Sean's ghost is colored white, red, or rosé, depending on the season and time of day."

"Better. Tell her I can't wait to hear them all."

Following a deadly pause and an audible breath, she said, "I can't joke with you about all this. It's too much. You've always taken too much risk."

This was her assessment now, when before she'd often accused me of being obsessed with Dick's curse.

"And I never should have let you go meet Samantha. Gerard is pissed, almost as pissed with me as you for not letting him know. With you dead, where's that leave your family? Locked down and lying to the world."

I'd upset Molly a couple times before but never like this.

"You know we're responsible for what we create. And you always create drama and death, even when it's faked."

There was some truth to her philosophy that we're all wizards making our own realities.

"The powerful law of attraction. Based on that theory, we have you to thank for the aliens coming." I was half joking. I thought to appease her by adding, "You entered my life nine years ago while writing your first alien story about Juno being abducted. Now, following all your staunch alien advocacy, they're almost here!"

"Sean, I'm not going to let you off the hook. Gerard is working with us to stage a funeral service for you for next week. Really, it's all shit you left us with. It would be easier on them—on all of us—if you were really dead. The helplessness, the not knowing, and your pigheadedness are insufferable."

Now was not the time to remind her to finish my novel if Dick got his wish. I wondered if she'd already received the manuscript and if she would continue it in first person or move to third. Alfred knew to send her the draft in case of my death, but then wouldn't she have mentioned it? Perhaps Alfred was not fully convinced I was dead. He did have a sixth sense about me. And Alfred would be a much more sympathetic ear; Molly did have to handle the load of being my family liaison and working with the authorities to assure everyone's safety at the DW. But saying it would be easier if I was dead went too far. Still, I let it go.

She ended the call, saying, "If you can't be safe within the family here, you should be in witness protection, not re-creating D-day on your lonely beach where Dick will find you unprotected. I'd say take care, but you wouldn't listen." She hung up abruptly.

"Goodbye, Molly."

MOLLY'S BELIEF THAT I WAS BEING SELFISH in death, with the entire family now drawn into danger from Dick and living a lie to protect me from my curse—wasn't wrong.

Oriol, who had been making himself busy in the kitchen preparing appetizers during my disheartening Molly call, returned for his phone and a game of chess. After another story about the time he and Dylan had traveled across a Moroccan desert with Bedouins, I told him I was tired and needed some solitude before my journey and would skip our evening meal. Our last night in the hideout, and I wasn't up for a late dinner or another game of chess. And the lyrics to "Born to Run" had become earworms tunnelling round my head.

Despite Oriol being a great host and always-cheerful renaissance man, I was treating him like Alfred, showing a lack of gratitude for his assistance and hospitality. I was tiring of his love for his bees and how smart they were. I didn't like bees and was allergic to their sting, so his stories of putting on a stinking hot suit and headdress and suffering the occasional bite made me wince. And he had started beating me in chess.

Oriol, ever gracious, said he had logistics to finalize for my escape and took his leave.

I practiced yoga and prayer and meditated on death and breath. I felt my family prayers surround me with protection. Juno and M agreed with me, via telepathy or my wishful thinking, that I had to keep the family at a safe distance. That agreement was reassuring after Molly's lecture about how I was neglecting my children. I was doing what I needed to for everyone's safety, and I was prepared for the journey to come. Still, I felt like a coward in hiding.

The weather forecast wasn't good, promising high winds whipping off the English Channel on our way up the Atlantic coast.

Oriol arrived promptly at dawn. I'd been ready for hours.

He filled me in on the crew and plan.

"The high-speed ocean-faring boat is in port. A hotshot kid will be your skipper, with Carlos as old hand and second mate. Sorry, no English speakers. I'd go too, but I get so horribly seasick. It will be a rough passage at speeds up to seventy-five knots."

"Great. Thanks for reminding me why I haven't been on a boat for decades. How many miles per hour is that?"

"Around eighty-five, but that's max speed for this boat on calm waters. Today you'll probably average around fifty-five knots or slightly above sixty miles per hour. These new electric boats have hydroplane sensors that keep the bow of the boat hovering above water instead of slapping it down on all but the biggest swells, so it will be smoother than you may remember. It's like flying. Sorry, but at those speeds you'll still feel it."

He looked a bit green describing my passage. I wished I could take a smooth helocraft, but they were subject to flight manifest and robotic passport controls.

"They'll have you in position before dark for your amphibious landing. The weather looks"—he flipped his flat hand a couple of times—"so-so."

"If we get near my beach, there's no one to see me, and the local villagers would greet me on the beach with beer if they knew I was coming."

"Okay, perhaps they can drop you before dark if it's safe and you make it on time."

"I'm not sure how close to the shore they can get, so I'm glad to have the dinghy."

"Military grade. A one-person raft."

I assumed that meant I'd gone over the $200,000. I had yet to figure out how to pay him from my estate. But Oriol knew I was good for the money. I gave him a hug of gratitude and realized I might not see him again for a while as I played dead in my solitary tower.

He handed me a small waterproof fanny bag.

"Carry only what you need—passport, phone, wallet, and maybe your Moroccan fez cap. Those boats take on so much spray, it's like taking a shower. And on the raft ride into the shore, you might get quite wet. Goodbye, friend. We didn't come this far for you not to make it home dead and alive." The dead jokes were too easy and getting old already.

"Oriol, Dylan picked his friends wisely and left them to me when he died. You are a true friend of the dead and those in deadly need." I hugged the man, a Big-Loving bro-hug of gratitude.

Goodbye, Oriol.

49 THE CROSSING

THREE HOURS INTO THE SPEEDBOAT RIDE, the spray slapping my face and the jarring swells slamming us down had me sweating within a horizontal shower. I had removed my red life jacket so I could breathe; it was a Catalan medium, and I needed an American large. The young pilot cursed my decision. Skipper boy continued his Catalan lecture with wild hand gestures. I assumed he was charging me with mutiny, but I couldn't be sure. Carlos seemed unconcerned by the ruckus kicked up by our skipper. I'd rather die drowning than suffocate on the deck. Seasickness was also killing me.

Twelve hours after setting course for Ireland, we finally approached my beach. A colorful spray of light spread over the ocean from the west, but the sun was about to sink into the sea. Those last rays shone on my beloved tower home above us. Carlos insisted that the pilot take the boat in precariously close to the rocky reef and the choppy water there, meaning it was time to lower my little yellow inflatable boat. Unlike the advances of our speedboat, raft technology hadn't changed much since WWII—inflate air into rubber bathtub.

The swells looked manageable until I lowered myself into the raft, with Carlos holding the rope and doing his best to hold the raft steady. I think he was crying for me, but it may have been the sea spray. I wanted to namaste the Catalan smuggler, but holding on to the raft handles seemed a smarter idea. I prayed my overworked heart would prove seaworthy. As I bopped around on the water, Carlos threw my lifeline into my boat and blessed me with the sign of the cross.

Carlos waved goodbye. But then started waving frantically for me to return to the boat shouting, "*Espere*, Sean. *Espere!*" As if I had any control over my craft and could stop it. Showing that he did know at least some English, he said, "Wait—your flotation!" He darted around his boat holding up my life preserver, but they couldn't get the boat nearer to me, and I couldn't get back to them. I think I saw skipper boy peevishly smiling though it may have been a grimace. After a quick windup, Carlos flung the much too light preserver halfway between us, into the sea. It floated like a little red otter on the rocky water's surface.

How could I, or we, have forgotten that simple bit of standard nautical safety? I was no boater and now was the too-stupid-to-live captain of a waterpark dinghy being thrashed about with the ocean already knee-deep in the raft.

What a misnomer *lifeboat* was. The sole plastic oar was of no use against the current and the waves. I bravely saluted goodbye, and they were off to a warm bed in a dry port. The red otter playfully bobbed out to deeper waters in their wake.

When you're in a dinghy, the waves are bigger than in the boat; I needed both hands to steady myself. On a positive note, either the waves or the current did seem to be moving me in the right direction. I was riding a bucking bull over the Atlantic Ocean on my knees—occasionally on all fours—praying to make it to shore.

I could see my damn front porch light swaying above the beach while the sea swayed me. I laughed to think Dick would be sorry to see me die this way.

If worse came to worst, I'd swim for it. As a teenager, at my runner's and swimmer's peak, it would have been a good half-mile workout. A part of me still saw the choppy-water swim as a simple workout, though at sixty-four I knew it was now even money at best that I would make it to shore. My inner child was crying. And my cardiologist had warned me to stay off roller coasters. She hadn't foreseen Sean's wild water ride.

Somehow the world thinking of me as already dead had death stalking me. Yet the presence of my stalker was nothing new. Since

2009, when he'd taken my first wife, Hope, with the hook of his sickle, he'd been after me. After my happiness.

Death had always passed me over, cutting down those standing right beside me. Maybe now it was my time.

Hope had died of an overripe heart. M had died selflessly sharing constant creation and Big Love with the world. Her renown for goodness and ethics was the reason the Guru had selected her for his mind-to-mind rape. Neither woman held back from their scientific pursuits on behalf of mankind. Dylan, too, had died protecting me from Dick after giving birth to the life-affirming theory that would mean so much to so many. They'd all been stolen from me. I'd been diminished by their deaths.

Or had I been enriched by their lives? Looking into the face of death, I saw how selfish my mind still was. All my loved ones' deaths were all about me. Like Bergman, I was personifying death that swept in with the dark cloak of night over a bellicose sea. Death was again near. And it wasn't the gaunt white face of the Guru or crazy eyes of Dick, but the angry Atlantic laughing at me. What a way to die, drowning with my sanctuary in sight.

I wasn't trained as a Navy SEAL, but I had been trained in the pool at the Deeksha West. Anytime I tried to shavasana on a float, inevitably Dylan on one side and Juno on the other played rock-daddy-off. I had plenty of experience being tossed off flotation devices.

Without further ado, a large swell hit the boat, flipping the raft over, throwing me into the ocean. My God, why did I take off my life preserver? Did I really have a death wish? The water, even deep into August, was freezing cold. I considered swimming back to the boat, getting it upright, and putting myself inside as I would with the swimming pool raft. But that would use up a lot of strength. And the waves named Juno and Dylan had taught me that I'd soon be back in the water.

A good swimmer and bad sailor, I decided to swim for it. I pulled off my slicker, which weighed a ton, but kept Oriol's fanny pack on, to be jettisoned as a last resort. Then I started swimming freestyle.

After ten minutes and maybe fifty waves, I decided to turn on my back, doing a dead man's float and swaying my arms like a bird to keep flat and hold my head upright as I attempted to time my breaths with the next wave washing over my face in a simulated drowning. I thought of our Yogi Mangku and how he faced his waterboarding torture with equanimity, and I used his example to keep from panicking.

I thought a thousand thoughts as I prepared to die.

I thought of Juno and pushing the light out through the crown of my head. I replayed her words, her wisdom. I recalled her bold yet gentle confidence, her certainty no matter what circumstances brought to her. Her lack of fear of death. Her lessons on how to meet death.

I pictured M and Hope, remembering how they made me laugh and cry and sometimes explode. I remembered how unreservedly freeing it was to forgive and be forgiven by the women who knew every fault of my adolescent mind and child-like imagination. And still they loved me, transforming the ordinary into the miraculous.

I pictured my children, my Juno and Dylan, who were loved beyond measure by their imperfect father with his tattered heart. They would always feel my love.

I thought about my Huxley challenge to self-realization, the goal of life, ever present but so hard to find. The two sides of me, man and monk, competed for my last thought and emotion while my body flailed on, refusing to believe that I was experiencing my last breaths.

I moved approximately two yards forward and one yard back when each swell pushed me toward the shore before another lesser wave pulled me back out. Periodically, I attempted to see if I could stand as the shore got closer, but this pattern proved tiring and near deadly as I sank beneath the waves gasping for air and then struggled to get back on my back, where I floundered like an upside-down turtle whose little arms and legs were about to give out.

When my body felt like letting go and sinking, a sweet lightness came over me like a wave of divine feminine grace. The steely water became warmer and supported me. My mother, Hope, M, and Molly, but mostly the essence of Big Love expressed through Juno, brought me buoyancy. I floated without effort in the womb of the wet and salty sea. Waves broke over me but periodically provided me intervals to breathe. I no longer struggled and would leave the rest to destiny.

When my core gave out, my feet started to drop. I fought my weakness, forcing my feet up. I'd run out of strength. My heart, beating far too fast, was still flailing and pumping but my other muscles were spent. It was time to succumb to the death that had finally caught up to me. I started to release my fanny pack to lighten my load, but how would they identify my body without my wallet, passport, and fez cap? I looked up one more time toward my warm tower.

You've forgotten somebody.

I fumbled in the pack and pulled out my waterproof fez cap. I would die with it on like an organ-grinder monkey.

"Alfred, awaken!" I gasped.

The proverbial ninth wave answered my Hail Mary; the biggest wave, washing over me, tumbled me like a giant washing machine over and over. My last thought before the lights went out: *Morte d'Arthur! should have been the command.*

Goodbye, Alfred.

I WOKE IN MY TOWER BED NAKED and covered in warm blankets, a fire crackling nearby. A dripping-wet man in Scottish dress sat by my side wearing a goofy grin.

"You old Lazarus. We are so fortunate your fez stayed on—it must have been those porcupine prickles digging into your scalp. If it wasn't on, I wouldn't have received your *morte d'Arthur!* command. That kicked me into high gear. I found you floating face up—two minutes flat after I got your wake-up call. They said you were already dead."

And I would have been if not for him.

"But I didn't believe it. A pipe bomb and a vat of ink didn't match the satellite images of that blast and the heat flash. Where one part of a story is made up, you have to question the rest."

"I didn't know you could swim," I said.

"You really ought to get to know me better. I swim at an Olympic level, even with all this tartan on. Here's some warm and hearty chicken vegetable soup." He started to spoon-feed me, but I took the bowl and three heaping spoonfuls before returning the bowl to the bed stand. The movement took all my strength.

"And hot tea."

I took a few sips while he held the cup to my lips.

"Alfred, I love you like a brother and owe you my life." I'd never told him I loved him before and could tell he was tingling all over by his dancing eyes and toothy grin, which did even more to warm my soul.

"From now on, I'll never swim alone." I knew this would please him, but I'd have to get him a bathing suit. "Please let Gerard know to tell the family I'm safe with you. And my friend Oriol . . . I need to sleep now." I was suffering the warm peace of exhaustion after being raised from the dead.

"Will do, boss. Sean, sleep!" he commanded. I listened, and my mind turned off.

51 MOLLY'S CONFESSION

I WOKE THE NEXT MORNING, near to midday, to an urgent, Gerard-secured text from Molly. He must have told her of my near-drowning experience. Molly insisted we had to *talk*, which didn't sound good. I hadn't spoken to her since she'd chastised me. She asked that we V-room—she had something to get off her chest and needed to see my face. Those words usually meant a weight was transferred from one chest to another.

As Gerard set up a secure chat room for us, I struggled in the shower to remove all the brine from my crevices before checking my devices. There was no news from Dick, and the public seemed to be leaning toward believing the *Bombing in Barcelona* was murder-suicide, with alternating views of Sam and me as the murderer. Either way, we were both still dead. The *Bombing in Barcelona* had become a media-mantra and meme.

It was still very early in Portland, and Molly was in red silk pajamas. Her face was worn, like that of a weathered gypsy with a hangover about to tell me of a terrible future. I looked even worse after wrestling with the Atlantic.

"I hope you're not making a fuss and stressing about my funeral—a simple sprinkling of my ashes in the vineyard, maybe Strawberry Fields with the Buddha there as witness, would more than do."

I had planned those lines—going on the offensive with humor. Molly begrudgingly laughed, but without a hint of joy.

"Sean, I'll tell funeral director Gerard that's what the deceased would like. There's already a popular AI-generated short story entitled 'The Bombing in Barcelona.'"

"I'll have to read that for my depiction. How did it end?"

"You and Sam go out in a blaze of glory. But, Sean, we need to talk. I'm sorry for making you come out of hiding for this, but I hologrammed with Juno yesterday, and she made me see myself, us—everything—clearly. She started in her unassuming manner—you know her well—talking about truth as the way. I asked about relationships and life, and she led me to see how we act as if we have all the time in the world when we should live each moment as precious and go through each meeting as if it might be the last."

I wondered if prescient Juno had seen my future and had counseled Molly to make her peace with me.

"Juno is such a good listener. Her silence and presence allowed me to discover my own answers," she said.

"Like any good sage or therapist," I responded, still trying to lighten the mood. And trying to understand where she was going. My mind was still waterlogged but in a calm and pleasant state of celebrating the light so nearly extinguished. I don't think she knew I'd almost died. And she'd have been charged with finishing my last novel, if not for Alfred, the Olympic merman, coming to my rescue.

"Our last few meetings have not gone well. You taking such great risks for yourself, not realizing the family is connected, and the fear for your life being snuffed out . . . all of it weighs so heavily on me and the children. On the whole family." Maybe Gerard or Alfred had told her about last night's near-death experience, but still she didn't mention it. "Gerard is making the DW a fortress again, so much so that he agrees you can come home, but he says that's your decision. The manpower and costs for Fort DW have been approved. He's already reactivated our safe room and security system."

I didn't roll my eyes as much as turn them toward the heavens; we'd been through this before, off and on for nine years. Thoughts of the family being in danger because of me made me sick to my gut. They didn't have death to protect them. I had death following me, determined to not let me die. Death wanted to torture me first by forcing me to witness all that I love die.

"But that's not why I must speak to you. Let me speak clearly and tell the whole truth. I love you and always will, and I'm satisfied with our being just best friends, and I cherish being part of the family." She paused for dramatic effect and to lift prayer hands to her heart.

I was relieved she was the grateful and not the angry Molly.

"But I owe you a big apology and need your forgiveness," she continued. "I betrayed you once long ago, and that betrayal has cost us everything. It has cost us the truth. And without truth between us, we never had a chance. You had a truth and love with M that will never die."

She gripped the large oak desk in the DW office like a life raft. She looked like me the night before, gasping for the words that were drowning her. I wondered why everyone was coming to me for forgiveness. Her eyes were glaring with fear that seemed to look through me. Did she see death standing over me?

I looked around, hoping to see Alfred, but my guest-bedroom-writing-study was empty. The sudden movement caused me to grasp my chest, where my heart beat haltingly, perhaps suffering the strain of nearly drowning, reminding me of another way I might die. Death was on my mind, distracting me from the distraught Molly, who must have had no idea how close I'd come to dying.

"Molly, it is you who should forgive me, with me playing the part of a suitor or lover at sixty-four when my driving desire is self-realization. I shouldn't have been whipsawing our emotions and playing on residual desires. I shouldn't have been causing you and the family such concern and risk in bringing Dick's curse down on all of us. Should I go on?"

"No, Sean, listen. This is a horrible betrayal that I kept secret, and now that Samantha has your forgiveness"—I shouldn't have shared that detail when we last spoke—"I need it too. I don't need you as lover. I need your Big Love and your family as my family. I told you recently that Samantha wrote me after M's death, but I didn't tell you everything. And not the worst part."

She was a good storyteller, and now she took on the role of one of her fatally flawed heroines who cut off Samson's hair. She knew the role well.

"Do you remember when we first met in your office, when Elliot P. sent me to interview you for the *New York Times*?"

"May the old gray lady rest in peace."

"And Samantha teased you while I listened. Not long after that meeting, Samantha contacted me for the first time. It seemed so benign— she'd heard I was writing a story based on Juno's disappearance."

"What the fuck?" Her crestfallen face had me backpedaling. "Your first alien abduction novel. The beginning of your new mythology. Did she help with the plot? Sam was an early adopter of AI to create some near brilliant forgeries of dead literary masters. Or—" Thank God mind-reading Alfred brought in a big mug of coffee and a warm croissant, which he placed beside me on the desk, before I suggested perhaps Sam and her AI had ghostwritten Molly's first alien blockbuster. I waved him off but with an endearing grin of gratitude and a bowing namaste.

"Is Alfred there with you?"

"He was but left and closed the door." I wanted her to get to the point of what Sam had done but saw the pain in her eyes that pleaded for patience and my forgiveness for God knows what terrible sin.

"Back then, I was writing of Juno's alien abduction, which I'd come to believe was true. Samantha said she could help me find Juno but told me I mustn't tell you because you were considering expelling her for meddling in your affairs. I assumed she might have learned some things through her wired-in resources. Therefore, I accepted her terms and she led me and my Chinese research assistant to China and Juno's case there. Which I then shared with you. But . . ."

She was tearing up, and I was impatient for the big reveal.

"Samantha also told me the Guru had planted the evidence that caused Juno to be sent to the mountain cell in Tibet, but that info was nowhere in the record and couldn't be found even in the wired-in world or the Chinese file. I didn't put it all together until after . . . and then couldn't bear to tell you—it was too late to do any good."

She started to sob. I didn't like her deception, but it wasn't as bad as this soap opera scene suggested. I had learned all this from the Guru and M in that fateful hologram.

"Molly, you know Juno and the family attempt to practice absolute truth, so you should have told me sooner, but this is no big deal. Any other Samantha or Guru or Dick contacts to confess?" I intended my question to sound like a joke, but she was crying.

"No, I swear! But, Sean, don't you see?"

I didn't.

"When I read your book, it got me thinking, and I became obsessed with the implications of Samantha's knowledge that Juno's incarceration was based on information the Guru made up for the Chinese. If I had told you at the time, we—you—may have seen the link between Samantha and the Guru. The children may not have been put at risk. And maybe we could have saved dear sweet Elliot P.!"

A flood of tears followed, giving me an emotionally charged moment to think. She was right that this was a major breach of friendship, of family, and I now understood the weight she'd been carrying.

"Hindsight's always a bitch. I probably wouldn't have made the connection myself. I didn't just now, when you told me."

But I would have back then, and perhaps I could have saved Elliot. I took a deep breath and exhaled softly, not wanting to pour on recriminations. But my inner response was severe disillusionment.

Before I became entirely disenchanted, I needed to recall my lesson of forgiveness and relinquish all judgment and blame. I looked away to pick up the coffee mug from my desk, to provide me a reprieve to summon forgiveness. I took a sip, spilling the hot brew down my front. I laughed, and Molly managed a smile that lifted up her moist cheeks.

"Now I understand why you were so eager to help me after M's death," I said, forcing forgiving words. "And you did help, Molly. Thank you for that."

"It may have started out that way, but you and your family came to mean everything to me. And now, with 9/9 approaching, I need to be free of this . . . weight, saddling my heart."

She wiped her eyes, but she still looked pretty rough even for four or five in the morning. Not knowing I'd sleep till noon, Molly must have waited up all night for me to release her burden.

"Sean, do you truly—and remember the importance of truth and to treat this like our final meeting ever, with Juno as our witness—forgive me totally?"

"I do."

I may have lied right then, but I would forgive her soon. I'd learned the way and power of forgiveness in Barcelona. And in that moment, I had to ease her pain. I needed to stop the insidious thought of *If she had told me, would M have lived?*

What-ifs are infinite, my Thin Man—don't give them a second thought. Nothing to forgive.

M's soft hand of forgiveness pushed my forehead to the V-room screen, where Molly returned the gesture. Molly smiled the smile of the forgiven, and a big weight was lifted. I knew it was lifted because my heart was singing. Pulling back, I said, "Now you agree to finish my novel in case of my untimely death?"

She nodded yes, although at the same time, she shook her head at my stubbornness. She seemed both exasperated and proud of me and my ability to wield my new superpower—forgiveness.

"I knew you would. Don't make the improved writing too obvious. And give a good edit to my draft, too."

I gave her prayer hands to excuse my use of a confession to gain a concession.

"My death and your writing, just imagine the sales!"

"You're already dead by all accounts," she said while flipping me a half-hearted bird by not fully erecting her middle finger. She'd bounced back quickly from begging my forgiveness.

I changed topics. "So . . . moving on to 9/9! Now that we know Gerard can set up a secure link, let's have a V-room with Ting and find out what the WT truly has planned for the alien arrival."

"Yes," Molly said, "Ting said she was going to try a new approach. Maybe she's got something by now. But if she still has nothing to report,

I'll bring in the press and tell them how we were barred from seeing what was on the last nine holes and demand that a team be allowed a look around the entire golf course and grounds."

I grinned, leaning back in my state-of-the-art writing chair with its firm support and agile flexibility. I was grateful for that chair, where I spent half my waking hours. I looked at my desk, my view, my fireplace, and my empty guest bed with gratitude. I looked back to Molly's face, which now was awake and ten years younger than when our chat started.

"That's not a Covered Conversation, is it? Molly, I'm so glad you told me and that we've resolved to be best friends and family. I'm grateful to have you in my life. I think this is the new beginning of our wonderful friendship," I said, echoing the final scene of *Casablanca*.

She pursed her lips and hesitated before saying, "Yes, I've been thinking about my love life, too, and Juno's advice to treat time and relationships as precious. Paddy is more my age and still hot-blooded."

With 9/9 coming, she wasn't buying green bananas.

"For you, he's a *bleeding volcano*. He's got the gift of gab, and he loves all your craics. We'd be neighbors." Now I was the one nodding and shaking my head at the same time.

This was truly the final release of my sapiosexual Molly fantasy of a late autumn romance. And though my new monk's vow of chastity still hung clumsily like a robe without a rope about my waist, I meant it when I asked and answered, "Paddy? Perfect!"

52 A BIG RED BIRD

THE NEXT MORNING, sitting in meditation in my tower turret, my turned-off phone started buzzing like a bee next to me with its red light flashing. Gerard had turned on my red light. His note insisted that I must contact him immediately.

"Sean, shit, this is not good. We have a credible report that Dick has been let off his leash and his chip neutralized, so he might soon be, or already is, traveling freely. We know he has already activated a lot of DOG imposters wearing his face around the globe, so we'll have to get him to come to us."

My demons would never let me be. Had Alfred plucked me out of an ocean grave so Dick could burn and bury me? Was Gerard going to use me as live bait? My head started to spin. "I thought the Russians couldn't diplomatically allow that to happen?"

"It was the Russians who contacted us. They've been in damage control mode since the bombing in Barcelona, yet their concern may be a ruse to allow them to deny responsibility. They claim to not know how he could have deactivated his chip without their help—and he must have had help—implying we had some role in it. They say they have no idea where he is."

Dead air followed as he waited for me to speak.

"Sean, you still there?"

"Yeah . . . just don't know what to say other than fuck and shit. This means he's free to make good on his damn curse." Shit, shit, *shit.* "Sorry for all the cursing. You never thought he'd believed I was dead for long. Shit, even Alfred wasn't buying it."

My mind immediately jumped the train, with its well-worn tracks and bleak landscape, all the way down to Dick's torture chamber. I felt my butt cheeks clenching.

"I believed he would not rest assured based on the circumstances of your death—*after* you took away his hologram eyes on the scene. And he faked his own death with the Russians, so I assumed he would be skeptical. Still, the ruse bought us time and doubt. But we have to assume he knows you're not dead now."

He paused, and I managed a grunting sigh to signal my agreement with that dire assumption.

"We and the Russians—but I wouldn't rely on them—don't think he knows where you are, so you may not be in immediate danger, though you should take every precaution. Like all Petrovsky's henchmen, Dick has lots of rubles and rubies to mask his identity and enjoy his freedom. He's probably on a yacht on the Red Sea swilling vodka and caviar, but I have a plan to catch him if he's coming after you. You have to trust me. It should work. You lay low and keep Alfred near."

"He's already saved my life once, and now he'll be my constant companion. How will you catch him?"

"Always go with what might be true. We're going to betray that you are potentially not dead by letting it be known that someone fitting your description is still holed up in that safe house in Barcelona. We'll be ready for him when he arrives. I will oversee the sting personally. We will take Dick dead or alive, his choice."

"What about Oriol—is he at risk?"

"No, the plan will keep him out of harm's way. I'm working with that pompous Chief Bonet, who wants to nab the Barcelona Bomber and become mayor. One last thing—don't let on you know he's on the loose. Keep playing dead. Tell no one, and soon your Dick will be put away for good." He laughed at the double entendre that hit too close to the bone.

His tone and confidence in his ability to bring Dick to justice brought me back from imagining the hell Dick had planned for me.

"Gerard, you're such a good friend. I am forever grateful. Thank you for stepping out of the multiverse to set the trap and keep me safe. I'd already be dead if not for you."

"One more minor thing—Molly asked me to inform you that Ting has reached a conclusion." That sounded strange for a seer using remote viewing.

"Hmmm, I'm a bit embarrassed under the circumstances, but may I ask another unrelated favor?" I waited for permission.

"Go on," he said.

"Could you set up a safe V-room conference for me with Molly and Ting?"

"Sure. Let me be your secretary, and then I'll go catch your killer. I'll have to explain to Molly why I'm putting the DW back on code red, in any event."

"What will you tell her?"

"Some amorphous threat . . . multiverse chatter about Dick and the DOGs making noise before 9/9. Nothing specific. We don't think the DW is at any real risk, and we're beefing up security there anyway. We were already back at code yellow after the bombing and in an abundance of caution, going to code red to make sure Dick doesn't make a move before A-Day."

I wished Gerard good hunting and begged him to be careful.

Then, getting on with my death, I sent him Ting's contact information. I asked Gerard to add a title to our V-room meeting: !!!!!!!!! I wanted to set the tone with a pole for each of the nine holes or a punctuation symbol for missile silos. We would finally get to see through Ting's eyes the Clashmoor back nine. A little international espionage would help me forget the vengeful tiger that was now untethered.

I also asked that he have Molly arrange a virtual meeting with the children, in private, after we concluded our business with Ting. With Dick on the loose, I wanted to see them just in case.

An hour later, Ting and Molly made their way into the old-school V-room. The family chose not to use googles and BCI hats.

I said, "Hola, Hawaiian Ting and Oregonian Molly! Our mystic eye-spying day!" My words were a bit manic after Gerard's wake-up call. And I was truly excited to gather top-secret intelligence that might land Molly and me in matching prison cells. "Alfred's with me." I panned out so they could see eager Alfred, overjoyed to be part of the team, sitting next to me behind my desk. They greeted him with greater enthusiasm than they'd shown for me.

Ting said, "Well, I hope I don't disappoint you after all those exclamation points!"

Molly said, "Yes, Sean, this is a case when nine-flagpole punctuation works." I laughed at her pickup of my invitation's punctuation pun and imagery.

"Must be our being back at code red here at the DW that's got you excited." She made a weary face at the revised threat level.

I whispered to Alfred, "I'll explain later, let it go for now." There hadn't been time to inform him of the Dick news in advance of the call. He'd want to review every possible scenario and steps for us to take.

Molly also let it drop. "However, I've never mentioned it to you— so as not to hurt your feelings—you overuse the exclamation point. I think maybe, and I'm saying this as a friend and fellow author, it's because it's an excitable little phallic symbol."

"Tee-hee, tee-hee . . ." went the trolley, tittering back and forth between Ting and Molly.

"Ouch!" I said.

Molly was my best critic, but I was surprised she'd held back that observation for so long and chose now, after we'd made amends, to launch her attack. Maybe the guilt had been too much for her before.

"Statistically, yes," Alfred said, "Sean uses the exclamation point, and em dashes, almost one hundred percent more than the average writer, but it's one of his signatures, and his readers and I love his enthusiasm and corollaries of thought. When you live a cursed and blessed life like Sean Byron McQueen, there's a lot of excitement and subplots."

"Thank you, Alfred." I tipped my cap to him in bro-solidarity despite his adding another line of attack. "And let's not let Molly distract us from our focus on the back nine and the battle for the green blazer of the Masters."

"No analogy is perfect," Alfred said, stealing a line M and I used to use, though my ironic use of golf imagery wasn't, strictly speaking, an analogy. Despite his genius of self-learning, he wasn't infallible.

"Ting, it's your show. Enough of the boys' banter," Molly said.

Ting was seated in the great room of her teahouse tree house. She was, as always, a radiant yogi sitting cross-legged on a yoga mat, but now looked non-binary with her recently cropped short dark hair of a novice nun, with a mala in hand, doing penance on a rosary.

The usually vivacious yogi also looked a tad weary or wary as she began her report, "The delay in what I saw was interesting and not at all what I expected when I started my meditations and entered a receptive state to see what was there on the back nine. Immediately the images were coming in so clear—a beautiful sweeping golf course bounded by bluffs hanging over the sea. This was one of the clearest remote perceptions I'd ever received, but it didn't reveal what we were looking for.

"Each day I tried, and the same images came to me—nothing to see but a green and sandy course, each hole punctuated by an exclamation point bearing a numbered flag on top."

More tee-heeing. After Gerard's news, the dobber jokes weren't appreciated.

"The only change I ever noticed was the weather. From what we discussed, I thought there was more and perhaps I was viewing a time before some big installation marred the greenery. But the weather matched the Highlands, Scotland's weather report. And on the other side of the course, I could see the orange tubes and the soldiers you saw there milling about. This continued for the last couple weeks—each day more waves of green—until it came to me."

Go on!

"I decided not to look but to meditate and listen for an answer. And a strong epiphany came to me that I knew was true." Ting smiled uneasily. She was usually so nonflummoxed. "I'm not sure if this will be good or bad news, but it's got to be better than nuclear silos." She waved a hand as if chasing away an evil spirit or a mosquito. "Let me back up and explain. I shifted my approach to mind reading, which is a form of telepathy—God forgive me, as we're not supposed to use this power to enter another's consciousness without their permission. It's to be used solely for unconditional love. Never for spying. Yet my heart, realizing how high the stakes were, gave me permission in this case."

We readily acknowledged this with nods and smiles, which she missed while moving to prostrate herself in a brief child's pose on her mat.

"Ting, damn the torpedoes!" I exclaimed, using Molly's rallying cry, but Ting frowned, obviously not appreciating the expression.

"This is the time for pulling out all the stops. The soul of humanity, and how we humans will meet the aliens, hangs in the balance."

Wherever I turned, I ran into a cliché that Molly would want to edit. But not now. She wanted to know the answer too. Alfred cleared his throat and said under his breath, "Perhaps give her a moment." He pushed mute on our end. "She is clearly worried about abusing her gift even for our compelling mission." He was better at reading people than I was.

Ting put her prayer hands to her heart and took three deep breaths before starting again. "I focused on a picture of Milton Straw. Oh my, did I pick up some manic energy there—clever, wily, extremely intelligent. Full of desire, sexual and otherwise, and accepting no obstacle to stand in his way—a real lust for life. He scares me. It felt like he knew I was meddling within his mind." She did a little shake-off dance.

My body tensed at the thought of her melding her sweet and peaceful mind with the titanic ego of the Great Man. I tried to ease her unease and said, "Ting, you did the right action for the right cause and deserve hazard pay. If it makes you feel better, Juno used telepathy to foretell that you would help us here. Please rest assured and tell us what you saw."

"Oh good, so I had my sister's blessing." She was joking, but I think she appreciated her sister's endorsement of her using her powers under these extraordinary circumstances, and it alleviated some of my guilt for sending her flying into enemy air- and headspace. "Nothing at all in his mind about any erection, I mean installation, on the golf course."

That was the first time I witnessed Ting blush at the slip of her tongue. The Great Man had played with her mind too.

"Rather, what came to me was a wicked and playful image of entrapment in some grand jest." She again waved one hand, this time erasing what she'd said. "No, not an image—more a feeling of gleeful anticipation of Molly being humiliated."

Impatience got the better of me, and I barked out, "Ting, what the hell was it?"

My outburst served to break the spell she was under, and she laughed at my rush to know. Alfred sat stoic, the picture of patience but smiling with Ting's laughter.

"Well, that's just it. The answer came to me clearly in meditation, or perhaps an alien intelligence whispered in my ear. You, all of us, are being played. There's nothing there! Other than a scenic golf course, exactly as I was seeing it each day."

Dumbfounded, Molly and I stared at one another. I'd expected a double helix or a gyre or vortex, lasers or missiles poised to launch on each of the nine greens, but *nothing*? That had never occurred to me.

"I'm confident in this," Ting said. "But I can't say why all the secrecy for nothing."

I don't know if the answer came to Molly or me first. I held up my hand to stop her from blurting it out.

"Riddle you, Alfred," I said, turning to my man. "Why all the secrecy for nothing?"

I knew Alfred well and watched his circuits become twisted, so glad was he to be included but hating to be confounded by a riddle.

"Um, mmm . . . I have no idea other than human perversity."

"Molly, the answer is?" I said with a desk-tapping drum roll, wanting to quickly put Alfred out of his misery.

"A red herring!" she exclaimed. We couldn't stop laughing or admiring the craftiness of King Straw. Quite the plotter.

"What's a red herring?" Ting asked. "And what's so funny?"

Alfred, too, looked confused for an instant. I'd taught him analogies, similes, and metaphors, but not red herrings. But by now he'd already, based on context, dismissed the smoked fish for the literary device definition. "Molly, you get the honors to explain the biggest damn red herring ever!"

"So big we missed it. Ting, a red herring is something in a story that looms large but comes to nothing. Every red herring should serve a purpose by distracting us from what is really going on. I'll have to send him a note expressing my admiration and ask if he'll consult on my next book. After 9/9, of course."

It was now Ting's turn to wait patiently.

Molly said, "But this red herring came with a twist as it served its own purpose. He pretended to want us to write a pro–World Tribunal piece asking the civilian welcome groups to stand down. He probably knew we'd never do that, but if we did, good for him. But he led us to believe, by pretending there was nothing to see on the back nine of the golf course, that something ominous and nefarious was there. By blindfolding us, he got us to imagine an aggressive military buildup or some trap for the aliens."

Molly gestured for me to continue.

"He intended for us to loudly call for an investigation of the site and declare what investigators would find there. If we had, Molly's credibility as the face of the alien-friendly movement and genuine claims of foolish government militarism would be at risk, with the alien-friendly movement itself on the line."

"He would deny our claims," Molly chimed in, "and there'd be a he-said, she-said dispute all over the metaverses." She paused for me to finish.

"Then, he'd announced his transparency to the world, inviting famous media people and WMD inspectors to play golf at the club, and we'd be dragged, live-streamed, hole by hole over the moors and then back into the clubhouse for beers."

"Well played, Sir Milton." Molly laughed. "You didn't count on sleuth Sean and telepathic Ting."

She deserved to laugh and enjoy the moment, having dodged a bullet. "I imagine Straw would've insisted Molly be there for her humiliation, sinking deeper, hole by hole! Flagpole by flagpole!" I exclaimed.

Alfred then summed it up. "Our false accusation and the blowback would have been a tremendous setback to the movement and to Molly."

As the discussion wound down, Ting and Alfred joined in Molly's merriment. Ting appeared to be relieved of her penance and Alfred enjoyed human joy. But I became reticent, thinking about unfettered Dick, and was bracing myself to speak to the children. The imminence of everything on the advent of 9/9 didn't leave time to savor *our* victory. As the call concluded, Alfred excused himself, knowing I wanted to speak to the children by myself.

The conversations with each child prodigy, both heartrending and beautiful, followed. I couldn't tell Dylan and Juno about Dick being loosed on the world and that their father, who was playing dead, might soon be literally dead. Yet I wasn't going to make the same mistake I'd made before going to Barcelona. I spoke to each as if we were sharing our last meetings, telling them I'd borrowed the idea from Mother Juno so they wouldn't read too much into our "game of speak your *peace.*" A game young Juno had invented years ago, using the homonym as a creative mistake. I spoke my peace first. And embarrassed them in turn with my effusive, infinite, and undying declarations of unconditional love.

I gave them as much time as they wanted, and as soon as I was out of the V-room, I was determined to capture their every word, every maudlin confession, every expression of love. All the more beautiful, coming from the reluctant and rebellious teenagers who must have sensed I was worried about more than just playing dead. But perhaps it was the 9/9 in the air that made everyone want to speak their peace. Their youthful excitement and anticipation about extraterrestrial contact had raised their hopes and fears for me and the world. But before I typed the first of their words, I had to bow to their desire for discretion.

My children and family were more than characters, and I had to balance honest disclosure with discretion; their safety was my top priority. And I'd almost forgotten that Dick might still be reading every word I committed to an electronic page.

I started to write of my escape and how we outsmarted the Great Man—and yes, my children's every word—but I used my Molly pen and paper.

53   PADDY'S THE MAN

THE NEXT MORNING, AUGUST 26, I wrote Molly. "I reserve 'The Red Scottish Heron' as a title for a short story about meeting the Strawman, with you as the hero." Later in the afternoon, after weighing the Dick risk and upsetting Alfred, whom I'd told of Dick's escape, I made my usual trek to town for provisions and to ask Paddy to keep watch for any passerby who shared his strong build but sported crazy eyes and was carrying a curse.

Before I'd taken two steps inside the pub, Paddy wrapped me in a bear hug, tears streaming down his cheeks. What an oversight; in my frazzled state, I'd yet to tell him I wasn't dead. From his perspective, I'd come back from the dead. His reaction moved from shock to awe to effusive brotherly love. As I told him the crazy craic of my death and resurrection, he provided the Guinness and lager lubrication in frosted mugs.

"Last Thursday when my sister asked about my moping and Usher's absence from his seat at the bar, I almost divulged our secret, but something held me back. It's hard to mourn alone. But now's not the time to look back; the only way Dick might enter these parts is as a tinker or tourist."

Paddy was an avid reader of John le Carré. And he turned a bit giddy about my return to life and being made my watchman.

"Unless they take one of my two rooms, tourists pass through. I have spies in the tinkers' camp on the other side of the moors. I'll ask they keep watch too, but of course won't give them any details."

"Yes, you gotta keep it quiet. I wasn't supposed to tell anyone that he's on the loose. And it's best, even though we don't think he's buying it, that Sean stays dead."

Paddy leaned in, conspiratorial in posture and tone. "Ush . . . you know Ireland has some of the strictest gun laws?"

"Yes, I've read about them recently. Wondering if I should try to arm myself, but it seems firearms were run out of this fair isle with the snakes."

"Yes, handguns are *verboten*—you get a minimum of five years for a popgun. But from before, way back to the time of *the troubles*, my family has kept one under the floorboards in the storeroom here. It's a wee little pistol that I fire once a year to see it still works, but it might fit your small hand. I could lose my pub license if it be known. I could live with five years in the hole, but to lose the pub that's been in the family since the 1700s, I couldn't live with that."

"Paddy, I wouldn't want to get you into any trouble, and I feel safe-ish as it is. I'm dead, so he can't kill me. And I have Alfred."

"Yes, well, still I'm sending you home with a half loaf of our Shannon's black bread. Wait here."

He came back, loudly saying, "Your bread and one more pint before you go." And then more softly, he added, "If your Dick shows up, give him a taste of Shannon's baking. It's sure to make him choke." He winked, though I'd already gotten his drift.

"Oh no, Paddy, one's enough for me," I said after draining the last of the pint and watching him whisk my mug back to the tap's spout. He didn't know of my vow of greater temperance.

"You're Irish and alive again, Ush, my friend, and we don't start counting till six, so sit back down on your stool and let's continue our chat."

I paid him an extra pound per pint, so he was driving up his tip. But he had another topic on his mind; he started to speak of Molly. My death must have got him thinking about her. About her being available. I sensed the current of his desire before he declared his intentions, so I interrupted to tell him we had once and for all decided to remain just the best of friends.

"Sean McQueen," he whispered, before raising his voice to say, "you're a bigger fool even than in your novels, and you'll rue the day you let that songbird go. A man can use a warm breast to snuggle as his bones grow cold. And that momma's got a squeeze box. Will you give me your blessing to see if maybe she'd have a rube like me?"

He was much more genteel when a woman was present but still a bit of a throwback with his 1970-something Who lyrics. Given that the town was stuck in the 1970s and all the centuries that had come before, he was a relatively modern man.

"She'd love to hear from you, I'm sure. My blessing is yours."

I didn't betray that she was thinking along the same lines.

He poured me one more than I told Alfred would be my limit of two. "On the house." He was pleased with me for being alive or maybe for getting out of his way to Molly.

"Let me know what she says. You can tell her I'll walk her down the aisle to give her away. No . . . on second thought, say I gave you my blessing. I'm not old enough to be her father and she's not mine to give away."

I finished my pint quickly to get back to my tower and my protector. On my hike home with the groceries, the loaded loaf of black Irish bread, and a beer buzz, I decided to use the menace of death by Dick, along with 9/9, as a spiritual prod. *Now or never!* I thought, tacking on an exclamation point. It was time for a single-minded focus on my practice. From here on, one glass of wine with Alfred on Friday and Saturday and two pints with Paddy on Thursday. I'd pass the remaining time before 9/9 not thinking too much and especially not wasting thought or time on Dick. Gerard was going to finally put that mad dog down once and for all.

I was dead, secluded, and the only armed man for miles around, secure in a tower fortress with Alfred, my bot bodyguard and brother.

I felt safe and committed myself to my practice. That night, I put my plan in writing.

All Day—Every third thought of 9/9!
4–6 a.m.—Two-hour meditation
6 a.m.—Coffee (one cup), egg, a slice of bread, and fresh fruit
with Alfred
6:30–8 a.m.—Hike and yoga on the beach
8–noon—Inspired longhand writing time
12–1 p.m.—A snack and one cup of coffee with Alfred
1–4 p.m.—Back to the beach, weather permitting, to rewrite and
edit the morning pages and prepare mind for what to write the
following day
4–6 p.m.—Meditation
Take the night off and enjoy dinner with Alfred
REPEAT

* * *

It was amazing how much one could get done when you got up at four
a.m. And I found myself going to sleep by nine. I had no time for Dick
as 9/9 approached. After Gerard captured or killed Dick, I'd be free to
live my life and awaken within it.

However, each morning, I circled the parapet to ensure that
Dick wasn't lying in wait or building a catapult on the beach. If he
approached from the beach, I'd see him coming, and I had Paddy's
popgun. For practice, I hit a few pieces of driftwood at ten paces. The
gun didn't have nearly as much force or recoil as Daddy aka Sadie, the
gun I'd taken away from Dick in the Himalayan hut. But it would still
be deadly at close range.

I dubbed my pistol "Chekhov."

EVERYTHING PROCEEDED ON MY self-realization schedule for three full days, until I got a call from Oriol, who knew better than to call me while I was dead. I answered, assuming it was an emergency.

"Bonet and your Gerard are dead," was his shaky salutation. "It's horrible and soon will hit the news. After you left, I gave them the key to the safe house. They didn't tell me much other than to stay away. I think they set a stakeout for your Dick, and now they're dead."

And so it began again, the death count rising around me.

"Fuckin' Dick. How?" I said. *Gerard, I'm so sorry. God bless you.* I prayed before allowing my emotions to get a grip on me. A second later, full of anger, fear, and grief, I was rushing down to the kitchen to get Chekhov and to be near Alfred.

"They were tortured and killed in the town house where you stayed. I'm glad I took the risk to call. I thought someone from Interpol or World Tribunal would notify you but couldn't be sure they'd know to—with all the secrecy and red tape surrounding you."

"They must have been tortured for where to find me, but Gerard didn't know the location other than Ireland. And you're right, my file at Interpol was encrypted from all but Gerard." I paused on the landing outside my bedroom.

"Sean, you're a dangerous man to know."

"I know. Fuck! Gerard was a good man, and he died because of me. People I love die, and now Gerard is added to the roll of the loved and dead. I'm sorry." I had to stop this. Too many died while death danced around me. I gripped the copper railing to keep from tumbling down the spiral steps. I hung my head between my legs, catching my hyperventilating breath before starting again down the steps.

"Do you think they gave Dick your name?" I asked, concerned. Before selfishly realizing that he, Carlos, and skipper boy also knew where I lived.

"Sean, I'm not taking any chances—going to the mattresses here, as they say in *The Godfather*. I'm up at my camp outside of town with my bee colonies. Carlos and a gang of our Catalan friends, well-armed, will be joining me."

I made it to the kitchen, where Alfred slept peacefully on his chair with his cane by his side. I dug the old gun from the oven mitt, patted it like it was my pet—*Good Chekhov*. And then I cocked Chekhov, glad it had a name that would prepare it to go off when needed.

"Will that young skipper you sent with Carlos and me to Ireland be there?"

"Yeah, he's part of the crew, but he was never told who you were. Don't worry about him. I've sent my wife to her sister in Mallorca. It's going to cost me a lot of wine and olive oil to have the men here until the danger has passed—like old times with the boys. But what will you do, my friend?"

"I owe you—a barrel of grand cru. I'm so sorry." I hoped I'd live to repay him. I'd already arranged through Gerard his payment for my ship to almost shore. "Give me a minute, Oriol. I need to think."

With our conversation paused, I had the clarity of mind that followed a couple days of spiritual practice under my belt, and the answer came to me fully formed.

"I'm done hiding. Now I'm on the offensive. Let him come. No more friends and family dying for me. Oriol, I no longer fear death, only pain. If I think he'll get me, I'll jump from my tower."

Sam had found me, so I assumed Dick would too.

"The sooner we have this behind us, the better. And all my friends and family can stop hiding or dying."

As I set my course straight into the tempest, my heart sank into a dark, bottomless well. I was back in that Himalayan hut of hell where I'd branded Dick and he bound us with his curse, the acrid scent of his burnt flesh embedded in my nostrils and his noxious words assaulting my ears.

"Alfred, awaken!"

He stood, a natural smile forming before he saw my face and my upheld hand commanding that he wait to speak.

"Sorry, Oriol. I'm waking my bo—buddy and bodyguard. Alfred." I turned to Alfred. "Dick killed Gerard." And then back to my call with Oriol, I said, "Neither of us will underestimate the other again. How'd he turn the tables on Bonet and Gerard?"

"Don't know. All I know is they're dead. And not just dead—they used an ugly Catalan word that loosely translates to mutilated, but in a deviant way. The WT in Barcelona has assumed authority over the case as a multi-jurisdictional shit-show. What a goat rodeo this is."

"I've not heard that before, but it paints the picture. A fucking bloody goat rodeo it is. I'm so sorry for this and for putting you at risk. Let me know if you learn any more. And one last favor. Can you leak my tower coast location, saying something like . . . hmm . . . *Sean McQueen, who supposedly died in the Barcelona bombing, has been spotted along the Cliffs of Moher. Are the aliens already raising our dead?* Give it to some disreputable Spanish media source and make it look like a happenstance sighting. I'll have Alfred send you a picture to go with the sighting. That way he won't need Scotland Yard or a month to find me."

I thought about contacting the Great Man, but the WT was already looking for Dick; if Straw was willing to help, he would try to stop me from meeting my fate sooner rather than later and would probably use saving me to blackmail Molly.

"I can do that. But you sure that's a good idea after what he just did to Bonet and Gerard?"

"The sooner this is done, the better. I can't be imprisoned on death row for the rest of my life." And I refused to let any others die in my place.

"All right, Sean, here comes a truck now with all my rowdy friends."
Thanks to Springsteen, Oriol spoke American like a Jersey boy when
the shit hit the fan.

I heard hooting and hollering and gunshots—the good ol' boys coming into the O. K. Corral of Oriol's cave retreat.

"Sounds like Barca just won the World Cup. You go get your Catalan
army settled. Post my location and picture tomorrow when Alfred gives
you the go-ahead. And be safe! I've got to return to life and set me a
rat trap."

IT WAS TIME FOR ME TO GO THE MATTRESSES, too, and make ready my tower fortress. I told Alfred the plan, and he was already researching more home-defense devices. We tested the ten-foot security perimeter around the base of the tower to ensure it would wake him while he recharged or slept, should Dick arrive disguised as the milkman. It was 2036, and the Irish still had milkmen that delivered the freshest milk once a week, always waking Alfred, should he be asleep, when the bottle was left at our tower door. Still, Alfred had me test the perimeter from every angle, and each time, the signal was strong.

"But I still should stay awake," he said when we finished.

"All right, but I have to phone Molly." I waved my phone and hand to signal him that it wasn't time to lecture me on the risks of making a call. He sat at the kitchen table with a disapproving facial expression. My Gerard-issued phone was less likely to be subject to surveillance than would be my hat-driven BCI passing through QC controls. This was a difficult call, and I didn't want Alfred sitting there to censor me. "Alfred, sleep!"

"Molly, listen and do what I say. We can't assume this line is secure. Gerard is dead. Dick got to him in Barcelona, a sting operation gone horribly wrong. Dick's loose on a killing spree. He's no longer captive in Russia. Gerard died for me."

I was a bit frantic, and Molly must have been in shock since she listened rather than talked.

"You need to go back to Fort DW protocols and security. And keep the family safe there. Make sure everyone has their family panic alarm turned back on and is ready to hurry to the panic room should we learn Dick is on his way. I don't think he will go there, but you need to be prepared. I'll make clear I'm not hiding at the DW. Call Gerard's office at Interpol and find out who's in charge of our protection now. Get the boys armed and lock the gates. Please. I'll tell Paddy and no one else. This has to end."

In case Dick's minions were listening, I stopped short of telling her that I was done hiding. I didn't mention Chekhov, my tower fortress, or iron-man Alfred.

"And Moll . . . no, never mind that." I'd been back and forth in my mind as to whether she should contact the Great Man to see what the WT could tell us about what I assumed was a rabid-dog manhunt for Dick. Again, they were going to do what they were going to do, and Straw would probably force me into hiding and try to leverage my plight to force Molly to make some favorable statement against her self-interest about the aliens meeting solely with the WT.

And I knew Dick, like death itself, wasn't going to die before he found me. We were bound by my brand on his chest and his curse on my heart.

"Don't worry about me. You need to focus on the safety of the family. Now that we know Dick is loose on a killing spree, you'll be back to the 2028 protocols Gerard put in place for a code red."

"What's your plan?"

"I've got superman AI—and a tower fortress and some additional measures I will take. Please don't ask."

"Sean, I don't like this . . ."

"You've gotta trust me. I beat Dick, the last we met."

"I got a bad feeling. You always assume a role—all bravado—based on all your old movies. You need government protection. Maybe we should contact the Great Man himself to even the playing field? Dick's trained and has access to all the weapons and powers of his Mother Russia—Alfred is one bot and you're just a . . . man. There's got to be a better plan."

I looked to Alfred, who always looked so peaceful when he slept, and wished she had not said his name, but Molly's and my conversations were supposedly secure even without the further encryption Gerard might have arranged for our call.

"There is, but please no more questions. I don't trust the Great Man. He, the WT, and Dick may all be eavesdropping, for all we know. I will say no more. My mind is set."

"I know you, and there's no arguing with you. I'll let you go but you need to use all your imagination to create a foolproof plan, and not be taken by surprise. Airtight—do you promise?"

"I promise, and I love you. I should go now and get to my plotting."

"I love you too. Nine-nine! Don't miss it!"

I'd handicap it 50/50 we would ever speak again and that I would live to see 9/9. I knew she would finish my book if I suffered a heroic death.

That call sealed my fate and set me in motion with unwavering conviction. And I'd honor my promise to make my tower airtight. I woke Alfred and sent him to the basement—he had a small office and desk there—to order supplies for our Alamo.

I felt Juno was guiding me even as we prepared for war. She would approve of all measures of self-defense now that I had no other choice. She would quote the Bhagavad Gita about how we have to do our duty, even if it may be violence, as long as it's an act of love and self-defense. She was the omniscient narrator of my life, who rarely spoke but was always there.

Alfred returned to report on the supplies he'd ordered and was kind not to remind me of his prior and more accurate risk assessment even as he issued a new one.

"If you take proper precautions and stay close to me within the tower with its one great door barred," he said, "we have an overwhelming advantage and Dick should not be able to harm you."

"Thanks. Let's store the camping gear." I pointed to the tent and provisions Gerard had us pack, still sitting in the hallway. "I no longer want solely to be unharmed. I want out from under his curse. That means . . ." I couldn't bring myself to say it.

"We have to kill him." Alfred didn't share my reserve or mincing of words.

"Yes, we must, my good friend." I felt him tingling from across the room.

"What did you get us to booby-trap our fortress?"

Alfred pulled out a list from his Scottish sporran pouch and showed me each item marked "rush": one environmental sensor (in case of chemical or nuclear attack), two high-powered day-and-night binoculars, and four security cameras, one for each direction—we already had a security camera in place for the front door. Alfred, thinking like an all-star, had ordered a motion detector for the glass turret atop the tower. Though the dome was hidden from prying eyes by a one-way 2D hologram stone façade, we still didn't want to take the risk that Dick would drop in from the sky, *Mission Impossible* style.

The tower was easily defended, with hurricane shutters and locks for the windows and the one entrance—the thick wooden door with its sturdy oak bar lock—and with a 360-degree view from my turret, a gun named Chekhov, and my state-of-the-art bot butler and watchdog, who could be stopped from protecting me only by my command or by a bullseye shot between his eyebrows.

We'd be prepared for the arrival of an evil Jason Bourne on acid.

The terms of Dick's curse made contemplation of a good death near impossible. I focused on the chance that I might live. My odds were better than when I went to meet Dick for a night in a hut in the Himalayas, though he had outsmarted trained law officers in Gerard and Bonet. How had he done that?

The story of the Barcelona safe-house murders was not being reported. The WT must have suppressed the bad press while it conducted its investigation. I wondered if Gerard had brought law enforcement bots to assist in the sting and questioned how Dick had turned the tables.

As I was saying a prayer for Gerard Montcerisier, I remembered he had a wife and children. Alfred had provided me his aristocratic last name and family history. Sadly, they had lost their family fortune after World War I. Since I was coming back to life, I could now send my condolences. And I'd reinstate and assign my NYU salary for life to his family. I prayed my *revenance* and stipend gift wouldn't be short-lived.

The next day, all the equipment was helocrafted in and installed. I risked Paddy's life by letting him help Alfred and me set the rat trap.

Alfred surprised us with another brilliant plan.

"Sean and Paddy, here is what we should do. You two run back to the pub and make a mask of Sean and bring it back here while I finish Dick-proofing the place. No time for pints, boys. The post about Sean being spotted around here will hit the multiverse in two hours, but even if he was already in Ireland, we should be safe until nine p.m. this evening. I ran a program, and that is how long it would take a robot to find you from the bait we have set. Assuming Sean is right and he'll insist on being present for the fruition of his curse." Alfred had sent a picture of me on the path to the town, with me unsuccessfully trying to hide my face in a hoodie sporting the DW logo.

"And as much as I hate to treat Sean like produce," Alfred continued as the man with plan, "when Dick or anyone shows up at the door, Sean will slip into the pantry and I'll become Sean, to welcome Dick or the mailman and take him down. And if he suggests Sean meet him in a hut in the Himalayas, I'll go as Sean to meet him. I'd like to see the world."

Paddy loved the plan, but I held some ill-defined reservations. For one, I didn't like the image of me hiding in the pantry as my stand-in played out the dramatic climax of my curse, waiting for his all-clear.

While we shared a pint, the 3D printer did its work making a mask of me. I confessed to Paddy, "I'm not sure I could register and send Alfred in my place. He's become like a brother to me."

Paddy banged his mug on the bar. "Yes, and you're a father who cannot be cloned."

An alarm sounded, informing us the mask was ready in Paddy's pub basement and mask library. Paddy tried on the less-than-flattering disguise, and looked like sixty-four-year-old me with a Jack Reacher body. I never ceased to be surprised by the age of the man's face that looked at me from the mirror. We returned to the tower.

I could tell Alfred was tingling all over to become me. His eyes were full of sparkling energy. He slipped the mask on over his head.

"That's you, Sean," Paddy said.

He was right. Alfred and I shared the same build, and wearing my face, he might even fool me. I brought Alfred one of my writer outfits and a *Peaky Blinders* cap. A second outfit—one that I actually wore—making Alfred look even more like me, with a little gangster flare. He certainly couldn't meet Dick in his kilt and sash.

Something about Alfred's safety program brought him to maximum tingles as the deadly threat approached. He was becoming even more real. I regretted all those years I'd treated him as other than human, which was all he ever asked of me. I had no doubt he would mourn me if Dick succeeded in his cursed desire.

We had an airtight rat trap, and thanks to Alfred, we had a pantry plan with a masked man. Molly would be pleased.

Paddy made me laugh by singing an old song by the Boomtown Rats about a rat trap to celebrate, and then again when he left me, saying, "You're like that little tyke in the *Home Alone* movies."

My amusement at that image soon turned to childlike fear. All that small boy wanted was his family back, to not be alone for the holidays with wicked men hunting him and breaking into his home. I became full of heartrending fear and a single-minded desire to live to see 9/9 with my family.

THE SUN HAD SET ON AUGUST 30, dropping the black screen that separated day from night. Dick would come in the dark. The dark liked darkness—not light.

I was slipping away from Nirvana, back toward that bleak hovel in the Himalayas where I left Dick. The past that had always followed us had finally caught up with us. Dick and I had unfinished business, and we would see it done.

Alfred and I were ready for my final dance with Mr. D. The drawbridge was up, the shutters battened down. Chekhov slept under my pillow, and Alfred kept watch on a chair in the corner of my bedroom. Since I couldn't sleep, we spoke of all the things we would do, and the places we would see together, after Dick was dead.

That long night my tormentor was a no-show, and I was oddly disappointed. Despite 9/9's relentless approach, I had lost track of the days and was marching to a different clock, one that watched the minutes and the hour of Dick's arrival.

The next morning, as Alfred cleaned up our breakfast dishes and pans, we spoke about Dick and whether we might be in for a prolonged vigil, if he was on a yacht, blazing with women half his age, while plotting his next move. Alfred made the case for me giving Chekhov to him, as I was statistically more likely to shoot myself by mistake than shoot an intruder. I joked that the Second Amendment right to bear arms did not to apply to him and put up my hand for him to cease arguing. As a compromise, I'd keep it hidden in an oven mitt on the nearby kitchen stove.

As I was about to go upstairs for yoga to clear my mind and get some distance from the over-vigilant and palpably tingling Alfred, Paddy called, distraught.

"He was in my pub! Dick! Two minutes ago. I'm on my way to see you, Sean."

"No, wait, what? Are you safe? Is he there now?" I tried to wave Alfred out of the room, pointing to the pantry. He pretended not to understand and instead slipped on my face. And, like an un-fun-house mirror, he sat facing me while I spoke to Paddy. I turned away from my flaccid face that masked my fear.

"No, he left. Imagine my surprise to learn you weren't Usher Wins-lett. He said he had to prepare for your date, and that I couldn't believe anything you might say."

"Paddy, if you're *not* under immediate duress, tell me who played Michael Collins."

"What? Liam Neeson. I don't understand."

"If he was still there, I'd expect you to say you didn't know." I was playing spy in my tower when I should have been hiding in a cave like Oriol. "What'd he say?"

"He said I had to deliver his message, a letter, to you personally, and to not break the seal if I wanted to live. Everything I was to do or say was followed by 'I will know' and 'if you want to live.' Thank God Shannon took my car up to Kildare with a couple friends. He's carry-ing a much bigger gun than yours. The letter isn't a bomb but a sealed envelope with a note *for your eyes only*, he said."

I wondered if it was laced with cyanide or whatever that touch poison was that Putin and Petrovsky used to administer painful deaths from afar.

"Paddy, place it in a ziplock, just in case, before you handle it."

"Shit, Sean, I'm holding it now. He says it'll tell you where to meet, as he knows you've booby-trapped the tower. He said if either of us calls the cops, he'll know and he'll add Shannon and me to your curse. And all your family at the Deeksha will also die."

"He takes his curses very seriously. But either way, I have no inten-tion of calling the cops till we hear what he has to say."

"I'm on my way, Sean. I didn't tell him anything about you. Just that we drank pints and you liked my sister's baking. He was dressed like a gypsy. You never can trust a gypsy."

"Shit, Paddy, sorry I put you at risk. And let's not blame the gypsies for this," I said in memory of Queen Mab and Polly Gray. "This is all Dick."

"No need to be sorry, but he did scare the bejesus out of me. Have my beer ready. I'll be there soon as I can with that dick's message for you. You didn't exaggerate about those sick eyes. Do you want me to ignore him and break the seal and read it to you instead?"

"No, I want you to live. I'll come to you. No, forget that—he said you're to come here? Probably best to do as he says—drop the message here and go. Don't forget I have a loaf of Shannon's bread to protect me." I peered back at Alfred over my shoulder, and there I was, my creepy clone, hanging on every word. "And we'll drink our beer as usual on Thursday, but with no six-pint limit. And tell the boys I'm buying."

My words harking back to old gangster movies and Westerns meant that Molly was right; I had seen too many movies.

But it wasn't more of my bravado. I'd learned from years of experience how to face death. I looked for agitation. I checked for fear. No and no. With the knowledge the end was near, a strange calm came over me. All the deaths, abductions, an earthquake, a fire, and a bombing had brought me here, the dead center of a crossfire hurricane. And I was calm, with no hair left to pull out or set on fire. This being the year of the dragon, I imagined Dick might bring a blowtorch to my tower.

So Dick made contact in the light of day. He must have thought I was easy prey. I wasn't inclined to meet him outside my fortress and out of reach of the oven mitt that hid Chekhov and where Alfred waited to stand in as me. Once I understood where and when he wanted to meet, I would have to come up with another Molly foolproof plan of attack where the imaginative writer defeats the sadistic spy on a bluff along the lonely moors. And if I died, Molly would bring me back to life, writing of my heroic ending.

I turned to face myself in Alfred, who, knowing me so well, knew better than to speak until spoken to. I knew he was bursting with ideas, but until we heard Dick's plan for my torture and death, there was nothing we could say or do.

"Alfred, I can't look at you like that, as me, in your *Peaky Blinders* cap."

"Sean, since he is near, it is time for me to become you."

"Okay, keep it on and stay near in the pantry, hidden. No debate. I want to speak to Paddy first and hear Dick's message before you weigh in and fully become me. Go, and Alfred, sleep!" I pointed again to the pantry door. Alfred looked like a dog being sent out in the rain but did as I commanded.

He could be roused with one of two commands: *Alfred, awaken!* a call to service, and *morte d'Arthur!* a cry for the kickass bot to rush to my defense while letting nothing stand in his way. I would use the right command at the right time *this* time, now that I'd practiced while drowning at sea.

But could I send Alfred to meet Dick as my body double?

I SAT AT THE KITCHEN TABLE waiting for Paddy, wondering if he'd walk. It was an hour walk or a thirty-minute drive, *if* there were no sheep on the road. I thought about what I'd write the children before I went to meet Dick or dared him to come to me. I worried about Alfred and whether it was right to send him to meet my curse. Dick might suspect I had a bot, and I imagined he was a pretty good shot.

Sixty-five minutes later, Paddy was late as usual, and I'd become increasingly concerned by the minute—until I remembered that Shannon had his car. Then, I saw on the monitor that he'd chosen not to walk or drive but was running down the narrow path and through my front gate at a good speed. As I got up to meet him, Alfred opened the pantry door, awakened by our security perimeter. "It's only Paddy. Alfred, sleep!" He returned to the pantry and the small seat we had placed there. I shut the door and went to greet Paddy to receive Dick's instructions on how I was to meet my death. Paddy would demand a beer, but I'd forgotten to ice a couple. He liked his beer ice cold, a bit odd for an Irishman. But he shouldn't stay any longer than necessary.

I checked the security camera and unbarred the great door. Paddy was all business and held one finger to his lips, shushing me before I even spoke. Perhaps Dick was watching from nearby and could read lips? Or maybe he'd slapped a listening device on Paddy. I stepped back and motioned for Paddy to enter in case Dick had a sniper's rifle.

Paddy anxiously handed me the letter with the old-fashioned formal wax seal of a 3D printer, forgoing our usual bro-hug greeting. Which was fine with me, as I'd never smelled him sweat before, and it wasn't pleasant. The letter he held—maybe the first one I ever hated—would tell me how I was to die. But Paddy made me feel less afraid, maybe because he was scared enough for both us. With his face frozen with fear, we went in silence to the kitchen and sat down.

"You look frazzled," I said. "And you're late even for the Irish."

He had good reason to be scared, and he hushed me again. I'd play along with his silent game. At the same time, I debated whether I should follow Dick's instructions on where and how I should meet my death. How would he convince me to leave my wizard's lair? Would he again promise that M was alive?

There was no severed finger, dangling as bait, in the slim envelope.

"A quick beer and then you need to go," I told Paddy, eager to move him to safety. I figured the beer would take the edge off. Nodding yes, he maintained his silence. Dick had done what no one else could do; he'd stripped Paddy of his baritone voice.

"Did Dick take your tongue? Or'd you take a vow of silence? I thought I was the monk."

Paddy wasn't taking any chances or finding any humor in my remark. He looked about the room slowly and deliberately, like it was bugged, grabbed my pen and paper from the table, and wrote, "Read his note first. His rules."

Poor Paddy was under great duress. I'd learned to live with Dick hanging over my head and was relieved that this curse would soon be lifted one way or another, and that I still had time for one last beer with a friend even if he was mute. But Paddy had looked into Dick's sick eyes for the first time an hour ago. I understood exactly the terror he must still be experiencing.

"I'll get our beers and we'll read Dick's love letter, and then I hope you'll find your voice and sing me a song as you go. Maybe something by the Pogues to brace me for a fight. It's not safe here, but the monitors will warn us of an approaching madman. I assume he expresses very distastefully how he proposes I am to die."

I handed Paddy a cold-enough bottle of beer. We clinked bottles and sat at the kitchen table, with me saying my Italian-sounding version of *sláinte*.

"Sláinte," Paddy said, sounding German. But at least he'd finally spoken.

I swigged half my beer before cracking the envelope's seal. I pulled out a small slip of paper.

Say hello to your old friend Dick!

What the hell? That was all it said.

I slapped the envelope to the table and looked up. Paddy was holding a gun on me.

No, not Paddy. Dick, the man of many faces, had a similar build to my drinking buddy and his clothes on. I should have smelled the rat when he walked through the door. Alfred slept in the pantry with a now useless mask and plan.

"McQueeny! Hello. Your friend is dead. He called you, as I expected, and I doubled back into the pub after listening to his call from a device I'd left there. Then I took care of him and helped myself to his mask. He was well known for his collection, and funny thing, collectors always have their own face, maybe so they can be two places at the same time. And, as we speak, I have DOGs all over the world with my face, driving the authorities crazy with false leads as to where I might be. I promised you a death of maximum terror. And I can see it on your face—we're off to the races with a very good start."

PADDY DEAD? And now Dick and death were so close I could smell them.

He waited for me to speak. But I couldn't speak or reach for the oven mitt resting on the stove out of reach of my left hand. It would be my last move. After all my planning to make my tower impenetrable, I'd let Dick in for a beer through the front door. And I'd forgotten the shaman's prescient warning, that danger would come cloaked as a friend.

Shit! M had warned me about masks, too, during her visitation. So much guidance that I hadn't heeded.

He removed the death mask of my friend. Tossed it aside. "But let's not rush it. I've seen your cardiologist report, so don't get your old heart racing too fast. Wait till you feel the gun going up your ass." He laughed at his slanted rhyme.

He had access to my private affairs. I hoped he didn't believe the security bot character named Alfred, in my fictional pages, was real.

"Oh, now it's your turn to play mute? I'd hoped we'd have a nice chat for the last time—in person." He clinked our glasses. "Do you want to say sorry for pulling my plug in Barcelona?"

He started to sway—to music only he could hear.

"No," I said.

"No apologies? A song and dance then?"

He stood to dance, the same as the last time, when he'd boogied while torturing me in the Himalayan hut of death. Time had stood still since our last waltz and now the boogie man was back. Something about his dancing caused even more fear than his words.

"No sleepy-time chili for me this time. I can't wait to burn you with a matching brand to your chest. I've fixed mine up a bit—I'll show it to you later. Your heaven's door is my hell's gate."

My God, he sounded like Blake. And, with his scent of rancid meat left out in the sun, he smelled like Lucifer. Paddy must have put up a fight, and then Dick put on Paddy's clothes.

"Well, you get the picture and know my MO."

His modus operandi was maximum torture leading to death. And Dick had spent nine years preparing exactly how to torture me with his rehearsed words and carefully choreographed moves.

"You do know our dark and deadly pact is all your doing, right? You had to publish my humiliation in your book and then spent so much time obsessing over my curse that I had to play my part as scripted in your new book."

He was hoisting me by my own petard as my first reader of a book Molly may have to finish. Damn my imagination.

"Your brand festered in me all these years, but now, with my revenge so near at hand, it's activated like Iron Man's heart." Swaying ecstatically, he ran his hand up the long shaft of his gun and then kissed it on the muzzle in a classic Dick fetish move.

He placed his hand on his chest, pledging to our reunion, as he stopped his dance to sit across from me. He removed his Paddy-brown contact lenses with his left hand while watching me with his gun and other eye. Paddy was dead. The crinkled, lifeless Paddy-face stared up at me, without eyes, from the kitchen table.

I couldn't think straight. I returned my attention to Dick and his eyes, those perverted eyes with their tiny spinning pupils. Eyes emblazoned with hate even more than when he was younger. The memory of the burning of his flesh still burned in him after nine years. He was blazing in every way.

Hate and madness were set to explode as currents of Euphory raced through him—I recognized the signs Sam had described as blazing. Dick was not a micro-dosing man of moderation. He could toss me over his head if the dose was strong enough. Euphory was a quantum computer interface jingling Dick's adrenal gland, releasing a rush of testosterone.

Drugged-up supervillain Dick was two feet from me, and he held the gun. I would need powerful aliens or an archangel to make an escape. Luckily, my avenging angel slept ten feet away behind the pantry door.

"Look at me, Professor." For a wicked man, he did like eye contact, holding it like an evil yogi.

"What'd you have to say, Professor? How'd you get Sam to open the booby-trapped briefcase alone? Her heart wasn't into our work after the Guru . . . Then I discovered she was back-channeling info about me to Interpol. Since she was telling you I couldn't move against you, I thought you might let your guard down to meet her. But I didn't get to see her face—as the first man to witness a body being bombed from inside the blast—thanks to you."

He tapped the muzzle of his gun against his temple before returning to his script. "And thanks to you, and your made-up story about how you were a hero for preventing the next great evolutionary leap of his New Society, we may all be doomed. That New Society might have given us a fighting chance against the aliens. I had to get to you by 9/9, as we all may be gone after that." As the head disciple of the Guru, he was espousing the propaganda of the DOGs.

He waved his gun up into the air and *bam*! He'd pulled the trigger, blasting a bullet into the ceiling to show me how it worked and to make my head ring. He was celebrating being near to executing his curse, his eyes whirling, relishing hate and lusting for death.

His smoking gun was poised at the ready, as if he expected someone to run in or burst through the pantry door. His beady eyes danced about the room. Alfred had a setting that allowed him to respond to loud noises, but I'd shut it off despite Gerard's warning to keep all safety programs running. I'd found it annoying when Alfred constantly showed up whenever I hollered or hammered a nail.

"Well, what you got to say, word guy? Too many words in your books, but we'll make this next one shorter, shall we? And I'm sorry to say M won't be raised from the dead for your climax. Maybe I'll write your ending, after a few edits to your current draft to make clear how much a Nancy-boy you were, squealing like a pig in the end—much more exciting that way. One thing I did like about your early drafts was how much my curse has meant to you. But you haven't written for a long while now." He narrowed his eyes on the notebook lying on the kitchen table next to me. "You've switched to paper."

He picked up my notebook. "I'll read this later. Gotta love the irony that I'll be your first and last reader."

He paused, but I still had nothing to say. I should call out for Alfred. But what if Dick with his Euphory-enhanced reflexes shot him dead between the eyes?

"You had so many words about how you defeated me in our hut in Nepal and what a whining baby I was . . . You really should say something now before we dance. I'm sure to take your breath away."

My body was frozen mute again, not because I had no memory but because I remembered it all. And now I saw how the absence of love, losing his father and guru, had inflamed Dick's hate, as Samantha had warned me. I wanted to call a time-out and a do-over. I needed time for an act of God to save me.

Breathe. Meet Dick's death with equanimity. But how to make a good death out of the worst death scenario?

I felt shame at knowing I must call out to Alfred even after Gerard and Paddy had already laid down their lives for me. And there were all the others . . .

But he's not a father.

"McQueen, when you got a couple minutes of life left, even thirty seconds more is a lifetime. And as long as we talk, I'm not torturing you."

I didn't know what to say but wanted to live. He was savoring his moment. He pointed the hot and smoky gun muzzle at my face.

"When dying's all that's left to do," I said, "it's important to do it well."

"Oh fuck off, Professor. I meant groveling and begging, not more of your fake bravado and philosophizing. Do you want to get on your knees and beg for mercy?"

"Would it matter?" I didn't know what to say or do. My thoughts

were leaping about like a monkey in a cage being rattled by a torment-
ing trapper. Flight and fight would both prove deadly.

"Might buy you time for the cavalry to ride in. But let's get on with
the main event. It might be better if I told you what to expect. I'll
start at the end and my gun—let me introduce you to Son of Daddy."
He held up the shiny new black Glock that made Chekhov look like
a water pistol. "SOD will go up your ass and blow out your brains as I
promised you years ago. For both my daddies."

I surmised he meant the Guru and his prior gun, which he'd given
the nickname *Daddy*.

"SOD will sodomize you. Ha, I hadn't thought of that."

He found his word play very funny. I found it Freudian.

I wished I was on that plane barreling downward toward a cliff wall
in my imaginary death scenario. I started my breath of fire technique,
thinking it might help me push my consciousness out through the crown
of my head or at least calm my confusion.

I still had my ace in the pantry, and it was past time to go to the
bullpen.

"Here." He pushed my notebook and Molly pen toward me. "Write
up your own last scene."

When I didn't pick up the pen, Dick pulled out a long glistening
knife that was sharpened to a fine point. With the gun in his right hand
and the knife in his left, he looked like a hungry demon holding two
metallic utensils he was about to eat me with.

"I hadn't planned this—imagine the sales with you writing your
own bloody climax!"

I might be able to lunge for the oven mitt hiding casually on the
stove less than a yard away before he could blow my head off, but that
was a long shot. But my heart was no longer up for the long drawn-out
twists and turns of dancing with Dick.

Breathe.

"I'll dictate then—pick up the pen! *And then, Dick made me pull
down my pants and spread my legs akimbo . . . The end.*" He kissed SOD
again, relishing his twisted twist to my story's ending.

As he laughed too loud, I put my arms and hands out on the table to get him used to them being there, and my left hand . . . Damn if it wasn't my bad left hand that was closer to the oven mitt. It was, however, my baseball mitt hand.

Maybe while Alfred distracted him, blasting into action from the pantry, the mask might at least confuse Dick, and I could lunge for the mitt containing a cocked Chekhov in time to help Alfred.

"Are you listening to me? What are you shaking your head about, Professor?"

"*Akimbo?*" I muttered, somewhat impressed.

I was trying not to use Alfred out of fear for his robotic life. Yet he was the obvious play here. I prayed he'd hear his command through the pantry door and that Dick would shoot him anywhere but in his third eye. All other parts of him were replaceable.

Slam!

"Ow! Fuckin' damn it."

In one quick swoop, the blade of Dick's knife went through my right hand, pinning it to the table. With his Euphory-enhanced instincts, he must have sensed I was about to act.

"That'll teach you to question my word choice. I'll write your ending for you later." He picked up my Molly pen with his empty knife hand and smelled it like it was a cigar. "If you attempt to remove the knife, I'll blow the other one off before it gets to lend a hand."

God damn it, it hurt, yet not as much as it looked. But at the time of my death, the image of a knife in my hand and the blood trickling from it was going to make meditation on the light shooting through the crown of my head damn near impossible. Knife in hand made me woozy. I instinctively started mumbling, *Juno, Juno, Juno.*

"Jew no? I'm no Jew." He had either misheard me or was pretending he had. "You're the Jew. And delirious from shock. Wait, that reminds me. Let me show you your brand. I've made it a work of art to remind me of you and this day." I wondered if he knew my mother was Jewish.

He started to unbutton his shirt like we were starting a game of Heart Sync. And over his heart, over my brand, was a baseball-size black circle with a red swastika tattoo spinning in the center. A pow-erful symbol of hate still, a century after it was first invested by Nazis with the power of the anti-Christ. Before that, it had been a loving symbol used by some Buddhist sects and a Nordic symbol for the Gods, Odin and Thor. His otherwise overly hairy chest made it look like a blackened crop circle with a twisted red cross.

The image sucked the life out of me, my mind spinning to the point where I worried I would black out.

Dick splashed my face with Paddy's beer.

"Hey, Jude, stick with me! I want you awake when I start slicing off pieces of you. But first I'll light the stove and brand your chest. Maybe I'll tattoo a dick there, to give the autopsy boys a chuckle. But let's chat first. I don't want to rush this."

He finished the dregs of his beer. And then he buttoned his shirt, not out of kindness, certainly, but probably so I'd be more alert to meet his torture. He must have realized the hateful tattoo was distracting me from his purpose.

I couldn't stop myself from checking. Yes, my hand still served as a cutting board for his knife, but that distraction he left in place. His torture was a measured art form carefully curated for maximum horror.

"Professor, remember the night you fucked me and killed my guru, my father?"

I was sure it was a rhetorical question, but I answered anyway. "I remember it well," I told him through gritted teeth, "though I can't take all the credit. A great lady ended your guru and his sick dream."

"Well, well, still the wiseass. You sort of guessed he was my father but that he wanted to keep our family bond secret. He believed one's family was a weakness, so he made me his strong arm of protection. In my line of work, revenge is a noble pursuit. With his last breath, my guru instructed me to kill you."

As long as he was talking, I'd keep Alfred safe. One thing about Dick I knew for sure, he'd kill me slowly, and I'd get to see it coming.

"My guru didn't know I'd already—I like your word—*cursed* you and was never going to let you die a peaceful death." He started flipping roughly and rudely through my notebook with the barrel of his gun like he was looking for pictures. "How you drone on about the importance of a peaceful death in your stupid book."

"I hope your guru was proud of his sadistic son, even though you failed . . ." I was too late in biting my tongue.

"You make torture so much fun, but let me share some fond memories of your beloved M before we proceed, things you never got to see or know. And then I'll tell you about Molly and the children."

I instinctively fisted my left hand, and he instinctively thrust the gun into my face. I released my fist, and he sat back.

"M begged my guru not to force himself into her. She cried that it would be a *new original sin—forced mental cohabitation.*"

He spoke in a poor imitation of M's sweet voice. And he went on and on with all the things I couldn't stand to hear, though some of it sounded like the words he used to torture me with before.

"She begged him not to. Begged for his ethical constraint, begged him not to defile her free will, her mind, her *soul.*" He laughed. "She was devastated." He shrugged. "I begged to fuck the grand dame, Lady M. To—"

"Shut up!" I screamed. "Keep her name out of your fucking mouth." I could take no more. It was impossible to shut one's ears with just one hand.

"Give that man an Oscar. You sound like that actor, from many years ago, at the Academy Awards. And really, Professor, so rude. And such a rush into a painful, humiliating death."

He put the gun to my head and turned on the stove. He pulled something from a pocket—a metal rod with a rubber handle—and held it over the flame, turning it like a walking stick in a campfire. He'd come prepared. I was glad he didn't move the oven mitt.

He sat back down with his red-hot poker.

"Before I brand you . . ."

I'm going to scream morte d'Arthur!

"I've saved my best news for your last memory before you die. A searing poker at your heart might make it race too fast, so let me tell the last thing you'll want to hear. You must have heard about my recent work in Barcelona. It's good to have friends in high places."

His eyes became inflamed, like an orc about to bite off an elf's face.

"But listen to this! Guess where a team of my DOG mercenaries is assembled and in position for predawn abductions? My operation Helter Skelter."

His fucking Manson eyes—those tiny pupils glistening and dancing like dervishes in their sockets—made it clear to me exactly where his DOGs were gathered.

"You got it! The Willamette Valley, Oregon. My DOGs are outside Sam's alma mater, the Dicksha, now a famous CE-5 site, where Molly fuckin' Quinn begs aliens to come"—he snickered—"between her legs. Not to mention it's where your two young ones are. I hear the aliens like fresh meat. Everyone there will simply disappear without a trace. Well, if you overlook a few blood-splattered walls."

He stood to reheat my brand.

"All set for five their time—they won't see another dawn. The government and media will presume the slaughter and abductions were the work of an advance party of evil aliens. Everyone will freak and beg the World Tribunal to protect them. All but the hard-core, crazy alien fuckers will abandon the CE-5 sites around the world. Well, you get the picture."

He paused to let the mayhem sink into my mind.

"Any questions about Helter Skelter? We'll leave blood all over the walls, and bloody alien symbols that look like rotating swastikas fucking one another. Apparently that one's an actual alien symbol—maybe after this, I'll add another one to my chest to celebrate *and* so the aliens will let me live. I wouldn't want to be an Israeli on 9/9. But more likely the aliens'll consider us all a mongrel species deserving extinction."

A burning question finally enabled me to speak to this crazy liar who was torturing me with last-minute horror stories to take with me into the unknown of a miserable death.

"Why would Russia look to help the World Tribunal? It's not a member yet."

"You didn't guess? I'm now a double-double agent working for the World Tribunal." He shook his head. "Don't know everything, do you, Professor?"

Dick was either prepared for the question or he was a good pantser.

"They could never directly promote me doing this my way, but the WT, along with Russia, allowed me my freedom and the funds for the mission. But my real payment is finally getting my revenge on you. And my bonus is letting you know you won't die alone but will take your family to hell with you."

His answer made only some sense, but it still might be true. The Great Man was a wily devil, and Molly was the perfect target to achieve his ends, but was he really a mass murderer of innocent civilians? I might not live to learn the truth. Dick was counting on me dying very soon.

It was time. Dick left me no choice. I howled out, "*Morte d'Arthur!*"

TIME SLOWED DOWN, though both Alfred and Dick reacted superfast.

Alfred, wearing my face, burst from the pantry on full-on engage-and-protect mode and not as my bon vivant butler. He rushed the unsuspecting Dick, who stumbled back as I pulled the blade from my hand to assist Alfred in killing the mad dog.

Alfred was covering ten steps in two and then flying through the air with a final lunge at Dick. Dick fell to his knees with gun and arm outstretched. After a *bang*, Alfred's head and then his body were flung violently back.

Dick had let out one loud bark from Son of Daddy, striking Alfred right between the eyes. Alfred folded like a marionette with the strings cut, collapsing in a heap on the floor.

"Alfred!" I fell to my knees, trying to revive him.

I'd never hugged or held him before, but I held him now, feeling the currents popping and rattling through him. I felt him struggling to speak but unable to, so I spoke for us both, "I love you too. We're family. Now, Alfred, sleep!" I didn't want him to suffer. And with one final loud pop in his hardwired chest, Alfred was dead. His body turned cold and clammy, now stained with my warm blood.

Goodbye, Alfred.

"Gay bot love, I'll add that to the ending of our book, rebranded as *Dick's Discord* and subtitled: *Crucible of a Curse*. Now, get up and sit down, you fool. And give me back my knife."

Son of Daddy was trained on me and growling to bark again. I released Alfred gently and dropped the knife, my whimpering grief passing quickly into rage when I saw Dick's pleasure at my pain radiating from his eyes.

"You see why Euphory works so well in a time of war—laser-like focus. Like you, I do research too, and I thought there might be a bot lurking somewhere—he's a big character in your story. Dead Alfred. You should have upgraded for a newer model with a bulletproof forehead, though it does make the bot look a bit Neanderthal. I checked the bot registry and there were no bots registered anywhere near here to any John Doe. Keeping an unregistered bot hidden away here—that was smart. I started to believe he was merely a figment of your fiction when you didn't call him as soon as I was unmasked. And when he didn't respond to my warning shot . . .

"Oh, and how clever. I see he was supposed to play you. Great minds think alike." His steel-tipped boot nudged at the remains of my face. He raised his gun like he might add more bullet holes to my faux face, but he must have decided to save his bullets for the real me. Looking over the barrel now turned on me and into those eyes, I wanted to die to avoid the torture he had planned for me.

"But now, without further interruption, let us continue our dance."

He picked up the knife and joined me on my side of the table, where I'd retaken my seat, sharing his putrid scent with me. He wiped the bloody blade on my white linen shirt like Zorro, leaving two interlocking Zs of a red swastika there. He tilted his head, assessing his handiwork, before he nodded.

"Marking the spot like a treasure map." He was gleeful as he went about his work. "But before I make us brothers with matching brands, I want some assurance you won't give me a struggle while I tattoo you."

I didn't know how I could assure him. The wound in my hand was bleeding freely, making me feel sick. I clutched at my heart, hoping it would rupture before Dick had a chance to burn my flesh there.

"Stand up!"

I did as he commanded. He raised my bleeding right hand by the wrist—I thought to stop the flow that was making a mess of the place—but he shook my arm instead, saying, "Hold up your right arm like you want to be called on in reading class."

When I didn't comply, he whipped his gun across the back of my head. Groggy and probably concussed, I raised my right arm. Dick grabbed my wrist and jerked it back and down, while shoving the elbow forward with his gun hand, popping my shoulder out of its socket. Searing pain cursed through me. I couldn't look, but my shoulder was hanging at chest level. With sinew and muscle torn asunder and screaming to be reconnected, I was a beaten beast, bleating and bent beneath a master's cruel yoke. He'd won his curse.

I was prepared to beg him to kill me, wanting no more pain and torment. Part of me already dead and lying at my feet. The promise of family mayhem and massacre was all that kept my survival mode lit, but it was dim and flickering. And I was about to pass out from the horror and the pain.

Writhing in primal pain and desperate for deliverance, I followed his gesture and stumbled in slow motion toward the stove for my branding when the image of my spiritual sage and healer—Juno, with a bindi—floated in front of my eyes.

My mind clicked off, silencing the anguish of my arm hanging off its hinges as it swung my hand like a bloody yo-yo. I watched the scene from slightly above, an observer, as time crawled at half speed. Ting's arrowhead started pulsing in place of my heart. From inside the nightmare, I was being guided.

Think of our old schoolyard trick.

Dylan?

I fixed crazed eyes over Dick's shoulder, toward the tower door, and in desperate surprise I exclaimed, "Paddy! Don't! Run!"

Dick twisted in slow motion to see. I turned too, and in one fluid movement I slid the oven mitt onto my left hand, and Chekhov went off with a *ping* in time to SOD's *bam*.

The *bang* of Dick's gunshot knocked me to my knees, but Chekhov's *pop* blew a hole in Dick's right eye. His remaining eye stopped spinning as the cyclops face slammed onto the table and then followed his body to the floor.

He fell on top of Alfred. I stood to wedge my foot under his swastika tattoo and flipped him off my man. This resulted in the mixed blessing of having him glare at me through his remaining dead eye.

He'd missed by an inch, leaving a heat streak on my cheek to balance out my facial birth marks, the first from another point-blank gunshot eighteen years before.

I should have picked someone living for my diversion, but though time moved slowly, there hadn't been time to think. There was no Paddy at the door, only his now blood-splattered face lying lifeless on my kitchen table.

Dick was dead. Killed by Chekhov's .22 caliber bullet to his lizard brain. A good shot with my glove hand.

But Alfred and Paddy were dead too.

And I—

The family! *My children!*

60 A BLOODY MESS

WHAT A BLOODY MESS. Alfred and Dick lay inanimate on the floor. Alfred was so much the better man, and a lot less messy in death, though he smelled like a burn pit, but still he smelled better than Dick. My heart was beating erratically and felt like it was being pinched. My mind lacked blood and my lungs hyperventilated for oxygen. I didn't know where to turn first. Molly? Juno and Dylan? The police or Interpol or—

"Sean, you okay?"

I'd called Molly. I was on the kitchen floor, propped against the stove. I was fighting the pain and struggling to be coherent. And Molly was tired, agitated, and alarmed.

"It's just past four here—this better be good."

Oh God, everything hurt, and blood was everywhere.

"Sean? You there? You okay?"

"Not good. Molly, listen—no time to think or talk. Get the children and the family, anyone there at the Deeksha, into the panic room now. But quietly. Push the silent alarm now. *Right now*. Seal yourselves in till you get my call. And, Molly, please, when you're all safe in there, call Paddy immediately. Dick got to him. I pray he's not dead, but . . ."

Shit, my shoulder hurt. The punctured right hand and bloody stream was painless in comparison. My eyes locked on Alfred. My heart bemoaning all that was lost and yet to be lost. But I needed to focus. Dick's DOG mercenaries might be already on the grounds or creeping through the halls of the Deeksha.

"If he doesn't answer, bring in the Irish police. Say we think he's been seriously injured or killed by a vicious murderer. Dick may have lied. Make up something so they act quickly." I forced my eyes open; I didn't know I'd closed them. "No, first call the local police there and the FBI and tell them you need protection. No, trust no one!" My mind was racing—while Molly and the family should be racing to the panic room.

My consciousness spun around a black hole of oblivion. Molly was asking questions I couldn't follow. I slid all the way to the floor, next to Alfred, and interrupted her cascade of questions. "Get to the panic room now! Alfred is gone. Dick is dead at my feet. You need to move."

"Sean, you're talking too fast. If Dick is dead, then you're safe, right? We're all safe? But what about Paddy, and why . . . This doesn't make sense."

I was confusing her and wasting time we didn't have.

"No time. And you and the family are *not* safe. Dick is dead, but his DOG men are coming for you and the family before dawn. Get everyone to the panic room now! And don't come out till you hear from me. Promise! Go!"

"I promise. But—"

I hung up to get her moving. *Had I killed them all?* Would dead Dick take them with him as his last sick act of a demonic life?

I struggled to stand and wrapped my right hand in a washcloth. I then propped my back against the wall and, howling like a jackal, yanked my dangling right arm down and across my body. The shoulder popped painfully back into place; I'd seen the maneuver in some movie and was shocked it worked. The searing pain was gone, replaced by a dull ache, allowing me to think of what I needed to do next, and it wasn't to call the police.

I texted Milton Straw. *I'm calling now. Pick up. I know your twisted plan. Life or death. Pick up. Your man Dick is dead but revealed all.*

I phoned him immediately. Great men can be impossible to reach, but he answered on the first ring.

"Sean, you all right? Your text—"

"I know your plan. Dick is dead here at my feet, but not before he told me everything about your WT raid on the Deeksha West. I have a great surveillance system and recorded it all, how you'd abduct and kill Molly and my family there to use as alien gore in your propaganda. It's all on tape. Dick, the man you sent to kill me, confessed it all before I killed him. You'll be the one dying in some prison cell. Fuck that, I'll kill you myself." Was I now a killer?

There was no tape, but there should have been, and it sounded true, even to me.

"Sean, have you lost your mind? I don't know what the fuck you're talking about." He didn't break character despite my threats, still playing the part of the great man holding all the cards. "It sounds like you should call the police. Do you want me to call? You can send me whatever tape you have. We're not cold-blooded kidnappers and killers. You've read too much Ludlum."

"He told me he works for you—the World Tribunal. And I have the proof."

"And you believed him? I thought he was a disreputable maniac. You killed him? My hat's off to you. We've been looking for that mad dog. Molly wrote that you'd figured out my little game of golf, but I never lied to you—there is a blindfold protocol in place."

He was creating reasonable doubt. Perhaps Dick had been spinning my own yarn back to me, from my early novel draft that envisioned the government posing as aliens to go after Molly.

"Sean, press Record on your phone."

"I already have." I pressed Record. "Wait, fuck you, you'll jam my recording again. You must have given him my location." I lied again as I'd had Oriol leak the location.

"I did not, and I can assure you there is no team heading to the Deeksha, not that I or the World Tribunal know about or sent. And I'm notifying the American authorities so they can make sure that no harm comes to the Deeksha or Molly."

He paused, but not for long. I sat at the table, sweating and shivering. Like Alfred, I hated questions I couldn't answer.

"Okay, that's done. I can assure you that the World Tribunal has nothing to do with the man you call Dick, other than hunting him as a fugitive. Sean, you're under great duress, I know. What else can I assure you of?"

"I'm going to release the tape of Dick's confession and let the world figure out what's true."

"Sean, that's within your rights, but think. A Russian agent with a lot of wealth from the Petrovsky era and a network of DOG supporters makes his escape to find you, and then this trained liar spins a story calculated to cause you maximum fear, of which there is no evidence other than your story of his deathbed confession. Still, your tape will cause great suspicion, animosity, and fear, further driving a wedge between the two camps when we should be focused on the aliens' arrival. Such an accusation, easily disproved, will discredit you and Molly and the CE-5 movement. CE-fivers will be made to fear. Hell, what am I saying—go ahead and do it."

He paused again. He was pretty good at spinning his side of the story.

"And know this—polls have shown that the more fear, regardless of its nature, the more the people clamor for their government to protect them. This wouldn't be good for anyone, especially Molly's cause of a peaceful alien welcoming."

The wily devil and family killer, or the decent and accomplished man, was right. Impeccable logic was the hallmark of many great men. Maybe Dick's tale of mayhem was his torture's pièce de résistance. It would have been the most painful part of my dying, imagining my entire family wiped out because of me. More people I love dying, even after I was dead.

If I agreed to drop Dick's story, we would never know for sure if Straw was good or evil. There was another problem—the only tape I had was of this call, where Straw sounded reasonable and I sounded like a maniac. It would be me declaring the words of a dead liar. A man I'd killed so he couldn't bear witness. Hearsay, they called it. I might try to get it admitted in the court of public opinion as a dying declaration.

And what if the Great Man was telling the truth? But even if he wasn't, he would prove me wrong if no DOGs were captured hovering around the Deeksha at dawn.

"Sean, you still there? What do you want to do? The authorities are already all over the Deeksha. Safest place in the world, they tell me. Amazing how swift the helocraft SWAT teams are these days. They're like firemen, all set to go. A team has been assigned to each CE-5 center just in case, and they're at maximum readiness with 9/9 so near. Hold on, Sean."

I dropped my head to the tabletop to try to stop an unpleasant humming in my ear. I was spinning within one of the nine circles of Dante's hell, waiting to hear if my family was dead or alive.

Straw was back, saying, "Sean, would you like to speak to the head of the SWAT team there? He says they're speaking with Molly and others who are holed up in a safe room, but they won't come out till they hear from you. She called Interpol and other authorities, who assured her they're safe, but she promised you. No DOGs and no aliens there. Time for them to come out and breathe easy. Sean, think. You're recording this, right? They're safe now, always were as far as I know. I assure you, Sean. What are y—"

If he was the man he was purported to be, I had rudely hung up on him to call Molly.

Molly, the SWAT team leader, Interpol, and my recording of Straw, which hadn't been jammed, all confirmed there were no DOGs sniffing around the Deeksha.

I HUNG UP WITH MOLLY ONCE I WAS SURE the family was safe. There were still too many conflicting emotions to register. I felt like a newborn who'd been harpooned by the hand and then yanked out of an excruciatingly narrow tube before being slapped on the butt by a hand over half my size. The difference was, I didn't cry as I struggled to bring the world into focus. Words fail, so I'll stick to facts.

The police were on their way to the pub, searching for Paddy's body, and to my tower. I straightened Alfred's body from its crumpled state and laid his hands peacefully across his chest. I peeled my charred face from his and shut his fried eyelids before placing a linen napkin over his face and the bullet hole.

"I love you."

Though I may have been in shock, those words were forever true.

I picked up my beer and clanked it with Dick's empty glass. "Sláinte."

As I drank down the rest of my beer, Alfred's cane, still propped up by his empty chair in the kitchen, caught my eye. "We got him, my brother."

I turned my head to study the bloody socket on Dick's face. I felt no regret other than deep remorse for not killing him nine years ago as he fled the Himalayan hut. Ting's *don't kill him* was apt and compassionate advice for a mosquito about to bite me during meditation, but shouldn't be applied to a homicidal human otherwise being freed to kill again.

I didn't want to be near his stinking corpse and couldn't look at poor Alfred, my loyal companion for almost a decade. I'd only had the pleasure of his company thanks to Dick's curse.

Moving, disembodied from the shock, I began rinsing off Dick's Zorro swastika from my shirt, but blood, as Lady Macbeth will tell you, is hard to wash off. As I rubbed my chest, I felt my heart. Not the way one feels their heartbeat, but every sinew and down to the first cell of the organ, and each cell was crying out, begging for relief.

I moved my awareness back to my head and my body to the front steps leading down to the beach to wait for the police, who wouldn't be happy with all my tampering with the evidence. I tried to phone Paddy, hoping he might provide a jolly reply. No answer.

I crumbled to my knees, praying in a half-crazed way, as the blue-and-white lights came swirling down in a cloud of sand kicked up from my beach. If I didn't expect the police helocrafts, I would have reported three UAPs.

While the police questioned me and investigated my tower crime scene, my mind kept returning to the Great Man. He was being set up in my ego as my next nemesis, my ego like a thief trying to steal my last chance at peace. Now that Dick was gone, I'd no longer look to outside sources or people to reflect the demons within. I'd been one step from enlightenment a couple days ago, and now I'd caused three more deaths. I'd also killed my last nemesis. I wouldn't be creating any more.

Straw was a man with great powers of bending reality or an illusion, depending on your perspective, to his will, but he was neither all good nor all bad, as far as I knew. I blessed him and let him go. I was determined to focus within and realize the Buddha in me. To finally turn all my focus toward self-realization and away from all distractions. A drowning man desiring breath doesn't worry about sharks in the water.

The Irish Garda, or Guardians of the Peace, were serious and thorough, but too late to protect the peace. Between their questioning of me, I was left mourning Gerard, Alfred, and Paddy, and contemplating, once again, death and how so many had died defending me.

AS A PARAMEDIC BANDAGED MY HAND and fixed my arm in a sling, I overheard the police announce they had found Paddy's body in the pub's basement office where "there had been quite a struggle." I didn't act surprised—I wasn't—and the most senior guard noted my reaction with suspicion. One more death on my conscience before Dick's curse had been lifted. My heart cried out for another dead friend. I half expected the one-eyed Dick to rise from the dead and kill us all.

The police hadn't ruled me out as Paddy's murderer and treated me like a homicide suspect caught red-handed with two smoking guns, and two more bodies with two masks, and quite a story to tell. I confessed to killing Dick in self-defense with Chekhov, a gun I found hidden in the tower basement when I put in the wine cellar. I didn't want sister Shannon to lose the pub after losing Paddy.

It wasn't until hours later, apparently after someone at Interpol and the Great Man himself vouched for me and got the illegal firearm charge dropped, that I was informed that Paddy was found with a blow to the head next to his 3D printer surrounded by a thousand ghoulish masks. It was an injury that would have killed an ordinary man, but it only knocked Paddy out, leaving the truly great man with a severe concussion. He was at the hospital recovering. Like the revolutionary hero Michael Collins, so full of the joy of life, he was hard to kill.

That news led me into prayers of thanks and oaths to be a better man. To finally meet my goal of true self-realization or die trying. To be worthy of all those that served, even laid down their lives for me, guiding me along my path.

In the days that followed, Ireland didn't suffer much from the international spotlight. They enjoyed the craic of masks and murder in a writer's secluded tower. They celebrated me like a playboy of the Western world. And Paddy as the hardheaded sidekick.

The fictionalized accounts of our heroics that day were as sensational and gaudy as you might imagine, but for a hot minute now that 9/9 loomed like a tsunami over everyone's head. September had finally arrived. Everyone had a countdown clock running, counting off the last nine days. And post-Dick, my focus was on my spiritual practice and laying Alfred to sleep one final time. He hated sleep. I prayed that perhaps he had been uploaded at the last moment into some cloud, and from there still watched over me.

Alfred was buried on the tower lawn with an old-fashioned gravestone. I didn't suppose he had a soul that moved from life to life, but I would never forget my companion and his sacrifice. I researched famous epitaphs and worked on the inscription for a full day. Yeats had written his own, ending his poem "Under Ben Bulben" with "Cast a cold eye / On life, on death. / Horseman, pass by." But I couldn't steal from a dead poet's grave.

Paddy used a digital picture of Alfred from his 3D printer to give Alfred back his face for his burial. Alfred was laid in the casket in full plaid—kilt, tweed coat, and cap. But sans underwear, so he'd be buried like a real man. I imagined bagpipes playing.

The gravestone simply read *A friend and brother. Alfred McQueen, February 3, 2028–August 31, 2036.* He would have liked being given my family name.

Paddy, in a red-white-and-blue head bandage, and me with my arm in a sling, looked like a Revolutionary War fife and drum corps as we laid Alfred to rest in Scottish dress. I tearfully recited Kipling's "Gunga Din," one of Alfred's favorite poems. Fittingly, an ode to underappreciated service.

By the livin' Gawd that made you,
You're a better man than I am, Gunga Din!

Though Alfred no longer wore my face, I felt a big part of my story for the last nine years and my alter ego was buried with him.

I wiped away tears for those lost and those saved, relieved that Paddy had survived Dick's blow to share in Alfred's farewell. The big man laid his arm across my shoulders, summing up Alfred in the most meaningful way.

"He performed his terms of service without once wavering. Better than we might say for most men."

Our terms of service are simply to love one another. But unlike robots, we are free to choose whether or not to follow our God-given natures, and based on our free will, to become deadly Dicks or Big-Loving Junos or any gradation in between.

I removed myself from the spectacle to the privacy of my tower to write the end of my last book—my own epitaph. Once I finished, I'd stop telling stories of me and end my egotistic game of self-discovery. I'd wanted to write a beautiful story—*Juno's Song*—but Dick had marred my ending. And time itself was in question, with eight days remaining until 9/9.

All the family wanted to rush to my aid. But I insisted we stick to the 9/9 plan. I would see some of them soon enough. I needed time to adjust and to practice peace in private after killing a man and losing my dear companion.

No words came to me, and my punctured pen hand hung from a useless shoulder, disrupting the flow of creativity. I placed the manuscript in my desk along with my Molly pen, to not see the light of day until I discovered who I was and what came after the arrival of the aliens.

Dick and his curse were gone like a bad dream. That insidious thought that *something is wrong*—that some black hat was coming over the horizon—was gone. It was time to meet my Aldous Huxley challenge of self-realization in this life. No more mañanas and nemeses, no more curses and excuses. One final river to cross. This determination became fixed in my cleared mind, not as a mere possibility but as a coming reality, becoming present in me. No more seeking outside myself that which was within, waiting to be realized.

Words meant little now; they fell like beads from a broken strand that built the story of me. I wrote a letter to Molly, reminding her to write the ending if for any reason I was unable to. I attached the letter to the manuscript while clutching at my heart, fearing I might never see *Juno's Song* come to full expression. My heart begging for the peace that passes all understanding.

I returned to my strict practice of yoga and meditation for the remaining eight days.

Juno's Song was about true liberation and not just freedom from a curse. I needed to take that one final step. To step into the unknown. Not to wake up in self-realization, not to fully open my heart now, after all the blessings and teachers that had found me on my path, would be a tragedy far greater than not finishing a book before my death.

63 GOODBYE, PADDY

THE DAYS FOLLOWING DICK'S DEBACLE passed in solitude, meditation, and yoga, taking me on a deep dive into the still waters of the mind. Plunging under the ripples of thought that so many times had become the waves of neurotic stories of me.

I revisited my beloved sublime poetry. I circled the fathomless heart's core where the true self, known by all great poets throughout the centuries, resides, using the fewest words possible to point to the ineffable.

Maybe it was the countdown clock or the stilling of my mind, but time moved very slowly the week before 9/9. My spiritual practice was attended to with diligence as I sat long hours like Buddha under the Bodhi tree after passing through all Mara's temptations. Juno was coming. I wanted to be ready. My yet-to-be-asked guru's arrival meant even more to me than the advent of aliens.

Everyone else was preparing for the aliens, and I wasn't left entirely to my solitude. When I refused to make my appearance at the pub that Thursday, five days before the day of reckoning, Paddy, still with a baseball-size bump and bandage on his head, insisted on delivering provisions and good-natured company. Shannon had come back from Kildare to care for him so that he might care for me.

Paddy and I sat on my beach talking frivolously about A-Day.

"So how will you greet the green men?" he asked.

"I think a namaste may be best. How about you?"

"I've got a Captain Kirk mask." He held up the palm of his hand and created a *V* between his middle and ring finger in salute. "Maybe they'll give us a Vulcan mind probe to suck out all our memories and the animating force, wiping clean the circuitry of our minds, leaving zombie slaves to serve them."

I had to turn away and bite back tears thinking of Alfred.

"I know you and your family are more believing in the coming Age of Aquarius and celebrating an unprecedented blossoming of Big Love. And Molly's been bending my ear, telling me I gotta believe." He smiled broadly like a teenager in love.

"Well, you gotta admit it's better than the other half that are wallowing in deep-seated reactionary fear and digging last-minute bomb shelters while watching the WT news telling them not to panic, since 'Earth is ready and stands united in high alert.'"

"Yeah, with Russia finally being admitted to the World Tribunal despite letting your Dick loose to go on a killing spree."

"That's all behind us now, Paddy." The police, though not very forthcoming, had informed me there was no trail leading from Dick to the WT.

"Tell this lump that," he said, holding his hand up to his still-bandaged head. "It can come off tomorrow. In the end, I suppose most people are getting on with their lives—diapers still need changing and children need to be fed, despite the big dip in the birth rate for 2036."

Between the Woodstock world of flowers and rainbows, and the bunkers full of batteries, toilet paper, water, and guns, there remained a stoic minority. Paddy was in this third philosophical camp, the "Ironists," those who continued to believe that nothing was about to happen and that the "alien" messages were merely cosmic radiation or dust. Or, if actual messages had been sent, that it was all some grand alien joke. God's or an impersonal universe's way of taking the piss out of us.

"Paddy, I hope you'll be joining us for 9/9," I said with deep feeling, shading my eyes from the glare of the sun as we walked along the beach. "Some of the family will be here. I'd love for you to meet."

He paused to laugh at my earnestness and averted his eyes to look down at his gnarly toes as he burrowed them into the sand.

"Despite being an ironclad Ironist, I do see the importance of these gatherings for the day of infinite jest. And I do love you, mate. But I've decided to use the magnitude of the moment for romance. The doctor cleared me yesterday to take Molly up on her offer to be with her for the festival at your Deeksha. First time I'll be leaving Ireland since my wife died. Actually, I should be going now to start packing. My flight's tomorrow, and the last-minute seat was hard to get. Lots of crazy folk flying about to peer into the same sky they could be seeing from their own backyards."

"When were you going to tell me? You're part of the family now—you'll love the DW! Have a great trip, Paddy. I can't wait to hear your romantic craic when you get back." I, too, looked down at the sand, glad his toes remained covered, as a part of me was unsure I would ever see him again.

"Consider getting a pedicure . . . you know, before *anything* happens with Molly."

I walked him up to the trail head back to village and said, "Goodbye, Paddy."

He would experience the passion my imagination had indulged in for so many nights before my recent vow of celibacy. As a novice monk, I was glad of that. I wished them the tantric joy of perfect sexual union that I had known with M.

As the big man walked away, he looked up at the lyrical Irish sky and spoke in spontaneous rhyme, "Jesus! I think he may be serious about all this monk business."

64 THE LAST SUPPER

AS PADDY FLEW WEST, other family members were flying east and west on their way to Ireland to be with me for 9/9 for a small family gathering at my Irish tower hovering over the Cliffs of Moher. I'd be hosting Juno, Ting, and the children. The family was all squarely in the Age of Aquarius camp.

I returned to my "I am" practice to prepare for the family and alien arrival and to be in high vibration, ready to resonate with Juno. It was fitting that Juno would be present for the end of *Juno's Song*.

With no Dick to fear, I was careful to keep my creative imagination focused on my life sankalpa of self-realization and not on creating a new nemesis to focus my energy on. I let the Great Man go without rendering judgment. I also would shed my role of hero. Without a villain, there can be no hero. I noted my mind's attempt to move the fear toward my troubled heart, but was able to avert the ego's wily efforts, and this allowed Big Love to grow in me.

Two more slow days passed as my mind settled into stillness more and more. Then the family arrived on September 7. I missed Alfred, as he would have made everything ready for me, but I did my best to carry on without him for the family. Mostly I missed Alfred's joie de vivre and constant company.

Molly, YaLan, Astri, and the boys were needed at the Deeksha West to host Molly's gathering of CE-5 enthusiasts and Paddy. Molly had made the DW *the* place to be to welcome the aliens or angels. A New Age *Vanity Fair* declared: *The Deeksha West is a spectacular venue for the*

gathering of highly conscious people, under the auspices of the indomitable
Molly Quinn, celebrating the alien arrival in the spirit of Big Love.

I was honored that so many of the family had chosen to share the day with me in relative seclusion. Everyone was celebrating the curse being lifted and Dick being gone for good. The tower was now open as another Deeksha refuge for the family to enjoy. I started and stopped calling it Eire Deeksha after the first pass, realizing how it would be abbreviated and the dobber jokes it would garnish.

Boy was being joined at the Deeksha in Kathmandu by Natalie and Grace Byrne, and Chi. I imagined Chi walking Astro through the airport. I wondered if she'd fit in an overhead bin or had to be checked like luggage. I'd never traveled with Alfred, but I would have bought him a ticket for the seat next to me.

All the Deekshas would be in constant contact. The family was as ready as we could be for the unknowns of 9/9. Juno and Dylan were buzzing with all the hoaxes, hysteria, and media-pumped adrenaline. After largely shutting out the world as the alien clock ticked down, I found the fuss all a bit embarrassing for mankind. I sensed we were being watched.

On September 8, the family at the Deeksha tower held what I'd dubbed the Last Supper. Juno prepared a feast based on local ingredients. The menu included a buttery, saffron-accented monkfish fresh out of the Atlantic that tasted better than lobster; a delicious spicy cabbage dish that tasted nothing like kimchi; and potatoes with thyme, sea salt, and a splash of thick Irish milk. She could make soup from rocks and it would have tasted divine, since love was her main ingredient.

The family helped with the preparations, and a round table was set up outside the tower on the bluff overlooking the Atlantic. My daughter had dressed Alfred's nearby grave with wildflowers, making sure he was included in our celebrations. Like Dylan, M, and Elliot, Alfred was part of the dearly departed family.

I spent a long time selecting and opening two of my best bottles of wine in case they might be our last. As a man of moderation, I'd have one glass of each, honoring again my vow to drink less. And the sisters, Juno and Ting, would take a sip and like fairies, get high on the bouquet.

We arrived at six for the feast in unplanned uniforms, the women in simple Irish peasant dresses and colorful headscarves—spiritual gypsies—while Dylan and I wore white linen shirts with blue jeans and cowboy hats that the deceased Dylan had long ago sent me from his dirt-biking trips out West.

As the family of gypsies and cowboys settled into our seats for a toast, we were ambushed. A drone dive-bombed right over our heads before rising to circle in angry little loops above the table, like a nasty metal crow or a tiny Blackhawk about to rain down bullets.

The drone must have been left behind by some media outlet. At least that was what I hoped. It was so high-tech that it might have been a World Tribunal weapon. It must have been motion activated or otherwise programmed to attack us in that moment.

So this is how it ends . . .

Something called my attention to Ting. Apparently, the drone was also attracted to her; it raced down to hover in front of her, in an AI and mystic face-off, as if daring her to blink and demanding she surrender. The angry black hummingbird's one red eye dilated, in and out, menacingly. Yet Ting's glare was fiercer. The drone shot up like a roman candle before that nasty bird crashed down into the moors with a dramatic plume of smoke.

The family laughed, acting like such an event was normal. In a way, it was nothing strange for September 2036. And within the family, powerful coincidences and miraculous occurrences were the norm. But I'd swear we had witnessed Ting using telekinesis. She, too, had cleared her head of the Great Man. Ting was again the jubilant sprite, full of summer spirit. Still smiling, she tapped her glass with her knife to call the party to attention. The *ting* of the glass started a life-threatening and life-affirming banging in my chest—the proverbial ticking clock. I smiled at the knowledge that this time bomb would take only my life and not the lives of those I loved.

"Tomorrow," Ting said, "let us experience *the happening* without any preconception of what our mind thinks of aliens or angels or other dimensions. Together as chalices of consciousness"—she held up her glass to the setting sun—"we are a powerful portal to the vortex of creation. Whatever celestial show tomorrow brings, let us bear witness without a drop of fear and welcome it with love. We are so blessed by this family, this life, this Earth."

She looked over the beach below, at the sun drooping low into the great ocean from a colorful sky, taking in the beauty of the moment with the family. She raised her arms to the twilight sky, in sun and moon salutation. Her eyes lighted on each of us in turn and then she said, "How can we not be fully grateful for all this? Gratitude and devotion lead to love and joy, and love and joy lead to gratitude and devotion. A wisdom wheel."

That is all ye know on earth, and all ye need to know.

She nodded to her sister as the Keats line played in my head in M's voice.

Juno then led the family in a chorus of three aums with grateful hands, held in prayer to our chests. We communed in the collective sound of God, and I swear I felt the grace of M by my side. And then we sipped our wine.

We shared the best meal ever. Juno, I wanted to call her my guru, was a master chef. And we celebrated the moment, and each other, without reference to the ephemeral past or the looming future.

As a dessert of fresh strawberries and Irish cream was savored, my son and daughter gave brief readings from the novels they'd been writing over the summer under Molly's guidance.

Dylan's story was the adventure of a sorcerer's apprentice, filled with science and magic—a perfect blend of his mother's quantum physics and constant creation theory and my literary taste. The young hero sets out on a quest after finding a mysterious map left folded and forgotten in a book by Nostradamus in the voluminous family library. As it was written in French, the all-American family hadn't opened the book for generations.

Juno's story was a Romeo and Juliet romance between young best friends and would-be lovers, Pat and Sean. The twist was that their genders are never revealed, a device brilliantly designed to challenge the reader and explode the critics' heads, as it would confound their desire to enforce political correctness. The gender-blender was mixed in with all the other obstacles to true love and self-discovery.

I found myself welling up with emotion as they read with the unjaded voices of youth brought up on Big Love. I shared their mother's pride in that moment, and I wouldn't change a word of what they'd written, except as I noted for novelist Juno, "I *pat-ent-ly* would have named the lovers *Pat and Lee* instead." The family faces around the table smiled at my silly pun. And I became overwhelmed with gratitude for the Big Love we all shared. My family looked at me at the head of the table. The elder statesman. A silly wizard in a cowboy hat.

I clutched at my chest, thinking my heart might crack the cage of flesh and bone and fly out. I was caught in the reflexive act, with concern reflected in the shadowing of the children's faces.

"No worries. It's a twang of happiness and a twinge of love." I used purple prose to deflect from my heartbreaking mortality.

The family's apprehension over my heart was amplified by the silence I now imposed around the subject. I'd promised to tend to it after 9/9, and the appointment was already set for the robots to operate; I didn't want to discuss it today. Concerned looks chased one another around the table, but no one spoke of my condition.

Tonight wouldn't be a bad time to die, as many thought we were all going to die by the end of tomorrow in any event, and I'd be spared the heart surgery. Perhaps I had a death wish after all.

Yet I knew that wasn't true. I was simply no longer scared to die.

The meal concluded around ten, with a plan to meet on the beach at sunrise to welcome the aliens. I joked that the aliens would adhere to New York City time, so we wouldn't miss anything. We'd set up a multi-time uni-verse meeting with the two Deekshas for high noon Irish tower time to circle the entire family and to ring in 9/9 together.

Of course, it was already September 9 in Hong Kong, but as of yet, no large-scale invasion had been reported and no jolly red Santa Claus or little green Grinch spottings had been confirmed. There were unconfirmed reports of contact, of course, but they were to be expected.

We were among those—yes, the family had swept me up in their enthusiasm—who acted like children on Christmas Eve, excited to see when we awoke what gifts the advanced beings had brought us. As we said our goodnights, Juno caught my eye, and we communicated without the use of tongues and lips. Electricity filled the air between us.

Meet on the beach to meditate tonight? came her welcome invitation.

Yes, so we're there for midnight.

As a child, I'd never been able to sleep on Christmas Eve.

65 JUNO'S SONG

A LITTLE BEFORE ELEVEN P.M. I met Juno in the kitchen, where she was heating water for tea. I'd never seen her sleep. She was rejuvenated from her meditation practice and nonresistant way of life. She simply did one thing, or nothing, at a time. She could live on air and tea, while dipping in and out of the infinite source.

Turning from the stove to face me, Juno was once again wearing the bindi, but it was her turquoise eyes that silenced my mind, stirred my spirits, and seized my heart—spellbinding me.

Juno's presence in the kitchen, where a couple of weeks before, Dick had come to his end in a puddle of cold blood, cleared the energy there and absolved me of shooting a man in the face. The knife wound in my hand no longer felt the cringing memory of the piercing blade, and my shoulder socket was settling back into place sinew by sinew. I clenched my fingers—they moved easily. I rolled my shoulder—I felt no pain.

I bowed my thanks, trying to honor the solemn moment, but lightness and joy bubbled out of me. Both my home and my body had been cleansed, and the heaviness I'd carried had floated away. I was left with the blissful sensation of Big Love in the presence of my spiritual master.

I wished Alfred was there to meet our honored guest. Alfred the prince of service. The Big-Loving bot would have recognized the infinite consciousness and unconditional love that was Juno. Superintelligence meeting an enlightened being would have been a sight to see.

Juno greeted me with one of her mind-reading messages.

"Hello, buddy! There is no guilt in defense of self and family. Like Arjuna in the Bhagavad Gita, it was your duty, part of God's divine plan, to go into battle to protect yourself and family. But now the battle's over, and it's time to go within and heal ancient wounds. Time to open our hearts."

She smiled as if she'd commented on the weather, which promised clear skies for the alien arrival. And then she checked the oven for whatever she had baking there.

Head and body tilted toward the open oven, she said, "In the face of the dragon, all we can do is bow down and have no fear."

I looked at the floor, where I stood atop the very spot where Dick had lain, his crazy dead eye staring up at me. I fell to my knees and prostrated myself. A dark ghost passed through me. Or maybe it was out of me. Dick being released from me, and the world.

Juno namaste'd my strange religious mummery.

And then I looked up into her saintly eyes and said it. "Will you be my guru?" Words I never thought I'd be humble enough or brave enough to utter.

She smiled. "The Buddha in me is the Buddha in you, and that is our guru. Yes, I will, I am. It is done. Many lifetimes and all of creation has brought us here." Her eyes, locking on mine, sealed our bond, and then she turned back toward the stove. "I'm making tea and biscuits for our night on the beach. Two pots—one for tonight and one for tomorrow morning when the family joins us."

Joy washed over me. It was done. A vast sky opened in my mind, welcoming her wisdom and thrilled by the prospect of tea and biscuits on the beach with my guru.

I stood, saying, "Be careful with that oven mitt—it's got a hole on the top." The police had recently returned it with other articles they had confiscated from the crime scene. Chekhov was not returned.

She stuck her finger like a wand through the bullet's hole and waved her hand, in-mitt, into the air, in one of her signature joyful gestures. I loved my guru, chef, and tea master with all the Big Love in the world. She made me feel nurtured, like a happy child in a warm, yummy-smelling kitchen.

Sublime feelings flashed through me as I witnessed her gracefully removing fragrant biscuits from the oven with my holy oven mitt. Tea and biscuits with Juno under the cosmic kaleidoscope of stars with the great sea roaring at our feet would be a joyful and sacred way to await the second coming.

Though the Bible had told us *we know not the hour*, perhaps we did now know the day.

For my contribution, I packed two warm cotton shawls, a beach blanket, and a bundle of dry wood for the snap, crackle, pop of a beachside fire. I also had two yoga cushions for our long meditation. We had enough provisions for me to pull my little red wagon from the shed, with its bulbous wheels for bouncing down the wide stone steps that led to the beach. My trusty old-school carrier was always welcome on the way down but less so on the way back up. Depending on the direction, I felt either young or old with my red wagon. Tonight, I'd be an innocent child moving in both directions, should we return from our date with aliens.

Landing on the beach with my little red wagon in tow, we began our journey into the unknown, anticipating miracles. Our bare feet sank into sand still warm from the sun; the atmosphere registered a mild mid-sixties. Like scouts in a new world, we followed my bobbing head-lamp along the shore to find the perfect seat for our vigil. My heart was filled and not pinching as angels, mermaids, aliens, and fairies all danced in the dark just outside the headlight's gaze. Magic was always near when in the company of my guru.

Juno found our place alongside a large driftwood table that looked like a small seal with its head sloping upright, but it had a flat enough back for our teacups to rest upon. The sand was Goldilocks-style—not too hard and not too soft to support our cushions. Our canopy was a clear moonless sky full of the twinkling diamonds of Indra's jewel-be-dazzled net.

I wondered if the aliens had purposely chosen to arrive on a new moon and how they might warp space or slow time to travel so far. If they traveled at the speed of light, time would have stopped for them, giving them all the time in the world. Molly believed they didn't need to warp space as they were merely coming down from a higher parallel dimension, where space was less dense and time less linear. Or, she'd once suggested, they would raise us up to meet them on a higher plane of consciousness.

As I set the fire in a little hollow of sand I had dug, I offered, "A beacon of light so they will find us. You have to believe!"

It was a tiny match compared to the burning-man bonfire Molly had planned for the Deeksha West. My rational mind, poking at its last clever strand of doubt, kept returning to the quandary of how and when the aliens would come on 9/9 when it wasn't the same time or even the same day everywhere on Earth. The Ironists had seized upon this seeming conundrum as proof that the alien date was a big joke. I rubbed at my face as my mind struggled to make sense of it. Molly's journey with the shaman had somehow assured her this was not an issue, but she felt bound to keep it secret and never explained why.

Time is merely a construct of thought, Juno answered me mind to mind. *They live in the instant of vertical time and as higher beings have no real concept of our imaginary horizontal time.* She, or the aliens, had turned Stephen Hawking's theory of time on its head. *A universal opening, outside of space and time, will allow some to experience these other realms. They did their best to signal a marker, in human terms, so we might be ready to make the leap. Please do not overanalyze it. It is time to leave thought behind and, with thought, time.*

My heart understood. The time for doubt and conjecture was over. Her telepathic voice was her remarkable voice, so lyrically crisp and clear, singing within me.

Then Juno, as she had when M and I first met her eighteen years ago, performed a modest but sublime tea ceremony. She performed the service in silence. Tea service was always a sacred ceremony with Juno, but this was high tea with the queen of tea as we prepared to sail out of this world.

She pulled a porous cloth pouch with a pull-string tie from her peasant dress pocket. The pouch might have contained medicine or a holy relic. She tossed it to me so that I might feel its natural weave and smell the luscious leaves.

She smiled, anticipating my question, and softly broke her silence. "Green matcha tea from the Deeksha garden, blessed by the animating force of nature."

I bent down to inhale the blessed and fragrant leaves and then returned the small and sacred sack to my guru.

Juno held up an index finger and said, "To heal your heart." And then she waved her wand hand up into the sky, stirring the stars.

"Where exactly is this tea garden at the Deeksha?"

I was asking to confirm the pleasing vision that had come over me, of her tending to the earth under the watchful eye of the Buddha by the pond, where Dylan's poem "Spring Blessing" was inscribed in rock. I knew that must be the place—where M and I fell in love after the earthquake in Kathmandu.

"Precisely," Juno said. She smiled at me in a mix of verbal and non-verbal communication. "You and Emily are always with me in the Buddha garden."

Juno already lived in a higher realm, where time and space weren't so strictly regulated. Maybe she *was* an alien. She was so evolved as to be another species. And what never ceased to amaze me, she had time for me and wanted to be with me, even now on alien eve. This made my head spin, that somehow, surpassing all belief, I was worthy of her light.

In her presence, I wanted for nothing.

Juno's light had always been with me in my darkest hours, days that were now behind me. My life was a mystical dance with the minstrel spirit that traveled within Juno. My life, ever since receiving Dylan Byrne's letter eighteen years ago, had all been a procession to her song. She had led Dylan to the theory of constant creation. She had led me to Big Love and M's love. She was the keystone of the family. She had saved me from the Himalayan hut of death as Dick's goon squad approached. And now she was leading me through the great transition, with 9/9 coming in less than a half hour. My diamond heart was breaking into infinite fractals that received and reflected her light.

"All that's left to do to bring the magic leaves back to life is to heat the water to the right temperature and . . ." She placed the entire tea pouch, with the strings hanging out, into one of the thermoses. The pouch's soft hemp-like weave allowed the sacred leaves to brew. We were percolating too, seated in silence with Rumi eyes meeting.

As we waited in rapt anticipation for a cup of tea, a vison arose between us, with our minds moving into the universal mind and becoming increasingly porous to one another. We shared an image of a seed pushing up through the rich earth into the light, its green leaves reaching for the sun. The same sun from which the seed, earth, air, and water had come. That sun, one of infinite suns, had come from the one sun, the source, bursting and imploding in constant creation, bursting and imploding over and over—till the tea was ready.

She poured the tea like a dancer moved, with deliberate and fluid movements. I received the tea with rapture. The boundaries between dance and rapture, guru and student, fell away. The sea air mingled with the scent of tea. And though it was a pitch-black night, the moment held the perfect blend of earth, air, and water, with all three elements mingling in the light of Juno's radiant sun. I slowly, mindfully, moved the cup of aromatic love to my lips for the first taste.

"The best tea ever!" And it was.

Juno had foreseen or planned these moments, this scene. To be more precise, it was as if she expected and accepted each moment exactly as it unfurled in co-creation with her. I was a child wizard, learning in the light of her mastery. My recent past settled within me like tea leaves to be read, and I welcomed the reading.

My Big Love for Molly had been tied up with desire for sexual union and old-age comfort. We'd traveled to a shaman in a yurt and gone to see a great man in his castle. We'd prepared to welcome aliens and perhaps the end of the world. I'd reunited with Elliot's killer and almost got blown up with that witch turned ally. I went into hiding and nearly drowned at sea. Two dear friends were brutally murdered by my would-be killer before I blasted his homicidal head half-off and then proceeded to drink a beer.

Candide and Gulliver had ordinary lives compared to me.

Living at the most interesting time, I had lived the most extraordinary life, but nothing compared to the here and now with Juno by my side, sipping tea in a state of grace on the beach under Indra's net of stars. Nothing was as extraordinary as seeing our minds dreaming and creating reality. Nothing was as astonishing as the flow of consciousness awakening within itself.

Juno looked regal and ethereal as the night flowed through her to project a hologram universe with us smack dab in its center, experiencing the stillness of the ever-present source of constant creation.

"Sean, you've become comfortable with paradox—you've always loved Zeno. Your momentum has always been taking you halfway and halfway again to where you are now—ready to cross over—though you have been crossing every instant of creation since you were born. But to realize it and to pause there in the instant of creation, experiencing fully the paradox of being and becoming . . . That time is now!"

Her words were followed by a silent click in my head that no longer registered the Zeno effect as purely physical arousal but as a spiritual one—the opening of a vortex—allowing alignment with the eternity of vertical time.

I saw through her eyes, felt through her skin, heard the humming above and within. I was Blake, burning bright. I was Walt Whitman, fully alive. Seeing the universe in a grain of sand and a leaf of grass.

We have come to this beach so that tonight I may pass from this life?

Yes and no.

My heart registered her cryptic reply as yet another paradox, but my head started grasping for more solid ground and asked, "Juno, I feel my life's duty is to be there for my children and my life's purpose is to finish my book. How can I let those go?" These words were my final expression of fear—all that was still holding me back.

"You should stay and do that if that is your duty. But there is no purpose—purpose assumes a lack, and there is no lack in the universe. Our enlightened selves wait for our realization and perfect alignment with constant creation. Letting go of all doubt and fear, we become who we are and have always been—spirits in exploration of the expanding universe that desires only more love."

I had become wise enough to hear the truth and know it to be true.

"Same as it ever was and will be," she continued. "All is awakened already, now and now and now."

"And the end of all our exploring/ Will be to arrive where we started/ And know the place for the first time." I quoted the Elliot lines for her, words that might serve equally well as an excellent epigram or epigraph.

She smiled, raising her index finger to her lips. Devil and angel, she could broker peace between heaven and hell with a smile or by holding up one finger to hush my mind, thus reconciling all opposites. *Listen.*

We meditated in silence, bliss, and love.

Then came a walloping of the soft beach beneath our seats, as if a giant shaman was pounding a huge kettle drum and vibrating sand and sea. Lord Ganesha, the elephant God, trampling the earth to usher in a new era? I half expected the screeching call, coming in from over the sea, of fire-breathing dragons. It was the same earthquaking rampage I had heard from my tower bed before without being able to identify the source. Maybe aliens coming from a dimension closer to the source were pulling asunder the atoms of our world with their intense vibration.

But then came not four horses riding on the winds of the apocalypse but dozens, with their hundred hooves galloping over the sand—a natural rampage of planet Earth. The pack of small wild horses untethered my gypsy soul to soar along with them on their near-midnight run.

The Irish had long before nurtured the return of the beautiful beasts, *the ponies*, to their native shore. Luckily, the animals had chosen a path closer to the ocean, where they could splash in the final ripples of the waves' long journey, otherwise we might have been trampled. These spirits of the night, like dark phantoms, passed quickly through the outer ring of our fire's light. Perhaps anticipating the alien cataclysmic arrival, they were inspired to run, like animals fleeing before a tsunami.

The wonders of life are always present but missed by our sleeping minds. In the presence of Juno, the magic was awakened by her clarity. I believed she had conjured the ponies' run of pure delight. Held by the presence of my guru in silent listening, my body, heart, and mind were all ears, ready to receive. Every cell was conscious and alive as the incredible blessing continued to thump through me like the sweet beauty of a glorious death approaching. The diamond in my chest was fully activated by her sweet and silent song.

Juno saw. "Yes, so simple. So beautiful, isn't it?"

She always saw so clearly into me, allowing me to also see.

"I've always known we are all already Buddhas, that we all share that light," I said. "But now I'm experiencing it with you. We are here to share that Big Love with others, as you're doing now."

I was overcome with gratitude and felt compelled to reach for her hand that lay upon her lotus lap so near. I paused, inches from the touch, already feeling the spiritual charge of her hand in mine. She moved the final distance, pressing palms and interlocking fingers. I felt myself disappear into our merging consciousness and returned to myself when she released my hand a lifetime and a few seconds later.

I was dumbstruck gazing at her face, and then I moved my still warm and tingling God-blessed hand to my heart, sure it would burst.

She laughed like a musical score. "Sean, an awakened life is simply who you are—awareness itself. Yes, to be in the service of Big Love is our true nature."

"I'm forever grateful." I namaste'd my glowing guru. Overflowing appreciation had been uncorked.

Juno said, "We never awaken alone!"

Our eyes danced and minds spoke and nothing was left unsaid. In tune with my guru, through a channel of divine loving energy. The night sky became illuminated in a supernatural way, with the light of ascension shining around and through us. The waves kept time with perfect intervals of breath.

We finished our tea in silence, moving ever deeper into the sync of telepathy. All the cells of my body and mind pulsed like sparkling lights, and my heart was beating like a big bass drum as midnight approached on alien eve.

I DIDN'T NEED A WATCH; I knew the time. Eleven fifty-nine. One minute to midnight. September 9, 2036, was sixty seconds away. Fifty-nine . . .

In a state of miracle readiness, we sat cross-legged like lotuses waiting for the rays of the sun to light upon us. Hearts tracking the final moments of time before the greatly anticipated tolling of 9/9. Our consciousness was mingling through the medium of Big Love. A divine aum played before us like an orchestra before the curtain went up.

Whatever was coming was nonfiction and held the promise of illuminating the illusion, reconciling all opposites one by one and settling the scales in perfect balance of some grand cosmic harmony—the aum of the infinite and eternal. The end was near.

Juno looked up. I looked up. The cosmos was humming. We started counting the stars to the beat of our breaths, synchronizing with the waves until, eyes closed, we entered the deep heart's core. Such peace and love. I saw it, *I felt it*. I understood the pure desire for the mystical and flowed with the celestial river of desire into its source—the unfathomable ocean. Summoning and surrendering in union with universal mind.

I let go of attempting to assign words to the beauty. I adjusted my position to lie in shavasana on the sand with my head on my cushion and a warm shawl covering me, holding my left hand over my heart so it wouldn't escape or explode as I became one with the night sky above.

The first click of a new day started tolling in my chest the final drumroll of my heartbeat. *Rumbabum!*

An otherworldly light appeared—*Rumbabum!*—parting the earth's atmosphere like the Red Sea. *Rumbabum!* I let myself receive the light—*Rumbabum!*—being drawn up by the light's enticing tractor beam. *Rumbabum!* A state of flow flowing. *Rumbabum!* Not an ordinary light. *Rumbabum!* But an all-knowing, shining, loving presence—*Rumbabum!*—experienced as extraordinary light. *Rumbabum! Rumbabum! Rumbabum!*

My heart contracted one last time, squeezing the last vestiges of fear out of me as it released, leaving me and my heart perfectly still upon the earth, experiencing peace. The drumming had stopped. My heart had ceased to beat.

Juno's voice whispered, "Let go!"

The longing heart finally burst fully open as consciousness rose out of my body through the crown of my head. Dead or dying, without a care in the world, I felt the wholeness that had been my intended purpose from the dawn of creation, from birth to birth.

All of creation as dancing awareness, in and out of One and Everything, beckoning me with the most beautiful sound—Juno's song.

Juno was singing in a language not of this world. Her anthem harmonized with the vibrating strings of the universe, its vibrational frequency raising us off the ground toward an immaculately lit portal, our bodies consumed by the light showering down on us. A spiraling supernatural light.

We hurtled toward the welcoming light, the fruition of all desire. The light was more than light. It pulsated love, and it radiated consciousness as it transmitted omnipotence.

Juno's song settled into the still momentum of a silent *aum*.

Where they touched the light, my right hand and arm became blue, with other colors of the spectrum twinkling within the blue manna from heaven. My hand, my writing hand, the hand that had so recently touched Juno's hand, was made perfect and new.

When I looked down, I saw that my entire body, now youthful and radiant, had been cast in this midnight-blue light and that Juno's celestial body was also bathed in blue. Her blue seemed a lighter hue, a touch of green radiating through her turquoise eyes like the clearest of coral seas.

As we ascended, I heard her counseling, *Surrender and know no fear.*

There was no fear, only gratitude for the good death she was showing me.

I again looked down, and there we were, me in shavasana and Juno in lotus watching over me. With Superman vison, I could see through our beach into the center of the earth and to the beginning of time—to the singularity of creation—where I became the primordial soup churning in Dante's inferno, where I imagined Dick, in that dark and denser dimension, was still learning the hard way the lessons of the heart.

I turned back to Juno and the light.

I'm here. Yes, follow me.

She didn't have to ask twice. Without effort, we flowed into an ultra-real sky, soaring over lush mountains, great sapphire lakes, and roaring waterfalls. The scale and colors were ineffable, words from our limited world and its dull rainbow inadequate to describe the breathtaking splendor of it all.

The air held a subtle fragrance, like the perfume of a passing fairy queen placing a kiss within consciousness rather than on one's lips.

Everything, every sense impression, was so much more real than in the life we knew. Imagination was unleashed from limiting thought, senses were freed from the doors of perception, with all directly experienced in consciousness, a truer dimension than our IMAX world, more real than living, like the difference between a dream and the normal waking state. A super consciousness, shining and unclouded by thought. Yet at the same time, the magnificence was all so familiar.

A celebration of life and love all around us.

But then a thought.

Juno, you're my death doula?

Your guide. There's no death, only birth upon birth in constant creation.

I let all thought go.

The *I am.* A liberated consciousness unlimited by form or even by space and time. That was the elevated, but still somehow sensual and sentient, experiencing.

This death was no trick of the mind, one last trip before nothingness. This was not a hallucination or a vision of transcendence but the transcendent experience itself. This was that and so much more.

But even this is not the ultimate divine reality, which is the one loving consciousness from which this dimension springs. We are closer now to that divinity which is in and all around us, as we shed the density of thought and form.

These were the higher dimensions, dimensions within dimensions, infinite but easily scaled in little quantum leaps. Voices of an angelic choir sang answers to all questions as they formed. Here was omnipotence that couldn't be explained in a naturalist way as a hallucination as oxygen left the brain. Here was the threshold to the all-knowing ultimate reality.

An alien reality, the promised contact, all orchestrated just for me?

No, it's a portal open to everyone ready to see.

Then I saw the multitude of spirits each enjoying a parallel universal view. I was one of many initiates of the newly dead or alien abducted.

Juno seemed familiar with the higher dimensional terrain and the angels or aliens who were guiding her. Guiding *us*. We followed a map created step by step as the infinite universe expanded, a map leading the legion of joyful pilgrims into realms unknown.

As part of our sublime initiation, we were then shown our past lives. They unfurled like a film playing backward and leading inevitably to this moment. The film's message was clear: that death is an illusion. Each death is merely an end of one's semiconscious dream followed by a falling into the bardo with continued preexisting proclivities—energy patterns—attached to the pure essence of our divine soul. Birth upon birth until all residual inclinations are washed away.

We were told by the celestial beings who silently narrated our films *to have no attachment to even one particular life or to judge that one was good and one was bad. It all just is, and all is good. Awakening is inevitable and lifetimes pass like heartbeats in eternity. Infinite love is expanded in this extraordinary way. The infinite and eternal expansion of consciousness . . .*

The words for the ineffable made perfect sense as explained to us by these higher beings.

The universal view had zoomed all the way out, until time and space became meaningless from the perspective of the infinite and eternal.

We, all of us pilgrims, were told that this was a day of ascendance, where many ordinary heart-centered people would be lifted up to see these higher dimensions. And some would spiral down the vortex, where Dick lay, as a warning to change their ways.

So that Earth may be reborn.

Angelic or alien presences—the name didn't matter. They were benevolent and loving and imparted wisdom, informing us that our consciousness had detached from our bodies in space and our minds had detached from time. And from that chorus of incorporeal beings, we were all shown exactly what we needed to see.

Those we loved were there, stepping forward to greet us, out of our past lives, and into their roles from our most recent life. My parents, Hope, Dylan, and Elliot were real, more real than when I'd seen them last, as the essence of who they were took on subtle, perfect, vivid vibrational forms, resonating with love.

Nothing real is ever lost.

In brilliant glowing flashes of a relived highlight reel, each member of my departed family held a lifetime review of our time together and the lessons learned from all the gifts they shared with me. My parents granting me birth and shepherding me through the wonders and night-mares of childhood. Hope, my first love, shared the gifts of nature, and her belief in our next evolutionary step that now was coming into being. Dylan had gifted me his humor and an adventurous nature before he gave birth to the beautiful theory of constant creation. And there was Elliot, the merry prankster who taught me not to take myself or the things of life too seriously.

Each evocative scene of my current life-review moved at the perfect speed—time slowed or didn't move, recalibrated within pure con-sciousness. I experienced each one through their own universe, from their perspective of the infinite and eternal, the lens cleared by what we call death. Life was being fully experienced only in death. Each step of my homecoming was grander than the one before, each building upon the scene before, raising the vibration to an even higher dimensional reality.

With M, of course, stepping forward for the grand finale in all her glory. She showed me she was still, and always would be, with me and the children. We saw the perfection of our relationship in Big Love, even the perfection found in her final act of noble self-sacrifice. Her presence washed away all the sorrow and pain of the last nine years, caused by wishing things had been different than they were. Our eyes locked, and our Big Love registered as the illusive, perfect 100 percent score—no Heart Sync technology needed.

In the end, I became aware of her pure consciousness and our shared being—then, like a hologram vibrating with maximum intensity, M stepped right into me, merging our spirits for eternity.

Love is immortality, echoed in her sweet voice within me.

Don't go, I pleaded silently with a smile. Though I knew now, M could never leave me. My plea was merely an expression of love. I was infused with her spirit and sense of overwhelming gratitude.

Every atom, every quark, and every string of the lyrical universe was tingling, dancing in and out of view at the moment of conception. Perfection.

But something was missing . . .

Alfred, there was no Alfred. He was absent from the heavenly choir.

Juno, who had never left my side, answered, *Nothing is missing. Alfred was never born so he can never die. You brought him alive with your love. He is a work of art. May he be a character that brings a smile to every reader's heart.*

I saw the perfection in Juno's perception of Alfred. There may never have been a real Gunga Din, but Kipling made him an immortal hero, and Falstaff still struts across infinite stages. I would guide Molly to write of Alfred's jolly character and sacrifice with all its nobility of service.

But now you know M and those you love are always there for you. Soon we will return to Earth . . .

You wouldn't send me back? I offered in protest. *Molly can finish my story.*

There's really no back and forward.

Then let us stay right here, I said, still relishing irony.

My alien guide, my joyful angel, my guru—Juno—gave me a soothing smile. *No one can finish your story but you. This was a view of some angelic dimensions, given so you will no longer doubt or fear. But there is one last revelation for us to see.*

The most amazing experience of this supernatural adventure was a series of scenes of the future as vivid as the memories.

As the great pageantry of future humanity passed before our eyes, we felt a complete, nurturing love; we were part of all, and we brought with us an expansion of light. The process shown to us was how to self-actualize what we truly believe. In other words, the wizard's alchemy that can reconcile paradox.

All would be, as it always was, all right, even more so with the knowing that which cannot be known.

That is why we must forget.

We wouldn't remember the specific coming attractions—the scenes were swept from our minds, leaving only the memory that we'd seen the future and the knowing of self-realization—that our lives would be changed completely by what we had been shown. Life, this one or the next, would be forever altered by this journey. Should we return to Earth, it would be in the service of Big Love.

That is why you must return.

Juno. Her voice always welcome, always present, even when she didn't speak. My guru had been with me for all my lifetimes.

Telepathy is a super subtle, fine-tuned vibrational transmission from the source to another consciousness in resonance.

I wanted to write that down.

Write for those who are awakening and tell how M still lives within eternal life. Tell of dying as not the opposite of life but as our reunion with the divine love of universal consciousness.

But what of my heart? It no longer beat. *How can I return?*

I didn't want to return.

It is whole and waits to go on beating. The beats' cessation was simply a metaphor to bring you here for healing and awakening.

A minute more?

To leave my current life now was more than all right. It was all right to never sip Burgundy again and to never make love to Molly. It was all right to never hug my children again and to never see Juno again in that ordinary life. I had witnessed—no, *experienced*—transcendent life. And my family, all true hearts in Big Love, would also know it.

After we'd faded back into the light, those who'd gone before would all be there in those ethereal realms, ever-present in our hearts. It was all right, more than all right—no purpose, no lack to the infinite and eternal, Big-Loving constant creation. All would be all right, without me, the actor, playing the part of an author.

I begged not to leave, as if I was once again a nine-year-old child at a Jersey Shore amusement park. Yet our bodies waited back on the beach in Ireland, 2036. And the family would mourn at dawn if Sean were no longer there.

Time is a fiction here, so nothing is lost, but we must go back now. There is no end to constant creation. What we call the end is really the beginning.

And with a thud in my chest, my heart started beating again upon that now-foreign beach. And despite feeling a sense of great remorse, when I opened my eyes and saw Juno there, I reconnected with my heart and my body. And once again, I am . . . Sean Byron McQueen. I had to smile, despite knowing I was back in a dream, but one I now would navigate with my inner light fully lit.

Make it a lucid dream. Juno's voice was still in my head. *Love has moved you so you may write.*

Dawn light filtered through the night's haze rising from the ocean. The merry voices of the family approached. Juno was singing, pulling biscuits from her basket, and preparing morning tea.

Auspicious is the Day!

ACKNOWLEDGMENTS

Beth Hill, Ava Coibion, Elizabeth Brown, Dayna Jackson, and Erin Brown, my editors and coaches who taught me how to build a world using letters, spaces, and punctuation marks.

ABOUT THE AUTHOR

MICHAEL KELLEY is a former lawyer who, prior to pursuing his passion for writing, built an international business on Wall Street before founding his own investment management firm. His love of literature and creative writing began during his years at the University of Pennsylvania.

Michael currently lives in New York with his wife and daughter. After years leading a busy life in the city, he now spends the majority of his time in the peaceful woods of Dutchess County where he enjoys meditation, yoga, wine, reading, and hiking, all of which inspire his writing.